WRITING
INTO
THE WORLD

WRITING
INTO
THE WORLD

ESSAYS : 1973–1987

Terrence Des Pres

Introduction
by Paul Mariani

Foreword by Elie Wiesel

VIKING

VIKING
Published by the Penguin Group
Viking Penguin, a division of Penguin Books USA Inc.,
375 Hudson Street, New York, New York 10014, U.S.A.
Penguin Books Ltd, 27 Wrights Lane,
London W8 5TZ, England
Penguin Books Australia Ltd, Ringwood,
Victoria, Australia
Penguin Books Canada Ltd, 2801 John Street,
Markham, Ontario, Canada L3R 1B4
Penguin Books (N.Z.) Ltd, 182–190 Wairau Road,
Auckland 10, New Zealand

Penguin Books Ltd, Registered Offices:
Harmondsworth, Middlesex, England

First published in 1991 by Viking Penguin,
a division of Penguin Books USA Inc.

1 3 5 7 9 10 8 6 4 2

LIBRARY OF CONGRESS CATALOGING IN PUBLICATION DATA
Des Pres, Terrence.
Writing into the world : essays, 1973–1987 / Terrence Des Pres.
p.   cm.
ISBN 0-670-80464-9
I. Title.
AC8.D566   1990
809—dc20   89-40799

Printed in the United States of America
Set in Galliard
Designed by Victoria Hartman

Contents

Foreword

I recall our first meeting: a young college professor of remarkable erudition and intelligence, eager for silence: at once its protector and detractor. Torn apart by contradictory forces, he struck me with an intensity that emanated from his entire being.

Bearded, hair tousled, sloppily dressed, Terrence Des Pres seemed to embody the radical sixties' student. Behind his tinted glasses, his eyes, at once gentle and demanding, probed constantly into those to whom he spoke. Serious yet given to humor, melancholy yet cheerful, his voice guarded, often cracked, no sooner would he ask a question than he would retract it in order to reformulate it in more pointed terms; then he would ask another, and a third. In the end, you realized that you had just listened to a long monologue made up of rhetorical questions.

The reason for his visit? At the time, while teaching literature at Colgate University, there beloved by students and colleagues alike, Terrence was preparing his major work: an analysis of the writings by or about Holocaust survivors. Did he seek my advice? I did not have any to offer. He knew his subject well and was assessing it in all its sorrowful and disconcerting complexity. How to reconcile language with that which refuses language? How to transform the unspeakable into simple words, which are never burning enough? Can poetry become the legitimate response to silence even as it becomes another form of silence? And then, on another level, what right does one have to speak of the "other" in place of the other, or even on the other's behalf when the other comes from a haunted place where human beings lived out not only their own death but the death of the multitudes?

For him—perhaps in him—the abyss was always present. Did he

attempt to fill it, to step across it? He was not satisfied to describe it; he wanted to understand its mechanism to reduce its evil power. Obsessed by truth, intoxicated by poetry, an impassioned defender of victims, Terrence relentlessly desired to penetrate the forbidden sanctuary of the nocturnal kingdom that was Auschwitz. Sometimes he would not think himself worthy of this: "After all, I wasn't there." I reassured him. "That is true: you were not there. But it is your part to study its gates and ditches. It is for you to observe, to reveal what you see within yourself." I believe that in the end he understood: he who listens to a witness becomes a witness. The secret pact between us was sealed. Having become accomplices and friends, we promised we would stay in contact. His quest brought us together more and more frequently.

Our principal grounds for disagreement: analogies with the tragedy of the concentration camps, which I then considered—and will always consider—unique, indeed ontological; while Terrence maintained that no event was unique. The proof? The Gulag. In his eyes, the two injustices reflected the selfsame evil, if not the same malediction. To a point, for ethical reasons more than philosophical ones, he perceived, as I did, in every tragedy, in every calamity, an intrinsic link with the Holocaust. But I insisted: a reference point, yes; a comparison, no. Because there was Auschwitz, it is up to us to combat the enemy of humanity whatever or wherever it may be. Because of the great catastrophe during the Nazi reign, we cannot invoke ignorance or powerlessness as an excuse or alibi. When men are persecuted, no matter where, we are there, either at the side of the torturer or at the side of the victim. From Auschwitz and all that it has come to signify, we know that the spectator is guilty. Terrence: "So we can compare!" Me: "No, we cannot."

Terrence was someone. Someone very special. Someone good. Often, in Washington or elsewhere, we talked about current affairs, never losing sight of their relationship with the past. Poet of memory, he was also one of action. I hear him still: "Men and women are dying in Central America. We must do something. We must . . ." And again: "Hunger rages in Asia, in Africa, and it is in the name of memory that we must end it." And also: "Nuclear annihilation threatens the planet. We must protest, sound the alarm. We must . . ." I see him again, his sadness, his pain, nearly enraged, voicing his appeals on behalf of some oppressed community, some persecuted people. Listening to him, I understood why he slept so poorly. It was because in thought he was elsewhere, with those who suffered and who despaired.

And he himself, did he despair? If he did, his despair was geared to sustain in others a possible need to act in order to justify the necessary hope.

Transcending despair in the face of the triumph of evil, Terrence Des Pres succeeds in his work to sing out his faith in mankind, what he would define as the sum of its possibilities.

Elie Wiesel

Introduction

Whenever I think of him now he is in shadow. Usually he is sitting across from me on the couch in my dimly lit living room, his rugged, handsome face already half-etched, half-erased by nightfall. He speaks softly but insistently, as if he had so much yet to say to the world and so little time in which to say it. Something like a dark brilliance seems to fall from him, the palpable, singular witnessing of this man to the fragility and preciousness of life and reason in this nightmare of a century. But then, suddenly, without warning, the face flickers, as if caught in the flare of a struck match, and once more disappears.

The abruptness of it all caught between the brackets of Terrence Des Pres's birth and death: 1939–1987. A call one autumn's morning that this vital flame was gone, snuffed out like that, two years short of fifty, and the chilling realization that there would be no more phone calls, no more visits, no more of those extraordinary, vital letters; that one of the too-few articulate witnesses to the horrors of our time—to those truths about ourselves we would just as soon forget, except for the moral imperative enjoined upon us that we must not forget—had suddenly, unequivocally, been silenced.

He had recently been remarried. He seemed filled with a new joy and several times told me that he was looking forward to beginning a new family. He had stopped drinking; he lectured me on the importance of dieting and exercise; and he had every expectation of being around for a long time. He was filled with projects and seemed to be reading everyone and everything. At the same time he understood, tacitly, that one might have to pay and pay dearly for staring for as long as he had into the abyss of human evil, and that bearing witness is a serious and costly business.

For fifteen years he taught at Colgate, in the beautiful but unforgiving Chenango Valley, his specialty a course on Holocaust literature, and lived in a few cloistral rooms (bare mostly except for his books) of a large, university-owned farmhouse. I imagine him at his desk there, the scholar of a single candle against a vast, inhospitable backdrop of stars, hungry for consolation, but hungrier for truth. Alone on New Year's Eve 1980, in his forty-first year, surrounded by the silence of those frozen snowdrifts, he writes a friend:

> I got on sweater and heavy coat and boots and went out into the bright star night and looked and to the south there was indeed an uncommonly bright star, flickering like stars do, just to the north of Orion's Belt, but that will never be overhead, so that's not the star of Christ's coming, and then I could see through the tree branches to the north a star, which ordinarily would not show up at that level with that mass of forest to show through, so maybe that is *it,* and I shall set my alarm for 5 in the morning and if I am alive and with enough courage against the cold and this terrible tiredness I'll go out and see *it* grandly there, intense in the middle of that vast blackness which is . . . the nothing that is something: all these ideas [recall] the power of my religious youth which suddenly I wish I could recover.

In retrospect and too late I have come to realize that Terrence's life was an attempt to recover something he must have known was irrevocably lost, something taken from him in his youth, an innocence, perhaps, but something taken—violently—from him. This is why he seemed to identify so passionately with the millions of victims which this century has seen. Victims of the concentration camps primarily, but victims of the gulags as well, victims of the monster bombs dropped on Hiroshima and Nagasaki, victims of repression and totalitarian rule, as in South Africa, Ethiopia, Northern Ireland, the Soviet satellites. In short, wherever on this globe the strong have lorded it over the weak.

The twenty-two essays included in this book cover fourteen years, from Terrence's early "Memory of Boyhood," which appeared in *Sports Illustrated* in 1973, to a talk he gave in April 1987, half a year before his death, on the problematic question of the use of satiric laughter in dealing with the Holocaust. Much of Terrence's prodigious energies during that decade and a half were given over to the completion of two books which often seem to have been written in blood. The first of these, *The Survivor: An Anatomy of Life in the Death Camps,* published in 1976, went through four editions in five years, and became at once a small classic on the topic of the Holocaust. Some of it—his chapter on the psychological uses of excrement to debase one's victims—had never been adequately articulated before. The second book, *Praises & Dispraises: Poetry and Politics, the 20th Century,* Terrence had virtually completed at the time of his death.

"I think of you / north," Carolyn Forché has written in the moving and deeply troubling poem which closes her book, *The Country Between Us:*

> I think of you
> north in the few lighted rooms
> of that ruined house, a candle in each
> open pane of breath, the absence of anyone,
> snow in a hurry to earth, my fingernails
> pressing half moons into the sill
> as I watched you pouring three
> then four fingers of Scotch over ice,
> the chill in your throat like a small
> blue bone, those years of your work
> on the Holocaust.

Always in these years the Holocaust was with him, something so horrible and yet so present that he never seemed able to shake its plaintive, silent, accusing ghosts for very long, no matter what he did, no matter where he was. For years John Berryman tried desperately to write his own black book about what had happened in the concentration camps. Each time he came up short, breathless, glimpsing those ghosts with his face averted, each time leaving his black book in shards and fragments. Instead, he dealt with the horror as he could with brilliance and sardonic wit in his *Dream Songs,* where, always, the dead, come back now in the guise of schools of barracuda, waited in the shallows for him.

Often, too, Terrence would have willingly turned from the nightmare of the Holocaust. But each time something in him made him turn back again, the imperative to bear whatever witness he could urging him on until once again he was staring at those terrible realities, far worse than those Dante managed to summon in his imagining of hell. The humiliation of the defeated, the terrible arrogance of the victor, mud, vermin, gray skies, every hope abandoned, the bodies of the victims stacked like cordwood to be fed into the screaming ovens, the horrible attempt to deprive the victims not only of their lives but of every vestige of their humanity. Again and again Terrence came back to the texts, reading and poring with the intensity of a Talmudic scholar over the unforgiving documents, the statistics, the diaries, the letters, the Orwellian officialese, the obscene euphemisms, until he was compelled to offer his own witness for those no longer able to witness for themselves.

But there were many other occasions beyond the specific focus of these two volumes when he was called upon to speak. Terrence began where many teachers of his generation began, with a critical inquiry into the literary nature of the text itself. But even from the start he questioned the assumptions and limitations of what too often devolves into antiseptic classroom discourse. Instead, he insisted we address the larger and messier issues of contemporary reality. The horror of the Holocaust, with its systematic program for the elimination of the Jewish people, consumed him first and last. But, as time went on and the map of Terrence's concerns became ever more global, the occasions of men's inhumanity to men—instead of being exorcised and laid to rest—likewise became even more urgent. The box had been opened, the demons swarmed, elbowing their way out, and Terrence was never again able to shut its lid.

Nor did he choose to. Even a quick glance at the table of contents and their dates will verify this spiraling of concerns: the linguistic and ethical limits to any literature of commitment, no matter how well meaning or well intentioned; the difficulty of adequately expressing the idea of the good, given the insane, diabolical realities of our century; the whiplash consequences for the nation that would compromise and subvert truth for its own ends (those *ragioni di stato,* as Machiavelli had it); the duty imposed upon the individual to speak out against genocide wherever it occurs, but particularly for Terrence in Europe, Armenia, Vietnam, South Africa; and, too, the particular and often ineluctable circumstances, as with the novelist John Gardner, as with Des Pres himself, as with so many, that surround and sometimes cloak the hour of one's death.

Terrence wrote with a rare combination of eloquence and power, more often than not with stunning effect. I remember once, in the summer of 1983, reading a copy of his essay "Self/Landcape/Grid," which he had just sent me. It was a hot afternoon, with the sounds of weekday traffic in Greenfield, Massachusetts, a town larger than Terrence's Hamilton, but smaller than his neighboring city of Rome with its SAC base, which adjacency was the occasion of Terrence's essay. I was waiting to have some work done on my car and figured I'd pass the hour reading what Terrence had to say. There was nothing special about the day or the place. It might have been any one of a thousand towns in America. Which was exactly the point: weather over a busy Pompeii on a sultry August day in A.D. 79, Vesuvius rumbling in the background.

But even as I read Terrence's essay, I was made aware that this particular Main Street on which I was walking, with the 300,000-year-old hills of the Pioneer Valley rising to the west and the maples and pines shimmering in the distant heat, this Emersonian transcendentalist's landscape, was part of a nuclear grid pattern on which a Russian nuclear missile was trained, even as American missiles in silos in Kansas and Nebraska were trained on Russian installations and other military and population nerve centers. I stood there reading, transfixed, unable to move out of the blinding noonday sun into the shade, as the familiar landscape shifted to another, more terrible configuration before my eyes, until the I who was reading—in one awful, blinding, transfiguring moment—saw itself obliterated.

Awe and terror. Terror and awe. Attributes once reserved for the Highest Being, but now, seemingly, transferred to those in authority. The State, yes—but the State is still made up of individuals, Des Pres reminds us, and individuals have a moral imperative to bear witness. No wonder, then, that one of the topics that consumed Terrence throughout the last decade of his life was what he saw as the abrogation in this country of the poet's responsibility to witness. For him this inability or refusal to commit oneself to a poetry of witness had resulted in a plethora of poems of inconsequentiality and indeed of decadence, a poetry which hid itself in a discourse of self-referentiality, self-pity, self-aggrandizement.

Among Americans there were exceptions—the Marxist-agrarian response of a Thomas McGrath, the feminist response of an Adrienne Rich. Terrence's personal library—which, when I saw it for the last time shortly after his death, was filled to overflowing with the latest in poetry and fiction as well as nonfiction—is an eloquent reminder that he was continually searching for a language that mattered, especially among American poets of his own generation. Among those he listened to with interest were Carolyn Forché (on El Salvador), Peter Balakian (on the Armenian genocide), Marc Kaminsky (on Hiroshima and Nagasaki), and William Heyen (on the Holocaust). But he also learned early on to cast his net wider, to include the poems of Auden and Hardy in England, Yeats and Seamus Heaney in embattled Ireland, and Breyten Breytenbach in South Africa. Then, beyond the borders of his own language, he reached out to figures known to him largely through translation: the Latin American poets, Miroslav Holub among the Eastern-bloc poets, Bertolt Brecht in Germany, Nazim Hikmet in Turkey.

Did this almost single-minded search for a poetry of witness leave him blind to other excellences in poetry? At moments, but no more so than the rest of us who search. And always, even at great personal cost, he was ready to listen, to debate, to enter into technical and linguistic territory that was unfamiliar to him. In doing so he sometimes stumbled or (infrequently) drew too rough a map of the contemporary scene. But he was forever refining his understanding even as he refined his style, reevaluating 3000 years of classics in the context of the living moment.

When an Air Florida plane crashed into the frozen Potomac River in the nation's capital during the bitter winter of 1982, and a passenger—a tall man whose name nobody seemed to know—helped five other passengers before he foundered and disappeared himself, Terrence wrote me that he could not help thinking of the tall nun in Hopkins's *Wreck of the Deutschland* calling out in witness even as she and the other nuns were swept under by the waves. Terrence was amazed at that kind of courage in the same way he was amazed at how some had managed to hold on even in the death camps. But his heart could be lifted at the example of those who risked and even lost their lives to help their Jewish brothers and sisters during the war, "amazed," he wrote, "every time . . . life and poetry reclaim each other, when it *happens*." He had the highest regard for poetry, and desired more than anything to deliver it from its status as an inconsequential plaything on the periphery of our vision. Indeed, he wanted to see poetry returned again to its ancient and sacred calling.

Language, he believed, used with reverence and precision, might—*might*—allow him to pay a respectful, tentative homage to what would otherwise be better served, as Elie Wiesel has said, by the final authority of silence. Like Wiesel, whom he so deeply admired, Terrence believed that if we did not speak out the truth about what had happened, others might forget—or, worse, like Orwell's O'Brienists, or like the Turkish government with the Armenian genocide of 1915, or like some revisionists with regard to the Nazi concentration camps, revise what had happened out of the history books altogether.

What alternatives to speaking do we have? In the camps, in gulags, in prisons, in torture rooms around the world, men and women were (are) raped, bludgeoned, electric-prodded, garroted into silence, including the terrible silence of death. There is something particularly horrible about those in authority and power beating their victims into guttural inarticulateness. In so doing the torturer's aim is to take away the very thing which distinguishes our kind and binds us into community: speech. For speech is the ability to say out who and what we are. Silence may be a strategy of dealing with one's enemies, but, as William Carlos Williams has reminded us, you do not get far with silence.

To catch Terrence's dark, rugged handsomeness in the waning summer light, that bearded, black-leather-jacketed charisma astride a Suzuki 1000, was to sense an announcement of power which was, one soon learned, a form of self-protection. I remember the first time I ever saw him, one August afternoon in 1981, along Route 125. It was the beginning of the Bread Loaf Writers' Conference, and I remember thinking to myself that this man looked like one tough cookie. Quickly, however, I came to see beneath Terrence's mask an extraordinary sensitivity and vulnerability, a man who had been somehow deeply wounded, as if some trauma in his life, real or empathetically imagined—more likely both—had given validity to his witnessing to the pain of others.

But how, I ask myself, can any of us carry the weight of so much collective pain: the deaths of so many in the camps, tortures, silencings, those headless, handless torsos sent floating down the rivers? Terrence grew up in half a dozen little towns throughout southeastern Missouri, moving whenever his father, a school superintendent, moved on to a new school district. Terrence had been raised a Catholic, and though he'd ceased practicing his faith long before I knew him, he still hungered after the church's mysteries and certitudes and especially its music. What he still believed in, I think, was the staying power of friendships and the ability of the word to manifest the truth and, ultimately, to heal.

He worked and worked hard, desperately, continually, searching for a consolation, a light at the end of some very long tunnel. It is no mistake, I think, that one of the last essays he wrote was on the topic of Holocaust laughter. Is it ever permissible, he asked there, to use the consolations of laughter on a topic as horrible and mind-numbing as the Holocaust? The question behind that question, I believe, was whether the mind could survive, with dignity, with only the barest traces of human warmth and caring. His answer here, as at the close of *The Survivor,* where the question was answered even more problematically, is a very tentative yes. It is a yes, I believe, because he needed that yes to warm himself against the intense, plate-buckling cold he felt everywhere around him at the submerged level where he forced himself year after year to work.

It was characteristic of Terrence to write out into the world, a world where pain is the daily staple of life. But he wrote there because he believed that, like Father Damien among the lepers at Molokai, he too was one of the afflicted. It is because of this felt sense of shared suffering, I believe, that he was able to write with such authority and conviction. After his death, Terrence's sister sent me a photograph of Terrence as a boy, fishing somewhere on the great Mississippi. It is a quintessential American picture, something out of Mark Twain: Tom Sawyer fishing, innocence captured in the friezing of an image. So this selection closes with the earliest of Terrence's essays, an essay in which for once Terrence can bathe in his sunwarmed boyhood memories.

The book begins, however, with a short essay Terrence wrote in 1985 while writer-in-residence at the Loft in St. Paul, Minnesota. In this piece he recounts the story of a nameless boy, a boy no different from himself, who, while hunting quail or deer in the same Missouri woods where Terrence once grew up, was shot and killed in a hunting accident (or worse), then carried in his killer's arms to a rock cairn and his body hidden in a shallow grave. It is that image, elemental, Biblical, a southern retelling of the tale of Isaac and Abraham, but with a far harsher ending, that undergirds and gives so much power to Terrence's own utterances about this century's countless victims. A father figure kills his son, then cradles the body, and tries to hide the evidence. It is the nightmarish story of those in authority destroying the weak who should be under their care and protection, as if by killing they could silence them.

But Terrence took pains that his voice would not be silenced. Here, then, are his own words, often wrenched from deep within himself. In truth, at their most intense they approach the level of poetry, the one genre Terrence thought denied to him. Sometimes, indeed, these essays manage to touch something like the sublime. It is then that we are most reminded of the power language holds to help us see things through.

Paul Mariani
Montague, Massachusetts
11 September 1989

WRITING
INTO
THE WORLD

Writing into the World

Like most writers-to-be, I started in my student days with verse. Already I was more than half in love with language, fascinated with the sounds of words, uplifted by the glory of my own forthcoming victories. Besides, poems were shorter than fiction, a good deal quicker in the making. Once on the page, furthermore, language at least *looked* like art. Free verse it was, very free. The deep inner meaning stayed inner, as hard to cipher as the inside of a stone. But pretense aside, I see now that I was opening literary space, testing a possible fate. Those early bouts with poetry kept me going until I could see for myself that the road not taken is sometimes the road one finally takes. If writing is a destiny, we hang on any way we can until the ordained calling comes.

There are few excitements as fine as those first walks at dawn after a night spent writing. I remember them still, the filmy lights and chilly smells, the visionary dignity of empty streets, the uproarious feuding of the birds—and further off the diesel pounding (which seemed the river's slow deep heart) of barges pushing upstream through the Mississippi's lifting mist. The work of those nightlong sessions is now lost, thank goodness, but the excitement remains. There *is* this thing about writing, any kind of writing, which makes the hardship and waiting small cost. I mean the perpetual sense of promise, of what remains—everything!—to be done.

From that time only one poem, or rather the attempt to write it, still sticks in my mind. I remember I wanted to find redeeming wording for an event that happened somewhere in the hill country of west Cape Girardeau where, in the autumn of 1960, I was living. People called it a "hunting accident" of which there were sure to be several when men with big guns invaded the backwoods to blast away, during deer season, at anything moving. What happened, according to hearsay, was this: A boy or young man had been discovered dead, presumably hit by a hunter, with a wound like the path of a fist between shoulder and neck. To judge from the blood, the body wasn't found where it fell, but rather some twenty yards uphill in a sort of natural cairn, a clump of man-sized rocks where—or so the hunter must have hoped—no one was likely to go. There, arranged against stone, the victim lay buried in leaves. The awful thing, to me, was the moving. There was no evidence of dragging, which meant that the dead or dying boy had been carried by the man who shot him. Carried! That was the detail that forced upon me the seeing of what happened. The man had taken the boy in his arms. Had held his prey against his thumping theart. With some kind of care the hunter had lifted the broken body to its resting place within the outcrop of rock.

For weeks I fought with words for what happened. I felt possessed by the need to *say* something. Not a diatribe against guns, not a sermon on bloodlust, but the clean formality of a witness presenting what took place. I wanted, maybe, to bless the boy's death, to appease the image of a tenderness so terrible. In any case I felt obliged to write what I had *seen*—although, of course, I hadn't seen it in fact. If I had been a witness, I was there in imagination only. What had taken place in the world seemed to take place in or near me—a disturbing state of affairs. Why this event? Why me near it?

The poem didn't prosper. I did much rewriting, but the right words never came. I was aiming to be poetical about an experience that mocked my notions of fine language. I wanted to be unworldly about something very much a part of the world, not knowing that for events of this ugly kind, as Wilfred Owen would show me, the poetry is in the pity. Nor did I know that, to discharge my obsession, it would be enough to trust, as writers must, the occasion itself—*this* event with me oddly *near* it—to inspire an adequate diction. Above all I did not yet know, as I would learn from Wordsworth, that imagination does its work by seeing what's there. Much of what counts isn't, upon first inspection, visible, neither to the mind nor to the eye. We therefore need to stop and look into; imagine options, connections, networks, and in this way—through creative labor of this kind—recollect the telling facts.

If today I were to write about the hunting accident, I would move from the known to the unknown, which is to say I'd start by using myself as reference point. Hunting was something that, from the Nimrod years of my youth, I knew intimately. Later, reading Faulkner deepened my early experience, and Ortega—comparing the hunt to philosophic inquire—gave me meditative distance. These influences, in turn, turned almost upside down as I began to doubt the American obsession with guns. The venting of violence, it seemed to me, had mostly replaced the hunter's totemic rapport with his prey. Mere sport, often drunken, had suborned the valor of an ancient needful action.

Viewed thus, the hunting accident was more than accidental. There are always, for any subject under the sun, worldly conditions to be met— social, political, cultural—when asking: Why this event? At some point, also, one must ask: Why me? I mean to say that if some part of the world hits home, we are right to expect connection between the external event and an interior drama, a timeless dreamlike tension trailing back into the mystery of self. In the case of the hunting accident, my attention was called—I would underscore *called*—by the image of the hunter carrying in his arms the wounded boy. That, for me, was the understory within the details of an apparently random incident. Freud might go on about sons killing fathers, but Freud's own argument, and especially the myth he used, makes clear that the master of understory was avoiding the fact that in *Oedipus Rex* the plot begins with the father's attempt to sacrifice the son. This story is as old as Oedipus or Abraham; as filled with terror as God commending His son to the cross; as endless as old men making the wars that kill young men. To write about the hunting accident, therefore, would be to uncover my own relation to it—an unknown knowledge, an obsession peculiarly mine. Here is the stricter sense in which, from the beginning, I would stand near the event and feel its call.

What we select to write about, I'm suggesting, isn't a matter of choice so much as being chosen. Writing of every kind begins, as Henry James said, with its *donnée,* the something given, the one small thing that cannot be refused. Often the initial term is unremarkable to others, so slight as to pass unnoticed except for the one person who, feeling instantly implicated, is delighted or appalled by its nearness. Bearing witness is a neighborhood activity. If I wonder why some particular part of town feels familiar, I must answer, as would any child, that I live (or did once live) there. When, therefore, I endorse the notion of imagination as seeing what's there, imagination as exact inspection of the actual, I mean to work with that part of the world revealed to me because of who I am concretely—place, time, heritage, my existence entire. That, after all, was Montaigne's way, he who invented the art of nonfiction.

Writing may or may not be done on assignment. My obligation, however, isn't to an editor or institution, but to occasions that I know instantly are *mine,* if only I allow them to engage me. My cardinal concern, therefore, is less the business of selecting material, which takes care of itself, than decisions about *how* I shall write—the choices that artifice entails, disposition of form first of all. The creative aspect of nonfiction resides in questions of craft. The facts are the facts, but how I write them up will be the measure of my art. Different forms, of course, dictate different solutions. Faulkner, I like to think, would have taken the hunting accident to heart. An incident as seemingly simple as this one could be made to show forth, in his kind of tale-telling, the vast mythological torment of the Old South in decline. If James Dickey, on the other hand, took up the same event he would forge the loose ends into an image beyond time or context—a moment of violence with its own dark beauty impervious to blame. Neither Dickey nor Faulkner would need more, by way of hard information, than the basic scenario. In fiction or poetry, a few facts go a long way. That's not the case for writers of nonfiction prose.

When it comes to kinds of nonfiction, there are countless varieties, all of them worthy. One distinction, however, needs keeping in mind. When someone like Carol Bly, for example, writes about rural life, she doesn't go to colorful stories about Ozark hill folk or the Beans of Maine. She stays with Minnesota circumstance, using her own response to what she sees. Her country letters might at first seem similar to other rural writing, the work, say, of Wendell Berry or Noel Perrin. But no, there is a difference. Bly bears witness to the untoward givenness of things nearby; she works to reveal a weave of life and custom that constitutes, to her amazement and dismay, a whole hard world. By contrast, Berry develops a program; he aims to endorse an American version of pastoral complete with noble savage. Perrin, meanwhile, simply has fun playing; suitably countrified, the university scholar becomes, as he calls himself, a sometime farmer. To see the difference, I trust, isn't difficult. It resides in the value of writing that gets at the integrity of lives nearby yet separate from our own. Bly's writing, in consequence, possesses a hard-edged dignity not to be found in Berry or Perrin. She also reveals the further impulse in writing of her kind, which is to *tell it like it is* with an eye to possible change. Allegiance to the real, for some of us, provokes a dream of redemption.

My claim for an aesthetic of witness goes no further than this: Wordly writing depends on the imaginative energy facts inspire—and it goes without saying that not everyone is moved to creation by facts. I should add that one's reaction to factual situations is usually also ethical; depending on the degree of threat or unpleasantness confronted, moral response can be a potent force in the kind of writing that, as I like to say, announces against. And finally, in work of this kind the writer's need to know, to have information at hand, is more than useful; for prose of witness, knowledge is one's job's first duty. To see what is there, imagination must have concrete points of entry.

No doubt rafts of reasons kept me from finishing my early poem about the hunting accident. I saw less than I thought I did, mainly because I didn't use my own information to the full. In my youth I lived with guns, as everyone did on the farms about, and when the accident happened my own experience could have taken me a good deal farther than I went, or maybe cared to go. I mean that by virtue of standing nearby, I knew more than I put at imagination's disposal. The key fact, after all, wasn't the shooting but that the hunter was never identified. Here, then, imagination's real work began—to gather the given facts into a sort of primal scene, and at the heart of it place the figure of the hunter. He could be the same age as his victim, a hunting buddy, a brother even. The shooting, furthermore, did not have to be an accident; it could be the outcome of a local feud taking its toll. Down south, lest we forget, tribal fighting (one of my in-laws died this way) is not uncommon. And the accident, finally, could be just that—the unhappy outcome of plain hazard. Two men out hunting, savage for big game, occupy changeable positions. How their fates play out is up to chance.

Worldly writing begins with fact, but relies on imagination to arrive at the heart of the matter. And one should start out instantly! Events constellate and dissolve. Things moving move away. In the case of the hunting accident, I can no longer grip what once gripped me. Now I'm pressed by other objects, other obsessions, and the nearness that I then felt is gone for good. This reminds me that when I set out to say what happened, I find myself limited by passing opportunity to inquire and search out. The force of time, for some kinds of writing, can't be escaped. Transcendence, art for art's sake, writing for the ages—these take care of themselves. Good writing will always survive. Meanwhile, the prose of witness responds to the world, finds its work in the occasions that call it forth. Its method is exact attention to the actual. It depends on respectful reading of detail; on imagination making connections and seeing what's there. It also depends upon art—right words to station the mind and hold the heart ready.

Prophecies of Grace and Doom

The Function of Criticism
at the Present Time

In *The Anxiety of Influence* Harold Bloom argues that "the meaning of a poem can only be another poem." He means that the poet spends his time rewriting works of earlier poets, an activity inherently perverse because governed by the poet's maniacal need to dispossess— by tactics of "misunderstanding, misinterpretation, misalliance"—the suffocating priority of his great precursors, whose presence he experiences as the absence of himself. The feeling of deadweight and deadend is strong in Bloom's book, and the revelation he offers—that we are witnessing the "death of poetry"—comes as a foregone conclusion. The past piles up, fewer and fewer poets can hope to breathe freely, and "it seems just to assume that poetry in our tradition, when it dies, will be self-slain, murdered by its own past strength." The vitality of art is thus a negative life, a life experienced as death; and what Bloom puts forward, finally, is his version of The End. I say *his* version, for although his solipsistic terms sound new, the same cannot be said for the sense of death informing his ideas (he describes critics, for instance, as "necromancers, straining to hear the dead sing"). Ihab Hassan has informed us in *The Dismemberment of Orpheus* that literature is a suicidal process; soon it will self-destruct and deliver us into that happy silence for which we yearn. And just to take a last example, Leslie Fiedler wishes us to know that "serious" literature is dead, so now we can go back to the true stuff, to a literature of gut response, by which he means pornography.

To mention Fiedler is to suggest another round of iconoclasm. But no, that would be misleading. Boredom is more to the point. These supersaturated men of letters are bored. Upon their days and thoughts the demon of noontide rides, the *acedia* of the desert saint whose cave has ceased to shimmer with divine intent. Belief in art-as-religion and literature-as-salvation, which inspired the evangelical tone in criticism from Wordsworth through the New Critics, has gone down with the leveling wind. Grand prospects no longer lend import to the critical enterprise, no longer sanction the literary overload of brilliant minds, and in the path of their comedown stand practical questions. What more is there to read? What more to say, write, teach? What more, in short, can "make it new" mean now?

But that, again, is only a part of the problem. If we were moved by works of literature the way Rilke was struck when he beheld the Archaic Apollo—*Du musst dein Leben ändern*—there could hardly be this prevailing sense of déjà vu. There would be no projection of a death in the heart, no symptomatic plaint of ennui and loss. Literature does not die, no more than the world itself goes down, despite the claim, two thousand years of it, that doom impends. Never, perhaps, has literary creation been more fertile, diverse, or just plain plentiful. No, the prophets of doom have something else in mind, and the persistence of their cry is a measure of genuine pain.

In youth the reader comes to literature as to a world of wondrous truth. He consumes book after book of poetry and prose, and ranging thus the heights, borne onward by joy, he comes to acquire fields, disciplines, methods. He becomes critical—and at some point, finally, he becomes aware that his fundamental relation to literature has changed. The large works are behind him, naïve delight is gone. The realms of gold have receded and no new world, no second dawn, no alternate route to transcendence remains. And now he grows to covet that first look into Chapman's Homer; he begins to envy the young their innocence. What has died, in this case, is not literature, but the capacity for naïve response, that state of openness and wonder which is necssary to literature *as an experience*. The "monuments" become monuments merely, and the realm they occupy begins to look like a graveyard or, at best, a museum.

Not a happy situation. But let us not revive the old excuse and say we murdered to dissect; not dismiss the problem by calling criticism the villain. Let us rather examine a strange bit of literary experience, a fact more common than the silence surrounding it suggests: that at least for some of us, a day comes when we admit to more pleasure, and often more fine satisfaction, from reading criticism than from reading original texts. Literature, that is, begins to engage us less than the realm of critical discourse. Of course there are exceptions: new publications, new discoveries, texts in areas of intense concern. But for literature in general the case is otherwise, especially for those big works which make The Tradition. These we discuss in class, write about in journals, build books around in order to keep jobs and maintain prestige. But we do not, I think, come to them freely, in need, or with that earnest joy of youth. Among those who care for literature, many will read the next book about Greek drama or Milton's art, but very few will ever go back to *Philoctetes* or *Paradise Lost*. And quite possibly those who continue to read Shakespeare will delight as much in the critical activity his works inspire; books like Barber's *Shakespeare's Festive Comedy* or Brower's *Hero and Saint*. Without intending to, and often half in guilt, we find ourselves preferring works of criticism—Auerbach's *Mimesis* or Benjamin's *Illuminations* or even, God knows, Fiedler's *Love and Death*—despite sure knowledge that everything in these matters depends on the text.

Spinoza defined philosophy as "the intellectual love of God," by which he meant the never-finished approach to reality through thought. Recently Lionel Trilling has applied this definition to criticism, describing it as "the intellectual love of literature." Behind Spinoza lay the gnostic belief in mystical ascent to godhead. No such faith animates Trilling's claim, and yet the case is similar. The problem is one of *approach*, a term to be taken in its double sense; method, nearing. And central to both Spinoza and Trilling is the idea of absence and motion—a movement of the ardent mind perpetually toward and around that which it *has not* but *knows of*, toward some distant plenitude which, apart and in itself, seems all but out of reach.

Aesthetic objects tend in any case to generate their own mediation. Works of art complete their existence in the world, come finally to contain the consciousness which views them, by this capacity to surround themselves with concepts. So sure is this process, that Welleck and Warren could define "the total meaning of a work of art" as "the result of a process of accretion, i.e., the history of its criticism by its many readers in many ages." There is something decidedly Hegelian in all this, Hegel being the first (as I shall suggest in a moment) to attempt a solution to the problems of Romantic and Post-Romantic consciousness. Which is to say that the relation of criticism to art, or of thought to essence, is a specifically "modern" problem. Criticism has always flourished, yes, but the rise of criticism as an occupation with its own discipline and methods, as a universal and in some sense *necessary* activity, has assumed its definitive form within the last two centuries.

To be "critical" means to turn from immediate to mediated response; and this has been the mark and burden of Western thought since Kant, who brought the thrust of the Enlightenment to a head when he decided no longer to do philosophy, in the old ontological sense, but rather to examine the limits of that doing. The range of consciousness, Kant argued, was narrower than commonly supposed. Mind could account for surfaces, for the phenomenal aspect of things, but it had no formal access to numina or essence. In consequence, surface and depth split apart, and the world's substantial presence began to recede. It faded into the famous *ding an sich,* a realm apart, to be known by faith alone. And *there,* rather than *here,* everything of ultimate concern—God, freedom, the ground of selfhood—was henceforth to be located. Or was all this a consequence? For the gap Kant described did not open only in metaphysics. What had come about was an end to the feeling of rapport with essence, an end to the immediate reception of things in depth. This predicament has been accounted for in every conceivable way: attributed to, for example, the collapse of belief; the rise of reason; the dissociation of sensibility; revolution; the move from rural to urban order, and so on. But that a change occurred seems evident; and when it did, the joy of plenitude gave way to nothingness and dread. Substance vanished into the void, leaving in its wake that sense of absence—*le néant des choses humaines,* as Rousseau put it—central to Romantic and therefore to modern consciousness.

At some point in the eighteenth century, that is, an obsessive awareness of loss and emptiness began to haunt men's deepest thoughts; and by the beginning of the Romantic period, the condition of absence had become one of the principal determinants of aesthetic representation. The development of modern painting—its collapse of perspective, its celebration of texture and surface, its denial of any world beyond itself—is one example. Modern literature, with its emphasis on symbolism and language-worlds, is another. In *Blindness and Insight,* Paul de Man goes so far as to suggest that literature, by its very nature as a self-conscious fiction, is a representation of absence. Literary works take their origin in "the presence of a nothingness," de Man argues; and "poetic language names this void with ever-renewed understanding." The assumption here is that all signification, whatever else it may serve or point to, signifies finally the absence of that which is signified. Any text is the image of something *not* present; or as Valéry said of poetry, it "never speaks but of absent things." De Man puts it this way: "here the human self has experienced the void within itself and the invented fiction, far from filling the void, asserts itself as pure nothingness." Literature, therefore, which was once the supreme concentration of truth and ineffable presence— "In the beginning was the Word"—now becomes an embodiment of the world's emptiness. As in Beckett's work, there is only the word, nothing but the word, the word persisting in its own nonbeing.

Among the principal bearers of meaning in human experience are the self and other selves, the world as a bounded totality, and, of course, works of art; all possess a surface (the medium of their concrete being) which conveys a corresponding depth (the feeling of significance), such that the presence of surface *is* the presence of depth. What has now been lost is the capacity for immediate engagement with surface-as-depth. This, as I have suggested, is the situation which Kant brought to focus. He left it to Hegel to bridge the gap, and Hegel was equal to the task. Having lost its immediacy, essence would have to be reconstituted in thought. The immediate would have to be mediated and thus delivered anew. The split between subject and object would be closed by mental labor, and here Hegel was truly prophetic. For what he acknowledged is what literary criticism, or indeed all critical discourse, covertly admits: *The need to reestablish response in depth through conceptual mediation.*

Naïve reception is beyond us. Myth is only myth; fictions are fictions; and their generative power, which depended on taking them for real, on accepting their surface as their truth, has drained away. How hard, for example, Yeats worked to keep the aura of those "sacred books" he loved in his youth. How stridently he insisted, against his ingrained skepticism, upon the force of symbols, upon the mysterious heart of mere stories. He arrived at a sort of truce, neither side claiming victory, and so with ourselves: we too strive to read the depth of surfaces and stay in the presence of meaning. This striving is the activity we call criticism. Of course criticism concerns itself with history, biography, social milieu; with analysis of style and linguistic structure; with judgment and interpretation and methods of scholarship. But beyond these, or precisely in the doing of these many things, criticism achieves its deeper aim. It becomes the medium through which we reenter the great works of art. It is how we hold beauty before us, how we share in its life, how we live again in its presence.

And often criticism is the prior, or concomitant, act of perception which allows the margin of genuine enjoyment we feel while reading. Take, for example, Pater's remark in his essay on style: "one of the greatest pleasures of really good prose literature is in the critical tracing out of that conscious artistic structure, and the pervading sense of it as we read. Yet of poetic literature too; for, in truth, the kind of constructive intelligence here supposed is one of the forms of imagination." For many of us, in other words, the exercise of critical perception has become a habit of mind as we read, and may even be the device through which we are *able* to read. When T. S. Eliot remarked that "criticism is as inevitable as breathing," he was suggesting that reading and criticism have become aspects of a unified act, the mutual conditions of each other. Northrop Frye makes a similar point: "it is not possible for any reader today to respond to a work of literature with complete or genuine *naïveté*. Response is what Schiller calls sentimental [self-conscious] by its very nature, and is hence to some degree involved in criticism." Surely this was not the case for Shakespeare's audience, let us say, or for the readers of Richardson. But if criticism has become "inevitable," we hardly do justice to the problem if we say, as many do, that the critical faculty has crushed all purer response. On the contrary, the mediating act of criticism allows, as if by stealth, entrance to the power of the work itself.

I am assuming, then, that the amazing proliferation of critical activity amounts to a cultural phenomenon in its own right; that it is a mode of mental behavior rooted in our time and plight; or that, as Roland Barthes describes it, "criticism is not at all a table of results or a body of judgments, it is essentially an activity, i.e., a series of intellectual acts profoundly committed to the historical and subjective existence (they are the same thing) of the man who performs them." Barthes goes on to define criticism as "a second language, or a *meta-language* (as the logicians would say), which operates on a first language (or *language-object*). . . . It is the 'friction' of these two languages which defines criticism." Criticism, in other words, is the act of penetrating a text by refracting it through another text, the former concrete and inaccessibly vibrant, the latter conceptual and as readily applied to the density of its object as, say, mathematics is to the otherness of multidimensional space.

Barthes stops short with a formal definition. The relation of criticism to spiritual need is left to others, to Paul Ricoeur for example, a French theologian who goes to the heart of the matter by defining criticism as a means of provisional grace. "We are in every way the children of criticism," says Ricoeur in *The Symbolism of Evil*, "and we seek to go beyond criticism by means of criticism, by a criticism that is no longer reductive but restorative." Having lost "the immediacy of the symbol," we resort to criticism as "the modern mode of belief in symbols." By means of this strategy we participate once more in the depth and sensation of meaning. As Recoeur puts it: "I can still today communicate with the sacred by making explicit the prior understanding that gives life to the interpretation. Thus hermeneutics, an acquisition of 'modernity,' is one of the modes by which that 'modernity' transcends itself, insofar as it is forgetfulness of the sacred. I believe that being can still speak to me—no longer, of course, under the pre-critical form of immediate belief, but as the secondary immediacy aimed at by hermeneutics." What is hoped for, and already partly achieved, is the birth of a "second naïveté," a new fullness of response made possible through criticism. Ricoeur concludes: "In every way, something has been lost, irremediably lost: immediacy and belief. But if we can no longer live the great symbolisms of the sacred in accordance with the original belief in them, we can, we modern men, aim at a second naivety in and through criticism. In short, it is by *interpreting* that we can *hear* again."

There is, of course, an altogether mundane reason for the compulsiveness of modern criticism: we do it as a trade, as a job like any other. It is also the form of warfare which self-interest takes among factions contending for dominance in academic and literary worlds. These are decisive factors, and in the context of economic necessity the older justification—the pursuit of excellence—looks silly indeed, especially when (as Edmund Wilson liked to point out) much of critical energy spends itself on second- to tenth-rate works. At some point, however, the pursuit of excellence becomes its own end; it fulfills the desire to participate in greatness and wonder, and here the critical enterprise turns back to the deeper need it nourishes. To take at face value most of the claims scholars and critics make in their own defense has become, to say the least, difficult. Criticism has not purified language or sensitivity, nor established a canon, nor upheld quality; nor has it convinced students of literature that in the neighborhood of genius, as Matthew

Arnold put it, "the great thing for us is to feel and enjoy his work as deeply as ever we can." For the critic himself this may be true, but then his effort is private, and what it comes down to is an admission of the *need* to "feel and enjoy . . . as deeply as ever we can."

Enjoyment springs from enjoinment, and criticism is the medium through which we regain connection with art's vitality. Arnold confessed as much, in his famous essay on criticism, when he concluded that "to have the sense of creative activity is the great happiness and the great proof of being alive, and it is not denied to criticism to have it." Criticism becomes a mode of possession, or of being possessed; and if I have turned the meaning of Arnold's statement slightly, I have hoped to touch the source of his admitted urgency. What troubled him was the loss of connection with great art, and the possibility that contact could be lost completely. Recently Frank Kermode has voiced a similar fear. He foresees a possible world in which "*King Lear* will be forgotten like the tulip mania"; and in "Survival of the Classic" he argues that criticism is the medium through which the classics remain present. "Classics," Kermode says, "are works of art that survive," and the "urgent question is, how does survival work?" It works because "critics, teachers, adapters, all, however original, are committed to the transmission of the classic." Preservation of the great works is vital because "we know that when they depart the other gods go with them, so that we can say quite soberly that they have the quality also of the palladium."

To call literature a *palladium*—a sacred object having the power to preserve the city, the state, or in this case the spiritual content of a culture—and then to see the crisis of our time in terms of a struggle to keep art present, is also to suggest the larger context of the problem besetting "our sect," as Kermode calls those who practice criticism. "Survival of the Classic" was presumably written in the middle to late sixties, years when the apocalyptic fury of the young was reaching its peak and the coming generation seemed bent on a New World having no "communion" with the past. A world with "no place for *Lear*" is of course a fearful prospect; but an end to the alienation of man from his own creations is something quite different. Marx, for instance, never for a moment wished to sweep away the classics. Far otherwise, he would have all men participate in them to the full. Liberated man would be aesthetic man, man in substantial rapport with himself *through* his works.

This is not the place to treat of causes and cures; but in order to grasp the situation of criticism we might at least keep in mind that criticism itself did not precipitate our complaint. Already in the eighteenth century a sense of loss and then of emptiness began to invade the self and its creations; and surely it was less than coincidence that during this same period there arose the split between self and society, which, since then, has become a condition of existence for almost everyone. Rousseau, proclaiming *le néant des choses humaines,* lamenting the deceptiveness of surfaces, was also the loneliest of men. Loss of plenitude, and the pain of isolated selfhood, are the major themes of Romantic consciousness; and what these kinds of experience suggest by their conjunction is that, in a profound way, capacity to perceive the world's solid presence—to feel substance and depth in the self, in art, in other selves—depends on rooted participation in fundamental human relations. We may at least speculate that the perception of plenitude wanes as soon as we lose touch with the energies of social existence; as soon, that is, as men are no longer embedded in their social matrix *beyond reserve.* But who lives without reservation? The alienation of man from his works has been compounded by a world of relations so dishonored and unjust and ironic, that estrangement itself, a willful holding of the self apart from its transactions, becomes a necessity of moral survival. No wonder nothingness haunts us. So long as we cannot belong to the life of society, life as much theirs as our own, works of art will be present, at best, as silence. Which is to say that the condition of absence, to which criticism addresses itself, has social and therefore political determinants; and that the function of criticism at the present time—to grant a provisional grace—is provisional only.

War Crimes

A Review of Marcel Ophuls's The Memory of Justice

Marcel Ophuls, the French filmmaker and son of Max Ophuls, has taken the documentary and turned it to original use. His last three films have focused on events of major historical import; but in each case Ophuls has been less concerned with the event itself than with its impact upon the private lives of the men and women involved. *The Sorrow and the Pity,* released in 1971, reconstructs the complicated agony of France under Nazi occupation. *A Sense of Loss,* made in 1972, records the cost of Ireland's civil war in terms of personal grief. These are strong accomplishments, but *The Memory of Justice,* released in the autumn of 1976, works on an even broader plane of ambition and scope. Starting with the trials of the Nazi elite at Nuremberg, *The Memory of Justice* examines the nature of war crimes, then and now; it seeks to understand the character of the perpetrators, then and now; and perhaps most unsettling, it insists upon probing German guilt in relation to the guilt of the victor nations, then and subsequently. Insofar as the film sets more recent atrocities within the context of Nuremberg, it encourages argument about its political "message." But insofar as its primary vehicle of connection between now and then is the memories of the many people Ophuls interviews, the film gives us testimony rather than argument, experience rather than political formulations, and if the film succeeds—and it does, despite the considerable risk it runs—its success has much to do with Ophuls's extraordinary skill as an interviewer.

At least in America, *The Sorrow and the Pity* received nothing but praise. But then, this earlier film stayed within the boundaries of France, and it worked almost entirely with the victims' points of view. *The Memory of Justice,* on the other hand, includes three wars and a dozen or more nations, and it works mainly with the victors' perspectives, the implication being that if the Nazis were evil, the rest of us—those with the power to defeat and judge—are not *therefore* good. Victory breeds its own sins, its own contradictions. Within the context of Nuremberg, for example, amnesty for recent draft resisters becomes an inevitable issue, since the argument for amnesty derives directly from the Nuremberg precedent. It is bitterly sad that the same country which, thirty years ago, condemned men for participating in an immoral war, should now condemn men for refusing to participate in an immoral war, or that the liberators of Dachau went on to set up free-fire zones.

This web of tragic contradiction is the material which gives *The Memory of Justice* its form, and Ophuls is relentless in his comparisons. Auschwitz, Dresden, My Lai—all are seen in relation to Nuremberg; and it has been precisely in this connection that controversy has arisen. It can be argued that the film minimizes the evil of the Hitler years, that it obscures the nihilistic nature of that war and undermines the uniqueness of the Holocaust by comparing these enormities with the lesser atrocities of Algeria, Vietnam, Kent State, and so on. What happened at My Lai is not what happened at Auschwitz, even if the numbers of the dead are left uncounted. To fail to clarify this fundamental difference does damage not only to truth, but, perhaps worse, to our future capacity for moral discernment.

Or one can take the opposite view; war crimes are war crimes and must be identified as such no matter on what scale or to what end they were perpetrated. Horror has followed horror up to the present moment, and to insist upon distinctions when the whole of mankind is threatened can only complicate solutions and increase the danger of a final holocaust. But what both of these interpretations overlook is the film's structure, its multiplicity of partial vision corresponding to the spectrum of possible response. *The Memory of Justice* is composed of testimony from so very many witnesses, each searching memory in order to speak his or her truth (or his or her lie); it holds so many points of view fixed within the perspective of each other, that no single interpretation can claim to be final.

By weaving together footage of Nazi and American atrocities, Ophuls does imply a relation, a comparison. But as he himself has said, to compare is not to equate. On the contrary, comparison can function to dramatize distinctions. And by making Nuremberg the principal event, a sort of absolute image to which the film constantly returns and against which other events can be recognized, measured, and judged, Ophuls implies that *this* event, for which *these* men are being tried, is special, unique, and central to everything else. Yet this uniqueness might end up entirely beyond belief or comprehension (as is often said of the death camps), were the incredible crimes of the Nazi regime not thus boldly placed *within* the spectrum of realized evil. There is, then, an unavoidable dialectic at work in the film: nothing is as final as we might wish, and within this shifting perspective the small, infinitely important drama of personal involvement and personal response replays itself in the faces of the men and women Ophuls interviews.

Although Ophuls uses conventional documentary footage from various archives, and although he implements this basic material with newsreels, headlines, popular songs, and photographs, his principal resource is the interview, which he manages to conduct in such a way that the encounter between camera and witness becomes, both for the viewer and the person interviewed, a moment of striking revelation. Beginning with the camera's capacity to study the human face, the nature of film as a medium is remarkably suited to Ophuls's artistic needs. Through the technique of montage he can juxtapose different scenes, different interviews, different moments in time, and thereby reveal aspects of a given situation which might otherwise go unnoticed. Through the technique of crosscutting he can break long sequences into shorter segments which may then be inserted at strategic places in the film. Both techniques allow for control of pace and momentum, and thereby give this basically spatial form (different times and places gathered around a central event) the character of narrative.

The manipulation of these effects is of course a matter of preference. Everything depends on editing, on deciding which images will be juxtaposed at which point in the film. The film is thus "set up," as are the places and settings which Ophuls carefully selects for his interviews. This has led critics to question the "objectivity" of a supposedly objective form. But, of course, there is no such thing as "objectivity" in the strict sense, if only because, to make sense at all, some perspective or point of view must be maintained. Ophuls certainly has his own view, but he constantly counters it by juxtaposing contrary images and by interview-ing people who hold conflicting beliefs. His art is based on the kind of spontaneity generated by tension and disjunction, even when—as his critics contend—particular sequences are obviously contrived.

But what about this contrivance? At one point we see Ophuls standing on a dock at the edge of a windswept lake, talking with an old man who holds a fishing rod in his hand. The man is admitting to Ophuls that he was a Nazi and that even now he will not be shamed by his past. As he talks, a fishhook dangles from his line, moving as the wind moves, a vaguely ugly, vaguely menacing object at the very center of the screen. And this scene, furthermore, is intercut briefly with another scene—the man's wife up by the house, listening to the interview, her face cold and crumpled with fear, her head unconsciously shaking slowly no, no, no. That is the whole of it, and in its simplicity it is enormously effective. Or again: while Ophuls interviews Lord Shawcross, prosecutor for the British at Nuremberg, Shawcross explains with a sort of academic de-tachment the correctness of bombing civilian populations. War is war and everyone must pay. As he speaks he sits in a luxurious leather chair next to a large fireplace in which flames flicker cheerfully. Intercut with this scene are brief shots of Shawcross's country home— a modest rural mansion impeccably kept (elsewhere in the film we see the ruins of Dresden and Hiroshima). All of this is "set up," to be sure. But these people agreed to speak in these settings (which are, after all, their actual circumstances of life), and they are openly stating convictions.

Or take, finally, the way in which Ophuls penetrates the very different worlds of two men who died in Vietnam. He interviews Barbara Keat-ing, a woman whose pride and pleasure in the fact that her husband died a War Hero is evident not only in her crisp words, not only in her expensive dress and finely styled hair, but also in her substantial suburban house, in the special cabinet where she displays her husband's war med-als, and finally in the fact that Ophuls, throughout the interview, stands on the stairs with Mrs. Keating at some distance above him on the landing. By contrast (and these interviews are juxtaposed by much cross-cutting), Louise and Robert Ransom are deeply hurt and humbled by the death of their son; for them it was a meaningless sacrifice, as stupid as the medal from President Thieu which Mr. Ransom scorns. Their sorrow and antiwar sentiment are evident not only in their painfully hesitant words, but in their working-class clothes, their unself-consciousness on camera, in the plain kitchen in which they are interviewed, and perhaps also by the fact that Ophuls has joined them around the table as they talk.

Contrived, yes; but Mrs. Keating was surely free to dress as she liked, to stand where she liked in her own home, and take a hard view of those who in her eyes failed their country by refusing to fight. In the same way, the Ransoms were free to dress, to sit or stand as they liked, to speak with bitterness about Vietnam; and their kitchen does indeed suggest a way of life that could ill afford their loss. The viewer might accept either argument *as* an argument for or against the war. But in both cases the argument is personalized by the kind of people being interviewed as well as by the character of their surroundings, so that finally the viewer makes his or her choice on the basis of human values (humility versus pride, care versus complacency) rather than abstract principles merely.

Ophuls is an artist of "second sight," a craftsman who creates through recollection after the fact. He is a man who believes that the more complex, contradictory, and many-voiced an issue becomes, the more likely it is to yield its residuum of truth. *The Memory of Justice* hinges on the fact that many of the nations which sat in judgment at Nuremberg had committed their own war crimes, and that the prosecutors themselves were not without fault. At the trials the Russians were in favor of mass execution—as usual. Lord Shawcross pronounces the bombing of Dresden a good thing. Edgar Faure, prosecutor for the French, admits to an admiration for Göring, and in an offhand moment remarks that, after all, no evidence was uncovered that could link Adolf Hitler directly to the death of a single concentration-camp victim. Telford Taylor, prosecutor for the United States, comes off somewhat better by insisting that no matter how shabby the effort, the principles of justice must be upheld. Unfortunately, the force of his statement is weakened by that peculiar brand of easygoing righteousness, or let us call it indulgent generosity, which only victors can afford.

There is much in the film which undermines the authority of the judges at Nuremberg, not least a *March of Time* newsreel which gloats most crudely over the American capacity to bomb Dresden back to the Stone Age *twice*, once at night and once the next day. Nevertheless, Ophuls is working on a double level at this point, and working very carefully. He knows that Nuremberg established invaluable precedents: that, for example, conscience may have legitimate claims against the state; or that when those in command never kill, and those who kill are only following orders, then both are guilty. These are ethical advances of world importance, despite their constant violation. But Ophuls also knows that Nuremberg has become a cop-out. We prefer to see the trials as proof that good men win, that bad men get what they deserve, or that they do not (it comes to the same thing), but that in any case Nuremberg marked an end of vigilance and of the need to remember.

But if it was the end of the Third Reich, it most certainly cannot be taken as the end of our need to recognize and condemn inhuman actions. And thus Ophuls endeavors to change our awareness of Nuremberg, from a piece of history to an internalized image of our struggle for a clarity of moral vision which has not yet risen, and may never rise, to its conclusion. Above all he seeks to discredit the easy Nuremberg—the one in which Spencer Tracy and Marlene Dietrich exchange high talk and tragic looks. And this is why, finally, memories of Nazi, French, and American atrocities are made to collide in the film; not for the sake of comparison only, and still less to suggest that the Marines are *Einsatzgruppen* in disguise. Through the simple device of rapid juxtaposition, subsequent acts of inhumanity are now fixed within a frame of knowledge whose reference is Nuremberg, and Nuremberg itself assumes this kind of authority not because justice prevailed, but because *its* reference—absolute, intractable, timeless in enormity—is the horror of the death camps.

Midway through the film the following sequences occurs. A young woman, slender and nude, stands for a moment under a shower in a darkened room. The scene shifts to a brightly lighted sauna, a closed room in which men and women, all nude and of different ages, discuss the moral problems of postwar Germany. One man remarks that in this place, stripped of clothing, all are equal, all are the same. The conversation gets around to Nazi atrocities and someone starts to speak of gassing, but then stops in midsentence to rephrase what he wishes to say. At this precise moment the camera moves upward to the fixtures on the ceiling. The scene shifts to another darkened room, this time with a swimming pool. Three nude women come through the door and splash into the pool. That is all—except, of course, that Ophuls has given us a parody of the death sequence at Auschwitz—the showers, the sealed steaming room full of bodies, the final throwing of the dead into pits.

Behind Nuremberg stands the Holocaust. In *The Memory of Justice* the real issue is so thoroughly present (especially in the minds of those Ophuls interviews) that the film contains less than a full minute of actual footage from the camps. No bulldozers shoving piles of bodies into pits. No ovens jammed with bones. All this is not necessary. Ophuls is working with a state of mind, a new kind of awareness created by the Holocaust and made public at Nuremberg, in which consciousness—simply knowing what happened—becomes conscience. Schopenhauer, in his treatise on morality, said that conscience is man's knowledge of what he has done, and that is exactly the point. Marcel Ophuls seriously intends to re-create the conscience of our race.

In an age of atrocity, Nuremberg becomes the sounding board for what we *know*. That is why the French deserter went over to the Algerian side; in French uniform, he says, he felt like an SS man. That is why young men refused to kill in Vietnam; and that is why the picture of those bodies in the ditch at My Lai hits us with a shock of horrid recognition. And that, finally, is why the face of Albert Speer, through all his lengthy interviews, yields no expression. He too knows, as all of us know, that after Nuremberg there is nothing more to say or learn, but only a memory to preserve. For Speer it is the memory of a guilt too great for atonement. For Ophuls it is the memory of our common struggle to see that the will to judge justly survives.

The Authority of Silence
in Elie Wiesel's Art

Reading back through Elie Wiesel's work, I am reminded anew how much and how diversely he has written. In addition to the novels there are the essays, the dialogues, the pieces of personal testimony, and, more recently, the finely crafted parables, portraits, and legends. Wiesel's output, in other words, is considerable, yet from a critical point of view he continues to occupy an odd position. As a survivor and a witness he is accorded a respect bordering on reverence. But as an artist Wiesel has received little recognition, especially when compared with contemporaries like Malamud and Bellow. Lack of critical attention may be explained partly by the fact that, until recently, most literary criticism operated on the principle that a novel or story should be self-contained and self-sustaining, without extraliterary reference. Neither the author's life nor the import of actual events, from this point of view, should be allowed to matter in judging a work of art. But of course, in Wiesel's case the separation of the man from the artist, and even more, the separation of his work from events in the world—one event most especially—would be senseless. On the contrary, what makes Wiesel and his work outstanding has to do first with his unique position as a writer *and* a witness, and then with the fact that everything in his work relates directly or indirectly to that overwhelming event we call the Holocaust.

Wiesel's position is therefore paradoxical from the start. In the spring of 1977 he was asked how he could continue so stubbornly to write about the Holocaust. His reply was unexpected: "I do not write about it." Here is a man whose personal and artistic vision has been shaped indelibly by experience of the death camps; a man whose voice, for most of us, seems to issue from the inmost center of that darkness. Yet he can say that he does not write about the Holocaust. On one level, of course, he means that most of his books are fiction rather than accounts of fact. But that is hardly the point; for, except in *Night,* which is autobiographical, Wiesel does indeed avoid direct description of the Holocaust. He does not write novels like, say, Rawicz's *Blood from the Sky* or Ilona Karmel's *An Estate of Memory.* Even in a novel like *Beggar in Jerusalem,* which includes a massacre of Jews by Nazi soldiers, the direction of Wiesel's vision moves elsewhere—to Israel and, as in *Dawn,* to the relation between the European catastrophe and the birth of the Jewish state.

Yet having said this I must immediately offer a correction. For certainly *Dawn* and *Beggar in Jerusalem* are "about" the Holocaust, so much so that without clear knowledge of the Holocaust, the reader will make little sense of either book. And this, I think, is one of the essential characteristics of Wiesel's writing: it is the product of an artist who is also present in his own work as a witness, and its power resides in the way, either by allusion or brief reference or strategic omission, Wiesel makes the sheer fact of the Holocaust the omnipresent—we might almost say omnipotent—background for everything else. The Holocaust, in Wiesel's work, is absolute and the point from which all else shall be measured. It is so absolute that, like God, it need not be mentioned. It is *there,* a monolithic presence against which all human endeavor—spiritual, historical, artistic—meets its boundary.

And that is why, if I select one single aspect of his writing that gets to the heart of the matter, I would say that silence, and the tension between silence and the need of the witness to speak, is the matrix of meaning on which Wiesel's accomplishment stands.

Speaking of "the impact of the Holocaust" in his *Legends of Our Time,* Wiesel makes the following remarks:

> Those who lived through it lack objectivity; they will always take the side of man confronted with the Absolute. As for the scholars and philosophers of every genre who have had the opportunity to observe the tragedy, they will—if they are capable of sincerity and humility—withdraw without daring to enter into the heart of the matter; and if they are not, well,

who cares about their grandiloquent conclusions? Auschwitz,
by definition, is beyond their vocabulary.

Wiesel means that in this special case, our traditional categories of
value and interpretation have been demolished by the very event so
massive and complete in itself, that concepts drawn from tradition and
civilized experience—in short, the key terms of *our* world—become, if
not useless, then extremely problematic.

What, for example, can justice mean when genocide is the issue? As
an act of bearing witness the Eichmann trial was effective, but as an act
of justice it was farce. And what of forgiveness? Can the victims, or for
that matter can we, forgive those hundreds of thousands of guards and
informers and collaborators and bureaucrats and loyal members of the
Reich for the death camps? If not, if these people are condemned and
cast out, what has become of the ideal of human solidarity, of the human
community as such? And what, again, of our "faith in humanity?" Over
and over the survivors tell us that one reason they did not resist was
that, until it was too late, their "faith in humanity" made the prospect
of such monstrous inhumanity impossible to imagine. And evil? On the
scale of the concentration camps it seems satanic, even cosmic, and yet
it was the product of men and women no different from ourselves—
people small, ambitious, afraid, or even, as Albert Speer insists, idealistic
and not without intelligence. Suffering?—all the pain we justify by
saying that it ennobles, that sorrow refines the soul? In Auschwitz,
suffering was as empty as the dead eyes of the *Muselmänner*.

That kind of list is very long. Possibly it does not end. Think of any
key concept in the vocabulary of civilized discourse and immediately, if
its sounding board is the Holocaust, you are in trouble. And the problem
is not with terminology alone, but likewise with traditional structures
of narrative art. Such time-honored structures of meaning as, for example, the quest, the tragic resolution, the significant death, make no
sense at all in the Holocaust Kingdom. Yet here we are, men and women
aware of our inadequate means, earnestly dedicated to a firmer understanding of Elie Wiesel, and through him, of the Holocaust itself. The
paradox—if not the downright contradiction—is obvious; and our situation is not unlike Wiesel's own predicament as writer and witness.
What artistic apparatus can he possibly employ, when by definition the
function of cultural constructs is to mediate, to domesticate—i.e., to

transform terror and nothingness into modes of value and meaning by which we may then stay human and sane?

To confront the experience of the Holocaust directly would seem to be possible in one way only, namely, through the straightforward testimony of the survivors themselves. But as Wiesel observes in *One Generation After:* "Reading certain books by [survivors] who do not know each other, one wonders: they describe the same scenes, the same partings. It all begins and it all ends the same way. It has all been said, yet all remains to be said." Yes, anyone who has looked at the vast documentation left by survivors knows that each story is the same story, one story to be told six million times. And having told it in *Night,* Wiesel must surely have wondered how, without merely repeating himself, he might more keenly come to grips with his urgent feeling that, having said everything sayable, "all remains to be said."

His solution has been to mobilize silence; to use silence as a category of relation to primary aspects of the Holocaust experience; to render silence in ways that make it—and therefore what it embodies—present and meaningful to us. His job, as writer and witness, has been to make silence speak.

Referring to the documents written by survivors—the "precisely kept ledgers of horrors," the "accounts told with childlike artlessness"—Wiesel says that "they waver between scream and silent anger." The scream, which transmutes itrself into the voice of the witness, is born of shock and pain, of rage and the overriding need to "let the world know," as survivors always say. Silence, on the other hand, is born of terror and sustained by the knowledge that the truth of Auschwitz can never be communicated, or that in any case a guilt-ridden world prefers to ignore this kind of truth. There is, as Wiesel notes, a "conspiracy of silence" against the testimony of survivors, in which the survivors themselves, through a socially induced guilt and through their own sense of having failed to make the world listen, are forced to join.

And thus on numerous occasions Wiesel has himself called for silence, as in his essay "A Plea for the Dead," in which he defends the dead against the kind of revilement and condemnation now current—e.g., "they went to their deaths like sheep"; they "regressed to infantile levels"; they behaved like "incompetent children"—and in which he concludes: "The world kept silent while the Jews were being massacred, while they were being reduced to the state of objects good for the fire; let the world at least have the decency to keep silent now as well." And in the same essay he says of himself: "I prefer to take my place on the side of Job, who chose questions and not answers, silence and not speeches."

Yet the voice of Elie Wiesel is ever with us. The books, essays, and articles continue to appear. Wiesel's commitment to silence is countered by his commitment as a witness, the latter drawing its strength from at least three sources. First, survivors feel compelled to scream, to warn, to remember, and record. Second, Wiesel believes that unless the world's guilt is openly acknowledged and the implications of Auschwitz are made an active part of general consciousness, the Holocaust will have indeed signaled the death of man; for if this unacknowledged guilt is not faced, the trauma it generates will grow until nothing less than nuclear war will suffice as atonement. A third reason Wiesel finds it necessary to violate the silence is to avoid betraying himself. In *One Generation After* he has one of his *personae* say: "In the beginning, I thought I could change man. Today I know I cannot. If I still shout today, if I still scream, it is to prevent man from ultimately changing me."

One of the special characteristics of Wiesel's writing is his wisdom, and wisdom, as T. S. Eliot pointed out in his essay on Goethe, is something very few of us possess, something not to be confused with intelligence or mere worldly knowing. In Wiesel's case, moreover, it is a wisdom born of silence and despair. He who speaks does not know, he who knows does not speak. Certainly Wiesel knows this, and by trying to transform silence into a mode of utterance he has revealed to us one of the most striking consequences of the Holocaust. Here was an experience so terrible that despair itself is inadequate; or rather, it was an experience of such permanent disturbance that even in despair the spirit, simply *as* spirit, continues to struggle, to respond, to confront. And in consequence, another important aspect of Wiesel's work is his *tone*. We actually hear the silence from which he speaks, and we cannot avoid the sense of words uttered in despair even while, by the very act of speaking, this despair is made to join with, if not hope, then something beyond hope, which survives and persists and is all the more convincing because there is no false comfort. I am really speaking of Wiesel's peculiar style; and if problems in stylistic analysis sound grossly out of place in the presence of the Holocaust, let me at least say that style, in literary art, is the verbal manifestation of character, of a particular configuration of spiritual being—in Wiesel's case a strange mix of despair and something beyond despair, a mode of utterance that includes, or is surrounded by, silence.

Some of my literary friends have remarked to me that Wiesel is not an especially fine writer. By comparison, they argue, other writers handle language better. They mean differently, of course; but comparison of this sort is suspect in general, and in this special case that kind of judgment can be made only if Wiesel's unique position—the "place" from which he speaks—is ignored. To read a book by Elie Wiesel is one thing; to read it with knowledge of the man as a survivor and a witness, and further to read it with at least some knowledge of the ghettos, the cattle cars, and the killing centers, is another, very different experience, even from the perspective of a purely aesthetic response. This is at once the weakness (from a critical point of view) and the strength (from a human and artistic point of view) of Wiesel's art. Much of the time the full impact of his prose depends on knowing *who* is speaking and *what* he is speaking of, while neither is actually clarified. Here, too, we might raise the whole pressing question of "art after Auschwitz," which is to say that any vision of the human condition will now be haunted by the Holocaust and its implications. Wiesel evokes it constantly, but often by suggestion, or seemingly innocent statements, or even by deliberately not identifying the source of his anguish and concern.

This, then, is what I mean when I suggest that silence is central to his art. Not silence as a vacuum or emptiness, but as *presence*—of memory, of the dead, of an evil so overwhelming and unspeakable that only silence, in its infinitude, can begin to represent it. In novels like *The Accident* and *The Gates of the Forest,* there is very little direct description of experience connected with the Holocaust, and then mostly in small bits and pieces. We have to imagine the implications, we have to recover *the story behind the story,* and it is Wiesel's use of silence that stimulates the imagination to do so. Likewise with *Messengers of God;* one reason Wiesel has been increasingly drawn to the Midrashic tradition of parable and commentary is that he can retell these tales largely by asking questions, and yet in a way that allows this bewilderment of detail to suggest—without open reference—aspects of the Holocaust or of man's relation to God and himself after Auschwitz. As if, in fact, it were all there from time's beginning.

No doubt some people will object that I am "reducing" Wiesel's work to its aesthetic dimension, that I am treating matters of ultimate concern as if they were merely artistic products. I have suggested that silence is an artistic strategy in Wiesel's work, an effective solution to an aesthetic problem, which is to say the problem of meaning and communication. Let me qualify this by stating that art is one of our few approaches to truth, one of the ways consciousness is allowed to focus on otherwise unreachable kinds of experience; therefore craft and calculation in art are matters of first importance. Wiesel himself must know this: it is evident in his decision to write, to be an artist—only, in his case, an artist always in service of the witness.

Let us agree, then, that he *uses* silence. But he could hardly do this if silence did not already have profound meaning for him. Here we move from the work to the man, in particular to the man who has demanded and pledged silence over and over again, as if it were the central mode of relation to the Holocaust. I do not mean silence on the thematic level; not, that is, the dramatization of silence as a mode of behavior, as in *The Oath* and *The Gates of the Forest,* although here too Wiesel's fascination with silence is evident. No, the kind of silence from which his writing springs is more than idea or theme; it is an experience and a condition, a cause for existential response and metaphysical implication.

In *Legends of Our Time,* immediately after the passage concerning our lack of vocabulary, Wiesel goes on to say: "The survivors, more realistic if not more honest, are aware of the fact that God's presence at Treblinka or Maidanek—or, for that matter, his absence—poses a problem which will remain forever insoluble." There are three phrases here that, if put in conjunction, figure in one of the primary meanings of silence for Wiesel. *God's presence, his absence,* and out of these two, the *insoluble problem.* This is very much like the contradictory but nonetheless authentic response that Wiesel expressed through *Night:* there is no God, and I hate him. After Auschwitz, in other words, God's presence is most strongly felt through his absence, which may indeed be an insoluble problem for the intellect but which, as experienced, is known and expressed as that eternal silence of the universe in the face of human agony. Quarreling with God is part of Jewish tradition, usually a one-sided quarrel in which God, when put to the question, answers only in the whirlwind. For Wiesel in any case—and let us not forget that he is a deeply religious man—for Wiesel this silence has become a permanent source of pain and the surest proof of God's existence.

On the human level, as I suggested earlier, silence is a symptom of our failure to comprehend and make sense of the Holocaust. But it is also, for Wiesel, the palpable presence of the dead, the purest voice of those millions murdered, who are most insistently present in their absence. One of the ways Wiesel deals with this aspect of silence is through those dialogues with the dead that continue to appear in his work. To acknowledge the dead thus, to address them as present, with respect and humility and also—as in *Beggar in Jerusalem*—with a yearning to join them, can be done, after all, only in silence.

By way of conclusion, let me repeat that silence is Wiesel's solution to questions about the Holocaust. There are no answers, no meanings to be discerned, only the intolerable weight of the event itself, to be faced in the quiet of an endless sorrow. And yet, knowing this, to stand in such a relation to the Holocaust is to take up an important, perhaps supremely important, position. For then silence and the Holocaust become one, each invested in the other—a situation in which each failure of mind and tongue, in which the stillness of despair no less than the soul's struggle to transcend its impotence, all serve to keep us in vigilant contact with the terrible truths of our century. In *Messengers of God* Wiesel makes the following remark: "One recognizes the value of a text by the weight of its silence." That is the measure of his own work as well, his burden and his aim: to evoke the unspeakable, to allow the dead their voice, to acknowledge God in His absence, and finally to make this kind of silence heard.

Poetry and Politics

The Example of Nazim Hikmet

Considering that in his homeland Nazim Hikmet was never free of police harassment, that he spent almost half of his mature life in prison and much of the rest in exile, he nevertheless managed to do a great deal of writing. Plays, journalism, a novel, more than twenty volumes of poems: his *Human Landscapes from My Country* alone runs to seventeen thousand lines, and at its best Hikmet's poetry possesses a bold grace and an eagerness of statement suggesting that for this poet the labor of words as needful as breathing. Already in 1933 there were phonograph records of Hikmet reciting his work; and in Paris in 1950, when Turkish students were called in by their embassy to be lectured on the "dangers of communism," they chanted a poem by Hikmet in protest. Better than anyone else, Hikmet caught the radical spirit of the new populism in Turkey; and despite their government's long disapproval of him, his countrymen have declared him their greatest modern poet. Since he received the World Peace Prize in 1950, moreover, his reputation has spread through Europe and the Near East. Only in America—for reasons I shall try to identify—has recognition been slow. Now, however, five books of Hikmet's poetry are available in English translation.

The recent acceptance of poets like Hikmet signals an important shift in American literary affairs. Editors, translators, and poets of a new generation have made their entrance, men and women doubtful of fixed opinions and inherited rules, who have found it impossible to ignore the work of poets like Pablo Neruda, Anna Akhmatova, Czeslaw Milosz, and Yannis Ritsos—to name only a few of the poets in whose company Hikmet belongs. To speak of Hikmet's poetry is necessarily to consider this "other" world of literature, a kind of art sometimes called political, sometimes called a poetry of engagement or commitment, which is strikingly different from the kind of literary product most of us have been taught to esteem. What needs to be noted at once is the growing attention to traditions other than our own—chiefly South American and Eastern European—the effort of younger poets, now writing in English to gain definitions and a sense of renewal by contact with examples outside the standard British-American-French tradition.

It seems that the temporal influence of our own past has begun to give way to the spatial influence of contemporary examples from different origins, some of them decisively foreign. Something like this happened before, of course, but only (if our French connection is put aside) up to a point. Looking again at what poets like Eliot and Pound did with Eastern texts, we see that with no care for the local economy they grabbed and picked like thieves at a bazaar. Eliot thought it better to steal than to borrow, Pound's *Cantos* are high-handed imperialism, and for Wallace Stevens the world's wealth was a bin of symbols at imagination's lordly disposal. Today, on the other hand, we seem closer to a truly global consciousness, and there is new respect for the integrity of the traditions to which one turns.

Much of the poetry of this "other" world, furthermore, has never worried about keeping life and art separate; it fairly thrives on energetic confluence of the literary, the political, and the plainly human. Most students of Anglo-American poetry have been trained on principle to distrust political vision in art—as if Milton, Shelley, and Blake had never writ a word. But poetry of this other kind is as valid as the sort we have been instructed to defend, and it may even be, in times as vicious as ours, more valuable. For Nazim Hikmet, in any case, there could be no fast line dividing art from life and political commitment—which accounts, in part, for the vigor and capacious humanity of his work.

Hikmet was born in Salonika, of Turkish parentage, in 1902. His childhood and early youth were spent in Istanbul, the city which would remain a central presence in his poems. Most of the time between 1922 and 1928 he lived in Moscow, where he studied, wrote plays, and, following Mayakovsky's example, learned to break words and the poetic line to suit his own vision. Between 1928 and 1938 Hikmet was in and out of Turkish prisons for a total of five years. His crime was never more than outspoken loyalty to Marxist ideals, but the constitution of the republic naturally outlawed intent to overthrow the government, which is what Marxism came down to in official eyes, and Hikmet's legal situation was exacerbated by centuries of bad feeling between Turkey and Russia.

Hikmet must surely have known what he was getting himself into by writing poems with a revolutionary ring, and through experience he would learn that when a person ends up in jail for writing poetry, there can be little room for thinking of art as something divorced from politics. In 1938—allegedly because military cadets were reading his poems and threatening to revolt—Hikmet was again sent to prison, this time for twelve years straight. Only in 1950, after a heart attack and the appeals of an international committee including Sartre, Neruda, and Picasso, was Hikmet finally released. He was then forced into exile (the government planned to draft him into the army), and he died in Moscow in 1963.

The first sample of Hikmet's work in English appeared in 1967, translated by Taner Baybars for one of the elegant little Jonathan Cape editions published in London. The selection is small, there are *parts* of poems, and a fair number are to be found in the broader collections published more recently by Persea Books in this country. Nonetheless, the Cape edition of *Selected Poems* stands as a laudable venture, and it contains one poem that any reader of Hikmet will appreciate—the twenty-page "Letters to Taranta-Babu," written in 1935 after fascist Italy's invasion of Ethiopia. Although much of Hikmet's poetry takes as its situation the circumstances of his own experience, this poem, like other of Hikmet's long dramatic pieces, makes fictional use of a real event. An Ethiopian man, trapped in Rome, watches the fascists take control and comes to realize that the Italians are preparing to attack his own country. He writes about this to Taranta-Babu, his wife at home, whom he "knows" will be killed. He must also know that these letters will never leave Rome.

One of the moving things about the poem is that although the speaker can vividly imagine the devastation in personal terms—his goats slaughtered, his villaged sacked, his wife's intestines upon the sand—he does not bear malice toward the men who will bring this to pass:

> They're coming, Taranta-Babu,
> from the heart of a conflagration;

and once they have flown the flag
    from the sunbaked roof
        of your earthen house
they may all go back—
but even then
                the lathe-turner from Torino
who's left his right arm in Somalia
will no longer work with his steel rods
as if working with bales of silk-thread.
And the fisherman from Sicily
            will no longer see the light of the sea
            through his blinded eyes.

Hikmet's sense of human solidarity is especially strong at moments like this. That the soldiers are themselves victims—of ignorance and fear, of official lying—is a fact that Hikmet will not treat ironically. This is a point of some importance, for facing disastrous events we either take refuge in irony (the measure of our detachment, our despair) or we suffer with the victims (the measure of our compassion). The latter requires patience and historical perspective; a commitment to the struggle of man against the state surely helps. Political involvement, that is, *can* support the poet in his need to remain human—open, caring, hopeful—amid dehumanizing circumstances. The poem itself is evidence that historical participation, refracted through an individual's immediate life, is as fit for poetry as any other subject.

The *Selected Poems* of 1967 was followed by two further volumes translated by Taner Baybars, both again published in England. In 1970 *The Moscow Symphony and Other Poems* appeared (published in this country in 1971, *The Day Before Tomorrow* in 1972. Both books were very small and relatively expensive, and, after the promise of the translations in the Cape edition, uniformly disappointing. With the exception of the long poem "The Moscow Symphony" (which is typical of Hikmet's more ambitious work, but not well organized and not well rendered), there is little worth reading. Either Baybars has selected poor poems or his translations are weak. The following lines are the concluding passage from a poem entitled "About Death," in which three of Hikmet's dead friends visit him in prison; one had died in a stupid industrial accident, one had died in ugly poverty, one had despaired of the world's injustice and drunk himself to death. And thus Hikmet concludes:

A Persian poet has said,
    'Death is just
    hits the poor and the rich alike.'
Why are you surprised Osman's son Hashim?
Or haven't you ever heard
    of a rich shah dying
        at the bottom of a cargo
            under a basket of coal?
The Persian poet says,
    'Death is just.'
Yakup, my dear chap, how well you laugh.
Never saw you laugh like that
    when you were still about.
A persian poet, Death . . . just—
leave that bottle alone, Ahmet Jemil.

Friends, your anger seems to be in vain.
I know:
    For death to be just
    Life must be just
        as well.

The dramatic monologue is one of Hikmet's favorite forms. This one is a meditation on the human result of class conflict, and its theme is (or ought to be) a truism: we die, yes, but as to *how*, under what conditions, things in death are as they were in life—the rich are indeed different. The political implication is that life, not death, must set things straight. These themes, at least in their idea, come across fairly well, but the lines I have quoted are surely not distinguished poetry. Either Hikmet often slipped into second-rate verse or Baybars is too often unable to capture the quality of the original. What eludes him is the immediacy of Hikmet's colloquial diction, when precisely this kind of language— direct, slangy, and offhand, the verbal equivalent of friendship and lively communal interchange—is central to Hikmet's aesthetic-political vision. Baybars deserves credit for introducing Hikmet to English readers, but he is simply not as successful as the American translators who have followed him.

Things I Didn't Know I Loved, published by Persea Books in 1975, was the first collection of Hikmet's work to appear in America. *The Epic of Sheik Bedreddin and Other Poems,* also from Persea, came out in the spring of 1978. With these two rich, inclusive volumes (both available in paperback), we are at last able to appreciate Hikmet's art. Randy Blasing and Mutlu Konuk translated both collections, and the poems they selected are representative as well as arranged chronologically— early poems, the long middle span of prison poetry, the late poems— to allow us a sense of Hikmet's range and development. The different stages of Hikmet's style are visible, which suggests that Blasing and Konuk have in some vital way stayed closer to Hikmet than Baybars with his more uniform and rigid translations. Even when the different translations are closest, important differences appear. Compare, for example, two versions of the same stanza, first from the Cape edition, then from Persea:

> At night I go knee-deep into the sea
> and begin to draw my nets;
> my catch: a mixture of stars and fish.

> All night I wade knee-deep into the water
> and pull the nets out of the sea:
> the fish get all mixed up with the stars.

I might argue that words like "wade" and "pull" bear more experiential weight than the more conventional "go" and "draw." Certainly "a mixture" is stiffer and more distant, more formal, than "all mixed up." The real distinction, however, has to do with faithfulness to Hikmet's special vision, which is at once historical and timeless. Marxist *and* mystical. This particular poem, entitled "Occupation," is chiefly concerned with the union of man and the cosmos through work, a theme which Baybars—by subordinating the "nets" and the "catch" to the "I," by breaking the moment into stages, by introducing time into a timeless human activity—subverts.

I would not wish to push such distinctions too far. In either translation the elemental level at which Hikmet finds his characteristic imagery is evident. He is, in the best sense, a writer of primitive poetry, poetry which depends for its power on primary techniques—repetition, contrast, line break, basic imagery of earth, man, and nature (which to the Western ear sounds Biblical), and finally a use of metaphor mainly to enlarge and enrich rather than to refine and complicate. These, along with Hikmet's directness of voice and mystical overtones, his moral energy and faithful delight in life itself, provide the foundation of his art.

I shall stick with the Persea editions from now on, and by way of moving to the heart of Hikmet's poetry, I want to look at some of his "prison poems." One of the signs of our time, it seems to me, is the large body of "prison literature" that has come into existence—a fact at once political *and* literary—and I would even suggest that the "prison poem," at least in the hands of a master like Hikmet, has become a genre of its own. Much of his best work was done while in prison, and a great amount of it refers to his own immediate condition as a political prisoner. "Letters from a Man in Solitary," which is addressed to his wife, begins:

> I carved your name on my watchband
> with my fingernail.

In such small sad ways does time take human shape. And that, of course, is the point: time passes, without structure or significance, as empty and endless as the Bursa plains which Hikmet could see from his window. Days pass, seasons, and that much more unused life is lost. One of the moments which, for the man in jail, most tempts him to despair is simply evening, another day gone:

> It's five o'clock, my dear.
> Outside, with its dryness,
>   its eerie whispering,
>   its mud roof,
> and with its lame, skinny horse
>   that stands motionless in the midst of infinity
> —I mean it's enough to drive the man inside crazy with grief—
> outside, with all its machinery and all its art,
> a plains night comes down red on treeless space.

The poem is built on such moods and seems to be moving deeper into darkness. But in the last section an abrupt reversal occurs; something happens which unexpectedly redeems the misery, cancels time and despair in one strong moment of transcendence:

> Sunday today.
> Today they took me out in the sun for the first time.

And I stood very still, struck for the first time in my life
                by how far away the sky is,
                how blue
                and how wide.

Then I respectfully sat down on the earth.
I put my back against the wall.
For a moment no trap to fall into,
for a moment no struggle, no freedom, no wife.
Just earth, sun, and me . . .
I am happy.

To find this kind of liberation in this kind of moment (which seems religious) is typical of Hikmet. He *will* find ways to make the pain and emptiness of prison life significant. And one of those ways is the ever-increasing awareness of nature as a source of strength and inspiration. In the following "Poem," whose first line makes full sense only when the entire poem is read, the poet's capacity to respond to the world's beauty is the index of his will to endure:

I'm inside the advancing light,
my hands are hungry, the world beautiful.

My eyes can't get enough of the trees—
they're so hopeful, so green.

A sunny road runs through the mulberries,
I'm at the window of the prison infirmary.

I can't smell the medicines—
carnations must be blooming somewhere.

It's like this:
being captured is beside the point,
the point is not to surrender.

The play on key words in the last two lines reminds us that such work constitutes a poetry of resistance, against the "enemies of hope," as

Hikmet calls the agents of tyranny, but likewise against conditions of prison existence which might cause the prisoner to weaken or give up. The fundamental structure of the prison poem is the stark division between "inside" and "outside," between life-in-the-cell and life-in-the-world. To survive unbroken, "the man inside" must maintain connection and rapport with the world's larger life. In this way self-pity can be overcome, and the reasons for imprisonment, the *real* reasons, remain firmly felt. The following lines are the opening of one of Hikmet's finest poems, "Some Advice to Those Who Will Serve Time in Prison," and notice how complicated the pun becomes when the title is read from the perspective of Marxist convictions:

> If instead of being hanged by the neck
>> you're thrown inside
>> for not giving up hope
> in the world, in your country, in people,
>> if you do ten or fifteen years
>> apart from the time you have left,
> you won't say
>>> "Better I had swung from the end of a rope
>>>> like a flag"—
> you'll put your foot down and live.
> It might not be a pleasure exactly,
> but it's your solemn duty
>> to live one more day
>>> to spite the enemy.
> Part of you may live alone inside,
>> like a stone at the bottom of a well.
> But the other part
>> must be so caught up
>> in the flurry of the world
>> that you shiver there inside
> when outside, at forty days' distance, a leaf moves.

One of the consequences of the gap between "inside" and "outside," or rather of the effort to close this gap, is Hikmet's characteristic imagery of absence: the leaf "at forty days' distance," the carnations "blooming somewhere," or this:

> Far away,
> where we can't see,
> the moon must be rising.

Hikmet's imagery might also be an extension of his Marxist faith that everywhere life goes forward, history moves, men work in concert to bring about a better world. But in the immediate case it is the outcome of his physical condition. Hikmet in prison *is* cut off, unlike the contrived isolation so dear to modern poets, which is metaphorical only. And since he cannot participate actively in the world, nor be in actual contact with the people and places he loves, he must find other means to restore relation, some legitimate way of keeping in touch. For Hikmet, in other words, absence is a condition of immediate existence, and how to make absent things present is his pressing need. His solution, of course, is poetry itself. Through an endless evocation of images, through the perpetual summons of imagination, he reunites himself with the world. Friends "visit" him, "letters" go out in all directions, he "talks" with his wife. Hence Hikmet's special reliance on the dramatic monologue: through it he reenters the world of human community.

When we speak of "worlds elsewhere" we usually have in mind private visions, fabulations rare and fine beyond the reach of ordinary life. Not so with Hikmet; he does not strive to escape reality but to attend upon it more dearly. In order to transcend the circumstances imposed by his jailers, he asks nothing more of imagination than that it restore to him a vivid sense of the world as it is. And thus in the poem "On Ibrahim Balaban's 'Spring Picture,'" Hikmet imagines the whole of Balaban's painting, item by item, until he has assembled—or reassembled—an entire world: light, clouds, mountains; foxes with "alarm on their pointed noses"; grass, water, bees, a stork "just back from Egypt"; rabbits, turtles, "a shimmering tree, / in its beauty most like a person"; mothers, wives, children, and finally *homo faber:*

> Here are his sandals, here the patches on his breeches.
> Here is the plow,
> here are the oxen, on their rumps the sad, terrible sores.

I would like, finally to look at two poems not written in prison. The "Gioconda and Si-Ya-U," composed in 1929, is an excellent example of Hikmet's robustly imaginative early style. The poem is an exuberant blend of fantasy and fact, whimsy and earnestness, in which the Mona Lisa—here a painting *and* a woman—falls in love with a young Chinese who asks her:

> "Those who crush our rice fields
>   with the caterpillar treads of their tanks
> and who swagger through our cities
>   like emperors of hell,
> are they of YOUR race,
>   the race of him who CREATED you?"

By way of answer, the lady with the mysterious smile leaves the museum to join the Chinese revolution. The poet himself lands an airplane on the roof of the Louvre to assist her escape. And although Gioconda and her lover are destroyed by Chiang Kai-shek's troops, the Mona Lisa's forced smile, frozen for centuries, has at last turned to real laughter. Hikmet implies that when paintings are enshrined in palaces and poems stuck away in academic tomes, their function is no longer to incite and inspire but rather to adorn and justify the status quo. Museums, from this point of view, are the ruling elite's method for containing art's naturally subversive power. The arts themselves need rescue, and Hikmet dramatizes his commitment by appearing *in* the poem as an accomplice.

The salvaging of truth by means of poetry is also one of the principal themes in "The Epic of Sheik Bedreddin." Written in 1936, after Hikmet had spent time in prison, this is one of the longest, most complex and impressive of Hikmet's poems available in translation. Bedreddin was an Islamic scholar and mystic who, in the middle of the fourteenth century, propagated the idea that mankind is a single community and therefore that the means to life should be shared in common. In practice this meant, among other things, the abolition of private property. Two of his disciples, Mustafa and Kemal, led a small revolt in the countryside, and for a time the peasantry—Moslem, Jew, and Christian—worked the land together. But then the sultan's armies arrived, the movement was defeated, Bedreddin and his disciples were executed.

The "Epic" gives a dramatic account of Bedreddin's rise and fall, but not as a story merely. What happened in the fourteenth century stands for the predicament of the revolutionary spirit, which must endure re-peated defeat and yet survive. Hikmet ties the fate of modern political prisoners to the fate of Bedreddin's followers, and thereby affirms the unkillable nature of his belief in the radical cause for which Bedreddin and so many others have suffered. For all its pain and sorrow, the poem celebrates the human will to revolt against injustice—and once again Hikmet makes his point by placing himself *inside* the narrative.

The poem thus begins with Hikmet in prison, reading a book by a professor of theology in which (viewed from the top downward, that is, from the standard point of view of the victors) Bedreddin and his disciples are reduced to the status of "common" peasants, to whom no special attention is due. For the professor, Bedreddin's movement was just another peasant revolt, short-lived, blind, at most an unfounded disturbance within the established order. The pressure of this lie, of history thus distorted and betrayed, is too much for the poet in his cell. He must *do* something, but what can a man in jail do? In a condition of near frenzy, he looks through the bars of his window and sees the white robe of a monk who had been one of Bedreddin's followers. The poet is suddenly outside his cell, outside of time itself, and with the monk goes back to the great days of Bedreddin as an eyewitness.

Only now is the uprising described, but this time with Hikmet himself as a participant. The poem ends with Hikmet back in his cell, where in the morning light he discovers that the white robe of the monk had actually been a cellmate's shirt hung out to dry. In this way Hikmet confirms the liberating power of imagination, and his imaginative participation in the rebellion is his way of authorizing the poet's role as true witness. In the poem's last section he and the other prisoners discuss the belief, widespread among the peasantry, that Bedreddin will one day come again to lead them from their misery. The poem concludes when one of the inmates admits that he, too, believes in Bedreddin's return, not in the flesh like the Savior of the Christians, but in the spirit of an entire people: "When we say Bedreddin will come again, we mean that his words, look, and breath will appear among us." And so, for Hikmet, it has.

One of the most interesting things about the "Epic" comes at the moment when Bedreddin and his followers are defeated, eight out of ten thousand killed on the spot. Especially curious is the way Hikmet, in his own voice—not as an imaginary participant, but as an outside observer—abruptly breaks into the narrative. It is as if this slaughter of innocence and hope were too immediately terrible to be contained by art *or* ideology:

The victors wiped their bloody swords
              on the flowing white robes
                    of the defeated.
And the earth that brothers worked all together
like a song sung together
was ripped up
              by the hooves of horses bred in the Edirne palace.
Don't say
     this is the necessary result
        of historical, social, and economic conditions—
                         I know!
My head bows before the thing you speak of.
but the heart
              doesn't understand this language too well.

The phrase "necessary result / of historical, social, and economic conditions" is a gross intrusion, something that a Marxist might expect, but of which the poet himself complains. At a moment like this, he says, don't try to console me with abstractions. Don't kill the spirit in its moment of transmission. Whatever may be the case analytically, within the borders of the poem the language of the heart comes first. Hikmet does not use ideological language in his poetry, except in occasional parody. He took pride in his Marxism, but at the same time he lived and worked by this simple formula: human first, Marxist second. This is clear from the footnote which Hikmet attached to the passage quoted above:

> Now as I write these lines I think of certain young men who pass for "leftists" and who'll be saying things like: "Well! He separates his head and his heart; he says his head accepts the historical, social, and economic conditions, but his heart still burns. Well, well—will you look at the Marxist!" . . .
> Marx, who knew that the Paris Commune would be overthrown, who knew the historical, social, and economic conditions necessitating its overthrow, didn't he feel the great dead of the Commune pass through his heart like a "song of pain"? . . .
> A Marxist is not a "mechanical man"—a ROBOT; he is,

with his flesh, blood, nerves, head, and heart, a historically and socially concrete person.

For Hikmet, Marxism was less a system than a way of seeing local injustice as part of a world-historical situation, and his own struggle as part of the struggle everywhere in progress. He was thus united, in spirit and in action, with men and women in every land, with every act in opposition to tyranny, with every hope for a better, a more justly shared world. At very least, a better world was *possible,* and this in itself made all sorts of sacrifice and loss worth bearing. With doctrinaire imperatives, with that rigid authoritarianism of the cadre, Hikmet had no affinity. He much preferred to sum up the whole business as Mao Tse-tung did when he defined Marxism—in idea and in spirit—as first and last "the right to revolt." As far as programs went, Hikmet's could be stated as follows: resist, oppose, defy, always keeping the will to freedom active, always remembering the goodness of life in itself.

In an introduction to Reza Baraheni's *The Crowned Cannibals* (which documents the torture of poets and writers in Iran), E. L. Doctorow describes the place of "political" art in these general terms:

> There is a kind of writer appearing with greater and greater frequency among us who witnesses the crimes of his own government against himself and his countrymen. He chooses to explore the intimate subject of a human being's relationship to the state. His is the universe of the imprisoned, the tortured, the disfigured, and the doleful authority for the truth of his work is usually his own body. . . . So let us propose discussion of the idea that a new art, with its own rules, is being generated in the twentieth century: the *Lieder* of victims of the state.

I am not sure that "new" is the proper word here, but certainly our time has provoked a vast body of literature concerned with political issues. As Doctorow suggests and Hikmet confirms, there is a vital part of human experience which is explicitly political and yet whose expression is not to be confused with propaganda, "social realism," versified doctrine, or any other sort of a priori utterance. Its ideological content cannot be denied, but neither can this be denied of any art whatsoever. The great difference is that while much traditional art remains unaware of its own ideological base, the kind of work a poet like Hikmet produces is deliberately explicit about the beliefs underlying the vision. Or put it this way: instead of invoking the consoling authority of "the human condition," instead of simply saying *that's how it is,* the political writer says yes, *that's how it is, but not how it must be.* The essence of a political fact is that it can be changed or at least modified in quality. We all die, as Hikmet notes, but in ways so very different as to suppose deaths almost different in kind. Some deaths are more human than others; imprisonment for political reasons is not *necessarily* an archetype of existence; and while all men and women must surely suffer, we ought all be allowed the means to bear our pain with dignity.

That a novel can be political and still a successful work of art has been conceded. Although a precise definition may be difficult, books like *The Charterhouse of Parma, The Possessed, The First Circle,* and Pavese's *The House on the Hill* have been generally acknowledged as examples of "the political novel." An equivalent term of poetry has not yet won currency. The fact, moreover, that an elemental experience like death can be represented in terms of the human condition *and* in terms partly political, suggests that political art depends on the kind of awareness with which it is invested. For this reason the novel more readily lends itself to political form: the author simply includes characters who embody some degree of political consciousness regarding the events they observe or experience. Their perspectives then clash with others, and the reader may make of them as much or as little as he or she pleases.

With poetry, especially poetry in the lyrical mode, the problem is more difficult. There is only one point of view, one kind of consciousness in the poem (even in a poem like *The Waste Land* all the voices are fragments of Eliot's intractably conservative point of view), and if the poet is not inclined to be outspoken, or if he prefers to veil his intent in irony to avoid jail or the firing squad, other means than direct statement must be found if the experience or feeling which the poem represents is to have a political dimension. And this, in turn, leads to the more vexing relation between the poet himself and the voice in his poems.

I am referring in particular to the autobiographical "prison poems," in which Hikmet simply uses himself, a real man in a real prison. He does not need to devise dramatic situations, nor must he invent appropriate scenes-as-metaphor. Authenticity is assured, and the seriousness with which he speaks is underscored by the authority of actual experience. In narratives like "Gioconda" and "Bedreddin," on the other hand,

Hikmet dramatizes his political involvement by sticking himself into the poem as one of its characters. Thereby he is able to express his personal allegiance and grief, not as an outside commentary, and not through a vocabulary alien to his essentially lyrical mode, but as part of the action within the poem's declared limits.

Nevertheless, we know that the character in the poem represents, or is continuous with, the actual person of the poet. And in the prison poems this kind of identification is more or less total. In these examples, at least, some knowledge of Nazim Hikmet—of his beliefs, his behavior, the major events in his life—is necessary to a full understanding of the poems. Now, Hikmet may be a special case, or, what is more likely, political poetry may be a special case, but either way the conclusion would seem to be—unspeakable as this is in academic circles—that unlike most modern poetry, which thrives on self-reference, ambiguity, and detachable personae, the political poem must be allowed to include, as a cardinal part of its meaning, the actual situation of the poet.

Back in the thirties and forties, largely in reaction to political upheavals of the time, the New Critics did away with any need to take the world or the author into account while reading poetry. During the McCarthy era of the fifties, this approach to literature re-suggested itself as perhaps the better part of valor. More recently, Harold Bloom has told us that poems are about other poems. The structuralists have decided that literature is a self-enclosed, self-propelled system responding to itself alone. And now the followers of Jacques Derrida refuse to admit that the author *or* the audience exists; a text, they argue, becomes a text only when the poet and the world are absent.

There are virtues to some of these ideas, and Derrida's arguments in particular are witty and a pleasure to unwind. But they are all, as their source and their continued support reveals, wholly academic. Men and women who know that they will be held accountable for what they write, that the cost of their art may be prison or death, cannot choose to separate themselves from their work. And neither should we. Osip Mandelstam is not a political poet by Hikmet's standard, and probably Hikmet is not so good a poet as Mandelstam; the point, however, is that Mandelstam's later poetry reads differently if we know that Stalin was pushing the poet to his death in a concentration camp. Or again, to listen to Victor Jara sing his protest songs becomes a decisively different experience when we know that for these popular poetic statements the Chilean police tortured him (they chopped off his hands) and machine-gunned him to death. In cases like these, there is a real difference in the interpretations we devise and in the seriousness with which we approach such works.

The conclusion may be that to write like Hikmet you must live like Hikmet. It follows that only certain poets will be able to write his kind of poetry. Or does it? Certainly we cannot write about what we have not been able to imagine, and to imagine something soundly we must have some degree of actual experience, however remote, of that which would inspire us to creation. Americans are not sent to jail for serious novels and poems, which are seldom political in any case. But that does not mean we are free of political experience. During the trauma of our Vietnam years, with social and political upheaval in every direction, there were more than a thousand poets publishing their work in America. Only the barest handful—Bly, Levertov, Dugan, Ginsberg, and Kinnell among them—passed briefly through what we might call their "Vietnam period." Why is this so?

This amazing gap between life and art is the more striking when we recall that a fairly large number of poets participated in rallies, sit-ins, marches, and protest readings, but nevertheless did not feel the pressure of this experience deeply enough for it to register in their work. How many books like *Body Rags* emerged? Why does a politically conscious writer like Mailer have to make of everything a joke before he can settle down to write? And why was a poet as powerful as Lowell unable, despite his political activism and his obsession with history, to free himself from that typically American torment of the solitary self?

Of course there are good but isolated examples of political poetry among the works of Tate, Frost, Warren, and Williams. And for poets like Oppen, Olson, and Reznikoff, there is always a degree of political consciousness present. We might even consider Robinson Jeffers, in his majestic negativity, a political poet of sorts. But overall, and despite Whitman's broad invitation, no tradition of political writing has been able to establish itself, and most histories of American poetry omit this side of our art altogether. There is, I think, something absolutely recalcitrant in the American character—a furious allegiance to the transcendental ego, a will to ignore history no matter what, a determination to behave more like Emerson's "transparent eyeball" than like a man or woman with real passions, involved in the very real problems of a society during dark and troubled times.

Generalizations about American poetry are bound to be suspect. I do not, however, think we possess—not yet—a tradition of political art sufficient to inspire and support a poem as big as *The Heights of Macchu Picchu* or a novel as brilliant as *One Hundred Years of Solitude*. Nor, in recent years, have we believed in the importance of poetry enough (Adrienne Rich's *The Dream of a Common Language* is a brave exception) to generate the kind of seriousness which political poetry may claim by virtue of its character not only as an art but as an agent of action in the world. Simply because in his art and in his person Hikmet opposes the enemies of the human spirit in harmony with itself and the earth, he can speak casually and yet with a seriousness that most modern American poets never dream of attempting. In the poem "On Living," for example, he begins:

Living is no laughing matter:
> you must live with great seriousness
> > like a squirrel, for example—
I mean without looking for something beyond and above living,
> I mean living must be your whole occupation.
Living is no laughing matter:
> you must take it seriously,
> so much so and to such a degree that,
> for example, your hands tied behind your back, your back to the wall,
> or else in a laboratory
> > in your white coat and thick glasses,
> > you'll be able to die for people—
even for people whose faces you've never seen,
even though you know living
> > is the most real, the most beautiful thing.
I mean you must take living so seriously
> that even at seventy, for example, you will plant olives—
> and not so they'll be left for your children either,
> but because even though you fear death you don't believe it,
> because living, I mean, weighs heavier.

And lest we conclude that Hikmet's seriousness is too much the function of his political cause and not truly rooted in the tragic depth of the human condition, not fully possessed by the love of life in itself, let me quote the last lines of the same poem:

This earth will grow cold one day,
not like a heap of ice
or a dead cloud even,
but like an empty walnut it will roll along
        in pitch-black space . . .
You must grieve for this right now,
you have to feel this sorrow now,
for the world must be loved this much
        if you're going to say "I lived" . . .

Hikmet's otherness, in terms of our tradition, is part of his value. To speak with irony, to deploy ambiguity like a many-sided shield, to pretend that anything uttered or even perceived issues from the invented voice or persona merely—these, until recently, have been the ways of most poetry in America, ways of orchestrating private vision while refusing the responsibility it entails. Hikmet, on the other hand, says what he means straight out. He places himself inside the story, or speaks in his own voice from the conditions of his own life. Thereby he offers himself as an example; and if he believes what he says, he must try his best to live an exemplary life.

In such ways art and existence meet, at risk no doubt, but at a risk worth taking. I am speaking of aesthetic risk, but for Hikmet the risk was, finally, seventeen years of prison as the cost of speaking freely. He would never have dreamed of disowning what he wrote. This was just the way any man or woman writing poems would act. And this way of living, as it resides in Hikmet's poetry, is perhaps the chief benefit of reading him. "He is the rock of defense of human nature; an upholder and preserver, carrying everywhere with him relationship and love." That was Wordsworth's idea of the poet. Hikmet took it for granted.

Introduction to
Jean-François Steiner's
Treblinka

T he particulars of the Holocaust are endless. Blunt shovels as a
preferred method for hacking prisoners to death. Children
dumped living into ditches of flame. Medical experiments. Lampshades.
So perverse are such details that simply to mention them seems shameful.
Statistically the Holocaust is less immediately sickening because less
sharply seeable; but here too, reality takes on a feeling of unreality which
terrifies. Extermination of nine million people in five years, at least six
million of them Jews, a million of them children. Death camps so efficient
that twenty thousand human beings could be "processed"—turned from
flesh to smoke—each day. The boast of Treblinka was "from door to
door in forty-five minutes"—from opening the cattle cars to slamming
shut the gas chambers. As an itemization of evil truly demonic, the
record of the Holocaust goes on and on, nor can we sum its meaning,
nor does it cease to haunt us deeply.

At Yale University in the early 1970s, for example, Stanley Milgram
performed his famous "obedience experiments," the aim of which was
to determine at what point a person would refuse, against "official"
directives, to continue in a process of obvious cruelty. The results were
unexpected. A full two-thirds of those who volunteered (people of different ages and jobs) did exactly as they were told: under the guise of
a "learning test" they followed the instructions of a man dressed as a
"scientist" and applied higher and higher charges of electrical shock to
"subjects" who were failing to "learn" properly. This process went on,
in some cases, until the "subjects" appeared to be having heart attacks.
The whole thing was faked, including the electrical charges, but the
volunteers, who were the real subjects, did not know this.

One of the peculiarities of the experiment was that volunteers tended to suffer increasingly from stress as the voltage appeared to be increasing, yet they were unable to stop. In some cases they began to laugh hysterically, laughter so pained and jagged that the soul itself seemed torn. But the worst and most revealing part of their experience came later, when they were informed of the role they had innocently played. Disturbed by what they had done, they felt compelled to judge themselves and they did it in terms of the Holocaust. They suddenly saw themselves as men and women who could indeed behave as Hitler's SS troops had behaved—only following orders, to be sure, but following orders nonetheless. And although it is ludicrous to compare a clinical experiment at Yale with events in the death camps, the fact that we do make such spontaneous connections reveals a central truth of our time. At some unconscious level, the image of the Holocaust is *with us*—a memory which haunts, a sounding board for all subsequent evil—in the back of the mind not only for the normal, well-intentioned people who took part in Milgram's experiments, but for all of us now living: we, the inheritors.

For the victims of the Holocaust I cannot speak. Their agony, which to this day is visible in the millions of scratches made by fingernails on the ceilings of the gas chambers, is theirs with a finality none of the living can know. But for us who dwell in its aftermath, the most awful thing about the Holocaust is simply that it happened. It entered the world not of fantasy or science fiction, but of fact, of history, the world that is real and present and ours. And judging from things like the Milgram experiments, from the perpetual fascination with Hitler and the Nazis, from the sudden eruption of interest in the Holocaust itself, its presence in memory has not only lasted but—forty years after the event—has grown in force and authority. Simply as a fact and as a precedent it mocks our desire to affirm life's goodness and undermines our hope that never again will human beings gather in such vast and well-ordered numbers to commit mass murder. It stands as proof of the human potential for radical evil and therefore also as a prophecy of our possible future. Which is to say that after the Holocaust we know, we know full well, that life can be governed by death.

The first Nazi camps, which were set up soon after Hitler came to power in 1933, were designed as places of detention and as training grounds for the SS. Dachau and Buchenwald were among the most notorious, and although we cannot forget that thousands of people perished in these places, we should also keep in mind that camps of this kind were not intended or equipped to be instruments of genocide, nor were Jews their only victims. After the outbreak of the war, however, and as the Nazi policy of mass extermination took shape with the Jews as primary target, the major "killing centers," as they came to be called, began to operate. And all of them were located outside the Reich itself— as if in this way the Germans could indulge in atrocity without tainting German soil and thus, by some made logic, remain pure and remote from their own evil.

The great killing centers were six: Auschwitz-Birkenau, Sobibor, Chelmno, Belzec, Maidanek, and Treblinka, all of them named for rural villages near which, in the occupied territories of Eastern Europe, they were built. A camp like Auschwitz murdered very large numbers of human beings daily, but it also served as an administrative center for the camp system as a whole, and likewise as a source of slave labor for industries producing war materiel. Other of these camps, Treblinka in particular, were designed for one thing only: to kill as many people as possible, as fast as possible. These camps, often referred to as "death factories," embody a principle I would call demonic rather than merely insane, for insanity is without firm structure, not predictable, something you cannot depend upon. What went on in the killing centers was highly organized and very dependable indeed: routines were established, and different methods of killing were experimented with; solid bureaucratic systems implemented the extermination process at every stage of its operation, and large numbers of men and women went daily about their jobs fully aware that the entire aim of this gigantic undertaking was murder, that the main and final product of this modernized factory system was death.

The dedication of life's energies to the production of death is a demonic principle of the first degree. Concomitant with it is a second, similar principle, namely, that unlike any example of genocide I can think of from the thick history of mankind's inhumanity—the slaughter of the American Indians, for example, or the decimation of cities that dared to resist this or that "world conqueror" (as Genghis Khan liked to call himself)—the destruction of the European Jews had no rational motive whatsoever, neither politics nor plunder, neither military strategy nor the moment's blind expediency. Jews did not obstruct Hitler's war aims, nor were they in any sense a threat to national security. This was genocide for the sake of genocide.

The demonic irrationality of this policy becomes the more apparent when we observe that if the killing centers were geographically remote, they were nevertheless connected by a massive railway system which shipped "cargo" marked "special treatment" from all the corners of Europe, as far to the east as Greece. This geographic "sweep" involved the crossing of many national borders and is again an indication of the apocalyptic dimension of the Holocaust. For here, too, the point was not to get rid of this or that group, this or that population which had come into political or tactical disfavor, but to reach as far across the earth as possible in order that death, for the Jews, might be absolute. The frenzy and obsessiveness of this drive may be gauged from the fact that during the last days of the war, when Hitler's Reich was clearly collapsing and every soldier and every piece of artillery was desperately needed to defend what was left of the homeland, trains which might have been used to transport troops and war supplies were instead, and without objection, employed to ship the last large community of Jews—those of Hungary—to Auschwitz.

The Holocaust is an unparalleled example of power run wild, which is to say that once evil on this scale picks up enough momentum, once it establishes itself in a system of functioning structures, it cannot—after a certain crucial point—be stopped by any counterforce within itself. The greater the concentration of power, the greater the paranoia it generates about its need to destroy everything outside itself. The worst thing that can be said of vast power is not that it inevitably corrupts its agents, but that after some point its deployment becomes greater than the will of the men who serve it. What can be destroyed, will be destroyed—a lesson the Holocaust confirms and which we, with our B-52s and nuclear submarines, our talk of "death yields" and "overkill," might wish to remember.

When we think of the Nazi camps (of which, by the way, there were hundreds), we tend to think of the most notorious examples, Auschwitz in particular, and further to think in terms of a few compelling images. In the mind's fearful eye we see long lines of men and women digging their own graves. We see Doctor Mengele immaculate in his SS uniform, standing before endless columns of people on a railway ramp, slowly moving a single finger of his gloved hand to the right (death), to the left (temporary life), a judge more almighty than God. We remember, from fragments of documentary film, open ovens full of ash and bone, and perhaps most persistently, the gigantic piles of the dead being bull-dozed into pits. All of this is true, of course, but such images are them-selves so overwhelming, so final in their autonomous horror, that the mind stops, defeated in its effort to comprehend. The dramatic nature of the Holocaust, that is to say, and especially when it becomes manifest through isolated images, obscures one of its most important aspects.

For the concentration camps were not only factories of death, they were worlds in which many thousands of men and women *lived,* their ranks continually depleted by death from starvation, from beating, from random killing, from sickness and exhaustion and sometimes from sheer suffocation in horror, but ranks immediately refilled with other prisoners who then went on with the work of running the camp, laboring in the factories, sorting the tons and tons of clothing and utensils left behind by the victims. The death camps were a world unto themselves, and the worst thing about existence in such a place, apart from the filth and pain and constant danger, was that those prisoners who had been "cho-sen," who had been sent to a work detail rather than the gas chamber, stayed alive only by involvement in the process of killing.

When we try to imagine such a world, three questions of furious significance arise. How did the inmates of the death camps stay alive at all? What did living under such conditions do to their souls, their sense of themselves as human beings? And why did they go on with their horrid work when, as survivors tell us, it was so much easier to die, and the temptation to slip into permanent oblivion or deliberately get oneself killed was infinitely more appealing than the wavering will to go on?

Chief among the virtues of Jean-François Steiner's *Treblinka* is that it answers these questions. Not in their entirety perhaps, nor to every-one's satisfaction, but with a degree of passionate envisionment which provides an overall picture of the death camp as a world of its own. More than that, however, from amid such darkness *Treblinka* projects an image of human strength and human goodness so frail yet stubbornly persistent, so ravaged and mutilated yet rebellious against its own defeat, its own extinction, that the Holocaust itself begins to look different when the story of this camp becomes known.

There are many studies of the concentration camp system (Eugen Kogon's *S.S.-Staat* is especially instructive), many maps and statistics, all of them valuable. There are also many excellent, indeed invaluable, accounts by survivors themselves, personal acts of bearing witness which allow us to see, if only narrowly and in fragments, what survivors themselves saw and experienced. But so far as I know, except for *Treblinka* there exists no *story*, presented from the *inside*, of the origin, the business-as-usual, and the final demise of a major death camp. By "story" I mean exactly what Aristotle meant: a human action through which the agents themselves are defined, an action with a beginning, a middle, and an end, with all its parts—in this case all those free-floating images which haunt us—subordinated to a wholeness which gives the details at least some degree of perspective and meaning.

Steiner manages to reconstruct the reality of one of the principal killing centers by giving us the story of the men who built it, the men who ran it, the men and women who destroyed it. He did this by personally interviewing all the survivors he was able to find or who would permit themselves to be found—a distinction I make only to suggest the difficulty of Steiner's undertaking, since to this day there is uncertainty about the precise number of people who came out of Treblinka. The number is somewhere around forty. Forty out of the 800,000 who died there. Forty out of the six hundred who revolted. The number is pitiful, yet without this tiny remnant the facts about Treblinka would never be known. The whole thing would never have happened. Where there is no story, there is no reality.

This method has its drawbacks, and since its publication in France in 1966, *Treblinka* has remained controversial. Because telling the story from inside requires novelistic techniques, Steiner freely portrays characters, reconstitutes conversations, and fills in missing details in order to convey the essential spirit of the events on which the story depends. He also substitutes fictional names to protect the names of survivors (the names of the killers are not changed), and there has been heated debate over particular characterizations. But these are not, I feel, serious objections so long as the structure of the story as a whole remains true to known facts. And in this respect, *Treblinka* is as close to the facts as we are likely to come. A more vigorous criticism has been Steiner's insistent theme of Jewish passivity in the face of impending disaster. But again, the central event which sets the story of Treblinka apart and makes the book special—the eventual revolt of the prisoners and the destruction of the camp—tempers if not boldly contradicts the theme of inaction.

New information has come to light since *Treblinka* was published, but none of it discredits or seriously qualifies the story Steiner has given us. The possible exception is Steiner's depiction of the meticulous care with which the "technicians," as he calls them, went about perfecting their infernal machine. The architects of the death camps appear as master planners who, except for their misjudgment of the Jewish will to resist, ran the camps with a technical expertise at once detached, controlled, and precise. To some extent this was true, and Steiner uses his portrait of the "technicians" to give us a sense of the deliberateness, the famous German attention to order and efficiency, with which the higher officials—men not themselves directly involved in the day-to-day madness—nevertheless oversaw the operation as a whole.

We now know, however, that a great deal of sloppiness, of trial and error, and also much heavy drinking undercut the idea that these nameless men were as fully in command as they were thought to be. The most valuable evidence comes from Gitta Sereny's series of interviews with Franz Stangl, who had been the commandant of Treblinka at the time of the revolt. Having escaped to Brazil by way of the so-called "Vatican route," Stangl was extradicted in 1967 (the year after *Treblinka* appeared) and sentenced to life imprisonment in Düsseldorf Remand Prison. During the last days of his life he agreed to talk with Sereny, and *Into That Darkness,* the record of their encounter, reveals a man for whom fear and bewilderment had always been springs of behavior. Intelligent and in some ways genuinely humane, Stangl was a man never sure of himself, a man who was only, and often with much hesitation, doing his job as administrator—a job which involved paperwork more than action, but which also, in Stangl's case, required a large glass of brandy so that sleep might come after the stench and outcry of a typical day in Treblinka.

There are, as I have indicated, scattered accounts of survival in Treblinka. But only in Steiner's book do we get the story of the camp from its beginnings in the summer of 1942 to its abrupt end on August 2, 1943. And what makes this story important is above all its ending. So neatly does our habit of blaming victims mesh with the idea that the Jews "went to their death like sheep" that evidence to the contrary goes unnoticed. Bruno Bettelheim, himself an "early" survivor of Buchenwald and surely not a sheep, has contributed more strongly than anyone else to this mistaken notion by insisting that camp prisoners could not see themselves "as fully adult persons," that they fell into an "anonymous mass" and behaved like "incompetent children." Such proclamations ignore the carefully calculated, fully adult tactics which, everywhere in the concentration camps, the prisoners used to create and sustain underground organizations and networks of resistance, thus saving thousands of lives. Certainly the Bettelheim thesis does not account for the small revolts within various camps, all of them doomed from the start, not to mention the Warsaw Ghetto uprising, the destruction of Sobibor, or the hopeless revolt of the Auschwitz *Sonderkommando,* which was able, before battalions of SS troops machine-gunned them down, to blow up one of the main crematoria.

The story of Treblinka not only discredits the "sheep" theory, it instructs us anew in the capacity of the human spirit to endure. Men and women brutalized beyond human recognition, hopeless as we shall never be hopeless, and with absolutely no help or encouragement from outside forces—these people were nevertheless able to regain a sense of their own worth as human beings, organize a system of underground resistance, suffer setback after setback as members were killed, secure arms under very tight surveillance, and then move together, with one spirit and one aim, to successfully shoot down their captors and blow up the camp. Their aim? The "mission" which carried them through months and months of despair in a project which from the beginning seemed insane? To bear witness. To rise up and fight against impossible odds so that one—at least one person among them—would survive in absolute obligation to "tell the world" what the name *Treblinka* had come to signify.

Consider the cost, the moral damage, of such an undertaking. A successful battle could take place only through the collective action of prisoners who had stayed alive long enough to organize themselves into rigorous fighting units. You cannot wage war without planning, without leaders, without a strike force divided into specialized squads, each with its appointed task. But any such organization, especially if it must start from nothing, takes *time,* and time in Treblinka meant one thing only: survival. Prisoners stayed alive by killing others *so that* the killing itself could be stopped and the crime be made known. The logic of this predicament was as terrible as the place itself, an intolerable torment somehow to be borne if life and resistance were to support each other.

Given the extremity of their initial degradation, the stages through which the prisoners passed on their way to open revolt can be seen as a regeneration of spirit amounting almost literally to resurrection. The first stage of revolt, the first humanly positive act in this demonically perverted world, was suicide. At some point, prisoners began to see that by taking their own lives they could thereby say no to Treblinka, and during the early months there were many suicides each night. But then the second stage asserted itself. As prisoners began to know and trust each other, escape became possible. Trains loaded with the clothing and possessions of the dead were continually leaving the camp, and with the coordinated help of comrades, a prisoner could at the last moment leap into a loaded boxcar. Or, again with the help of others, a prisoner could make his way to the open ditches where the dead were piled, and lying there as if dead await nightfall to crawl from the grave, slip under the wire (not electrified as in Auschwitz), and break for the forest.

Some attempts failed, others succeeded, and their success tells us two things. People outside the camp certainly did know what was going on inside. But also, in this second phase of defiance, small units of cooperation became established among the prisoners, which not only generated a rebirth of hope but started the process of trust and collective organization without which the third and final stage could never have occurred. And just as escape ruled out suicide, the stage of armed revolt ruled out escape. Where the help of everyone was needed, suicide and escape became personal luxuries. To burn down the camp and release prisoners in numbers large enough to ensure the survival of least a few, nothing less than an absolute community of struggle, transcending personal hope, became the one way to victory.

And hence the value of *Treblinka*, its historical import *as a story*. Through time a definite sequence of action grew and asserted itself, culminating in one of the most unlikely triumphs in the history of human struggle. And with the story comes a new definition of heroism. For if, in this age of totalitarian government and mass murder, we are to speak of heroism at all, it makes sense only in terms of collective action deliberately and often hopelessly pitted against enormous structures of evil. It cannot be framed in terms of the old heroic ethic, wherein the individual, as an individual, defies power and willingly dies for a glorious cause. There is no glory, and in a world where death rules, dying for anything at all becomes stupid, becomes abdication. Very few of the participants in the Treblinka revolt survived, but what they fought for was life.

We live in dark times and the story of Treblinka is worth knowing.

It is worth holding to with all the soul's strength. It is, that is to say, an example of what a handful of human beings *can do,* of spiritual damage sustained without capitulation, and likewise of absolute power which turns out to be less than absolute. And it reminds us, lest we overlook a significant fact, that in the Milgram obedience experiments, which I mentioned earlier, if two-thirds of the volunteers did as they were ordered, one-third did not.

The structures of evil grow more sophisticated, more finely tuned and organized. They proliferate and interlock and aid each other and cover the planet and begin, like the Holocaust, to appear overwhelming. When governments across the face of the earth, not excluding our own, are prepared to sacrifice populations and shoot down protest in any form, when darkness begins to seem total, proof to the contrary becomes invaluable. What happened at Treblinka is proof to the contrary, and on such hard, rare proof our humanness depends.

The Bettelheim Problem

Here is an example of the Bettelheim problem: In William Styron's novel *Sophie's Choice*, which the narrator calls a "stab at understanding Auschwitz," we find listed "a few of the most eloquent who have tried to limn the totally infernal in their heart's blood." Included are names like Tadeusz Borowski and Elie Wiesel, men who knew Auschwitz firsthand, but also Bruno Bettelheim, a name which presumably carries equal authority. Bettelheim, however, was never near Auschwitz, and nowhere in his publications about "the camp experience" does he provide sustained discussion about the worst of the death camps. Is Styron's reference to Bettelheim therefore eccentric? Not at all. The general view has long been that Bettelheim speaks from a privileged position, and he himself has fostered this attitude. He has always stressed his own "camp experience" as the basis for his authority in such matters. And by calling himself "a survivor of the camps" he suggests a kind of archetypal identity which might include any camp, Auschwitz, Treblinka, Belsen, from which survivors of the Holocaust emerged.

That, at least, is how we have received him, and to judge from laudatory reviews of his 1979 book, Bettelheim's position as a representative survivor and as an authority of "the camps" is intact and persuasive. A reviewer for *The New York Review of Books,* for example, said of Bettelheim's essays on surviving that "here Bettelheim speaks with absolute authority." This is mysterious not only because other survivors, in books like *Fighting Auschwitz* and *Values and Violence in Auschwitz,* have discredited or severely qualified his views; but also because Holocaust survivors have at last gained a hearing and they stress that Bettelheim (who by 1939 was already in America) cannot claim, as he does claim, to be speaking for them. The problem is compounded by the fact that, whereas survivors take exception to Bettleheim's assessment of their experience, the literary and scholarly community still largely accepts Bettelheim's position as the final word on men and women caught in extreme situations.

The conflict between Bettelheim and other survivors is worth examining. So is the conflict between eyewitness testimony and academic theorizing. I shall look at both and further, since Bettelheim has attacked my own work on survivors and has thereby granted me vantage, I shall use his attack as a touchstone for examination of his work in general. In *The Survivor* I offered a critique of his theories at the level of theory. Here I shall attend chiefly to his methods, and the place to begin is with the way Bettelheim *crosses worlds,* and the way he invests his arguments with *personal* content.

Camp and School

More than that of most thinkers, Bettelheim's work is rooted in historic locations, the concentration camp first of all, and then the Orthogenic School for autistic children at the University of Chicago. Both are uniquely self-contained worlds, both are constituted by extremity, and more than once (as in *The Empty Fortress*) Bettelheim has aligned the two as inverse forms of each other. I shall therefore use the term "world" in a technical sense, and be especially alert to occasions on which Bettelheim crosses from one world to the other. Speaking of children at the school, for example, he says: "it occurred to me that once before I had not only witnessed, but had also partly described, the whole gamut of autistic and schizophrenic reactions—observed not in children, but in adults in the German concentration camps."

Seeing one world in terms of the other allows Bettelheim a singular perspective. It also leads to suspect practices, in particular his habit of equating survivors with psychotic children, and his summoning of moral and emotional endorsement for his ideas by presenting them within the framework of his identity as a man who endured "the camps" and as a sort of miracle worker with "hopeless" children. But then, Bettelheim's work *is* bound to his private history. It is in the nature of survivorship to bear witness, and in large part the story of the Orthogenic School is Bettelheim's story. This is one of the conditions that make criticism or objective measurement of his work problematic. What makes it a problem, however, is the way Bettelheim uses his special status in order to discredit people whose position questions or intrudes upon his own.

The essay "Surviving," in which Bettelheim attacks Lena Wertmuller's *Seven Beauties* and my book *The Survivor,* appeared first in *The New Yorker* (August 2, 1976), and has been reprinted as the centerpiece in *Surviving and Other Essays.* Here is the heart of Bettelheim's case:

> When a large and significant segment of those who speak for the American intellectual establishment seems ready to accept the most basic principles of Nazi doctrine and to believe the suggestion—present in carefully camouflaged but convincing forms in *Seven Beauties* and Des Pres's critically celebrated book—that survivorship supports the validity of those principles, then a survivor must speak up to say that this is an outrageous distortion.

Bettelheim's basic contention—that the film and the book depict survivors in terms of Nazi doctrine—I shall analyze later. The thing now to note is that by presenting himself as a survivor Bettelheim can claim to be a spokesman for all survivors and, in their defense, allow himself vigorous bursts of moral indignation, as when he goes on to say: "Survivors won't be around much longer, but while they are, they cannot help objecting—not to their being forgotten, not to the world's going on as usual, but to their being used to bear witness to the opposite of the truth." The incongruity of Bettelheim's stance, in this case, is that he more than anyone has worked to establish an image of survivors almost identical to the kind of survivor he asserts that Wertmuller and I are defending. His major argument, in a book as influential as *The Informed Heart,* is that behavior in the camps was characterized by "infantile regression" and that most survivors stayed alive by adopting "a personality structure willing and able to accept SS values and behavior as its own." "They prided themselves on being as tough or tougher, than the SS." "Old prisoners came to identify with the enemy, and tried to justify it somehow in their eyes. But was the SS really just an enemy any more?"

By arguing that prisoners identified with the SS, Bettelheim openly declares that survivorship supports the validity of Nazi principles. That he should attack others for his own theory is a contradiction worth keeping in mind. The issue here, however, is that, having appointed himself the advocate of survivors, he goes on in the same essay to criticize their achievements. His argument against the accomplishments of the underground resistance in Buchenwald, his insistence that the takeover of the camp by the prisoners was "a non-event," is based on a misuse of facts characteristic of Bettelheim and therefore revealing in a way worth examining, as I shall, in careful detail. The present source of confusion (in an essay which purports to take up the cause of survivors) is the way Bettelheim denies survivors any self-determination, or respect for their struggle:

> The completely misleading distortion in *Seven Beauties* and articles excerpted from Des Pres's book is the pretense that what the survivors *did* made their survival possible.
>
> Any discussion of survivorship is dangerously misleading if it gives the impression that the main question is what the prisoner can do, for this is insignificant compared to the need to defeat politically or militarily those who maintain the camps—something that the prisoners, of course, cannot do.
>
> . . . not more than a dozen or so of the many millions of concentration camp prisoners managed to survive by their own efforts—that is, to escape from the camps and get away with it before the Allied forces triumphed. All others, including me, survived because the gestapo chose to set them free, and for no other reason.

Escape depended on collective action, as many survivors testify, but that is hardly the point. To define survival as Bettelheim does, and declare that men and women who managed to help each other stay alive for months and years in places as hopeless and dangerous as Auschwitz nevertheless did *not* survive by their own will and struggle, is a distortion which, were it less pointed and cruel, might be written off as irresponsible. Nowhere in Bettelheim's major publications about survivors, furthermore, do we hear about Treblinka and Sobibor, two of the major "killing centers," which the prisoners themselves destroyed through armed revolt. At least two hundred escaped from Treblinka, although only forty were alive by the end of the war, which says something about the difficulty of survival even after escape.

Successful revolts were of course too rare and improbable to stand as a type of survival behavior, although they do dramatize a *tendency* everywhere at work in the world of the camps. To defeat Auschwitz militarily was plainly not possible, although from the beginning a group of prisoners had organized themselves to *try*. What counted for survivors was finding *ways to live* in places like Auschwitz, then to endure the death marches, and then, in camps like Belsen and Dachau, to hold themselves together in body and in spirit against sickness, against extreme exhaustion and starvation *until* the Allies arrived. How ordinary men and women, with no resources but themselves, were able to do this *is* a "main question," and even provisional answers can give us invaluable information about man in extremis.

As might be expected, there was a wide range of behavior in response to camp conditions; but most striking is how often, amid such thoroughly dehumanizing circumstances, men and women stayed alive by staying human, as if collectively and over the long run there is a real and necessary link between humanness and survival in extreme situations. When we think of existence in Auschwitz, the fact that many men and women survived by keeping their humanity intact seems extraordinary to the point of heroism.

Not, however, according to Bettelheim. He criticizes *The Survivor* because it makes "the survivors appear as unusual," and because it "draws our attention away from the millions who were murdered, and concentrates only on the all too few who survived, and survived only because the Allied armies rescued them at the last moment." He implies that living in the concentration camps was nothing out of the ordinary, and again he suggests that the struggle to survive—what men and women actually did to keep going—does not count. As for drawing attention away from the millions who were murdered, Bettelheim himself has had little to say about the victims, and the following passages from *The Informed Heart* suggest that even against the dead Bettelheim maintains reproach:

> Walking to the gas chamber was committing suicide in a way
> that asked for none of the energy usually needed for deciding

and planning to kill oneself. Psychologically speaking, most prisoners in the extermination camps committed suicide by submitting to death without resistance.

Millions of the Jews of Europe who did not or could not escape in time or go underground as many thousands did, could at least have marched as free men against the SS, rather than to first grovel, then wait to be rounded up for their own extermination, and finally walk themselves to the gas chamber.

Remarks like these are primary examples of the blame-the-victim syndrome. After Hitler had defeated the armies of Europe, how were the Jews to "march as free men against the SS," the old and infirm, the one million children, sticks and stones against the tanks and aircraft of the Germans? There is something here entirely characteristic of Bettelheim: whenever he speaks of damage and destruction, he describes it in ways which make it appear as if the victims did it to themselves. Survivors, he tells us, stayed alive by being "willing and able" to imitate the SS and accept Nazi values. Being driven into the gas chambers was "suicide." Or of the dead: "they had given up their will to live and permitted their death tendencies to engulf them." Anyone who still believes such ideas without very complex qualification should read Filip Müller's *Eyewitness Auschwitz*. As a member of the *Sonderkommando* Müller was one of the very few survivors to actually see, month after month, the unspeakable travail of the victims, their confusion, rage, blind terror, but never anything like "death tendencies" which they "permitted" to engulf them.

How then, do we measure Bettelheim's claim to speak for other survivors, especially this remark: "All others, including me, survived because the gestapo chose to set them free, and for no other reason"? Bettelheim was in Buchenwald and Dachau for one year, before the war, before extermination of Jews became fixed policy, at a time when prisoners could still hope for release. In Buchenwald at that time the inmates could receive money and letters from home, they could buy extra food, they *still had families*. None of this was true in the death camps. Let us, therefore, see in his own words how Bettelheim managed to survive:

Up to the time of the war, practically every week—at times every weekday—a few prisoners were released. During 1938/ 39 quite a number of Jewish prisoners were among them, in their case if all their possessions—often including also some large sums paid by their relatives—had been turned over to the Nazis and they could show that they would leave Germany immediately upon release. These conditions were met by me. . . .

So I have no idea why I was among the lucky ones who were released. It may have helped that one of the most prominent American public figures intervened personally and also through the American legation in my behalf.

If I read him right, Bettelheim is saying that through money and political influence at the highest level, including a special invitation to come to America at a time when ships like the *St. Louis* were being turned away, he got out of the camps. Elsewhere he observes that "no country, not excepting the U.S., let more than an entirely insignificant trickle immigrate to it." Through sufficient wealth and high connections, Bettelheim managed to be a part of that "insignificant trickle."

If Bettelheim escaped the Final Solution through uncommon use of privilege, his identification of his fate with the fate of Holocaust survivors in general is exaggerated. His claim to speak for other survivors is limited and misleading. Saddest of all is the way he uses his own experience to generate an authority which in turn allows him to discount and often condemn—I shall cite other examples—the awful struggle of those who survived, sometimes for years, the infernal torment of the death camps. Which is to say that Bruno Bettelheim is neither a spokesman for survivors nor an authority on "*the* camps." How he came to be taken as such is the core of the Bettelheim problem.

Prisoners and Children

His first description of survival behavior, a long essay entitled "Individual and Mass Behavior in Extreme Situations," was published in 1943 and again in 1944. Large portions of it were incorporated into *The Informed Heart,* which appeared in 1960, and the essay has again been reprinted, without serious change, in *Surviving and Other Essays.* In 1943 survivors who would later disagree with him were fighting for their lives in the camps, and the narrowness of Bettelheim's view owed something to the fact that studies of "the camp experience" did not exist. But by 1979 a vast literature about the Holocaust had come into being, and the fact that Bettelheim has elected to reprint his 1943 essay without qualification suggests that despite new evidence he prefers his earliest ideas. This is another part of the Bettelheim problem, and in what follows I shall simply take him at his word.

Bettelheim's basic assertion is that "the prisoners developed types of behavior which are characteristic of infancy and early youth." Camp conditions "destroyed their adult frame of reference" and "contributed to their disintegration as adult persons." He concedes that exceptions existed, but the only example he offers of sustained adulthood is himself. The final impression is that "regression to infantile behavior" was universal, or as Bettelheim sums it up: "this regression would not have taken place if it had not happened in all prisoners."

But even apart from isolated acts of heroism like the Warsaw ghetto uprising, the Buchenwald takeover, the burning of Sobibor and Treblinka, or the revolt of the Auschwitz *Sonderkommando,* prisoners reduced to "regressive" or "childlike" modes of behavior could never have organized the collective tactics or created units of underground resistance which, everywhere in the world of the camps, aided the general struggle for life—or as Anna Pawelczynska describes it (she is an Auschwitz survivor and a trained sociologist): "the whole great network of mutual aid, communication and information, which was partly the outgrowth of decisions and strategies coordinated by the conspiratorial organizations operating in the camp, but even more, perhaps, the consequence of spontaneous human reactions."

All the same, through the prism of psychoanalytic observation Bettelheim insists that everywhere around him he could detect "childlike behavior," and here is one of his examples:

> The prisoners lived, like children, only in the immediate present; they lost feeling for the sequence of time; they became unable to plan for the future or to give up immediate pleasure satisfactions to gain greater ones in the near future.

Plan for the future in the death camps? Of course Dachau and Buchenwald were not killing centers, but by the time Bettelheim wrote *The Informed Heart* he had maneuvered his local observations into a perspective of universal application, which is how scholars have taken his theories—not, that is, as a limited case but as *the* case.

At this point, however, I wish only to illustrate Bettelheim's misapplication of the psychoanalytic approach. Every day, in the camps, hundreds of prisoners died from starvation, and tens of thousands could feel their strength failing for want of minimal nourishment. Yet in *The Informed Heart* Bettelheim makes this observation:

> Prisoners were obsessed with food and hunger beyond all reason. To a large degree, this too can be explained by their reverting to infantile attitudes which made them turn to food as the most available and basic symbol of security.

The insufficiency of this approach is apparent. Why, then, does Bettelheim persist in this way of thinking? Possibly because it allows him a theoretical basis for the central charge he makes against survivors, which is that although they "usually did not directly admit this," nevertheless "old prisoners accepted Nazi values as their own." Or again, "When a prisoner had reached the final stage of adjustment to the camp situation, he had changed his personality so as to accept various values of the SS as his own."

Identification with the aggressor, as Anna Freud first observed it in her work with children, is integral to the theory of infantile regression. This is the vital link in Bettelheim's argument, for example when he states: "It seems that once prisoners adopted a childlike attitude toward the SS, they had a desire for at least some of those whom they accepted as all-powerful father-figures to be just and kind." In this way Bettelheim arrives at his negative image of "old prisoners," by which he means survivors; and to the extent that he imposes his own vision upon contrary facts I find it worth notice that when he sums up their behavior he makes survivors speak *his* words:

> The prisoners' feelings could be summed up by the following sentence: "What I am doing here, or what is happening to me, does not count at all; here everything is permissible as long and insofar as it contributes to helping me to survive the camp."

That sounds like the protagonist of *Seven Beauties,* but not like other survivors who were in Buchenwald at the same time as Bettelheim, but whose testimony contradicts his. Among key witnesses were Eugen Kogon, Ernst Wiechert, and Ernest Rappaport, the last a psychiatrist, the first a leader in the underground. Another survivor-psychiatrist, L. Eitinger (he went through Auschwitz), has offered a critique of Bettelheim's emphasis on "negative coping," in particular the idea that survivors identified with the SS. In an essay entitled "On Being a Psychiatrist and a Survivor," Eitinger points out that "identification with the aggressor, as far as it occurred, was a negative coping mechanism, leading to the destruction of those involved and—in the few cases where they survived—to deep pathological changes in personality."

Bettelheim would agree that in such cases pathological change occurred; but he is wrong, in Eitinger's view, to suggest that negative coping was the *prevalent* form of behavior. Nowhere in Bettelheim's major statements about survivors do we find sustained attention to the fundamental form of *positive* coping, to behavior which promoted life and spiritual resilience. I am referring to the prisoners' tendency to organize and help each other, to participate for mutual support in each other's struggles. We could never guess, from Bettelheim's work, that *social* response to extremity was in fact the key to survival in the camps. At issue is his consistent refusal to elaborate upon "coping where attachment to others was a central concern," as Eitinger points out, or to acknowledge the kind of radical humanness which Anna Pawelczynska describes in her study of Auschwitz:

> Regardless of how isolated a prisoner felt or of how aware he was of the support of his fellow-prisoners, that support existed. In the beginning the chance to give material help was almost nonexistent, but there was at least human sympathy. With time, newer and better-organized mechanisms of collective defense made their appearance. The chances of their succeeding depended on the attitudes of large numbers of prisoners and their capacity for cooperation and loyalty in the face of the most acute terror.

Parents and Destroyers

Bettelheim's *The Informed Heart* focuses on survival as an act of individual self-assertion apart from collective effort. He gives himself as an example, and perhaps the oddest thing about his depiction of his own survival is that it entailed a crucial occasion on which Bettelheim managed to act in a way "acceptable to an SS soldier," a kind of behavior which "did not correspond to what he expected of Jewish prisoners." This rather strange example suggests the degree to which Bettelheim sets himself apart from others like himself. The following statement occurs in three of Bettelheim's major publications; he is referring to his fellow inmates in Buchenwald, and his relation to them, as he describes it, is an example of a typical me-against-them attitude in Bettelheim's work:

> Now they appeared to be pathological liars, were unable to restrain themselves, unable to separate clearly between reality and their wishful or anxious daydreams. So to the old worries, a new one was added, namely, "How can I protect myself from becoming as they are?"

If this were said solely of survivors we might take it at face value. But the fact that a me-against-them formula appears in any situation where Bettelheim is confronting someone who occupies or enters *his* world, suggests that his view of survivors is part of some deeper, more intimate vision. In his work on the treatment of psychotic children at the Orthogenic School, for example, the same stance is taken—this time in terms of a battle between Bettelheim-as-healer and parents-as-destroyers. In *A Home for the Heart* he discusses the relation of parental care to the child's development of "basic trust" in this way:

> The determining factor is whether the infant feels that he can depend on his parents' intentions and have confidence that he will be reliably well taken care of. Nobody who has experienced this basic trust will ever need a mental institution.

He implies that almost all severe psychological disturbance is caused by the failure of parents to manage their most elementary obligations. What is at stake, for Bettelheim, is the child's soul in dramatic contest between himself as the chosen parent ("possible precisely because the figure has been selected by the child") and the actual, but unworthy, parents. In *Love Is Not Enough* he states that "the difficulties of almost all emotionally disturbed children have originated in the relationship to a parent," and that recovery cannot be hoped for until such children receive "assurance first and foremost that we intend to protect them from their parents." In an essay entitled "Schizophrenia as a Reaction to Extreme Situations" Bettelheim says that one of the chief functions of the Orthogenic School is to "protect the child from any hostility coming from the external world, particularly from his parents."

Only in *Truants from Life* does Bettelheim relax his antagonism toward parents, perhaps because the book is a description of case studies, which is to say stories of children who have been through the experience of the school and for whom, therefore, Bettelheim has become the "true" parent, the giver of new lives to children whose original lives had been shattered by their parents. This hostility toward parents goes a long way toward explaining why, in *The Children of the Dream,* despite his own observations of emotional detachment and what he takes to be an "other-directed" personality structure (which elsewhere he abhors), Bettelheim nonetheless is strong in praise of child-rearing practices on the Israeli kibbutz. Here was a situation in which, at least as Bettelheim saw it, children were free from close parental control: "My conclusion must be that despite published reports to the contrary the kibbutz system seems quite successful in raising children in groups by other than their mothers, and this from infancy on."

Bettelheim's negative view of parents is consistent with psychoanalytic principles and cannot simply be dismissed. What is troublesome is the vehemence with which parents are singled out, in Bettelheim's "universe of the School," to play the role of villains. This might stem from his deep commitment to suffering children. But too often his antagonism toward parents erupts with almost violent vigor. In an essay apparently written in the late 1970s, he compares, without qualification, the predicament of the psychotic child with the situation of concentration-camp inmates:

> The rebuilding process is the same . . . whether the traumatization is due to the Nazi holocaust or to having been forced to exist in a most private hell; whether one has been destroyed as a person by a government using all the machinery and power

of the state for this purpose, or by the psychological abandonment and rejection of parents who, more often than not, are themselves deeply unhappy people, incapable of doing otherwise.

At issue here is not similarity but outright identification; and apart from conceptual confusion there arises the implication that parents are Nazis. And, in fact, Bettelheim does not hesitate to forge this identity. Using the demonic phrase "black milk" from Paul Celan's famous poem about the Holocaust, Bettelheim says:

> When one is forced to drink black milk from dawn to dusk, whether in the death camps of Nazi Germany, or while lying in a possibly luxurious crib, but there is subjected to the unconscious death wishes of what overtly may be a conscientious mother—in either situation, a living soul has death for a master.

Equating parents with "the death camps of Nazi Germany" is an extreme example of Bettelheim's habit of crossing worlds, an instance which shows forth the obsessive character of his vision and opens others of his well-known pronouncements to question. If hostility toward parents, and the will to save children from their parents, are constants in Bettelheim's world, then his famous attack on Anne Frank's family, so unfair in itself, takes on an added dimension. Anne "had a good chance to survive," Bettelheim tells us, "but she would have had to leave her parents." Anne Frank's parents would seem to have lent Hitler a helping hand, and elsewhere "the parent" is directly equated with Hitler:

> The parent seems omnipotent because he has the power to withhold the substance of life—food. Under Hitler, the state had exactly the same power. Living in such a society, all citizens were as dependent as children for the substance of life. Or again, if the parent can inhibit his child's freedom of movement, the mass society can do the same to its recalcitrant citizens. And the parallels follow throughout.

In Bettelheim's work, certainly, "the parallels follow throughout," and that he continues to make these comparisons reveals a central strategy for dealing with those whom he sees as his opponents. They are, without further thought, Nazis. In the late 1960s, for example, when Bettelheim spoke against students involved in campus protest against the war, he was "convinced that Vietnam and the Bomb serve youth as a screen for what really ails them," and what really ailed them was simply "the adolescent itch to confront for the sake of confrontation." That the war was generating spiritual damage, especially among the young, did not count. Student protest, in Bettelheim's view, was a "threat to the integrity and true calling of the university," in other words, a threat to the institution which was actively supporting Bettelheim's world of the school. He therefore compares students to the youth "in pre-Hitler days," and condemns them for this reason:

> Student Fascism of the Left (particularly when, as in the U.S., it is combined with black Fascism such as that of the "Panthers") could bring a right-wing backlash that would quite possibly strangle the democratic order.

Bettelheim's support for the status quo against dissent is not important here. The main problem, as before, resides in his readiness to call anyone entering his world a Nazi. Bettelheim has written hundreds of pages exhorting us to "march like free men" and resist the pressures of "mass society." And if there is one emphatic theme through all his books, it is the call for moral and personal "autonomy." When "autonomy" shows up at his doorstep, however, it becomes "Fascism."

Kalman/Kogon

It is perhaps less than surprising, then, that Bettelheim lumps together Wertmuller and me as purveyors of "principles . . . by which the Nazis, and particularly the SS, lived, or at least tried to live." In different ways, *Seven Beauties* and *The Survivor* are invasions of Bettelheim's exclusive world, the former as an autonomous refraction of the camp experience, the latter an explicit challenge to Bettelheim's version of survival behavior, especially his unwillingness to see significant good in survivors or in their achievement. I shall not waste time discussing the film, nor question Bettelheim's interpretation, except to say that he plainly puts no stock in the idea of art as *criticism of life,* but rather clings to the Romantic notion that the protagonist, simply by virtue of occupying center stage, carries the endorsement of the artist and audience (the problems this attitude creates may also be seen in Bettelheim's treatment of "amoral" fairy tales in *The Uses of Enchantment*).

That art often sponsors and instructs is clear enough, but so too is the artist's capacity to turn both aesthetic resources and response of the audience against a given subject—a point which ought to be apparent from Wertmuller's use of parody and displacement, or from the almost textbook formality with which she structures her indictments. *Seven Beauties* is clearly *about* a vile and loathsome man, but the conclusion does not follow, as Bettelheim would have it, that the protagonist is "made to stand for the archetypical survivor, the image of us all."

Let us, however, take Bettelheim at his word. Let us assume that *Seven Beauties* does endorse and celebrate a creature whose "nihilistic vision . . . is a Fascist vision." What then? In the whole of his argument against *The Survivor*, Bettelheim does not once quote a complete sentence or produce a concrete example of the Nazi doctrine he says the book embodies. Each time he makes a charge against the book he illustrates his point by reference *to the film*. In particular he takes three isolated phrases, uproots them from their field of reference (quotations from the testimony of survivors), and confers upon them a contrary meaning by setting them within a context manufactured by reference to *Seven Beauties*:

> Des Pres leads up to this dictum ["to embrace life without reserve"] by saying that we must "live beyond the compulsions of culture" and "by the body's crude claims." Wertmuller's film gives these principles visible form and symbolic expression. Pasqualino embraces life without reserve as he accepts without compunction Fascism, murder, rape. He lives beyond the compulsions of culture as he rapes a mental patient who is helplessly tied down, and as he hands over other prisoners to be deprived of their lives to secure his. By voluntarily managing an erection in intercourse with a ruthless killer, he survives by the body's crudest claims.

This method of argument, which Professor Paul Robinson calls "devastating critique," is doubly suspect in view of the fact that Bettelheim never mentions that the book he is condemning contains direct criticism of his own work. Professor Robinson's ready acceptance of such tactics (in *The New York Times Book Review,* April 29, 1979), reveals an added dimension of the Bettelheim problem, in particular the way influence of ideas and thinkers is perpetuated through the academic habit of suspending judgment when in the presence of recognized authority. In this way Bettelheim's ideas have stabilized and spread to shape our attitudes toward survivors. In this way also, Bettelheim has exercised his kind of "devastating critique" and gone unchallenged in cases far more serious than those in the "Surviving" essay.

A central strategy in *The Informed Heart* is to develop ideas which take their origin in Bettelheim's own experience and then support them not with incidents he himself observed but with dramatic examples taken from the testimony of other survivors, Eugen Kogon in particular. Kogon's *Der SS-Staat,* translated as *The Theory and Practice of Hell,* is an official report, prepared at the request of Allied investigators and cross-checked by a committee of other survivors. In *The Informed Heart* Bettelheim cites Kogon's testimony seven times, incorporating significant parts of Kogon's book into his own, and then he proceeds to discredit Kogon by suggesting that inmates with "privileged" positions had "a greater need to justify themselves":

> This they did as members of ruling classes for centuries have done—by pointing to their greater value to society because of their power to influence, their education, their cultural refinement.

His specific example is Kogon:

> Kogon's attitudes are fairly representative. For example, he took pride that in the stillness of the night he enjoyed reading Plato or Galsworthy, while in an adjacent room the air reeked of common prisoners, while they snored unpleasantly. He seemed unable to realize that only his privileged position, based on participation in human experiments, gave him the leisure to enjoy culture, an enjoyment he then used to justify his privileged position.

That sounds convincing, but let us look at Kogon's description of the same event:

In the winter of 1942–43, a succession of bread thefts in Barracks 42 at Buchenwald made it necessary to establish a night-watch. For months on end I volunteered for this duty, taking the shift from three to six o'clock in the morning. It meant sitting alone in the day room, while the snores of the comrades came from the other end. For once I was free of the ineluctable companionship that usually shackled and stifled every individual activity. What an experience it was to sit quietly by a shaded lamp, delving into the pages of Plato's *Dialogues,* Galsworthy's *Swan Song,* or the works of Heine, Klabund, Mehring!

Such books had been seized by the Nazis and dumped as waste in the camps, and although there is genuine pleasure in Kogon's account, there is not a trace of what Bettelheim calls the "need to justify." Kogon's book is an extensive record of the achievements of the political underground in Buchenwald, including methods of organization, strategic use of functionary positions, and a detailed account of the takeover of the camp by the prisoners. The episode Bettelheim singles out is, in Kogon's view, just another small example of resistance in action. The reason he is there is not to read Plato and Galsworthy, but to enforce "the bread law"—a rule endorsed by the prisoners which absolutely forbade stealing food from each other—in order to help keep a sense of moral order, and thus of their own humanity, alive among the inmates. Kogon does not, as Bettelheim states, refer to air which "reeked of common prisoners" but to his "comrades." His private enjoyment is a by-product of responsibility, and if there had been no books Kogon would have volunteered all the same, going without sufficient sleep "for months on end" to do his duty as a man committed to the general struggle.

To reduce Kogon's act to "privilege," and further to declare that it was "based on participation in human experiments," are perversions of truth to a very grave degree. Kogon was a prisoner in Buchenwald for seven years. He was a leader of organized resistance efforts, and by working in the medical block (a job he undertook at the request of resistance members) he did not participate in "human experiments" but used the strength of the underground to bring successful pressure to bear upon SS doctor Ding-Schuler, who became instrumental, through Kogon's influence, in helping the underground negotiate with the camp commander, thereby subverting the possibility of general liquidation of the prisoners in Buchenwald at the end of the war.

How do we know these facts? Partly from Kogon's report, which of course Bettelheim read. But also from another book which Bettelheim also read and quotes from. And here, finally, we come to Bettelheim's determination to deflate the "myth," as he calls it, of how the prisoners in Buchenwald successfully took command of the camp in the war's last days. Referring to *The Survivor*—which discusses resistance movements and underground activities in the camps—here is how Bettelheim argues:

> The statement about the "taking command of Buchenwald" by prisoners "during the war's last days" is partly correct because the event referred to did occur—on April 11, 1945, which was indeed one of the last days of the war in Germany. But as far as the prisoners' taking command is concerned, it was a non-event that Des Pres has made to appear an event of the greatest import. What actually happened has often been described accurately, but it has more often been turned into a myth. . . . What happened was that when two American tank columns had reached the immediate vicinity of Buchenwald, the camp commander, to save his life, turned the camp over to the SS-appointed top prisoner of the camp and ran away with the rest of the SS. Only then did the prisoners "take command."

Bettelheim, of course, was not there. He relies on other witnesses, in particular a British officer who was imprisoned in Buchenwald during the last fifteen months of the war and who was himself a leader in one of the two main groups of resistance fighters in the camp. His name is Christopher Burney, his book is *The Dungeon Democracy*, published in 1945, and the most amazing thing about Bettelheim's use of *this* book— to destroy the idea "that what the survivors *did* made their survival possible"—is that Burney gives a detailed account of many actions through which members of the underground functioned successfully to keep the SS at bay, in particular the heroic efforts of a prisoner named Emil Kalman, a leader in the other underground group, whom Burney praises for his "unbelievable clarity and coolness of mind and his ability to take risks which would have daunted most ordinary heroes," and whom, finally, Burney calls "the principal savior of the 23,000 prisoners who were there to greet the tanks of the American Third Army." What Burney could not have known in 1945, but which Bettelheim should have noted, is that Emil Kalman was Eugen Kogon.

Kogon escaped shipment to Auschwitz three times, switching names in the process, and each time his rescue was secured by the help of fellow resistance members. It was this same backing by the underground which gave Kogon the power to deal openly with Ding-Schuler, who preferred to hedge his bets in the event of a shoot-out or a battle with the Allies. And Burney, contrary to Bettelheim's use of his report, provides evidence that a shoot-out nearly came to pass. There was one SS plan to have aircraft bomb the camp, and another which at the last minute dispatched a special squad of SD with flamethrowers (they got as far as Weimar) to demolish Buchenwald. Through Ding-Schuler, meanwhile, Kogon and his group were able to negotiate covertly with Pister, who was commander of the camp, causing Pister to vacillate, to allow prisoners not to obey camp commands, and to postpone orders from Berlin. At one point the four top leaders in Burney's group (himself included) were listed for immediate extermination and were hidden by Kogon's group. Soon thereafter, both groups cooperated to stop the murder of forty-six political prisoners also named for immediate execution.

Most important was the letter—quoted by both Kogon and Burney—sent from an Allied commander to Pister, in which Pister was threatened with personal retaliation if he allowed the prisoners in Buchenwald to perish. This letter was a forgery, composed by resistance members in the camp, and then posted from Weimar by Kogon/Kalman, who had been smuggled out of the camp with the assistance of Ding-Schuler and the concerted effort of the underground. Both Burney and Kogon give the details of this pivotal event: Pister took the letter seriously and was even less willing to liquidate the camp.

It is true, as Bettelheim says, that Pister finally turned Buchenwald over to "the SS-appointed top prisoner of the camp." He could hardly keep face and hand things over to known resistance leaders. It is also true that as Allied forces approached, the SS guards retreated and vanished. And although Kogon does not record this, I am prepared to believe Burney when he says (Bettelheim quotes this as evidence of the "non-event") that he saw prisoners with weapons from the hidden arms cache acting "very childish, forming bands of different nationalities and marching about as if they had defeated the entire Wehrmacht." This sort of behavior does not discredit the long-term struggle of the underground, nor is it, on the day of liberation, as irresponsible as earlier "talk of open rebellion" against three thousand fully armed SS troops, which would have ended in massacre and provided a real excuse for wiping out the camp. From Bettelheim's constant talk about the need to shoot it out with the SS, we might suppose he would have favored such a move. The underground, on the other hand, rejected open confrontation *for the moment,* but kept it as a contingency plan *if* the SS began destroying the camp.

I have been relying on the same sources Bettelheim cites, and the point to be made is simple: the last days of Buchenwald were a touch-and-go affair, and as Burney says, "every moment gained was lives saved." The crucial fact is that in Buchenwald the prisoners had managed to build and sustain a reliable resistance organization; they armed themselves, they gained enough power to negotiate with the camp commander, and by their *presence* were sufficiently strong to forestall SS plans to demolish the camp. This is the essence of effective action under extreme conditions—collective action rigorous enough to subvert the logic of destruction and hold a vastly more powerful enemy at bay until help arrives.

The reports by Burney and Kogon supply ample evidence that against overwhelming odds survivors of the camps could take action and *do* things that saved lives. So we are back to the Bettelheim problem: Why does he insist that what prisoners were able to accomplish on their own was not important to their condition as survivors? After reading and quoting from both Kogon's book and Burney's account of Kogon/Kalman, how can Bettelheim say that Kogon owed his survival to "participation in human experiments," that his "life depended on keeping his position of privilege," or finally that Kogon's behavior "is another example of the truth of an often repeated comment: that in the camps, not the SS but the prisoners were the prisoner's worst enemy"?

Existence Was Resistance

Not the SS but the prisoners. It is true that I have written this essay out of personal concern, but what makes my own care more than private is our common need to question the authority of Bettelheim in matters concerning survival and survivors, and, through these ultimate issues, how we think about human nature and finally ourselves. Any theory that promotes the idea that in extreme situations the majority of men and women will regress to childlike behavior, accept the values and intentions of their assailants, and go to their death "like sheep" is not merely misleading, not only a slander against the decency of survivors; it also fosters nihilism and radical loss of faith in our own humanness. In *The Survivor* I suggested that Bettelheim has been the outstanding exponent of the "sheep" theory, a suggestion Bettelheim rejects with the following remarks:

> To say that the victims of the gas chambers "went to their death like sheep" is a scandalous use of a cliché, not only incredibly callous but utterly false. Nobody who knew the camps and thought about them could possibly give credence to it.

True, Bettelheim never uses the words "like sheep." He prefers to speak of infantile behavior, of collaboration with the SS, of victims who "grovel" and allow themselves to give in to their "death tendencies," and of entrance into the gas chambers as "suicide." He also, on at least one occasion, has called the victims something rather worse than sheep:

> Strange as it may sound, the unique feature of the extermination camps is not that the Germans exterminated millions of people. . . . What was new, unique, terrifying, was that millions, like lemmings, marched themselves to their own death.

Like lemmings. And again it is the victims rather than the killers that are faulted, "not the SS but the prisoners." The millions who died are thus implicated in their own destruction, and survivors must bear the burden of their complicity with the SS. Such is the essence of Bettelheim's vision, the most disturbing consequence of which has been the readiness of scholars to accept his authority without question. In *Slavery,* published in 1959, Stanley M. Elkins developed his slave-as-Sambo thesis by comparing the condition of American slaves to the situation of inmates in the Nazi camps. The comparison is ludicrous, but Elkins nonetheless argues that what held for prisoners in the death camps held also for blacks on Southern plantations, and by leaning heavily on Bettelheim, Elkins arrives at this model:

> A truly childlike situation was thus created: utter and abject dependency. . . . Everything, every vital concern, focused on the SS. . . . It is thus no wonder that prisoners should become "as children." It is no wonder that their obedience became unquestioning, that they did not revolt, that they did not "hate" their masters. . . . Their masters' attitudes had become *internalized* as a part of their very selves. . . . they could, when commanded by their masters, go to their death without resistance.

Elkins maps out a world in which no resistance, no social bonding, no network of relation among the victims existed or could exist. Subsequent studies of slave society—books like Genovese's *Roll, Jordan, Roll* and Gutman's *The Black Family in Slavery and Freedom*—have perhaps gone to the other extreme but have at least done much to correct Elkins's fundamental error, inherited from Bettelheim, that men and women can live *without social foundation,* debased, dehumanized, entirely submissive to the power destroying them. Criticism of Elkins's theories ought to have led more recent scholars to question the uncritical use of Bettelheim's work. But as recently as 1978, Barrington Moore, Jr., has taken Bettelheim at face value to support his own methods in *Injustice: The Social Bases of Obedience and Revolt,* and here are some of Moore's conclusions:

> . . . prisoners in the concentration camps have cruelty and suffering imposed upon them with a maximum of violence and coercion. Under such circumstances one might expect that the suffering would seem most unjust and would have no moral authority whatever. Such is not the case.
>
> The SS was able to pervert to its own cruel purposes the networks of social cooperation that did arise spontaneously, and that otherwise might have formed foci of opposition to, or disintegration of, camp society.

> From the standpoint of the present inquiry the most significant aspect of the prison camps' social organization was the way it worked to inhibit any action that smacked of heroic resistance. . . . The SS, Bettelheim observes, was usually successful in preventing martyrs or heroes from being created.

That a scholar of Moore's caliber should be so misled suggests more than lapse in scholarship. It is evidence of the power that Bettelheim continues to wield. Like William Styron and others, Elkins and Moore assume without question that Bettelheim is *the* authority on "the camp experience"—that what Bettelheim claims held for Buchenwald and Dachau before the war holds also for the worst of the death camps through 1945. It is as if the following words, spoken by an Auschwitz survivor, had never been uttered: "Oppression as violent as that under which we lived automatically provoked resistance. Our entire existence in the camp was marked by it." In the world of the camps, existence *was* resistance, every day, all the time.

The Heart of the Problems

My aim in *The Survivor* was to see what goodness might be found in the worst of possible worlds. Having initially accepted Bettelheim's view, I was surprised to discover that behavior in protracted crisis takes its structure from fixed activities including social interchange, collective resistance, shared will to keep dignity and moral sense active. By "the compulsions of culture" I meant symbolic systems forcing upon us a mind-body split which denigrates physical existence in favor of spiritual transcendence. By "the body's crude claims" I meant the dignity of physical being, of the body as something intrinsically valuable. And by "embrace life without reserve" I meant willingness to accept the goodness of life in itself, life sacred and final, apart from religions and ideologies which justify existence by negating it, which demand that we die for this or that cause, which transform mass murder into the acceptable means to a "glorious" goal. In *Mein Kampf* Hitler spoke at great length about the power of symbolic manipulation, and he was in deadly earnest when he argued that only through "idealism" could a nation willingly spill the blood required to reach "higher" ends.

To call people Nazis is a serious matter, and when Bettelheim says that survivors identified with the SS, that parents reduce their children to the condition of camp prisoners, or that genuine dissent in a free society is Fascism, he is making damaging charges. When in his "Surviving" essay he attacks *The Survivor* without mentioning that the book contains criticism of his own ideas, he is misleading readers in a way which, from the perspective of professional standards, is unethical. And when he says that Eugen Kogon survived by "participation in human experiments," he demeans a man who by all accounts was exceptionally decent and brave.

And yet. Even in an essay like "Surviving" Bettelheim's moral indignation seems so fervent and sound, his blunders are so vulnerable, that to say he has calculated all this, that his misrepresentations are "deliberate," is somehow to miss the point. When he writes, "From the beginning of time, those who have borne witness have been an embarrassment. To those who have been carried away by Wertmuller's film, or by Des Pres's writings, what I have written here has perhaps caused embarrassment," his self-appointment and sense of vindication are so vigorous and unreflective that we cannot but wonder if in some fundamental way he does not see the unhappy and misleading statements that abound in his work.

And that is the heart of the Bettelheim problem. He will look neither right nor left but say what has to be said to keep his world free of intruders. Anyone with whom authority might have to be shared— other survivors, parents—shall be discredited. In the world of the camps Bettelheim is the only true survivor. In the world of the school he is the only source of adequate care. By constantly crossing these worlds, planting one upon the other, Bettelheim derives an identity which, at least in his own eyes, is much like the mythical Just Man, the One who shall bear all suffering, the One on whom the existence of the human world depends.

Bettelheim's theories of survival behavior have too long reinforced our sense of impotence and despair in a world so wildly beyond comprehension or control. With the historical authority of the Holocaust to back it up, his image of the survivor has too long confirmed the prevailing sense of victimhood. For these reasons especially, we can no longer afford to accept Bettelheim's authority without question. With so much opposite evidence, we cannot afford to believe that *in general* men and women regress to a condition of childlike incompetence or

endure violence and injustice by siding with the assailants. What survivors were *able to do,* with only their humanness and each other for
support, was remarkable in itself and remains an example worth knowing
when we contemplate the darkness ahead. Of course survivors sustained
deep damage, but let us now consider, despite the damage done, the
strength revealed.

Goodness Incarnate

A Review of Philip Hallie's
Lest Innocent Blood Be Shed

Horror swells around us like an oil spill. Not a day passes without more savagery and harm, and from all the earth's corners, instantly or within hours, the media alert us to what has occurred. Unlike any generation before us, we are wired into history, and this kind of immediacy, global in reach, is bound to alter the way we feel about ourselves and the world. Assassinations, bombings, nations spewing blood in war and civil strife—atrocity becomes a déjà vu affair. Political imprisonment, "torture seminars" run by the CIA on methods learned from the Nazis—it's everyday stuff. Against the speed and mass with which such ugly information hits us our defenses collapse. Where is reason, progress, any firm evidence to support our faith in humanity? We stand naked before terrible events that not only shock and unnerve us: more and more, they begin to define what we perceive as reality. Their shadow deepens, crosses any path we take, stretches into endless night. And over everything, prophetic and implacable, the memory of the Holocaust hovers to mock us, the *Schadenfreude* of history.

Ours is an age of aftermath and we live by an infernal logic. We are maimed in spirit by the brutality and suffering we witness, or we close off care and don't give a damn, and either way our humanness diminishes. In his account of how he came to write *Lest Innocent Blood Be Shed*, Philip Hallie, a professor of philosophy at Wesleyan University, expresses our common predicament this way:

The pattern of the strong crushing the weak kept repeating itself and repeating itself, so that when I was not bitterly angry, I was bored at the repetition of the patterns of persecution. When I was not desiring to be cruel with the cruel, I was a monster—like, perhaps, many others around me—who could look upon torture and death without a shudder, and who therefore looked upon life without a belief in its preciousness.

Yes, *mon semblable, mon frère,* he is right. Rage and despair on the one hand, a dead soul in a worthless world on the other. Keeping faith in human worth, insisting upon the efficacy of care, has become extremely difficult. If, for example, the great oil companies can wreck the world economy for their own advantage and no single government can check them; if terrorists can shoot down schoolchildren and still be hailed champions of justice; then the momentum of evil would seem beyond stopping, and life, if life needs decency and hope, is defeated. Again, Hallie:

If only such things were possible, then life was too heavy a burden for me. The lies I would have to tell my children in order to raise them in hope—which children need the way plants need sunlight—would make the burden unbearable.

From where can salvation come? How shall the burden be lifted? By chance, while looking through documents about the Holocaust, Professor Hallie came across a brief article about "a little village in the mountains of southern France." He began reading with the scholar's expected "objectivity," but the utter simplicity of what he read disarmed him:

I saw the two clumsy khaki-colored buses of the Vichy French police pull into the village square. I saw the police captain facing the pastor of the village and warning him that if he did not give up the names of the Jews they had been sheltering in the village he and his fellow pastor, as well as the families who had been caring for the Jews, would be arrested. I saw the pastor refuse to give up those people who had been strangers in his village, even at the risk of his own destruction.

Then I saw the only Jew the police could find, sitting in an otherwise empty bus. I saw a thirteen-year-old boy, the son of the pastor, pass a piece of his precious chocolate through the window to the prisoner, while twenty gendarmes who were guarding the lone prisoner watched. And then I saw the villagers passing their little gifts through the window until there were gifts all around him—most of them food in those hungry days during the German occupation of France.

Out of what circumstances could this small event have risen? What kind of community would run such immediate risk? For in fact, during the entire period of the Nazi occupation, first under the nervous eye of Vichy, then directly under Gestapo surveillance, the people of Le Chambon—about seven hundred villagers and two thousand peasants from outlying farms—had used *themselves* to welcome, hide, and keep from harm more than 2,500 refugees, most of them Jews. Under the leadership of their Protestant pastor, and with financial aid from the American Quakers, the members of this community *voted* to make of their homes a "city of refuge." They would open their doors to anyone in need, and would organize their small resources for the express purpose of saving as many Jewish children as possible. They would also work with the Cimade, an underground organization run entirely by women, to smuggle Jews across the border into Switzerland.

What took place in this remote mountain village was certainly not broadcast to the world; everything was done quietly, covertly, to all appearances as if nothing were happening. It was the kind of event easy to overlook because it needed to be overlooked. Nor was it heroic in the inflated man-against-fate sense of that word; rescue operations were a day-to-day business, crucial decisions were made at the level of the family by ordinary people in their kitchens. Nor was this the saga of a great leader merely, for although André Trocmé was the spiritual center of the village and a very forceful man, his power rested with the villagers, who *permitted* him to carry forward plans for their city of refuge. He was committed to nonviolent resistance; the villagers endorsed his view—fortunately, because against the Nazi war machine a stationary group could not use tactics like those of the mobile Maquis: that would have meant confrontation and disaster. Resistance to evil, when the odds are so grossly one-sided, means resistance to the policies of evil. If Jews are to be turned in, then no Jews will be turned in. Once these conditions are understood, the thing that makes the story of this village supremely beautiful is simply that it happened. These events took place and therefore *demand place* in our view of the world. If awareness of history has pushed us to the point of losing faith in ourselves, the case may also be, as Professor Hallie says, that "redemption lies in remembering."

It also lies in simply finding out. Professor Hallie spent three intense years among the people of Le Chambon, talking at great length *with* them, getting to know them as individuals, as friends, allowing himself to abandon the scholar's detachment so that, to the full depth of his being, he might come to understand "The Story of the Village of Le Chambon and How Goodness Happened There," which is the book's subtitle. And Hallie's reason for writing the book is also ours in reading it. "I needed this understanding," he says, "in order to redeem myself— and possibly others—from the coercion of despair." To know that goodness exists, like the myth of the seven just men on whose existence the existence of the human world depends, is more than knowing merely. In times as brazenly brutal as ours, it is among our deepest needs.

Lest Innocent Blood Be Shed is important not only for the story it tells, but because it does just that, it gives us a *story*. In *The Poetics* Aristotle insisted that in the telling of a story, character remains subordinate to plot, to what happens, not because fate rules or because we blindly run like rats in a maze, but because only through plot, through a sequence of interlocking actions, does character reveal itself concretely as a force *in* the world. Some novelists still know this. Historians knew it once, although recently they, along with sociologists and the new breed of literary critics, have given up on what human beings actually do, preferring instead statistics, systems, data tabulation, and "deep structures," as if in crucial situations (i.e., in life) the union between event and character had nothing to do with historical understanding, let alone historical outcome.

Professor Hallie, with his strong respect for persons, with his passion for "ethics incarnate," has reminded us of one of the oldest open secrets in the world: that goodness, like other constituents of human character, does not simply exist, it *happens,* stage by stage, decision by decision, and the best way to understand it—and thereby be blessed and inspired to faith and emulation—is to behold it in action. And once we see that events do not *just* happen, that they have beginnings, middles, endings, we are ready to appreciate doubly the strength of Hallie's book: the "Story of Le Chambon" is a wonderful example of goodness in action, but it is also a mode of analysis and revelation, a way to grasp concretely the ineffable character of human beings committed to decency and care. Without story—specific persons doing specific things—the moral dimension of reality is lost.

And so there is André Trocmé, the Huguenot pastor urging his people to be mindful of the crisis upon them, a man of mystical fervor, aggressively loving, almost explosive in his rush to save lives. And there is Magda Trocmé, as commanding as her husband, wholly absorbed in the daily nourishment of life, disdainful of ethical precepts apart from action, a woman who could never manage to think of herself and her friends as "heroic," but only as human beings doing what, at that time, in that place, needed to be done. André conceived the idea of hiding refugee children in the village, and it was he who went to get help from the Quaker office in Marseilles. But Magda best sums up the spirit of the village itself: "I do not hunt around to find people to help. But I never close my door. . . ." And it was she who said, when the first Jew abruptly appeared at the door timidly hoping for help, "Naturally, come in, and come in."

Around these central figures a small knot of active organizers gathered, those who ran the schools, those who turned *pensions* and boardinghouses into the "funded houses" that received financial support from outside the village and in which large numbers of Jewish children survived the war (only one of these houses was found and destroyed by the Gestapo). Then came the villagers themselves, each with a home into which one or more refugees came, sometimes to stay, sometimes to wait until accommodations could be arranged elsewhere. And surrounding the village, there were the isolated farms where many Jews found safety and work. Connections were maintained with partisan fighters in the area. Someone (never identified) supplied blank copies of the indispensable identification cards that each refugee needed in order to pass as a villager or at least as not a Jew. And a fast voice (also never identified) would call on the phone to say that a raid was coming, that the Germans were on their way for one of their "sweeps." Goodness would seem to be contagious, for throughout the whole of this operation, even after Le Chambon became known as a "nest of Jews" and the villagers lived in fear of their lives, not one person turned informer.

Individuals got arrested, got killed, but in the main the rescue mission of Le Chambon was successful, and this brings us to one of the central points of Hallie's book. These people did not simply wake up one day in the middle of the war and decide to start saving Jews. They began at the beginning. When the Germans occupied France the villagers would not salute the Vichy flag. When loyal citizens were commanded to ring the bells of their churches to celebrate official events, no bells rang in Le Chambon. And at a time when to preach an ethic of non-violence was forbidden by law and by the Protestant Church itself, Trocmé and his fellow pastor regularly broke this law. The risk was relatively slight in these cases, but that is hardly the point. The village was in small but active revolt long before the first Jew arrived, and when that frightened woman knocked on the Trocmés' door—when the point of no return came—they were ready to carry out in practice what they had already been doing in spirit.

One of Professor Hallie's most pursued observations has to do with the impact of the Huguenot experience upon the village during the war. We tend to remember the Saint Bartholomew's Day Massacre of 1572 and forget that for most of their four centuries' residence in France the people of Huguenot faith were harassed, discriminated against, and persecuted constantly, often to the point of extreme bloodshed. To them, the "law of the land" had never been worth respecting, and when the Vichy regime started laying down new laws, this was only one more case of law-as-abuse to which this people, this tradition, would respond as of old—with "the resistance of exile." At least in this case, not doctrine merely, not faith passed on untested, but the memory of a people's collective past determines their behavior in crisis, especially when torment and persecution—the need to act and endure—had been the cost of their faith in the first place.

To say that the past counts may sound like a truism, but the example of the Huguenot tradition in Le Chambon leads Professor Hallie to his most valuable insight. He believes (and so do I) that ethical norms tend to arise from, and be clarified by, the experience of victims. Human beings under protracted pressure are best situated to see and feel (not just propound and discuss) what hurts life and damages the spirit. And out of this negative moment a positive morality is born. In this situation, the condition of victimhood has so long persisted that morality and resistance become identical in the struggle to transcend (or simply survive) the fact of always being open to harm. To test this we need only consider that although the ethic of Classical Greece, based on the celebration of strength and magnanimity, is extremely appealing, it could not save its own culture and has not entered the heart of Western morality half so much, or so persuasively, as the combined ethic of the Jews and the early Christians—both of whom, in terms of empire and persecution, were victims.

Nietzsche had great fun with this idea, but he somewhat missed the point. In *The Genealogy of Morals* he argued that Christian morality arose from the plight of a people who had neither the political nor the economic means to defend themselves, and therefore advocated an ethic of peace, equality, and neighborly care. Taking this to be a strategy of *ressentiment,* the envy of the slave for the "noble soul," Nietzsche preferred to celebrate the classical virtues of largess and restraint, the decent usage of wealth and power, on the very mistaken assumption that wealth and power can be managed wisely, without corruption or abuse. The downtrodden of the world know otherwise. They know that the noble soul is self-absorbed, that the wealthy can afford not to care, that restraint and good judgment are forgotten as soon as power feels threatened. Above all, they know that human beings are easy to debase and easy to kill.

In long possession of these latter truths, the villagers of Le Chambon knew that to be on the side of the victim is to be on the side of life, which is what morality in practice comes down to. They also knew, from centuries of experience, that victims do not have the leisure to act "in due time," but must do what they can "in time," in both meanings of that phrase. With their Huguenot tradition to guide them, the men and women of Le Chambon were ready in advance to put their beliefs into action. Goodness happens when human beings know ahead of time that one day they will be called upon to act. Our humanity remains tragically tied to the inhumanity we oppose and endure. The preciousness of life is a function of death. Goodness is a function of the harm it resists.

Goodness. When was the last time anyone used that word in earnest, without irony, as anything more than a doubtful cliché? *Lest Innocent Blood Be Shed* is one of the rarest of books, the kind that can change the way we live. It is conceived and written on a modest scale, but Philip Hallie knows full well the wisdom of starting small—that is one of the book's themes—and among other large accomplishments he has restored to the word *goodness* its rightful moral beauty. We can begin again to use it with confidence. We can—with the example of Le Chambon to remind us—begin again to believe that decency is possible.

Against the Under Toad
The Novels of John Irving

It has seemed something of a mystery that out of nowhere a serious, highly sophisticated novel with the unlikely title of *The World According to Garp* became, in the States, a runaway best-seller. But of course, *The World According to Garp* came out of the novels which preceded it, and among readers alert to talent, John Irving has been known with admiration since the publication of his first book ten years earlier. Irving was born in 1942 and has produced four remarkable novels; but the mystery, if there is one, arises from the avidity with which Americans at large "discovered" and took such vast delight in a book as ruthlessly unhappy as *Garp* certainly is. Presumably this kind of response to Irving's fiction tells us something about America or even, I should think, about the farcical ferocity of life as we live it anywhere.

Garp is Irving's best book, a comic masterpiece which draws much of its strength from setting styles and forms against each other. But Irving's will to come at the world from different directions—stories inside stories, genres circumventing genres—is already handled with mastery in *Setting Free the Bears,* published in 1968, and with a freedom almost wanton in *The Water-Method Man,* which appeared in 1972. Only *The 158-Pound Marriage* departs from mixed form; published in 1974, it is as lean and concentrated as a mine shaft.

One of the results of Irving's multiple manner is that each of his novels is wholly distinct, in conception and style, from its companions. We might almost mistake them for books by different authors. But only at first glance. For what informs them all, inspiring each with intense consistency, is John Irving's peculiar vision, his singular way of seeing the world. Friendship, marriage, and family are his primary themes, but at that blundering level of life where mishap and folly—something close to joyful malice—perpetually intrudes and disrupts, often fatally. Irving takes for granted that the world is mucked up beyond even provisional redemption; that personal destiny is again and again derailed by impersonal forces; that no leader, faith, or ideology will arrive to save us from the mess in which we founder. Harm and disarray are daily fare, as if the course of love could *not* run true. As if existence were governed by caprice and mockery, by the perverse power of some yet to be observed tenth planet. And if a sign or emblem were wanted for this new ruler of the zodiac, there is no doubt, in Irving's universe, what name and shape it would take.

In *The World According to Garp* the hero, along with his wife and two small sons, spends summers in a family house (later a feminist headquarters) on the New Hampshire coast. Because one of the boys, Walt, is very young, there is much warning about the undertow along this stretch of shore. The undertow, his parents remind him, is terribly wicked today. Look out for the undertow. One morning they spot Walt alone on the beach, staring intently at the incoming waves. When asked what he's doing he says: "I'm trying to see the Under Toad." All along he had mistaken the proper term and mythicized the fear it signaled into a creature of invisible but monstrous being. And Walt is right. Arising as if from the sea, the Under Toad squats upon the world's rim, bloated and watchful, the sign of a new star under whose baleful dispensation life must henceforth proceed.

Novel by novel, Irving has moved steadily toward more intimate knowledge of this sinister energy. His relish for German words, together with the way Vienna ("a museum housing a dead city") haunts everything he has written, gives an almost historical tremor to the pun on *Tod*, while the corresponding pun on *Unter* suggests a depth of being which in theology has been called "the demonic," by which is meant life perversely pitted against itself, a will to mockery and mutilation, eruptions of exuberant spite. These are the forces to which Irving has adjusted his vision, hence his insistence on bizarre events and sad outcomes—on stories "rich with lunacy and sorrow," as one of Garp's friends says—and hence, too, Irving's mix of disaster and farce, his blend of gravity and hardminded glee. He aims to confront the habits of the Under Toad directly, and fix the perception of life's demonic undertow at exactly those points where, any day, any one of us might slip and be sucked down.

A world at war is the worst world possible, and this is where, in *Setting Free the Bears,* Irving starts. There are plenty of horrifying moments in this novel, yet from such unhappy material Irving produces nonstop laughter. The impact of war upon civilians, its chaos and rapidity of event, its deadly whirling force—all this comes across with convincing power. So does the maniacal behavior of ordinary people trapped in a world of seismic upset. How does Irving make this funny? How, without the aid of tragic resolution—for in an age so warped and bedraggled there is no hope of high closure—can crass, undignified suffering be turned to catharsis? The answer is in good part the secret of Irving's art. He knows that under grotesque pressure and robbed of choice, men and women respond to their fate in ways that are brave but also ridiculous, jerked this way and that by shifting circumstance and an acceleration of coincidence that renders attempts at sane action ludicrous. If this is indeed the case, and if no one is exempt, then the determination to laugh *at* becomes likewise the duty to laugh *with,* the sole mode of compassion, of human communion, available in a world whose overseer is the Under Toad.

But *Setting Free the Bears* is not, properly speaking, a "war novel" at all. The book's main line of action, which culminates in animal apocalypse when the Vienna zoo is "liberated," takes place in the sixties, and here Irving's love of stories within stories becomes especially effective. The novel is composed of three separate layers, each story bearing strongly on the others, but each distinct in content and stylistic presentation. The "Pre-History" covers wartime Vienna and partisan scrambles in Yugoslavia. The "Zoo Watch" contains some of the most original writing in modern fiction and celebrates Irving's strange fellow feeling for animals, as if in his view our humanity is not complete without acknowledgment of the animal dimension of being. Finally there is the picaresque tale of the two young men who ramble about the Austrian countryside, planning their "zoo bust," heading for hilarious ruin.

The picaresque mode is freewheeling, unpredictable. In its explosive brutality, so is war. And so too, in its certain uncontrollability, must be the release of a zoo full of animals, the fierce and the timid alike, some to eat, most to be eaten. But to see things this way is also, indeed inevitably, to behold life as foredoomed, in which case the novelist becomes, as T. S. Garp will say of himself, "a doctor who sees only terminal cases." The tendency in Irving's fiction is toward epilogue, and one of the most remarkable things about his novels, viewed from the vantage of *Garp,* is that they can be read as one extended fictional enterprise. Together they track our spiritual passage from its origins in reaction to the inhuman revelations of the Second World War, through the anomie of the fifties, the radical rampage and self-destructive experiments of the sixties, toward the struggle for adulthood and survival which characterized the seventies.

To argue that Irving planned this bildungsroman of our time would be excessive. Nonetheless, his deep sense of demonic turbulence, his comic reception of life as "a ludicrous and doomed effort at reclassification," and his steady sympathy for those who sustain damage and maimed hope and still fight to be normal—to love, raise children, stay sane—combine to make Irving especially suited to record the havoc and madness we everywhere witness during these last-gasp days of our century. Thus while those who screw up in *Setting Free the Bears* pay with their lives, the screwed-up hero of *The Water-Method Man* persists through his folly and earns a second chance. The bitter outcome of *The 158-Pound Marriage,* however, suggests that a second chance is only, after all, a chance, and that the perversity of human heart is sufficient to ensure that the Under Toad will more than likely have its way, leaving its victims to laugh or curse as they can.

The Water-Method Man takes its young protagonist through two wives and a side trip to Vienna on his precarious approach to adulthood. The zany freedom of male companionship ends in a ghost tank at the bottom of the Danube, making way for the beginning of serious male-female relations as the hero, nick-named "Bogus," gets his penis back to normal working order. Children and the responsibility of parenthood begin to figure importantly, and perhaps because these are fundamentally hopeful themes, Irving's second novel is also his most relaxed piece of writing. It is likewise—apart from *Garp*—his most intricate, a virtuoso performance in juxtapositions. Script and scenes from a cinema verité film replay the story in parody. And against these, like the backdrop of night, Irving unwinds the blood-and-guts saga of *Akthelt and Gunnel,* an epic poem in "Old Low Norse," in which, as in cartoonlike dream, the Under Toad rules.

For its dextrous comedy, for its energetic play with form, *The Water-Method Man* provides happy relief. It also serves as a bridge from the kind of world determined by impersonal forces to the closer, more self-inflicted world of private championships. But if history is a field of ruin, so too is the shut sphere of marriage—marriage, that is, as an experiment and a test which some survive and others do not. In this latter sense, *The 158-Pound Marriage* is surely a black and ruthless book. The title refers to a middle-weight wrestling match, where falls are fast and expected, where expertise counts more than brute force, where consequences may be dire but scarcely the substance of champions. Starting with the commonplace of adultery, Irving traces the soul's unrest, its stupid preference for pain and complication, through two couples who switch partners and pursue their odd indulgences to the point of no return. There is no overt violence, but the outcome can only be buffoonery and hate, with the hint that this particular "match" was fixed from the onset—that one of the couples may have played this game before.

Roped off from connection with the larger world, Irving's ménage à quatre is strictly a collision of personalities. And whereas sex in the earlier novels was an easygoing gift, in *The 158-Pound Marriage* sex becomes the source of subtle disruptive powers, the occasion for setting free something a good deal more brutal than bears. Which is to say that Irving's humor, as strong as ever, has moved closer to the tears which such sad and twisted goings-on must, if released from comic check, draw forth from the unhappy heart.

The peculiar power of *The World According to Garp* arises from the way both the author and his characters resist external intrusion—politics, fame, other people—and fail. Beginning with the decision of Jenny Fields (Garp's mother) to have a child without committing herself to a man, the life of T. S. Garp unfolds through his years as son, husband, parent, and writer, ending with his assassination at the age of thirty-three. His mother, whose autobiography, *A Sexual Suspect,* makes her a hero among feminists, is also assassinated. Along the way many other people die, mostly in ways unlikely and bizarre, as if Garp's world were a slaughterhouse fitted up with funhouse mirrors, and his story a string of epilogues. Here is a hero who singlemindedly sets out to live quietly and sanely, to keep his children free from harm, to write novels with absolutely no bearing on his own private existence; but for all his intelligence and decency, the "world" will defeat him.

The 158-Pound Marriage was Irving's third novel, but it is the first time in his fiction that women start to move, to have their own sphere of being. They certainly move in *Garp,* where rape, feminism, and finally "sex reassignment" are central issues. One of the finest characters in the novel had been, before her sex-change through surgery, a pro football star. Jenny Fields successfully resists her allotted "role" as a woman, and in Garp's family, Helen, his wife, goes off to work while Garp cooks, cleans, worries about the kids. But "reassignment" will not forestall disaster, and Irving's novel, like the brilliant "Pension Grillparzer" which Garp writes, depicts everything as a "ludicrous and doomed effort at reclassification." By tracing the relationship between wife and husband, and then again between parents and children (and how these two sets intersect to cause catastrophe), Irving is able to handle a large range of human hope and fear and final insufficiency. He is excellent in his portrait of Garp's sons, Duncan and Walt, whose view of their father is often hilarious, whose dialogue is true without fail, and whose vulnerability in a world of numberless hurtful things causes Garp a brooding, prophetic dread.

And of course it happens: midway through the novel an accident occurs, infinitely improbable but absolutely fated by the behavior that brings it about, leaving in its wake death, dismemberment, and a world that for Garp grows darker, wilder, more open to demonic intrusion. A penis is bitten off, an eye is poked out, an arm is severed, a child's neck is snapped. Garp's mother is shot at a political rally, and Garp himself will die for writing a sensational novel about rape *(The World According to Bensenhaver)* which makes him famous but also enrages a group of radical feminists, the "Ellen Jamesians," whose sign is their amputated tongues. Mutilation is the Under Toad's signature, its little joke the way dignity constantly collapses into melodrama. Garp watches his mother's murder on television and thinks: "the event was an X-rated soap opera from start to finish." Perhaps the finest thing about Irving's skill as a writer is his use of comic means to keep a book about sensational and melodramatic events free from the contagion of its lunatic content.

That a serious novel like *The World According to Garp* should become so widely read is rare, at least in America, and I do not think the popularity of *Garp* rests entirely with the obvious benefits of a good story and the accessibility of wonderfully straightforward prose. John Irving belongs to a small group of American writers, chief among whom must be included Kurt Vonnegut, Joseph Heller, and Thomas Pynchon, novelists whose work has inspired respect for the plainest of reasons— these people write a kind of fiction useful, as genuine art must always be useful, to spiritual need. Fiction speaks to us, touches our deepest fears and wishes, in so far as it articulates our embattled sense of being *in* the world, thereby confirming the self in its struggle to face and endure the besetting difficulties of a time and condition. One critic has suggested that the key to Irving's kind of novelist is the mobilization of paranoia as a mode of universal insight. Given the threat of terminal wreckage—helpless governments and collapsing economies, nuclear befoulment and the possibility of a Final Solution that shall be truly final—little wonder that those who take their stand vis-à-vis the Under Toad have gained our special regard.

Facing prospects so oppressive, Irving's kind of novelist has worked out a number of strategies. Vonnegut combines a so-it-goes stoicism with the cosmic perspective of science fiction. Heller penetrates infernal darkness through the hysterical drain-off of a central insidious event. Pynchon seems openly to side with destructive energy, celebrating its negative splendor, reveling in its promise of doom. But whereas Vonnegut and Heller accept our condition of victimhood as final, and Pynchon identifies with existence-as-aggressor, Irving has stubbornly refused to capitulate. Rebellion, defiance, even derision, inform his art. He confronts threat with jeers, perceives pain in terms of farce, rebukes fate by playing with the ways the Under Toad plays with us.

Reading Irving's novels, we are so engaged by their exuberance, their humor and what appears to be sheer delight in mischief, that the world seems almost jolly, a hell of an entertaining place. And this, it seems to me, is Irving's victory. As an artist of utmost earnestness, he tells the hardest kind of truth, but in the telling insists upon the freedom to have fun. Critics have sometimes missed the horror at the heart of Irving's vision. They have observed his high-spirited frolic and have presumed, mistakenly, that Irving's whole point as a writer is play. Maybe, but with one decisive difference: this kind of play, defiant, boisterous, recklessly brave, is Irving's hardminded prescription for survival.

John Irving's fiction comes down to this: it serves our need for spiritual defense. Is this no more than a bag of brilliant tricks? Possibly, but against an adversary like the Under Toad the tactics of the trickster—prominent in myths of every culture—are indispensable. Without them the enormous pressures of dread and savagery would surely grind us down to nothingness. All comic artists are tricksters. They skate on thin ice, they make us laugh, they help us hang on. And the survival value of laughter, in times like ours, cannot be too highly prized. For sanity, for endurance, for necessary pleasure, no other stance works half so well.

The Dreaming Back

Über allen Gipfeln ist Ruh. —Goethe

Über allen Wipfeln ist Unruh. —Brecht

Beneath clouds calm in autumn light, quiet farms lie open to the sky. The grain has ripened and been stacked in sheaves, the green-gold stubble of the fields glows softly. Wild ducks pass low in flight, and far off a village, barely visible, hovers among trees in the afternoon haze. The wind stirs faintly, but otherwise the land is motionless, silent, at rest in its bounty. The world seems timeless and untouched, as if amid these peaceful fields the innocence of earth could never be lost. But now the foreground comes into view, and with it appear knots and strands of barbed wire. Concrete posts crook up like claws, post after post in lines that extend without end. Guard towers arise, chimneys, barracks row upon row as endless as the wire. In ordinary sun, the kingdom of night declares its dominion.

The place is Auschwitz, the scene just described is the opening sequence from *Night and Fog,* and as Resnais's famous documentary unfolds, engines of death and mutilation cancel the elemental peace with which the film began: ovens, bloodgutters, cement ceilings of gas chambers scratched and torn by the victims. These things exist as they did when the death camps were active, as mute and fixed as memory itself. And now, using film from the Allied liberation, Resnais shifts back in time and allows the event to speak for itself. Kapos carry severed heads.

Cleanup squads drag corpses as weightless as rags. Bulldozers push gigantic piles of the dead into pits, their bodies twisting down upon each other. The film ends by moving from a rusted torture machine to the rubble of a crematorium. The desolation is that of civilization itself. Earth's power to nourish and console is pointless now, and the happy fields do not return. Goethe's oak stood in Buchenwald. *Über allen Wipfeln ist Unruh.*

The juxtaposition of quiet farmland with Auschwitz is bitterly ironic, as Resnais intends it to be. But to behold the film's initial movement—from life's beneficence to the machinery of genocide—is to witness something very much like the Fall, an end to grace and innocence not as described in legend and myth but through the historical event which actually brought it to pass. And as the remainder of *Night and Fog* makes clear, this is a Fall without promise or even prospect of redemption. We live, that is to say, in the unrest of aftermath and we inherit the feeling that something has been taken that cannot be restored. I am not speaking of the victims, whose lives and world are indeed gone, but merely of ourselves and the impact of the Holocaust upon the way we think and feel. We are infected by a sense of terminal defilement, and this kind of loss is the symptom of a deeper damage: we suffer from the radical diminishment of our capacity to accept and forgive, to bless and be blessed. What has been lost is the kind of transcendence which allows the spirit to recover innocence and reside once more in the purity of its first and rightful estate, as in these culminating lines from W. B. Yeats's poem, "A Dialogue of Self and Soul":

> I am content to follow to its source
> Every event in action or in thought;
> Measure the lot; forgive myself the lot!
> When such as I cast out remorse
> So great a sweetness flows into the breast
> We must laugh and we must sing,
> We are blest in everything,
> Everything we look upon is blest.

Lucky Yeats; he died in 1939, when destiny could still be conceived in personal terms and events were still, more or less, measurable. Not that he didn't witness terrible things, the bloodletting of Ireland's civil war especially. "Nineteen Hundred and Ninteen," published in 1928, is one of the darkest poems in English; but alongside Paul Celan's *Todesfuge*, Yeats is mild by comparison. We cannot fault him for that. We might rather envy him, living as it were before the Fall, when genuine affirmation, and rapport with the world as a sacred living whole, were not yet denied. There was as yet no "wound in the order of being," as Martin Buber has described the damage we feel. And notice, in the experience Yeats portrays, that when the worst has been faced and the process of recapitulation and forgiveness is complete, the "I" expands to "We." The shift has occurred in us too, but through collective catastrophe rather than joyous transport. Where now is that exuberant conviction of communion?

The predicament of aftermath defines us, and not merely as individuals but as creatures of an age that has never been able to assimilate the implications of the event we call the Holocaust. And we may fairly assume that the spiritual dimension of our problems has something—perhaps very much—to do with our failure to regain, after 1945, necessary capacities of spiritual balance, in particular the capacity to judge *and* praise, to be morally responsible *and* able to celebrate "everything we look upon." In one of his bizarrely prophetic moments, Nietzsche took our situation to extremes by arguing that to affirm existence wholeheartedly would be to will everything over again and again without end. Everything? We see Nietzsche's point. But after the Holocaust his cosmic logic, correct in itself, is the logic of insanity.

What may be inferred from Nietzsche's myth of eternal return, and confirmed in the lines from Yeats, is that the spirit liberates itself from history by working back through the whole of its past, confronting *in the mind* events which took place *in the world*. In aesthetic form, Aristotle defined this as catharsis. The church recast it in sacramental form and called it Confession. Freud rediscovered it in the "work" of dreaming, and made it the basis of psychoanalytic treatment. Some version of recapitulation or "reliving," followed by return to innocence or "rebirth," is essential to spiritual well-being. The problem now is that events which block regeneration are collective rather than personal, much too large for individuals in the solitude of their separate lives to manage. Like it or not, we are involved *beyond* ourselves. To be in the world but not of it, to recover innocence after Auschwitz, plainly will not work. The self's sense of itself is different now, and what has made the difference, both as cause and continuing condition, is simply knowing that the Holocaust occurred.

The self's new relation to events beyond itself is easily observed. Show *Night and Fog* to a group of young people and when the film is done and the lights go on, notice that no one speaks, no one seeks the eyes of his or her neighbor. Dishonor and diminished dignity are palpably present. Yet none of these people knew the Holocaust firsthand; they took no part and were not alive when it happened. But that such feelings are "normal" responses to knowledge of the death camps can hardly be denied. We are in no way guilty but we do not feel blameless. We live decently but not without shame. We are entirely innocent but innocence, the blessedness of simple daily being, no longer seems possible. The peaceful fields are gone. *Über allen Wipfeln ist Unruh.*

The kind of spiritual restoration which Yeats describes in "A Dialogue of Self and Soul" is an instance of a universal process which, in his mystical book *A Vision,* he calls "the dreaming back." Keeping in mind our sense of urgency and blockage when facing matters of the Holocaust, here is Yeats on "the dreaming back":

> In the *Dreaming Back* the *Spirit* is compelled to live over and over again the events that had most moved it; there can be nothing new, but the old events stand forth in a light which is dim or bright according to the intensity of the passion that accompanied them. They occur in the order of their intensity or luminosity, the more intense first, and the painful are commonly the more intense, and repeat themselves again and again.

We dream back through events until, having at last understood and made peace with the past, we transcend our bondage to history. The specific work of encounter, which has about it a kind of compulsion, Yeats calls "the return," by which he means the spiritual reliving of events "until all are related and understood, turned into knowledge." Each moment of return involves "a periodic stoppage of movement" and the action of the dreaming back as a whole is summed up this way:

> After its imprisonment by some event in the *Dreaming Back,* the *Spirit* relives that event in the *Return* and turns it into knowledge, and then falls into the *Dreaming Back* once more.

Imprisonment and compulsive return, reliving and final transformation of event into knowledge: these are the stages of the dreaming back, nothing more disturbing than the sheer time this may take:

> After each event of the *Dreaming Back* the *Spirit* explores not merely the causes but the consequences of that event. Where the soul has great intensity and where those consequences affected great numbers, the *Dreaming Back* and the *Return* may last with diminishing pain and joy for centuries.

All of this is metaphor, to be sure, and more than a little bizarre. But in our present state of foundering, unorthodox perspectives are worth testing. I am not, furthermore, using Yeats's concept of the dreaming back exactly as he sets it forth in *A Vision.* There it has mystical significance, it implies literal belief in reincarnation, and in the main it is a personal, indeed a very solitary affair. I would rather see it as a spiritual or psychic process conducted at the cultural level, in which all of us join to resolve the turbulence caused by the Holocaust and its aftermath. In this latter respect, the concept of the dreaming back works remarkably well as a perspective on our current "imprisonment," as Yeats would say, by an event. Most intense and painful, the Holocaust preempts all lesser events, demands that we confront it again and again in our attempt to turn it into knowledge; and so long as this process remains incomplete we may expect our spiritual condition to be characterized by deep unrest. The point to keep in mind is that the spirit feels compelled to return and work through events for which it feels responsible, but also events by which it feels polluted and maimed. And if we allow this kind of usage, then the principal manifestations of the dreaming back in relation to the Holocaust are currently *denial* and *obsession*—with a third development, the creation of a new kind of *conscience,* starting to emerge.

Denial is reluctance of the spirit to initiate its own painful passage through the events which define it. In the case of the Holocaust this has been a three-stage strategy. Allied governments refused to believe their own evidence that the Jews of Europe were being destroyed. Then came the decades of silence and taboo, when the death camps were not to be mentioned nor survivors heeded. More recently pseudoscholarly publications have appeared to argue that the Holocaust never happened. Outrageous as all this is, it is a natural response to terrible events. And it will not prevail. Denial has developed from stupidity and fear to its present status as a form of negative recognition. The Holocaust has entered general consciousness, and while a few scramble to escape through denial, most of us work toward relief through earnest understanding.

More destructive than denial are the dangers of obsession—despair, nihilism, madness. After such massive evil there is no redress, no justice, and to fix upon irreparable horror leads to despair. Nihilism then follows naturally, and with it the conviction that nothing matters, that civilization is a sham, that to kill men and women in such numbers "proves" that human values are useless, that life has no especial worth. One's own life then becomes worthless, and from here but a brief move remains to perverse delight in the spectacle of evil and the prospect of doom. A surprising amount of post-Holocaust fiction has gone to this extreme, perhaps most significantly Thomas Mann's *Doktor Faustus* which examines, and Thomas Pynchon's *Gravity's Rainbow* which celebrates, the negative splendor of destructive energy.

The temptation to despair is always present, but more subtly ruinous is the protracted torment of aftermath itself, the stuckness of spirit in its will to face the worst. Neither able to advance nor to retreat, we become imprisoned by the event we struggle to transcend. The Holocaust becomes the only reality, its darkness blots out all light, its implications ramify into the world and into the deepest reaches of the soul until entrapment becomes total. And here true obsession, a species of madness, begins. This is the condition which Arthur Koestler explores in a short story entitled "Confrontation." Koestler's protagonist begins by resigning his post to protest his government's refusal to prevent circumstances that will result in genocide. His gesture changes nothing, but from that moment he finds himself helplessly obsessed by the evil of our time. Digging a ditch in his garden, he imagines masses of men and women digging the trenches into which they will fall when they are shot. Chopping wood, he remembers how the losers in some partisan scrimmage were axed to death. Sitting before his fireplace, he watches the flames curl upward and sees bodies twisting as they burn alive.

By way of "experiment," the narrator discusses his obsession with a certain Dr. Adamson. That he is going mad becomes clear when we discover that Adamson is the narrator's projection of his own rational self, that part of him which would, but cannot, control and calm the deeper self's pain. The emblem of this condition, as infinite as the suffering it contemplates, is what Koestler calls the "block-univese":

> Did you ever read Pascal, Dr. Adamson? Do you remember his agonized cry: "The eternal silence of infinite space terrifies me"? I am even more terrified by the universe of a fourth dimension, which contains the frozen past, present, and future. We crawl along inside it like blind maggots, and because we can only move in one direction, which we call the future, we believe that the past is wiped out. In reality, everything that happened is still happening; everything that was, still is. The agonies of the past are preserved through eternity, the gas chambers are still working to full capacity. . . .

That is obsession become madness, an example of dreaming back with a vengeance. Precisely because he is a good man, Koestler's narrator is possessed as, in earlier times, people were said to be entered and possessed by invisible demons. He represents a kind of consciousness which suffers from its own capacity for responsibility, and at moments we must all feel trapped in something similar to Koestler's "block-universe." The more we examine the facts of the Holocaust, the more insistent its horror becomes. But this kind of obsession, like other kinds of derangement, is solipsistic; and the fact that Koestler's narrator gradually cuts himself off from all human contact contributes decisively to his decline. Which is to say that for an event as universal as the Holocaust, the task of dreaming back will necessarily be shared. We work together in mutual encouragement, creating thereby a community of response stronger than any man or woman alone could possibly summon.

The recent growth in Holocaust studies is evidence that the process of the dreaming back—of spiritual struggle to turn history into knowledge—has picked up momentum and begun to address its task with new dedication and rigor. The Holocaust will certainly serve as a sounding board for reexamination of ourselves, a point of ultimate reference by which to measure the failure and need for revision of any moral or cultural category we care to investigate. Whether we shall understand the event in itself remains to be seen. That we shall gain indispensable knowledge is clear enough, but I doubt that *through knowledge* this particular event can be put to rest, and for the following reason: the more we know of the Holocaust, the more *we* change, the more we find ourselves circumscribed by the event we sought to transcend and from which we had hoped to pull free. The chances are, in this special case, that the process of the dreaming back will not complete itself. We shall not reach freedom, we shall not recover innocence nor escape the stark unrest of aftermath. The more we learn, the more we shall fear. The more we know, the more we shall remember.

What ruins innocence is not guilt but memory. Bearing witness is a form of memory. The dreaming back is memory in action. And so is conscience, which in Schopenhauer's definition is our collective knowledge concerning what humankind has done and suffered. In exactly this sense (as in Santayana's much quoted remark), remembering the past becomes, through disturbance and revulsion and also fear, attention to the present and care for the future. It follows that knowledge of the Holocaust becomes the source and inspiration for conscience in its post-Holocaust form. There are signs that such a conscience, collective and global, is coming into existence—the Nuremberg trials and establishment of the UN; the Eichmann trial and ad hoc convening of "world courts" to publicize and condemn international crimes; repeated efforts to set up an early-warning system to foresee and prevent future genocides—and in every case the reference is the Holocaust. We must not be misled by setbacks. The creation of what might finally become a "world conscience" is the slow product of our collective dreaming back, and the outcome shall depend not on success but on failure, or rather, on stuckness, on "reliving" the event again and again, keeping memory active, allowing the demise of innocence to be the birth of vigilance. The unpleasant fact is that conscience—now, for us who dwell in aftermath—has arisen in response to genocide and its strength depends on our willingness to live with memory's perpetual unrest.

Consider one last time Resnais's *Night and Fog,* only this time view it in reverse, as in memory, from end to beginning. The crematorium and the metal torture machine give way to brief scenes of denial in the courtroom. Kapos put down the severed heads and back away. And then the mass graves open. The dead push upon themselves upward, rising again to earth's surface, and so insistent is this obscene resurrection that the big bulldozers are themselves shoved backward. Our machinery of disposal fails, the dead in their multitudes are unstoppable. But then they vanish and item by item the implements of mass murder reappear and then pass from view, the low ceilings, the ovens, the black entrails of the barracks. The guard towers appear and disappear, the fences fall away and at last we return to the fields, the blessedness of earth before the Fall. But nothing now is right. *Über allen Wipfeln ist Unruh.*

Into the Mire

The Case of Bertolt Brecht

I f we hold with the sort of innocence still lingering in American literary criticism, then what Hannah Arendt called "the case of Bertolt Brecht" would seem to be closed. Nobody denies his genius. There is general agreement that he is one of our century's best poets and that his plays are the most significant contribution to serious drama since Ibsen. That ought to be the end of it, but just here the difficulties start. As Eric Bentley wrote to James Laughlin after Brecht had caused endless trouble over small details of publication: "Both you and I have a right to be out of patience with Brecht. But he is still important as an artist." Bentley's sentiments were voiced countless times during Brecht's life, often in terms much stronger, and this double attitude toward him—that he was a genius of doubtful humanity—has echoed in his wake ever since. I think Brecht's "case" comes out in his favor, but the crossover between life and art, or the way extraliterary matters play a part in literary judgment, has become a permanent element in our response to Brecht's work. Situations wherein the artist's life reflects importantly upon his art are on the increase, and Brecht would hardly have become the center of such stiff-necked debate were it not for the fact that what we make of him extends what we make of the art/life problem generally.

In the latest collection of *Paris Review* interviews, Francine du Plessix Gray warns that one of the most "alarming" developments since the Second World War has been "our ravenous appetite for the Artist's Personality." True enough, the fastest way to literary fame nowadays is not to write a book of fine poems but to interview a batch of poets.

Given the work, we want the life as well. Insofar as what we are after is dirty linen, then "alarming" is not too strong a word for the tendency Gray describes. But she is wrong in at least one respect; our need to measure life and art in terms of each other corresponds to an important shift in literary awareness, and it is not a recent development. What is new—and here Gray's reference to the Second World War affords insight—is the degree to which politics gives special import to the relation between the artist and his work. Prior to the sort of political intrusion which now infects everything, we had worked out a remarkably flexible method for handling art/life problems, a method now in doubt because of poets like Brecht.

Both Byron and Rimbaud, for example, share affinities with Brecht and might even be thought to prefigure him. Both, as a contemporary said of Byron, were mad, bad, and dangerous to know. They were antisocial, sexually wild, destructive to themselves, and hurtful to their friends. In other words, splendid examples of the *poète maudit*. They were, as I said, more than a little like Brecht, yet we do not hold their personal behavior very much against them. And when we pass judgment on artists of their kind we look to the importance of their art and allow it to redeem, or at least mitigate, the way they lived. To create great poetry takes great talent which, in turn, deserves special privilege. Or so we have supposed, subscribing to the cult of Art and Genius that has been the core of our Romantic inheritance. For at least two centuries, revolt and self-indulgence have seemed natural to artistic integrity, and if on occasion this sort of license causes local wreckage, we have assumed that the human cost is small compared to the largeness of spirit set free.

But artists themselves have so often abused this benefit—think, for example, of Mailer or Capote today—that we might expect only fools to keep faith. On the contrary, the cult of genius has survived not only internal betrayal; it holds its own against a countermovement which might have but did not demolish the myth of the artist's superior humanity. Ironically—since he so honored genius and loved art—Freud did much to put both in question. Quite apart from the connection between art and neurosis, Freud simply let loose the suspicion that a flawed soul can do fine work and still be flawed; or finally that creativity is as much a muddle as a mystery. Taken all the way, Freud's emphasis on the dark drives of the unconscious turns the venerable myth of the "daemon" into the disquieting idea that some force truly demonic directs the artist at his task.

Few of us are hard-line Freudians, but the "suspicion" of which I speak is now so widespread that no biographer, even with the best of intentions, would attempt a poet's portrait without first digging for unpleasant facts, some evidence of that necessary wound which allows art's mighty bow to bend full-strength. The aim of this process is to push past decorum in order to capture, as Coleridge said of the poet, "the whole man active." As it turns out, some of these poets are rather deplorable people. Robert Frost, for example, was pretty much the "old-stone savage armed" he described as his double in one of his poems; and Lawrance Thompson's big biography of Frost stands as a sort of landmark in the arena of serious debunking. More recently, Harold Bloom has carried the whole business to extremes by telling us that great poets are, well, monsters. At some fearsome psychic depth, poetic patricide is what makes the burning fountain burn.

We might thus suppose that our Romantic notions of the artist's high estate have undergone steep discount. But no, the wounded archangel is an archangel still. We know that art is essential, and if the golden egg comes flecked in dross the goose is still no ordinary bird. In general, then, we say for example that Dickens was an awful fellow, that the domestic damage he caused was unfortunate, but that thereby he did write those fabulous books. We are even beginning to believe that the monomania of a Tolstoy or a Wagner or a Picasso was necessary; work on such grand scale required egos that mistook themselves for God. And Byron, Rimbaud? Their sorry endings anticipate Brecht's, but the society of their times *was* degenerate, and not to rebel would have been capitulation. So now we have it both ways. If art justifies the way artists live, their reckless lives add credence to their art.

As a method for handling cases in which the artist's life puts his art into question, this has been a clever if slippery solution. It has been applied to Brecht, but never to general satisfaction. And it can also backfire. Martin Esslin, for example, has been one of Brecht's toughest defenders; his 1959 study is still probably the best short introduction to the man and his work. In *Mediations,* Esslin's 1980 collection of essays, he again comes to Brecht's defense. He praises the recent translation of Brecht's poetry, *Poems 1913–1956,* which is indeed excellent. Esslin's main business, however, is to save Brecht from academic cultists, who want to canonize Brecht's every word, and more importantly, to take Brecht out of the hands of his Soviet apologists, who attempt to deify him and use his fame for political advantage. In particular Esslin attacks the image of Brecht as the genial genius of East Berlin, the Marxist sage untroubled and at home in the world Stalin built. Esslin's strategy is direct; he quotes pointedly from Brecht's later prose (mostly unavailable in English) and demonstrates that Brecht was consistently critical of the Soviet system. To rid Brecht of any Stalinist taint is Esslin's aim, but by establishing moral distance between Brecht and Soviet reality, Esslin inadvertently throws the current method of handling art/life problems into reverse. For if Brecht knew the system was perverse, doesn't work inspired by Marxist ideals become suspect? Or, if his art is acceptable beyond dispute, can it redeem a man who remained silent during times truly terrible when, in fact, his artistic privilege gave him the chance to speak out?

Esslin is on Brecht's side and we understand his point despite the questions he raises. But the problem persists and has reached a high point in James K. Lyon's *Bertolt Brecht in America,* published in 1980, a book which in itself, and in the critical response it has provoked, has magnified Brecht's "case" wholesale. Lyon too favors Brecht, but his account of Brecht's American exile contains so much unfavorable material that late in the narrative Lyon breaks in with a special plea for Brecht's essential decency. And Lyon too relies on the current method of justifying the life and the art in terms of each other. He repeatedly excuses Brecht's offensive social behavior and his heedless treatment of colleagues by pointing to the way—admittedly amazing—those whom Brecht wronged so often tended to put up with him and give him the benefit of the doubt. The assumption is that only genius could merit pardon so sweeping. For example, Brecht confounded his faithful supporters again and again, Eric Bentley and H. R. Hays especially. Bentley admits to being badly used, but he never wavered in his assistance and readily calls Brecht "the most fascinating man I have ever met." Lyon says of H. R. Hays that "like so many collaborators who admired or were fascinated with Brecht, he continued to promote the writer's works and reputation until the end of Brecht's American exile." And when, as Lyon records, Brecht offended Joseph Losey so keenly that Losey quit his job as director of *Galileo,* Charles Laughton got on the phone to Losey and said, "Please come back." "I will," Losey replied, "if Brecht apologizes to me." Shortly thereafter, Laughton phoned again with this message: "Brecht says please come back, and he also says you should know Brecht never apologizes." Losey went back.

Responses of this kind suggest deep regard for Brecht's genius, and

Lyon goes so far in praise of this uncommonly demanding spirit—
hypercritical, adversative, uncompromising—as to assert that Brecht had
to behave as he did: "Brecht believed that goodness or friendliness, not
evil or anger, was man's normal state, and that indignation over injustice
tended to wear off in time. Therefore he resolved to remain critical by
exerting himself to keep his anger alive, i.e., to be the 'evil' one by
playing the role of the adversary." No doubt there is justice in Lyon's
reasoning, and ordinarily these would be acceptable arguments. Why,
then, does our standard method of disposing of the art/life problem
falter in Brecht's case?

The answer takes us into territory still largely unexplored—the unacknowledged but increasingly urgent relation between art and politics.
In poetry of Brecht's kind, literary issues are questions of conscience
and decency as well. Any aesthetic enterprise which claims to be more
than art for art's sake must ground its claim outside itself. It must
acknowledge, as most lyrical poetry for example does not, its relation
to social reality. Both tragedy and satire are instances of art ministering
to the social health of the community. Didactic art, on the other hand,
points either to the authority of the past or the promise of the future
in order to justify its appeal. It either expresses the ethic of established
institutions or, as in Brecht's case, it clarifies the moral vision inherent
in an ideology which, not yet actualized, has no concrete backing beyond
the poet's embodiment in his own life of what, through his art, he would
have others be and do. Which is to say that when art becomes overtly
political, we have some right to suppose that how the artist conducts
his public life will certify or jeopardize his work's authority; and we
may also suppose that excellence, while it excuses much, cannot condone
its own betrayal.

When in 1979 the English translation of Brecht's *Diaries 1920–1922*
appeared, response was predictable. Here was a portrait of the artist as
a young man, done in the artist's own hand; and what we see is mainly
an artist brazenly self-centered, a man in his early twenties whose chief
gift to others was havoc. Among initial reviews, I recall none which
took these diaries as an occasion for further questioning, namely, how
could an ego so seemingly insolent go on to produce a body of art
whose definitive mark is its moral intelligence, or have come in the later
journals, and especially in the later poetry to speak in a voice undeniably
compassionate and wise. Here again James Lyon's account of Brecht's

years in the United States offers unexpected insight. Lyon hit upon the opportunity for using Brecht's own theory that art reveals most when it presents familiar action in an unfamiliar context. Lyon gives us the portrait of an artist out of his element. And what happens in Brecht's plays happens in Lyon's book: two versions of reality are made to appear, to contend and provoke us to thought.

Exile wasn't the problem. Brecht rather liked the idea of being forced out by Hitler. What got him down was being on the dole, being a famous playwright suddenly unknown and unvalued, being at the peak of his creative powers without the means to exercise them, and being, finally, trapped in Hollywood, then the crassest corner of America. These were circumstances that Brecht never mastered; his predicament brought out the worst as well as the best in him, and his American experience may thus be used as solid ad hominem evidence against him. This is unfortunate and misleading, because those who thrive on gossip or whose idea of biography never gets past personal anecdote will miss the one time in Brecht's life when he was caught off his guard and allowed his soul to show.

From the time of his arrival in California in July 1941, until October 31, 1947, his last day in New York, Brecht's personal style created a flood of negative response. He was, according to one of his associates, "enormously energetic, enormously stubborn, enormously sarcastic, enormously difficult." His arrogance was as unbearable as the smell of his unbathed body. His lack of social grace was as glaring as his two-day's growth of beard, his omnipresent cheap cigar, or the fact, as one of his friends put it, that Brecht "ate very little, drank very little, and fornicated a great deal." In this latter respect, most of us know dozens of poets and writers who can match Brecht's performance—except, of course, for the drinking. This level of detail, nevertheless, is the matter that reviewers of Lyon's book have fastened upon, starting with Auden's remark that of the few people who might deserve the death sentence, Brecht was one and that he, Auden, could imagine doing it himself. The other de rigueur item in this Brechtian file comes from the occasion on which, in 1935, he came briefly to New York to oversee direction of *The Mother* and found that the American style of acting was as appalling to him as the reinterpretations that were mangling his original text. At rehearsal he finally exploded with the words that now stand as the slogan of Brecht's behavior in America: *Das ist Scheisse! Das ist Dreck!* That critics have simply presumed that stuff of this sort takes us into

Brecht's final character suggests not only our attachment to trivia, but the more serious error of mixing personal tics with conduct meriting real criticism—thereby making of Brecht not a complex case to be understood, but a mess to be endured or dismissed as we wish.

In the wake of such confusion we need to recall the serious case against Brecht, which was put forth most forcefully by Hannah Arendt in 1966 and is now included in her *Men in Dark Times.* Her argument—the only one that counts—comes down to this: while poets may go further than ordinary mortals ("more is permitted"), they may yet go so far ("sin so gravely") that they damage their authority and their art to a terminal degree. To her credit, Arendt views the vagaries of Brecht's private life as beneath the dignity of his "case" or of her own evaluation. She observes instead that the root of his art is compassion and that in his life he was utterly devoid of self-pity. Her main concern is therefore with acts and decisions which, for the poet with a political identity, may be said to constitute his "sins." And here Arendt approaches solid ground. Whereas Brecht was heroic in his stand against Hitler, and whereas his commitment to Marxist ideals was admirable and genuine, his failure to speak out against Stalin was an abomination pure and simple. And in Arendt's view, Brecht's failure came to its culmination when he returned from exile to spend his last years in East Berlin as director of the Berliner Ensemble.

Always the moralist, Arendt was also exceptionally sensitive to literature, and it is on literary grounds that she would make her final indictment. She argues that after Brecht's return to the Soviet sector of Germany this great poet ceased to write great poetry or anything else worth respecting. When he betrayed his muse, his muse abandoned him. And unlike Ezra Pound—that other "case"—Brecht was not a madman but a shrewd, extremely intelligent man who always knew what he was doing. That, really, is his crime in Arendt's judgment: he knew. Here is the sum of the serious case against Brecht:

> . . . it is precisely [his] extraordinary intelligence, breaking like lightning through the rumble of Marxist platitudes, that has made it so difficult for good men to forgive Brecht his sins, or to reconcile themselves to the fact that he could sin *and* write good poetry. But, finally, when he went back to East Germany, essentially for artistic reasons, because its government would give him a theater—that is, for that "art for art's

sake" he had vehemently denounced for nearly thirty years—
his punishment caught up with him. Now reality overwhelmed
him to the point where he could no longer be its voice; he
had succeeded in being in the thick of it—and had proved that
this is no good place for a poet to be.

The mark of a good argument is that it opens up, rather than closes
down, the range of issues involved; and since Martin Heidegger was
one of Arendt's heroes, we might go on to ask if for philosophers, too,
"being in the thick of things" is no good place to be. Arendt, in other
words, has touched upon one of the paramount problems defining the
life of art and thought in our century. The predicament is not new—
when he had his chance to be a second Socrates, Aristotle went Brecht's
way. But in our time the pace of events, the magnitude of catastrophes,
the increasing pressure of political forces make escape, or even a bit of
entirely private breathing space, less and less possible.

In the nineteenth century, simply fulfilling the role of the *poète maudit*
was sufficient; and once their revolt had been guaranteed through their
art, poets could—like their apolitical counterparts today—debauch, so
to speak, with dignity. Today that's not enough. If an artist takes up an
adversary stance his position is a sham unless accompanied by some
index of conviction that also touches upon the way life is lived. This is
true not only because social criticism spills over into conflict openly
political, but more deeply because the integrity of art is nothing if not
rooted in our common struggle for spiritual autonomy in a world where
governments of every stamp are determined to smash human rights,
silence dissent, and by using language for propaganda and "big" lies,
pervert that potency of words on which poetry and moral discernment
depend. Arendt's sense of how difficult the role of the poet has become
does much to explain her hardness toward Brecht.

But to what extent was she right? Brecht surely got himself into the
thick of terrible things, but a similar position has been endured by other
of our great modern poets, Mandelstam, Akhmatova, and Milosz among
them. It does not follow that political turmoil ruins art. Brecht's brilliant
early poetry was written in opposition to the Nazi rise, and after Hitler
came to power and Brecht went into exile he produced some of his
finest poems and plays. For the vehemence of his poetry against war
(his "Legend of the Dead Soldier" in particular) he earned the hatred
of Hitler's brownshirts long before 1933, and in that fatal year he wrote

his "Hitler Chorales," a group of satires to be sung to the melodies of famous Lutheran hymns, the first of which begins, "Now thank we all our God / For sending Hitler to us," and which ends:

> He'll paint the filth and rot
> Until it's spick and span
> So thank we all our God
> For sending us this man.

Brecht's irony, ferocious and jubilant, suggests the vigorous will with which he launched his attacks. He was, in all ways, a man on the offensive. What gives any body of poetry its character is the specific tension arising from the poet's private relation to the world. And in Brecht's case there is no doubt what this relation was. Keeping in mind that "the house-painter" was his term of derision for Hitler, here from a poem entitled "Bad Time for Poetry" is Brecht's position:

> Inside me contend
> Delight at the apple tree in blossom
> And horror at the house-painter's speeches.
> But only the second
> Drives me to my desk.

That was written in 1939; the previous year Brecht wrote the following stanza from "To Those Born Later," one of his most telling poems:

> All roads led into the mire in my time.
> My tongue betrayed me to the butchers.
> There was little I could do. But those in power
> Sat safer without me: that was my hope.
> So passed my time
> Which had been given to me on earth.

That is Brecht's view of his calling, and let us be sure we have heard him aright. Armed with nothing but his art, he declares a one-man war on the state. At first this seems ridiculous, a sort of unilateral suicide pact. But when we go on to consider the extent to which, in many countries, writers are arrested, shot, or forced into exile, the relation between the solitary artist and the state takes on the aspect of real war.

And even though there is something hard to credit—arrogant, delusional, even monomaniacal—about such a lopsided stand, Brecht is not alone. Solzhenitsyn is the most visible current example, but there are dozens like him—poets who sense that one of the profoundest battles of our time is between the individual and his own government, poets like Joseph Brodsky (Russian), Reza Baraheni (Iranian), or Kim Chi Ha (Korean), all of whom have suffered political persecution for their art.

But if that is Brecht's true position, and yet he never attacked Stalin with anything like the ferocity he leveled at Hitler, isn't Arendt right? He arrived in East Berlin on October 22, 1948, and he lived there six and a half years before he died in 1956 at the age of fifty-eight. That is a short time for any artist—especially amid political unrest on all sides— to begin a new life, to set up a theater company and see to its success. When he first returned he was refused entry to the American sector of Berlin, but he would have gone to the Eastern zone anyway. He was a Marxist and this would be Marxism on German soil, *his* nation's chance to rebuild itself from the rubble according to socialist principles. That is a cardinal point to keep in mind when weighing Brecht's return. Germany was not yet two nations and Brecht had enormous hope for a unified Germany. With a national theater in mind, and knowing the urgency of gathering the cream of German talent before it dispersed across Europe, Brecht urged Piscator to join him: "It is a good moment, one should not put it off much longer, everything is still in a state of flux and the direction things take will be determined by the forces at hand." Brecht desperately wanted to gather sufficient "forces at hand."

We now know for certain that Brecht was never bribed to live in East Berlin by the promise of his own theater. His most recent German biographer, Klaus Völker, is emphatic on this point. There was no "official invitation." In *Brecht: A Biography,* Völker states "it would be truer to say that [Brecht] forced his way in." The theater was Brecht's idea, and it met first with indifference and then with much difficulty before it opened officially, more than two years after Brecht's departure from America, and the Berliner Ensemble would not have its own building until March of 1954. The amount of time and energy that went into this struggle must have been very great; and even so, only six productions were staged before, in 1951, a new round of Soviet purges and the vicious atmosphere of the Cold War destroyed, once and for all, Brecht's hope for a national theater that would contribute to the creation of a new Germany. It was at this point that Brecht observed: "Time will show if pessimism is to be rated negatively."

During these crucial last years, then, Brecht was intensely busy. He was politically active, speaking, going to rallies, traveling in a semiofficial capacity. He was creating his own theater and keeping Soviet censorship at bay. He was building up a first-rate acting company. He was adapting plays to fit his own ideas of dramatic art. He had begun to write new plays. He was doing what he most loved and what he had missed most while in America—directing without interference, solely in accord with his own deepest principles. And he was also writing poetry. His last poems are spare and swift and might appear slight on first reading, but many are excellent, the "Buckow Elegies" in particular. And what chiefly characterizes his poetry during these last years is the increasing frequency and bitterness of poems bearing anti-Soviet sentiment, such as "Still At It," the theme of which—everything has changed and nothing has changed—was strong in Brecht's work at this time:

> The plates are slammed down so hard
> The soup slops over.
> In shrill tones
> Resounds the order: Now eat!
>
> The Prussian eagle
> Jabbing food down
> The gullets of its young.

Some of his late poems are sarcastic in the fiery early style, as is the case, for instance, in "The Solution"; after the East German regime had crushed the workers' uprising of June 17, 1953, Brecht writes that perhaps the best course of government would be to "dissolve the people / And elect another." More of the late poems, however, are muted and subtle, as if these were the last, half-uttered words of a man talking only to himself, a man, say, whose entire life had taught him that "As always the lovely and sensitive / Are no longer," and who steps into the ragged shade of an abandoned greenhouse to see "the remains of the rare flowers."

If most of Arendt's indictment is not borne out by the facts, that is not completely her fault; in time of upheaval, facts are hard to come by. But on one point—and here the mystery of Brecht deepens—Arendt was right. Brecht always knew. In Russia, personal friends had been shot or had died in concentration camps. In his late prose (I quote from one of Esslin's essays) Brecht contemplates the Soviet situation and observes that the whole vast system "still works very badly and not very organically and needs so much effort and use of violence that the freedoms of individuals are very limited." There is, he goes on, "compulsion everywhere and no real rule of the people." As for the goals to be realized, the violence and coercion "prove that all the basic elements of the *great order* are far from realized as yet, are far from being developed at the moment."

The repetition of those last phrases beginning "are far" gives Brecht's view a strange, almost mesmerized quality, as if he were evoking despair and hope in exactly equal measure. Without illusion, expecting nothing, he simply won't let go, won't foreclose on a dream gone forfeit. And this, I would now suggest, is precisely the element of character most strikingly revealed by Brecht in exile. As Lyon points out, Brecht waited so long to make his escape from Hitler's advancing armies that he very nearly did not make it. He sailed, in fact, on the last ship that could get him to America. Pondering this, Lyon remarks: "Few optimists have had fewer illusions than Brecht and remained optimists. He refused to quit Europe until the situation was hopeless." But wasn't this Brecht's style in all things?

The first two years in America were spent in Hollywood, where "to sell" was the cardinal verb in the new language Brecht confronted. Were this anyone but Brecht, the spectacle of a genius doggedly trying to turn out inane "film stories" would be pathetic. But not in Brecht's case. He eventually wrote more than fifty of these "stories," but with the partial exception of *Hangmen Also Die,* nothing he worked on succeeded. What was wanted was a "Metro-Goldwyn-Mayer Gospel for the Little Man," as Brecht referred to the prevailing formula, with its mandatory love interest and its taboo against any hint of class antagonism. But like Bartleby the scrivener, Brecht preferred not to. The more he saw what success meant, "the more steadfastly he resolved to write film stories for Hollywood on his own terms or not at all." That, of course, ensured his defeat, and for a man as lucid as Brecht, knowing what he was doing must have made him all the more irascible. But just here the Brechtian element comes plainly into view: he would have his art handled "on his own terms or not at all." Nothing could sway him in matters bearing directly upon his own work. And in this respect Brecht is perhaps the supreme example of what Lyon calls "obdurate genius."

Lyon's careful tracking offers much evidence that Brecht was "obsessed" with Broadway. Since his youth, America had exerted the deep pull of myth on Brecht's genius, and now he wanted American recognition for his work, which of course meant acceptance in New York. But here again the intractable Brechtian element asserted itself. When, for example, Le Gallienne, whom Lyon calls "the guiding spirit of the American Repertory Theater and one of the best-known American actresses of the day," asked to play the lead in *Mother Courage,* Brecht replied in English: "Over my dead body." He had seen her perform, and her Stanislavsky style was anathema to Brecht. *The Caucasian Chalk Circle* got as far as a signed contract, but Brecht withdrew when he could not persuade Auden to rework the translation. And when his old friend Erwin Piscator, who was already established, told Brecht he wanted to do *The Good Woman of Setzuan,* Lyon observes that a "New York production might have taken place without delay." Except that Brecht wanted Piscator to do a different play, and then haggled over the situation until all foundered.

The production history of *Galileo,* which did not reach Broadway until Brecht was back in Europe, is a summa of Brechtian resistance. At various points he turned down Orson Welles and Mike Todd, both eager to produce the play, either of whom would have ensured a hit. Perhaps Brecht's saddest run-in was with Harold Clurman, then a director who not only respected Brecht but whose political sense and willingness to work with experimental forms made him the perfect person to launch *Galileo* in New York. Clurman asked for the job and was turned down because Brecht saw him as a member of the Stanislavsky camp. Clurman persisted, suggesting that Brecht misunderstood him. He assured Brecht that he would be happy to "learn" the proper Brechtian principles of drama, but again no. Brecht thus spurned a talented and sympathetic man whose connections would have helped guarantee a warm reception for *Galileo.*

Brecht's behavior, in the examples just cited, almost amounts to a third case against him. Are we to interpret such action as egomania, as madness, as perverse delight in complication? Brecht's "obdurate genius" certainly caused trouble on all sides, but it was also the source of his greatness, the distinguishing characteristic of this artist's power. As Lyon points out, "The word 'compromise' was not in the vocabulary of a dramatist determined to change the existing theatrical world." And again politics is the heart of the matter, for by changing the theatrical world Brecht intended to release a powerful cultural force which would work to change *the* world. That Brecht did aim to change the world follows from his commitment to Marxism. The key, however, is that for a poet whose genius was profoundly rooted in the demotic authority of spoken German—language of the street, market, bar, and gutter, culturally grounded in Luther's lingual usurpation of the Bible—when Brecht spoke of changing the world he meant (at least first) Germany.

Unlike many of his fellow exiles during the war, Brecht was dead set against "Americanization," and he was not bothered by his status as a German exile. This, in fact, was the proof of his German as opposed to Nazi spirit, just as today, for example, the Russian poet Joseph Brodsky takes his exile as proof that against the Soviet perversion he is the true repository of Russian soul. There is much evidence, especially in his poetry, to suggest that Brecht identified his genius with the fate of his country, and beyond doubt his calling as a poet was at the service of Germany's downtrodden masses. In a way not presently apparent in America, poets of other nations—Poland and Hungary are strong examples—have traditionally identified themselves and their art with their country. We did have Whitman, and more recently Williams; but thinking of Eliot and Pound, or the suspect glamour of our expatriates, we might more readily see our poets and writers in pursuit, as a famous critic put it, of "a world elsewhere."

Brecht's fierce care for the destiny of his nation might therefore seem of little consequence, but, on the contrary, it was of absolute importance, and it accounts for much that has been questionable in his public conduct. The American acting style, for example, was dreck because it wasn't Brechtian, i.e., German, in Brecht's interpretation. And the most significant outcome of his relation to German identity was that Hitler loomed infinitely larger, more real and menacing, than Stalin. Toward Hitler there was hatred violently personal; toward Stalin, on the other hand, Brecht was perplexed, critical, horrified, but also detached. If Brecht identified as strongly with the German people as I think he did, then of course Hitler was more threatening than Stalin, despite Brecht's knowledge of the Soviet catastrophe.

One of the most instructive chapters in *Bertolt Brecht in America* describes the ugly conflict between Brecht and Thomas Mann. Mann called Brecht "very gifted, unfortunately." Brecht referred to Mann as "that short story writer." Hostility was mutual, and at least on Brecht's side it amounted to outright hate. Some of this arose from the usual antipathy of genius for its double. But Brecht could not abide the bourgeois basis of Mann's art, and he had been critical of Mann long before they arrived in America. When the two giants finally came face to face in California, an explosion was inevitable, and the form it took was, again, very revealing. The issue this time was whom to blame for the war, and the degree to which Germany in general should be punished.

Mann held that the Nazi movement was homegrown, the outcome of something demonic in the German soul. He went so far (if we can believe Brecht's journal) as to say that he "would not find it unjust if the allies punished Germany for ten to twenty years." This, of course, infuriated Brecht. He demanded a sharp distinction between the Nazi regime, which kept the country in tow through terror, and the German people at large, most of whom had suffered inhuman hardship since the defeat of the previous war. Brecht did not absolve the citizens of this culprit nation from their share of guilt, but he insisted that the Nazi regime had represented, and had been supported by, a very small portion of German citizens, mainly the industrialists and leaders of big business. Here Brecht's reliance on Marxist analysis failed him, for although firms like Krupp and I. G. Farben did indeed profit grandly, *this* government was not an extension of capitalist designs. Like the rest of us, Brecht could not account for the Nazi mentality. The point of the Mann-Brecht conflict, however, is the emphatic clarity with which Brecht revealed his need to save Germany from political division and from still more spiritual despair. The terrible irony is that because he identified his fate with the fate of his country, what happened to Germany happened to Brecht: both ended divided, at the center of endless controversy and international strife.

Quite apart from political questions, however, Brecht's artistic contribution has come to seem decisive; his influence has so thoroughly penetrated the vanguard of theatrical and cinematic techniques that he seems "modern" in a sense more commanding than his "modernist" contemporaries. This turn of events, while true in itself, blinds us to the special relation between art and life in Brecht's case and obscures his calling as a poet. His preference for forms like ballads, street songs, doggerel, jingles, and church hymns, especially within the context of an art that is overwhelmingly didactic, surely raises doubts about Brecht's apparent modernity. And, in fact, to understand him we must see Brecht as a poet of the traditional, premodern type—in other words, the poet as repository of tribal wisdom, as voice and conscience of the community as a whole, the magician whose capacity to praise and curse extends even to keeping kings and tyrants in line, but whose powers will also be called up, like the "rat-rhymers" of medieval times, to stand before the village granary and through poetic incantation drive out the rats.

This was Brecht's job as a poet—to drive out the rats, starting with his own barn. Esslin and others have argued that Brecht's Marxism was the intellectual consequence of his basic poetic disposition, a point which is fairly obvious from Brecht's journals and which can also be seen from his early poetry. In its ideal form, Marxism gave Brecht's explosive genius the discipline and clearness of aim he needed. It also gave him something even more valuable. For Brecht, Marxism was a form of mediation between himself as an alienated individual from the middle class, and the bedrock commonality of the German populace. If this sounds odd, let us recall that Romanticism was the point in the development of our cultural heritage when, for the first time, a literary movement and political awareness began to merge, as may be seen in Shelley and Blake, in Hölderlin, in Hugo, and in a host of others. And as the nineteenth century advanced, the poles of the modern predicament were increasingly defined in terms of two extremes: on the one hand social estrangement as fate, on the other the Marxist dream of harmonious community as historical promise.

That was the gap that poets like Byron and Rimbaud faced but could not close. And the hope of closing it has always been Marxism's secret appeal for intellectuals and artists who feel in the world but not of it. Certainly this was how Marxism helped Brecht resolve his major problem—how to allow the single individual and the communion of suffering humanity to meet, or how to warrant the collective validity of personal vision. Such was the function of Marxism in Brecht's case. Thereby the poet gave over his gift to the community he served, and thereby his commitment to a modern ideology took on the ancient, mythical identity of the soothsayer amid a people sorely afflicted.

Looked upon in this way, Brecht's "case" begins to be greatly more positive and offers an occasion for rethinking an array of presumed conclusions. Usually an ideology dominates the individual, but in Brecht's example the enormous power of this headstrong man dominated the ideology. His art never suffered reduction, or diminishment of invention, or any of the closing-down effects, including the sacrifice of private integrity, which critics (mainly in America) charge against any poet who is so bold as to confront in his art what all of us, every day, confront in our lives. Brecht's genius was equal to the theories available at his historical moment, and this accounts likewise for the fact that with no illusions about the Soviet defeat of Marxist ideals, Brecht would not permit his own vision of the Marxist dream to die. Defeat, yes; capitulation, no. There is thus a strong element of tragedy in Brecht's case, and there is evidence, as in the following poem, that he knew exactly where he stood:

> At the time when their fall was certain—
> On the ramparts the lament for the dead had begun—
> The Trojans adjusted small pieces, small pieces
> In the triple wooden gates, small pieces.
> And began to take courage, to hope.
>
> The Trojans too, then.

That is one of Brecht's late poems. His sense of failure and betrayal is bitterly present, and that amazing last line, by turning history back upon itself, captures in an instant the tragic dialectic between struggle and defeat. More deeply than Arendt intended, this poet *knew*. And knowing, he gathered his strength to survive and carry on. This, I take it, is the final character of Brecht's "obdurate genius." He was dead at fifty-eight, but had he lived as long as, say, Thomas Mann, who died at eighty, I cannot believe that Brecht's oppositional nature, or his Marxist idealism, or his care for his country would have allowed him to remain silent when, two months after his death, the uprising began in Hungary which the Soviets would so brutally smash, or that he would not have spoken out loudly indeed when, in 1961, the Berlin Wall went up.

If the "case" against Brecht persists, it feeds on the predicament that any artist with the courage to face political issues must endure. Art is perfect as life can never be. In terms of our ideals and convictions, all of us may be measured and found wanting. The political poet is thus caught in a double bind. No institution or society—think of the Church, think of America—lives up to the beliefs which inform it. And no poet can live up to those finest moments of vision which make the poetry itself invaluable. Political events, furthermore, can discredit in a day the hard-held convictions of a lifetime. When, therefore, we measure Brecht's life and art against each other or against our own standards, we can reject him for his faults or accept him with honor for his astonishing tenacity. And we might remember too, as Brecht wrote in "To Those Born Later," that commitment entails cost; that anger, even against injustice, makes the voice hoarse.

A History of Death

A Review of Philippe Ariès's
The Hour of Our Death

Any thinker determined to sum up an entire province of human experience invites doubt, or should. Ideas have their own logic, quite apart from the world they presume to explain. The worst that can be said of a good theory is that it demands—and receives—willing suspension of disbelief. Any system reaches beyond the facts for which it claims to account, and just as often the integrity of the whole will depend on methods not themselves systematic. On the other hand, without the focus of ideas and the heuristic thrust of theory we are nowhere. We don't have much choice, except to proceed with care, and perhaps also to prize ideas that make sense of many small details rather than ideas that provide epic uplift or seem to promise power. The small details, in turn, will endorse the theory which revealed their sense, and not as facts merely but as the units of a concrete language through which we articulate existence and gain as much as any intellectual effort can afford: placement and participation in a newfound totality.

This kind of discovery, this kind of reconciliation, emerges with overwhelming generosity from *The Hour of Our Death*. Philippe Ariès has used the study of death to produce a profound view of life, and he has done it by sticking almost completely to local details. To appreciate his achievement, however, we need to understand the limitations so vast a subject imposes. Ariès claims to have given us the "history of death" for the last thousand years. By "history" he means changing attitudes toward the dead, styles of dying, burial practices. This he has done within the limits of European Christian culture, mainly France, with now and then a glance at England and America. Of Jewish, Eastern, or African cultures he has nothing to say. His range of evidence, on the other hand, is very far-reaching, including the architecture and iconography of churches, tombs, and cemeteries; ecclesiastical, clerical, and municipal documents of every sort; personal and public testimonies such as wills, medical reports, letters, and so on. But then he does not hesitate to move from documents and artifacts to works of pure imagination, poems and novels, as if all sources enjoyed a common parity. To account for vast cultural changes he also relies on terms like "collective unconsciousness," not to mention the ease with which (granted his enormous learning) he jumps back and forth among so many centuries. There is, then, a discrete, well-considered expediency to his method, which might be characterized by an unfortunate pun (I presume unintended), as when he explains vestiges of the far past by saying that burial rites long abandoned had in fact persisted "underground."

But then, it is precisely the underground network of a culture that Ariès seeks to uncover. The methods he employs are more a function of his material than of preconceived ideas, and certainly he is careful. What counts in a book as big as this one are things like its cumulative texture, connections repeatedly sighted, and the degree to which Ariès does indeed earn our trust. And in every case his ideas are simple but decisive. His principal assumption is that how we face death affects the way we face our lives, or as Ariès puts it, that there is "a relationship between man's attitude toward death and his awareness of self, of his degree of existence, or simply of his individuality." This uncomplicated equation is made to yield remarkable results. As it turns out, death has not provoked timeless forms of response. On the contrary, much of our recent funereal behavior is of eighteenth- and nineteenth-century origin, and what at the graveside must seem ancient and universal turns out to be very different from other and earlier styles of interment. In all instances, however, relation of self to community emerges as the relevant factor.

Ariès's thesis amounts to a secular version of the Fall, and it comes to this: once we were on familiar and therefore favorable terms with death, but now we are not, and the change has been catastrophic to psychic balance no less than to how we value life. During the Christian Middle Ages death was "tame," which is to say, death was accepted, it was integral to the wholeness of life, it was an event public and communal, ordained rather than random, neither fearful in its coming nor horrid in its aspect. When one's time was up it was simply up, and terror's main source—the struggle of the will to circumvent fate—was entirely absent. In consequence, the dying person might feel physical fright, but death anxiety in its modern form was not known. And because eschatological belief in the form of the Second Coming prevailed, to die was to enter a realm analogical to sleep, awaiting the glory of general resurrection, when body and soul—the two were not yet thought of as separate—would rise together to dwell thereafter in beatitude. The degree of acceptance can be judged from the fact that even death's more extreme manifestations, including mass graves that stayed open until they were full, or the stench of burial in church, or the open spectacle of charnels jammed with human bones, were familiar to the point of inconsequence. The men and women of that far-off time took such things for granted, without undue fear and apparently without revulsion or even discomfort.

Today, on the contrary, death anxiety is pervasive, fear of dying is our deepest dread, and in consequence we are both obsessed with death and resort to stratagems of denial in countless ways. Death is not accepted, neither as an event continuous with life nor within the framework of communal continuity. It is private and invisible. And in the moment of agony the self is utterly alone. The dying person cannot count on institutional blessing or support of the community or any firm eschatological belief to lessen the despairing sense of nothingness that prefigures the self's nonexistence. This predicament dates from the eighteenth century, but its signs were already visible by the end of the sixteenth century, a change which Ariès describes thus: "The idea of death was now replaced by the idea of mortality in general. In other words, the sense of death that had formerly been concentrated on the historical reality of the moment itself was henceforth diluted and distributed over the whole of life, and in this way lost all its intensity." And this, in turn, began to change the quality of existence, as if to be alive were now less full than once it had been. As Ariès puts it: "This life in which death was removed to a prudent distance seems less loving of things and people than the life in which death was the center."

To say that life and death were once continuous, or that the dead and the living were then a single community, is very different from the idea that by denying death its intensity and specific moment, our sense of it infects the whole of existence. If this distinction is historically accurate, then Ariès demolishes the conventional wisdom in a single sweep, in particular our belief that in medieval times men were tyrannized by death in its gruesome and macabre forms, whereas today we are free from such depressing horrors. The view put forward in Huizinga's *The Waning of the Middle Ages,* a book that has long been on almost everyone's list of favorite reading, may have radically misled us. Ariès thinks so. Certainly the spectacle of the charnels is evidence, but of what? Huizinga takes *les Innocents,* the most famous of the medieval burial sites, as the sign of a society obsessed with death; and Ariès argues that Huizinga was simply wrong when he wrote that "Living emotion is paralyzed amid the realistic representation of skeletons and worms." The reference here is to the macabre character of medieval death imagery, culminating in the *danse macabre,* which is not, as Ariès points out, realistic at all, but rather symbolic of death in its communal, indeed its festive manifestation.

This takes us into one of Ariès's most startling reversals. *We* may look at the macabre imagery and presume that it represents terror and obsession; we may suppose that it expresses the morbid spirit of an age characterized by high mortality and general uncertainty; or finally that such blatant symbolism can only reveal stark defeat before the great fact of death. But these are our interpretations and what they reveal are our own attitudes. For medieval men and women, images of death and decomposition were "the sign of a passionate love for this world and a painful awareness of the failure to which each human life is condemned."

The emphasis, for Ariès, falls heavily on "passionate love," and he offers much evidence—from art, from wills, from the medieval habit of assembling one's earthly goods for contemplation as death drew near—that the medieval attachment to life was materialistic and wholehearted; that the clerical teaching of *contemptus mundi* was an elite doctrine which never became popular; or finally that "at no time has man so loved life as he did at the end of the Middle Ages." That the clergy, the wandering preachers especially, put so much stress on the macabre is further proof of the medieval care for material life; the Church worked frantically to instill in a people immune to fear of death a terror of the beyond which might then be used for ecclesiastical, which is to say political, ends. But the desire to devalue life by emphasizing death would not take hold until the sixteenth and seventeenth centuries, when contemplation of death did become pervasive. And surely, we need only look again at Chaucer's *Canterbury Tales* to see that Ariès has a point.

The principal reason that death was not feared as it is today arose from the topographical structure of medieval community, which in turn had everything to do with religious belief and the nature of burial. In pagan as in Christian times, children and common folk were buried in mass graves, a custom that prevailed until the end of the eighteenth century. In either case the cemetery as we know it today had not yet been invented. What counted, however, was the position of the burial place in relation to the community's physical layout. In contrast to pagan burial (for example, the endless lines of sarcophagi along the roads outside the Roman city), Christian burial took place inside the community and centered around the church. Each town or village had its church, which housed the remains of a saint; and as Christendom settled into routine, more and more people of wealth and social position wanted to be buried not in the common graves or on their own estates, but rather *ad sanctos,* in the immediate proximity of an actual saint whose beatific aura might be of substantial blessing to the soul of he or she who dwelt alongside.

To rest as near sainthood as possible meant, in practice, to be buried in the church itself, and that this kind of burial became commonplace can be ascertained from two sources: repeated records of clerical displeasure, in which case church burial is specifically cited; and the plain fact that even today in the old churches of England and Europe, one cannot move about at all without treading upon wall-to-wall graves. People who could not be buried inside the church wished to be as close as possible, in the walls, against the outer structure, in the immediate approaches, their graves spreading outward around the building itself in ever-widening rings which were not, officially speaking, cemeteries, but simply the overflow of the dead in relation to the church. And as the practice of burial in church indicates, this entire area was occupied by the living in performance of both religious and secular duties. Here the community truly met, the dead and the living together. As Ariès sums up the process: "Burial *ad sanctos,* development of faubourgs around the cemeterial basilicas, invasions by tombs of the towns and villages, where they coexisted with the habitations of men—these were so many stages in an evolution that brought together the living and the dead, who had once been kept apart."

The medieval capacity to face death calmly was rooted in communal selfhood and in the religious promise of general resurrection. Everywhere around them the living were reminded by the dead that they, the living, were part of a vast community which, at the time of the Second Coming, would encompass the totality of Christendom. The open pits for the common dead were within sight—and smell—of the church, and so were the charnels. These bins of bones declared the oneness of humankind in death, and so did the graves which were used and reused to accommodate new generations awaiting their turn to dwell in holy ground. The relation of grave to church replicated the connection between self and community, and this was not a matter of belief merely but of concrete topography. Little wonder that Ariès structures his study around the myth of the Fall. If death has a "history," its secret dynamic is the slow shift from traditional to modern concepts of self, the former embedded in society as a whole, the latter rootless, alienated, sustained by nothing but sheer will to be. And having lost the comfort and assurance of communal death, we rugged individualists have gained little compared to the unnerving nothingness which, because it is our final end, reflects our present existence like a mirror that casts no image.

We might suppose that for purely demographic reasons, as population expanded, or conversely, as war and plague robbed communal burial of its effective function, the medieval attitude toward death would weaken and collapse. Perhaps this is so, but Ariès sees the erosion of communal selfhood, and therefore the end of the "tame" death, as coming from another direction, indeed as coming from within the Church itself. By the end of the early Middle Ages, two distinct attitudes toward life after death had appeared: "The traditional attitude, common to the great mass of laymen, remained faithful to the image of an unbroken family of living and dead, united on earth and in eternity. . . . The other attitude was peculiar to a closed society of monks and priests, and attests to a new, more individualistic psychology." Emerging from "the hothouse environment of the cloisters," the "clericalized" death gradually supplants the "tame" death, and this development is second only to the great process of secularization that from the eighteenth century onward would determine attitudes toward self and death alike. An anticlerical bias, peculiar to the French, might be at work here, but Ariès does claim that the germ of modern selfhood, estranged and aware of the void, found its first fertile ground among the medieval clerical castes. The question of bias pales to insignificance before the enormous variety and richness of evidence, all of it drawn from burial practices, to certify the movement from communal to isolated, individualistic selfhood. The Fall did occur, and Ariès documents it in endless detail.

Consider, for a moment, the position of the clergy, elite and apart, charged with herding the faithful into heaven. Consider also the condition of acedia, that peculiar combination of boredom and melancholy which—then as now—has always been the intellectual's privileged blight, the source of a hypercritical consciousness which sees in all things corruption, failure, and doom. But unlike intellectuals today, the medieval clergy had real power, and to impose their own vision upon the masses was in fact their duty. And thus the stage was set. Throughout the early Middle Ages, the eschatological image that dominated popular imagination was the Second Coming, and in Romanesque art the damned are crowded out of sight by the community of the elect, their arms uplifted to greet the returning Christ. Starting in the twelfth century, and continuing for almost four centuries, emphasis begins to shift to the Last Judgment and "Christian iconography projected on the historied portals of medieval churches the film of the end of the world" with dramatic division between the elect and the damned. This was the triumph of the clergy and—outlandish as this sounds—the beginning of an identity crisis that would culminate in the modern concept of isolated selfhood.

For with the victory of Judgment over general Resurrection, the idea of individual destiny arose. Some members of the community will be saved, but others will not, and each must look with terrible care to the particulars of his or her own life. Life becomes a long legal process, and with the judicial attitude comes the new idea of existence as biography, each moment—or page—of which will one day be weighed and judged for all eternity. The symbol of the Book had always been central to Christianity. But whereas it had originally been the book of the elect, it now became the book of the damned, the register in which the affairs of men are recorded for judgment. That the book should underpin the biographical sense of the self may seem to us a pleasant irony, biography being the principal literary genre of our time. But for the medieval man or woman this was a fearful piece of news. And with eternity at stake, one had better read not only the fine print but between the lines as well.

Dying in a state of grace was no longer certainty of salvation; the whole of one's particular life, apart from the commonality of human effort, was now the crux.

Death, in a word, became personal. And now new customs and demands became common. The number of private tombs began to increase, as did the practice of composing a will, which would favorably settle one's earthly affairs and, more and more, leave personal endowments to charities and religious institutions as a hedge on salvation. The wealthy purchased masses to be said for the repose of their souls, one thousand being a common number, and on occasion as many as ten thousand. The coffin was introduced as a more personal style of burial than the winding sheet. Epitaphs appeared, growing longer and longer, including more and more detail, expressing the need to assert one's individual identity in death. Dates, too, began to appear—first the date of one's death, but finally the date of one's birth also; and one's life, so to speak, now occupied not only a specific site in space, but a niche in time as well.

As death became more individual, the effigy became an essential part of the grave, with increasing focus on the portrait. The tomb was no longer a place of interment but a commemorative monument, and as the idea of personality became more pronounced, churches filled up with portraits in the form of the bust, each proclaiming its own individuality amid the general declaration of separate self. Ariès describes this spectacle in a wonderful passage:

> When twilight fills the church, all the heads, arranged in no particular order along the walls or against the pillars, seem to lean out of their niches as if out of windows. The flickering flames of the candles cast patches of yellow light on their faces, and the fleeting contrasts of dark and light bring out the expressions of the features, giving them a kind of motionless and concentrated life.

For a very long time, of course, such practices were the prerogative of rank and office, commoners and the poor could still expect only the common grave and a shroud. But the process of individualizing death was real, and by the eighteenth century its sociopolitical outcome would be decisive: "Persons of humble rank—petty officials, craftsmen, and laborers—were no longer content simply to sleep in sanctified ground with no thought of the memory they left behind them. Now they, too, aspired to a visible tomb." Ordinary people "invaded" the burial grounds, and what they wanted was the beginning of burial as we know it today: a coffin, a private grave, a visible marker complete with inscription and—another innovation—a cross as the preferred symbol of death. Thus the self, spurred on by terror of private death, discovered itself through the symbols of its own demise.

By the sixteenth century, the new style of dying was also established. Whereas in medieval times the moment of death counted most, now the fact that one *would* die spread over the span of one's lifetime and touched upon every aspect of daily life. The result, as Ariès describes it, was not happy: "But what life? Not just any life, but a life dominated by the thought of death, a death that is not the physical or psychological horror of the death agony but the opposite of life, the absence of life, a death that invites man's reason not to become attached to life." Death becomes the emblem of life itself, the cause for meditation upon life's brevity and emptiness. It was at this point in our culture, the period of the sixteenth and seventeenth centuries, that distance between death and the self was introduced, but with this curious outcome: the more remote, the more imminent it became. Not being anywhere, death was everywhere. And now imagery of the macabre returns—pictures and objects meant to evoke life's sadness, the world's illusions, the vanity of all things. And this is indeed a turning point. The feeling of nothingness is gaining ground, melancholy dominates feeling, the lone figure contemplating a skull by candlelight becomes archetypal. The only substantial reference point is death itself, which now comes to have a positive fascination and might even, in thought, be more satisfying than life. As Ariès sums up the reversal:

> This world, so pleasant and beautiful, is rotten and precarious. Death, which hides in its recesses and shadows, is, on the contrary, the blessed haven, safe from the troubled seas and the quaking earth. Life and the world have taken the place of the negative pole that the people of the late Middle Ages and early Renaissance had identified with death. Death and life have switched roles.

The puritan reduction of life will now become respectable, the reformers will have their day. The age of reason dawns, but by refusing to credit death as either a haven or a sacred event, both life and death become part of nature's empty neutrality. For those who still believe in the soul, the body becomes a loathsome prison. For freethinkers the body, especially in death, yields a new fascination, and the gothic obsession with graves and decay becomes prominent. The body's inherent sexuality becomes an occasion for the eroticization of death, and the new interest in cadavers is only partly medical. The anatomy lesson becomes a form of entertainment; dissection becomes an art; grave robbery becomes common, and the general curiosity about purely physical existence leads, among other things, to perverse examination of the line between pleasure and pain, being alive and being dead. The dark spirit of de Sade emerges to rebuke Enlightenment optimism. And one of the oddest outcomes, beginning in the seventeenth century, reaching a sort of hysterical climax in the eighteenth, was the brief obsession with being buried alive. This may correspond to the belief that life is already dominated by death, but in any case the terror was real, it was widespread, and it produced lasting consequences. Autopsy, for example, and embalming were now in demand. What we call "the wake" became common, as did wills with specific instructions to leave the body untouched for a period of time, just in case. And by the end of the eighteenth century, "repositories" were established where bodies could be kept under observation until death was beyond doubt. These places were, in fact, our first "funeral homes."

Viewed in this unhealthy light, the age of reason and enlightenment looks less rational than we might have supposed. The eighteenth century did, however, make a decisive contribution to burial as we know it today. It faced the problems of demographic overload and sanitation, and by way of solution created the modern cemetery. The place of burial was moved from the center of the city to the outskirts. Landscape and architectural design were taken into account, and now that the cemetery was a secular, municipal institution, its actual site took on the aspect of a public park. By solving the problem of space, furthermore, a rational if abstract equality was at last achieved. Everyone might have a private grave and de facto concord prevailed as, side by side, row upon row, strangers dwelt together in settled harmony. This was, of course, the urban solution. In rural areas the place of burial was still the "churchyard," which acquired new significance as the age of Romanticism dawned. At this point the modern, alienated individual began to visit the country churchyard, a solitary figure in search of peace and intimations of the infinite. Death, in other words, was again changing its meaning.

It could hardly be otherwise. The sense of nothingness which overtook the self in the eighteenth century could not be tolerated without despair, and although these—despair, nothingness, the abyss—would remain modern categories, the Romantic revolt against secularization of death would produce countercategories which, at least until the First World War, successfully circumvented the void and restored to death a dignity, amplitude, and beauty that made it not only acceptable but positively attractive. Here again *The Hour of Our Death* is revolutionary for the insight it offers. Scholars have debated endlessly the origins of Romanticism—the rebellion against reason, the apotheosis of the individual, the discovery of originality and creative energy as resources necessary to society—but whereas the Romantic obsession with death has often been noted, and just as often been dismissed as morbid, the idea that death itself was one of the prime movers of the Romantic movement has had, with the exception of Mario Praz, few supporters. But after reading Ariès there can be little doubt. The enactment of "the beautiful death," and the further identification of death with infinity, were Romantic inventions which transcended dread and, by suggesting elusive mystical fulfillment, transformed death into a kind of experience that could be shared, not only at the actual moment of dying but beyond the grave without end.

The idea that death can be beautiful is part of a larger Romantic drama which Ariès calls "the death of the other"—death as a delicate spectacle, to be witnessed in hushed wonder and swelling tears by the living and performed with as much refinement as the dying person could muster. It was the privilege of the survivors to help the deceased die "well." Careful coordination and mutual encouragement were essential, pathos and self-pity were subsumed by the gravity of the occasion. And although Ariès does not mention it, not for nothing was tuberculosis the favorite nineteenth-century disease. Consumption, as it was then called, wore down the body gracefully, etherealizing the features with the sadness of death foreknown. It allowed small baroque details—spots of red upon a snowy handkerchief—to assume discrete significance. And as things advanced toward the deathbed finale, there was time enough for family and loved ones to gather, to begin mourning in advance, to indulge their feelings to the full. This, in effect, was death for art's sake, a highly

WRITING INTO THE WORLD

artificial arrangement, and if the "beautiful death" reminds us of opera, that is because a great deal of nineteenth-century opera took this particular style of death as its principal theme.

In consequence, death again became "tame," and within the private confines of the family it regained its communal character. Even so, this might have been no more than what its post-Romantic critics claim, a charade, were it not for the attendant belief, essential to Romanticism, that death was the portal to a realm transcending time and space. If in the nineteenth century love and death became inseparable, here was the reason. If suddenly family bonds became shockingly intense, and if the death of children gained an importance it had never had before, here was the reason. Being the entrance to eternity, death was not the end of affection but the promise of a perfection that only the dead could achieve. For lovers as for families, death would be the ultimate reunion. One could go gently into that good night because others were waiting with greetings of tremendous love. One could endure another's death because, in due time, one's own death would ensure perpetual union. Looked upon in this way, death itself was the source of consolation. And for the survivors there was an added bonus: being nowhere in particular, the spirit of the deceased could be anywhere and his or her presence might at any moment be felt or evoked by commemoration and ritual. There might then be actual rapport between the living and the dead.

This "cult of the dead," as Ariès calls it, is of course a strategy for denying death's finality, but it was remarkably successful and accounts for much behavior that even today we take for granted as the natural response to loss of family or loved ones. Regular visits to the cemetery, care for the actual grave, placing flowers against the headstone: these are acts of respect and commemoration, but they are also rituals of rapport which assuage sorrow, endorse faith in immortality, and facilitate the psychic process of mourning. Objects originally owned by the deceased are preserved and revered as when, in the extreme case, a room is maintained exactly as it was when the dead person still lived. And then there is funerary jewelry, the most common item being the locket which contains a picture or a strand of hair. Indeed, the function of photography in the battle against death has still to be assessed. But clearly, we are at the end of a process of evolution that through many centuries began with *memento mori* and concludes with the memento, the souvenir. As Ariès sums it up: "At the end of this evolution the subject is no longer death or the death of a loved one. Death itself has been erased, as it were, and all that remains is a substitute for the body, an incorruptible fragment."

Romantic death and the cult of the dead are still with us, but their authority has greatly diminished. Death as a personally shared event, or the idea that death is beautiful, require circumstances that are stable, private, domestic. No wonder Romantic attitudes have failed us: after the carnage of the First World War, after the horrid revelations of Auschwitz and Hiroshima, in a world where atrocity has become the norm and people die in droves, death is neither beautiful nor domestic nor even recognizably human. To the extent that Romantic practices remain, they linger desperately and are the proof of our poverty.

We are indeed in desperate straits, and on this note Ariès concludes his "history." Having exhausted our defenses, we have elected to deny death point-blank, without mediation, without psychic strategy. We shall simply push it out of sight and thereby keep it out of mind. We shall not acknowledge its presence in the world of daily routine. This is what Ariès calls "hidden death," and the reduction of death to invisibility depends on a three-stage process: first, concealment (removal to the hospital); next, the "lie" (refusal of family or doctors to inform the dying person of his or her true condition); finally, the general conspiracy of silence (no public recognition of death or grieving). Death in this form is thoroughly dehumanized, at most a technical event toward which we maintain calculated indifference. Genuine indifference, the medieval tolerance of death's immediate sight and smell, expresses sincere acceptance and, as we have seen, was rooted in the fact that during the Middle Ages the dead were kept inside the community. Now the aim is to keep death outside, beyond the realm of normal awareness. But as Ariès has also demonstrated, only by responding to death at the level of community can death itself be tamed. Having been cast out, death regains its savage otherness, against which the resources of the isolated self are simply inadequate.

Ariès observes that the outright denial of death has been most pronounced in America; not, however, because we are more cruel or uncaring than other societies, but because more than most countries we have maintained beliefs that make denial easier: "first, the belief in a nature that seemed to eliminate death; next, the belief in a technology that would replace nature and eliminate death, the more surely." The former was our nineteenth-century solution, the latter is with us today.

The idea of nature as a transcendent realm into which, upon dying, the self could be absorbed eternally was part of our Romantic inheritance; it can hardly mean much to an industrial nation of city-dwellers. Which leaves us with technology, and here we continue to be expert. The "hidden death," after all, depends on medical technology as its means and also as its excuse. And we do have machines which keep bodies alive after the person is dead. This manipulation of death by machines is grotesque, and as Ariès suggests, from the hidden or medicalized death a new image of the macabre is emerging: the human body neither fully alive nor fully dead, punctured by needles and entangled in tubes, the eyes drugged and empty. *Ecce homo.*

The new emblem of death goes hand in hand with the condition of community it reveals. In order that the hidden death stay truly hidden, all communal support must be withdrawn from the dying person. This abdication is as ugly and inhuman as its larger implication, which Ariès formulates as follows:

> But how are we to explain the abdication of the community? How has the community come to reverse its role and to forbid the mourning which it was responsible for imposing until the twentieth century? The answer is that the community feels less and less involved in the death of one of its members. First, because it no longer thinks it necessary to defend itself against a nature which has been domesticated once and for all by the advance of technology, especially medical technology. Next, because it no longer has a sufficient sense of solidarity; it has actually abandoned responsibility for the organization of collective life. The community in the traditional sense of the word no longer exists. It has been replaced by an enormous mass of atomized individuals.

That traditional community no longer exists is, of course, a truism. So is the loss of communal selfhood. So is our anguish as isolated individuals. But within the framework of death's history, these commonplace truths take on new urgency. If psychic balance depends on the balance of life and death, and if, in turn, this necessary symmetry can happen only when the community of the living, as a community, extends itself to include its dead, then our need to face death in order to love life will go unrealized. We shall live as ghosts. Death shall not count and if not death, then not life either. And once death becomes unreal or of no admissable significance, then any amount of it can be tolerated. That political leaders everywhere talk openly of nuclear war and argue that such a war is winnable is proof that death is meaningless. The current frenzy of our preparation for nuclear holocaust depends on our capacity to deny death's reality, and in terms of psychological repression, death-denial may be the source of our collective desire for destruction. *The Hour of Our Death* is richly instructive, and therein lies its terror. For if his basic assumptions are correct, then what Ariès tells us finally is that the hour of our death is very near.

Auden's Truth

Who among us does not know, has not often quoted, lines from W. H. Auden's poem which begins:

> I sit in one of the dives
> On Fifty-Second Street
> Uncertain and afraid
> As the clever hopes expire
> Of a low dishonest decade. . . .

Those are, of course, the first lines of "September 1, 1939," and they sound as applicable and right today as they did at the start of the Second World War. Like so much of Auden's work, the poem is full of indelible lines, the "huge imago" of a "psychopathic god," for instance; or the "error bred in the bone" which craves "Not universal love / But to be loved alone." And then there is that other line, by this time legendary, which goes simply: "We must love one another or die." It's not overly striking, there is no compelling image, but E. M. Forster took it for a great truth and today, with the chance of nuclear holocaust increasing, the line seems saner than ever.

Yet Auden abandoned it: the line, then the poem. It survives in *The English Auden* but does not appear in the *Collected Poems*. How the poem got dropped is well known and hardly needs retelling except for a larger point I have in mind. After "September 1, 1939" was published, Auden's inspection landed on "We must love one another or die," and then he said to himself: "That's a damned lie! We must die anyway." Auden fiddled with rewriting, and ended up discarding the poem. It was, he later remarked, "infected with an incurable dishonesty." What dishonesty? "September 1, 1939" remains one of the best poems in English, which manages to record and express, in an idiom wholly its author's, a characteristic but seldom touched kind of modern experience, a kind of emotional moment that can only be called "political," in this case the private response to an encompassing public event.

Auden's claim is that to make love and death a matter of choice isn't true. We see what he means, I presume; and we are also reminded that Auden rewrote and discarded poems the way he smoked cigarettes— always lighting up or stubbing out. But to him a poem's "truth" really mattered. That may sound strange to us (raised on the notion that poetry is neither true nor false), but it wasn't odd to Auden. For him a poem had to be *true*. The other famous example that flunked Auden's test was "Spain 1937." He might have disapproved because the poem urges ideals in which, after his own brief involvement in the Spanish cause, he no longer believed. As he said: "Nobody I know who went to Spain during the Civil War who was not a dyed-in-the-wool stalinist came back with his illusions intact." Then again, he might have rejected it because, as Edward Mendelson says in *Early Auden,* the poem is internally self-canceling, with images of choice and of necessity negating each other, the result being a betrayal of the political vision the poem was intended to embody. But no; for Auden the fault was that the poem's last lines were not true. To think that "History to the defeated / May say Alas but cannot help or pardon," suggests that might is right, that victory vindicates. That could not be true, not morally, and certainly not in Franco's case.

Auden's preference for *truth in poetry* over the more conventional idea of *poetic truth* led him to say, in 1964 when Stephen Spender asked him to contribute to a book on Yeats, that he was "incapable" of writing objectively about Yeats, and for the following reason: "he has become for me a symbol of my own devil of unauthenticity, of everything which I must try to eliminate from my own poetry, false emotions, inflated rhetoric, empty sonorities." No offense, but Auden's feeling about Yeats's poems was that "His make me whore after lies." That probably says more than Harold Bloom about the problem of influence. Poets had better stay on guard against taking another's style as their own. And again, truthfulness is the issue; along with the remarks about Yeats, Auden added this little verse:

> No poem is ever quite true,
> But a good one
> Makes us desire truth.

By "truth" Auden does not mean the Romantic poet's faithfulness to private vision, nor does he have in mind the sort of neither-here-nor-there integrity that I. A. Richards ascribed to poetry as "pseudo-statement." Our own *ars poetica,* that a poem should not mean but be, was for Auden plain silliness. He could appreciate the emphasis the New Critics put on fidelity to voice, persona, ironic resonance. And he could see, if not much care for, the phenomenological truth of the poem as verbal icon, as reflexive language-entity or any other such formulation so dear to the Modernist movement. But that was all by the way. By truth Auden means what ordinary men and women have always meant— the world, that which *is,* the impinging presence of persons, places, and things beyond the self, everything that makes the claim to purely private vision suspect. Henry James defined the real as "things we cannot possibly *not* know." That, I think, might serve as well for Auden's idea of the true. And in poetry, Auden's truth would lead him to value the mirror over the lamp; creation as engagement with *the* world rather than solitary envisionment of *a* world elsewhere.

What I've said so far is nothing new but only out of fashion. That Auden has received less critical attention than his peers is no accident; he alone was not Romantic. We must remember that for all their bluster against the Romantic movement, Eliot, Pound, and Co. were in that tradition, tougher perhaps, perhaps a bit wiser or just more conservative, but Romantic all the same. In their notions of poetic autonomy (no ties to the world beyond the poem) and of creative imagination (new emotions, new orders brought forth) they were pure Coleridge. The assumption that poetry demands "willing suspension of disbelief" still prevails, and it implies that a poem is something apart from, and often in contradiction to, the real or the true as James or Auden would have it.

But is that what Coleridge actually said? Yes and no. His famous definition comes from the passage in *Biographia Literaria* where he discusses "the plan" of *Lyrical Ballads*. Upon rereading, what Coleridge establishes is that there are *two* kinds of poetry, neither entirely distinct from the other of course, but each in its practice sustaining a principle that can be distinguished from its opposite. As Coleridge saw it, the joint endeavor of *Lyrical Ballads* amounted to a division of labor. To Wordsworth he assigned one sort of poetical work, to himself the other. For us, the point is not how finely each poet carried out his end of the job, but the theoretical distinction itself:

> . . . it was agreed, that my endeavours should be directed to persons and characters supernatural, or at least romantic; yet so as to transfer from our inward nature a human interest and a semblance of truth sufficient to procure for these shadows of imagination that willing suspension of disbelief for the moment, which constitutes poetic faith. Mr. Wordsworth, on the other hand, was to propose to himself as his object, to give the charm of novelty to things of every day, and to excite a feeling analogous to the supernatural, by awakening the mind's attention from the lethargy of custom, and directing it to the loveliness and wonders of the world before us: an inexhaustible treasure, but for which, in consequence of the film of familiarity and selfish solicitude we have eyes, yet see not, ears that hear not, and hearts that neither feel nor understand.

So: a "semblance of truth" and a "willing suspension of disbelief" on the one hand; and on the other "awakening the mind's attention," its object being "the world before us." We can set "The Ancient Mariner" or "Christabel" against "Simon Lee" or "Michael"—or, Auden, Williams, and Brecht against Yeats, Stevens, and Rilke—and see plainly enough the distinction Coleridge made. Auden's art does indeed address "the world before us," and aims, by "awakening the mind's attention," to awaken also the unfeeling heart. One of the most interesting things about Auden's poems—even those explicitly Christian—is that they alert the mind as well as the heart, and reading them we *feel* that no suspension of disbelief is required. Who believes that "Musée des Beaux Arts" is not true; that the tragedy of suffering—the victims enduring alone, ourselves unable to share their burden even if we would—isn't exactly that, a diminishment of human community which is constant and universal?

The difference between poetry which responds to the world and poetry which responds to inner vision has often been acknowledged through the overworked division of literature into Classical and Romantic modes. I am not bothered by the oversimplification (I too am being oversimple) but by the mounting confusion such terms create, as when a Romantic poet like T. S. Eliot thinks of himself as Classical, or pretended to. So let us, for the nonce, resolve this business by an image. The Romantic or visionary poet works by selecting a unique blend of colors from light's spectrum, usually those closest to the violet or even ultraviolet end; Auden's kind of poet works with unfractured light, preferring no color but that of sunlit air itself, as when in"Ischia" Auden celebrates Mediterranean lucidity:

> How well you correct
> our injured eyes, how gently you train us to see
> things and men in perspective
> underneath your uniform light.

Auden started out in the Modernist mode, but he grew beyond it remarkably fast. By the time he was twenty-nine, in 1936, he wrote his wonderfully breezy, rhyme-royal farewell to the packed cryptic style of his youth and declared himself a poet for all weathers, his subject humanity at large:

> To me Art's subject is the human clay
> And landscape but a background to a torso;
> All Cezanne's apples I would give away
> For one small Goya or a Daumier.

Letter to Lord Byron is Auden's first big poem; the tradition of Chaucer stands solidly behind it, and the "airy manner" of Byron's *Don Juan* should not divert us from the poem's earnest intent as a self-portrait and a manifesto. Auden wants "a form that's large enough to swim in," and speaks up for a kind of poetry as attentive to life as a Jane Austen novel. He pledges himself anew to the *human* landscape, desolate and forever scarred. And he will *not* be fooled by the make-it-new movement any more than he will believe that the brave new world of scientific splendor—"Where the smoke nuisance is utterly abated / And all the furniture is chromium-plated"—exists generally, in truth:

> Well, you might think so if you went to Surrey
>   And stayed for week-ends with the well-to-do,
> Your car too fast, too personal your worry
>   To look too closely at the wheeling view.
>   But in the north it simply isn't true.
> To those who live in Warrington or Wigan,
> It's not a white lie, it's a whacking big 'en.

> There on the old historic battlefield,
>   The cold ferocity of human wills,
> The scars of struggle are as yet unhealed. . . .

Thus Auden allies himself with experience that is permanent and collective, and with those who suffer and endure. He accepts the horror of history and politics—"The cold ferocity of human wills"—and takes it for granted that from these conditions very few can escape and none can count on remaining exempt. In *Letter to Lord Byron* Auden becomes himself; he can now enter his major phase and begin the great poems on which his fame justly rests. If life's hard issues, in his "chat" with Byron, are touched upon with comic poise, Auden's dedication is in no way lessened. Very soon he would have his task so thoroughly defined that he could rhyme "song" with "wrong" and fully accept the way, in his art, aesthetics and ethics merge. He could pit "his verses" against Europe's "horrible nurses" and see his own position not unlike Voltaire's. Except, of course, that the time is now 1939 with war coming, and with humbling hindsight he knows what Voltaire could not—that against great darkness poetry can console and defend but never prevail. Even so, Auden's portrait of the poet in "Voltaire at Ferney" endorses the kind of job any poet might take upon himself as the burden of his trade in a world such as ours:

> Yet, like a sentinel, he could not sleep. The night was full of wrong,
> Earthquakes and executions. Soon he would be dead,
> And still all over Europe stood the horrible nurses

Itching to boil their children. Only his verses
Perhaps could stop them: He must go on working. Overhead
The uncomplaining stars composed their lucid song.

It was at this time, too, the same month in fact, that Auden wrote
"In Memory of W. B. Yeats," and critics who are forever quoting one
line from that magnificent poem—"poetry makes nothing happen"—
are overlooking to a shameful degree what Auden says, in the same
poem, that poetry does do and, accordingly, what the poet must demand
of himself. No matter how dark the night or terrible the day, "With
your unconstraining voice / Still persuade us to rejoice," and here again
the rhyme is telling—poetry, as Auden often said, helps us the better
to enjoy life by helping us the better to endure it. That, of course, was
Dr. Johnson's dictum, rooted in the belief that art, by helping us to face
the truth, helps us also to transcend life's dehumanizing forces. To hold
such artistic principles in the twentieth century is no small victory. But
that these were indeed Auden's principles, his deepest convictions as a
poet, as a citizen of the world, cannot be doubted:

> With the farming of a verse
> Make a vineyard of the curse,
> Sing of human unsuccess
> In a rapture of distress;
>
> In the desert of the heart
> Let the healing fountain start,
> In the prison of his days
> Teach the free man how to praise.

Auden wrote those stanzas in answer to a time when "the living
nations wait, / Each sequestered in its hate." That was in 1939, catastrophe was already on the way. But this was, and would always be,
Auden's manner: let us have the truth however unnerving, then let us
find ways to celebrate existence nonetheless. In his great early sonnet
sequence, "In Time of War," Auden begins one of the poems with
"Certainly praise," and then he goes on: "But hear the morning's injured
weeping, and know why." That we should *know* is central to our capacity
for praise. Auden again refers his art to the true, and poetry itself will
be the vehicle through which such knowing becomes steady and whole.

Always face the worst, be it war or just the day's unpleasantness or, as in "City Without Walls," those three-in-the-morning debates we have with ourselves when, sleepless and insanely lucid, we allow the hard truths to slip past our weary defenses.

But of course, poetry is our best defense, and how Auden deployed his art was again the outcome of his insistence on truth. Being as tightly tied to life as words to things, Auden's kind of poetry frees itself, and us with it, by declaring the fact of its artifice openly, knowing that in itself it is not truth but *merely* art. I would stress the double meaning of "merely," or as Auden put it in one of his playful occasional poems:

> . . . only
> Those who love illusion
>   And know it will go far:
> Otherwise we spend our
> Lives in a confusion
> Of what we say and do with
>   Who we really are.

That art is *not* life is the grand theme that orchestrates all the magical parts of *The Sea and the Mirror,* and which, in a comic apotheosis of Jamesian gab, allows Caliban his virtuoso address "to the Audience." Sea and mirror need each other even while they constantly threaten to betray one another. In the case of a master like Caliban, art easily wins over life's dense profusion, yet in the end where is he, Caliban aping Prospero, but stranded still upon the artist's island, and so demonically fluent that he becomes the spokesman for his opposite, indeed *becomes* that opposite and so, as Ariel knows, needs saving from his own success. That *The Sea and the Mirror* is a concoction of the set piece enforces the victory of artifice. And yet, Antonio still broods unrepentant. Prospero's art—his "all"—is "partial."

That is the point likewise in "The Shield of Achilles." Art is the shield that protects us, grants us our moment in the sun, but in the end cannot save us. And even so, only art of a certain kind can help, not art that is visionary or that celebrates romance, but rather poetry which includes—tragically, comically, the means may vary but the aim must be sure—a comprehensive attention to the real. And accordingly, upon the shield where we would hope to see "Men and women in a dance / Moving their sweet limbs," we see instead "no dancing-floor / But a weed-choked field." We are shown not what we desire but what we cannot possibly (after reading the poem) not know:

> A ragged urchin, aimless and alone,
>   Loitered about that vacancy; a bird
> Flew up to safety from his well-aimed stone:
>   That girls are raped, that two boys knife a third,
>   Were axioms to him, who'd never heard
> Of any world where promises were kept,
> Or one could weep because another wept.

The poem insists upon its formal elegance, manifest chiefly through stanzaic symmetry and strong rhyme. The contrast between *this* beauty and *that* ugliness is not, however, an exercise in irony. Emphatically, the poem says of itself that art is one thing, life another; that form and content conflict; and that in the end art will not suffice. What a pile of heresy! Formalism, which has governed literary criticism in America for most of this century, cannot abide the split between form and content, and won't tolerate the belief that something called "life" or "truth" is out there somewhere to limit art's Romantic claim to dominion over all. Modernism subsumed content under form to insure that form was all that mattered, that life and truth couldn't count apart from formal subjugation. And so it went. "When we speak of technique," as Mark Shorer put it in 1948, "we speak of nearly everything." Or as Cleanth Brooks has repeated for decades, let us think of the poem as "a construct," or as an "artistic document," or even, pushing hard, let us say that "form is *meaning*." To which, of course, Auden could only say yes, yes, indeed yes. And then go on to talk about "truth," and to suggest that the modernist emphasis on form for its own sake was cockeyed. A nice irony, this; the virtuoso, the master of all forms, the finest wordsmith in modern English not playing the game. The happiest of artificers suggesting that artifice was but a way of engaging something more important, life, truth, Caliban's curse, the burden of our sorrow.

No, in "The Shield of Achilles" the sharp juxtaposition of romance and the real, the terrible marriage between horrid content and exquisite form, none of this is ironic. It is Auden using art to face the facts and saying so. It is artifice proclaiming its freedom despite its bondage to unhappy truth. Poetry is artifice and artifice which revels in itself is play and play, in a world as tragic as ours, is the only kind of transcendence we are likely to have. To rhyme "will" with "kill," as Auden says in "Horae Canonicae," is a chance of language, as all rhyme is, and in its surprise it bears an awesome revelation. Or again, in the stanza from "Voltaire at Ferney," to chime "song" against "wrong" is to celebrate art's power to engage the truth in earnest play and not be cowed or beaten down—but not to win either. Our humanity resides in that balance.

Of the great moderns, Auden is the only poet of whom we can say with confidence (and not be embarrassed) that his theme is the human condition. And here once more, Auden owes his success to his lover's quarrel with that which—immediately and for everyone—is true. If the true is what *is*, then it must be everywhere and will appear in every guise, frivolous and tragic, randy, stupid, heartbreaking, a matter of tears and laughter at every turn. Not for nothing did Auden master more techniques, and work in a vastly broader spectrum of forms, than any of his contemporaries. He had, after all, the entire world before him, nothing denied. Auden could write about anything (and pretty much did) because, as Georg Lukács has argued for Homer and the epic, he addressed a totality which might be entered at any point. And thus Auden's prodigal variety, his desire for "a form that's large enough to swim in." No single form would do, but that was a challenge Auden relished. He liked to think that poetry was comparable to human personality—capable of all registers, taking the heavy stuff along with light verse and even, now and then, a bit of doggerel.

To talk about "truth" or demand that a poem be "true" is surely asking for trouble. And yet if we approach Auden in good faith and see him as a poet engaging "the world before us," using his own life as a sort of backstage entrance rather than the main act, I think we can allow the problem of truth in poetry to rest and still rejoice in Auden's enterprise. Whatever it is, Auden's truth is endlessly diverse yet homing toward the general and the shared, and it afforded his poetry an authority that provokes immediate trust. In lines I have always cherished, Auden put it this way:

Even a limerick
ought to be something a man of
honor, awaiting death from cancer or a firing squad,
could read without contempt. . . .

Terror and the Sublime

I n Edmund Burke's *A Philosophical Enquiry into the Origin of our Ideas of the Sublime and Beautiful,* first published in 1757, the author is only nine pages into his argument when he offers his initial definition of the sublime:

> Whatever is fitted in any sort to excite the ideas of pain, and danger, that is to say, whatever is in any sort terrible, or is analogous to terror, is a source of the *sublime;* that is, it is productive of the strongest emotion which the mind is capable of feeling.

Burke elaborates upon this definition throughout his treatise; but as if to leave no doubt concerning his cardinal point, he added the following sentence to the slightly revised 1759 edition of *A Philosophical Enquiry:* "Indeed terror is in all cases whatsoever, either more openly or latently the ruling principle of the sublime."

In this paper I shall attempt to clarify how terror can be the secret heart of things sublime; why the mind does not experience dread or stunned diminishment but rather such positive emotions as (in Burke's vocabulary) astonishment, reverence, wonder, and delight; and why, in this special case, the mind may feel itself to be deeply satisfied or even sublime in itself. I shall be content to employ Burke's own empirical-psychological method; and I want to use the term *terror* exactly as I use the term *sublime*—both may refer to objects or external conditions in themselves terrible or sublime but both may also refer to an emotion or state of mind experienced either as terror or as sublime. This approach allows me to formulate the questions with which I am most concerned: What is the relation of terror to the sublime? What dynamic process might the mind undergo to arrive at moments of sublime experience?

We begin by remembering that in Burke's time as in our own popular reference to the sublime does not include recognition of the element of terror. Landscapes, sunsets, great works of art and architecture are called sublime. But nowadays so is an especially fine meal or just a happy night out on the town. When most people use the word *sublime* they use it with positive and enthusiastic intent to convey some expansive sense of grandeur, magnificence, or plenitude, or to name a beauty unusually impressive. Nothing negative attaches. Although such usage may reflect our current penchant for loose superlatives it also suggests a state of psychic elevation, which I would therefore call the *naïve* or *innocent* sublime.

Longinus's "On the Sublime," written sometime during the first century A.D., is the great defense of the innocent or noble sublime. The influence of Longinus began to be felt in Europe in the latter part of the seventeenth century, especially after Boileau's French translation from the Greek in 1674. From that time onward, culminating in the pre-Romantic stirrings of the eighteenth century, the sublime as Longinus defined it held undisputed sway as a principal category of literary value. Put simply, the sublime is that which produces, but which also resides in, the high style in literature. Its elements, as Longinus set them forth, include "elevation of mind," the "power of forming great conceptions," a kind of intensity resulting from "vehement and inspired passion," and finally, along with "noble diction," a forceful command of figurative language. In perhaps its most famous formulation, "Sublimity is the echo of a great soul." Greatness of soul was the central source of the sublime in literary art, and its chief effect on the reader was spiritual transport—a sense of being uplifted, of being carried beyond oneself as if one shared in or had indeed become sublime.

The naïve sublime may be lofty, noble, or grand; but nowhere is it said to touch upon terror. Longinus even remarks that some passions—pity, grief, and fear in particular—cannot be sublime. Here, then, is authority, if authority be needed, to partake of the sublime in all its high-minded innocence. Or so it seemed to many generations, and still does. But upon a closer reading of Longinus we notice that he backs up his concept for the sublime with specific examples. In twenty-one instances he quotes, with approval, lines from suitably sublime poets, usually Homer (usually from the *Iliad*), but sometimes from various Greek tragedies. The interesting thing is this: In all but two of these examples, the content of the poetry being quoted is blood, battle, rage and leaping flames, cleaving swords and piercing spears, or—in a word— the sort of mutilation, disfigurement, and annihilation that goes by the name of war.

Possibly Longinus was a member of a warrior culture and we might therefore suppose it quite natural that he would seek examples of the sublime from Homer, the greatest poet of a warrior culture. But that is not the point. Rather, if we consider the healthy, upright human image as the emblem of dignity and human worth, then Longinus roots his idea of the sublime in a kind of experience that does open violence to the human image. And if we can further agree that terror is that which diminishes, mutilates, and dissolves the human image, then terror *is* an element in the sublime as Longinus illustrates it. If his own noble stance obscures the connection between terror and the sublime, this is not bad faith on the part of Longinus but rather a consequence of the sublime in itself. Indeed, we may fairly conclude that the definition of the sublime, in Longinus's usage, is this: the lofty depiction of terrible actions. That the notion of the naïve or innocent sublime has so long prevailed owes much to the power of a style which suppresses the terror from which it draws its energy.

For Longinus, finally, the sublime is mainly a matter of rhetoric, an aesthetic category concerned with proper composition. Burke also approaches the sublime at the aesthetic level, as in his distinction between the *pleasure* of beauty and the *delight* of the sublime. But Burke then goes on to treat the sublime as a special kind of experience in response to objects and conditions such as the ocean, darkness, obscurity, the vastness of heights and depths, and above all, the forms of power which cause danger or pain and threaten self-preservation. With Burke the sublime is no longer principally a literary matter but rather the consequence of our response to things which, by virtue of the terror they thrust upon us, are perceived as sublime. And with the shift from Longinus to Burke we move irreversibly from the naïve sublime to another sort of sublime that is considerably less innocent and in some cases even demonic. Of real importance for Burke, furthermore, is the relation between external impact and internal response, as in the following passage:

> The passion caused by the great and sublime in *nature,* when those causes operate most powerfully, is Astonishment; and astonishment is that state of the soul, in which all its motions are suspended, with some degree of horror. . . . Hence arises the great power of the sublime, that far from being produced by them, it anticipates our reasonings, and hurries us on by an irresistible force.

That, as we shall see, is exactly the contrary of Kant's idealist position, as if Burke were anticipating Kant's later critique. For Burke, the forms and objects of the actual world count, and count mightily. And in every case, furthermore, Burke's sublime is a manifestation of power, as when he says, "I know of nothing sublime which is not some modification of power." Under the rubric of power he includes not only overwhelming natural forces such as storming seas and earthquakes, but also political power, as when he says, "The power which arises from institution in kings and commanders, has the same connection with terror." And in all cases, finally, the sublime is connected not only with spiritual distress, but as much or perhaps even more with physical threat, as when Burke says that "the idea of bodily pain, in all the modes and degrees of labour, pain, anguish, torment, is productive of the sublime," which leads necessarily to a hard connection between the sublime and death, as when Burke says that "the sublime is an idea belonging to self-preservation."

Burke spends so very much time describing the ways in which the sublime is terrible that we may wonder how, in moments of sublime experience, we could ever feel anything but utmost dread rather than the sort of exultation, or "delight," as Burke prefers to call it, that we do in fact gain. Burke attempts to solve this problem partly by playing heavily upon the concept of sympathy which we, the beholders, must feel toward victims or potential victims of terrible occasions, sympathy being a positive and uplifting emotion. More to the point but with perhaps less than sufficient logic, Burke simply insists upon the idea that "terror is a passion which always produces delight when it does not press too close." Elsewhere in *A Philosophical Enquiry* Burke expands upon this principle:

> In all these cases, if the pain and terror are so modified as not to be actually noxious; if the pain is not carried to violence, and the terror is not conversant about the present destruction

of the person, as these emotions clear the parts, whether fine, or gross, of a dangerous and troublesome incumbrance, they are capable of producing delight; not pleasure, but a sort of delightful horror, a sort of tranquillity tinged with terror; which as it belongs to self-preservation is one of the strongest of all emotions. Its object is the sublime.

The fact is, whereas Burke convinces us that terror necessarily provokes the sublime, he does not convincingly go on to establish why the encounter with terror *is* sublime—except, of course, to remark on the saving grace of aesthetic distance. And if we look again at the passage just quoted, it would seem that for the encounter with terror to be experienced as sublime, the mind must *do something* which allows it to look upon its own possible destruction while at the same time being certain that its own self-preservation is assured. Precisely what the mind does to effect this primal release remains to be seen. Burke does not account for it. The most he can say is that self-preservation in the face of terror is the strongest emotion the mind can entertain—and that this emotion generates the power of sublime moments.

Burke may not have had all the answers, but he must be credited for raising the central questions and for discounting, once and for all, what I have called the naïve or innocent sublime. After Burke, the element of terror cannot be ignored. And there is one last point, only touched upon now and then in Burke's analysis, which is central to my own estimate of the sublime. As I suggested earlier in reference to Longinus's imagery of war, there is, or can be, something demonic about the sublime—some delight in destruction which aims particularly at the diminishment and finally the annihilation of the human image. Burke, although he cannot account for it, is not unaware that this is so.

Two examples from *A Philosophical Enquiry* will suffice to reveal what terror really means for Burke. Burke constantly equates terror and physical pain, often with no attempt at qualification. It seems especially revealing, therefore, that directly after Burke introduces his first definition of the sublime (quoted above) he goes on in the same paragraph to assert that of all emotions, pain is by far the strongest. He makes the particular point that no amount of pleasure in one's life could ever justify or balance pain at the level of torture. No one, as he puts it, would be willing to "earn a life of the most perfect satisfaction, at the price of ending it in the torments, which justice inflicted in a few hours on the late unfortunate regicide in France." Burke's example seems mysteriously to come out of nowhere; it is, in fact, a topical reference to an attempt on the life of Louis XV, in 1757, by one Robert Damiens, who was subsequently put to death under torture in the particular style called *écartèlement*, which means "tearing to pieces." This awful episode was much discussed in English periodicals, and Burke thought enough of it to insert it in his 1759 revision directly after his initial definition of the sublime.

A final example: In the following passage Burke wishes to endorse yet again the intimate connection between terror and physical pain. And thanks to Burke's graphic prose, there is no denying that the pain-terror equation is presented in a manner that can only be called, once more, the disintegration of the human image. According to Burke:

> A man who suffers under violent bodily pain; (I suppose the most violent, because the effect may be the more obvious.) I say a man in great pain has his teeth set, his eye-brows are violently contracted, his forehead is wrinkled, his eyes are dragged inwards, and rolled with great vehemence, his hair stands on end, the voice is forced out in short shrieks and groans, and the whole fabric totters. Fear or terror, which is an apprehension of pain or death, exhibits exactly the same effects.

So now we know what Burke means by *terror*—that which, as it bears down upon us, collapses the human image, as when "eyes are dragged inwards" and the human voice "is forced out in short shrieks." This is powerful stuff, not to be tamed or transcended by the sort of delight which, at a convenient distance, Burke would have us believe effects sublime transport.

Burke's treatment of the sublime is empirical and, as we have seen, at moments almost intimate. Kant, on the other hand, proceeds at a level of abstraction which, in *The Critique of Judgment* (1790), acknowledges the importance of terror to sublime experience but which stays serenely above the unseemly particulars of actual blood and flesh. It could hardly be otherwise, since for Kant the powers of the mind reign supreme. Burke saw terror everywhere, even in suddenness, in smells, and perhaps most tellingly, in "the shouting of multitudes." Kant simply took terror for granted, not as something inherently significant, but rather as an occasion for a victory of the mind so grand as to merit, in itself, and solely *unto* itself, the name and character of sublimity. Objects in nature which occasion the sublime moment are, by Kant's definition, vast beyond comprehension—either in extension or in power—but that we comprehend them nevertheless reveals "a supersensible substrate (underlying both nature and our faculty of thought) which is great beyond every standard of sense. Thus, instead of the object, it is rather the cast of the mind in appreciating it that we have to estimate as *sublime*." That sublime experience arises from the encounter between the mind and some terrible object or condition is common to post-Burkean analysis. But Kant, when he considers this encounter, will not allow authority to anything outside the human mind. He concludes "that the true sublimity must be sought only in the mind of the judging Subject, and not in the Object of nature that occasions this attitude."

Kant is adamant on this point, but along the way he makes some interesting slips. If, for instance, the mind's sublimity rests on something "supersensible" that underlies "*both* nature and our faculty of thought," might some deep rapport between mind and terror at least be supposed? Equally of interest is Kant's observation that "the feeling of the sublime is a pleasure that only arises indirectly, being brought about by the feeling of a momentary check to the vital forces followed at once by a discharge all the more powerful." Both mind and vitality are brought to a dead stop by *something,* if only for a moment. This brief "check to the vital forces" would seem to be terror's hegemony, established only to be broken. And yet terror is what brings the vitality of our existence to "a discharge all the more powerful," as Kant puts it. Is it then too much to suppose that when, for example, we stand amid fierce winds and thunderbolts exploding on all sides, what we feel at such a moment, and only at such a moment, is *power?* And further, that this sudden surge of "power" or vitality is felt to be equal to, and perhaps also not unlike, the power in the terror we confront? Such questions are at least worth keeping in mind.

In Kant's view, however, terror becomes the mind's opportunity to transcend its ordinary limits and thereby recognize its own sublime dominion over even the worst threats—not excluding the threat to life itself. In one especially striking passage, Kant pits the power of the mind against nature's demonic forces (forces external, but also internal, to man), the outcome being that special moment when the mind reveals to itself its own sublime estate:

Bold, overhanging, and, as it were, threatening rocks, thunder-clouds piled up the vault of heaven, borne along with flashes and peals, volcanoes in all their violence of destruction, hurricanes leaving desolation in their track, the boundless ocean rising with rebellious force, the high waterfall of some mighty river, and the like, make our power of resistance of trifling moment in comparison with their might. But, provided our own position is secure, their aspect is all the more attractive for its fearfulness; and we readily call these objects sublime, because they raise the forces of the soul above the height of vulgar commonplace, and discover within us a power of resistance of quite another kind, which gives us courage to be able to measure ourselves against the seeming omnipotence of nature.

Against this massive inventory of terror, our own power might, as Kant says, seem of "trifling moment." But no; precisely in this predicament, provided of course that "our own position is secure," we come to "discover within us a power of resistance of quite another kind." From a position of security this resistance seems questionable, and exactly of what it consists is never quite made clear, except that it is rooted in some "supersensible" realm common to *all* things, the mind no less than objects terrible. But what needs emphasis here is that the sublime in Kant's interpretation is not just another moral-aesthetic category. On the contrary, it is a key to our humanity because in the confrontation with terror we discover "a preeminence above nature that is the foundation of a self-preservation of quite another kind from that which may be assailed and brought into danger by external nature. This saves humanity in our own person from humiliation, even though as mortal men we have to submit to external violence."

This, then, is the logic within Kant's analysis of the sublime. He knows from immediate experience that the sublime moment does invest us with a feeling of power equal to the powers that threaten to destroy us, and that in this moment we enjoy a sense of exultation altogether beyond the reach of terror's rule. For Kant the sublime thus becomes one of the rare occasions when the immortal soul reveals itself and "proves" that we possess within us something more and definitely superior to mere natural being. In the sublime moment a great revelation occurs, an essential victory is won. For if terror cannot shake us, nothing can.

Terror's significance, therefore, is that it "challenges our power (one not of nature) to regard as small those things of which we are wont to be solicitous (worldly goods, health, and life)." A degree of nobility is thus restored to the sublime experience; but even so, terror is *required* for this process of radical transcendence to complete itself. We might legitimately ask what sort of "mental movement," in Kant's phrase, the mind performs to find a strength that was not (or was not known to be) among its resources prior to the sublime moment.

By way of a start toward my own conclusions, I want to suggest, in response to the questions Kant has raised, that terror is indeed the necessary condition for the sublime; that the sublime is a drama or *agon* played out between the mind and that which terrifies it; and finally, that far from resisting terror by deploying a "supersensible" power of its own, the mind sheds its fear and exults in a strength it gained by internalizing, or identifying with, terror's own power—which is indeed, as Kant would have to say, "a power of resistance of *quite* another kind." Here the sublime experience is the product of a process more commonly known as *sublimation,* the same strategy on which culture itself rests and which, as Kant instructs us, "saves humanity in our own person from humiliation, even though as mortal men we have to submit to external violence."

If, now, we go briefly to Schopenhauer's analysis of the sublime, as he sets it forth in *The World as Will and Idea* (1818), we gain an added perspective on Kant; and here again we see the two sides of the sublime moment—the dissolution of the human image on the one hand, and transcendence and exultation through identification with overwhelming power on the other. For Schopenhauer, existence was pure terror. The "supersensible substrate" of Kant's position was simply naked self-devouring will, informing, supporting, and destroying all things. In short, life lives by preying upon itself in a nonstop spectacle of violence; this, I would suggest, is the true demonic. Given its horror, Schopenhauer's urgent question as a philosopher is very simple indeed: How to escape? There are three ways, each involving withdrawal into a state of pure, will-less contemplation. The first is that of the philosopher; the second that of the artist; and the third is that of anyone who happens to find himself or herself in the sublime situation.

Schopenhauer, not unlike Kant, viewed the sublime as more than just a moral or aesthetic category. For him, too, it afforded a revelation that might also function as a sort of salvation. He presents his analysis of the sublime in four stages, each more terrible, more encompassing, but also more fiercely sublime than those that came before. In each stage, however, the sublime moment is achieved by "the pure subject of knowing." All common humanity is shed and therefore also all fear. In a sort of pact with the surrounding forces of destruction, one "quietly comprehends the ideas even of those objects which are threatening and terrible to the will." As Schopenhauer observes, "[i]n this contrast lies the sense of the sublime."

Having traversed all manner of sublime desolation—deserts of terrible aspect, regions void of all life—we come at last to Schopenhauer's grand finale, which I shall quote at length, in order to set forth the sublime's essential dialectic: terror and dissolution of human individuality on the one side, and on the other "a power beyond all comparison superior" because the beholder, who is now also *the participant,* has completely identified with terror—so completely, indeed, that it seems his own idea. Here is Schopenhauer's summation of the sublime revelation:

> But the impression becomes still stronger, if, when we have before our eyes, on a large scale, the battle of the raging elements, in such a scene we are prevented from hearing the sound of our own voice by the noise of a falling stream; or, if we are abroad in the storm of tempestuous seas, where the mountainous waves rise and fall, dash themselves furiously against steep cliffs, and toss their spray high into the air; the storm howls, the sea boils, the lightning flashes from black clouds, and the peals of thunder drown the voice of storm and sea. Then, in the undismayed beholder, the two-fold nature of his consciousness reaches the highest degree of distinctness. He perceives himself, on the one hand, as an individual, as the frail phenomenon of will, which the slightest touch of these forces can utterly destroy, helpless against powerful nature, dependent, the victim of chance, a vanishing nothing in the presence of stupendous might; and, on the other hand, as the eternal, peaceful, knowing subject, the condition of the object, and, therefore, the supporter of this whole world; the terrific strife of nature only his idea; the subject itself free and apart from all desires and necessities, in the quiet comprehension of the Ideas. This is the complete impression of the sublime.

In this passage we see not only vast powers blotting out the human voice, but also the "individual" in the process of becoming "a vanishing nothing." References to the beholder, who is now thoroughly involved, shift from "He" to "it," at which point the "knowing subject" and the realm of terror become identical through the vehicle of the Idea. The suggestion is that terror has been incorporated and transcended by a very thoroughgoing dynamic of identification. As Schopenhauer puts it: "The vastness of the world which disquieted us before, rests now *in* us." The essential strategy of sublime experience could hardly be clearer, arising, as Schopenhauer says, from "the felt consciousness that in some sense or other . . . we are one with the world, and therefore not oppressed, but exalted by its immensity."

One last point: Schopenhauer's imagery of the sublime in the passage above is the stock-in-trade of the gothic novel, as it also is in the landscape painting of people such as J. M. W. Turner, John Martin, and Caspar David Friedrich. The gothic novel emerged as a prominent genre at precisely the time when the category of the sublime became central to art and philosophy. And as I believe, with Hegel, that any serious idea or form releases its own perverse counterpart, I presume that the phenomenon of the gothic novel is not without significance to my argument. I am thinking now of classics like *The Monk* (1796) and *Melmoth the Wanderer* (1820). Both books employ Schopenhauer's imagery of terror; both provide striking scenes of the human image in the process of disfigurement and decomposition; and both aggrandize protagonists whose superior power derives from identification with the source of terror, in these particular cases a pact with the devil.

A similar if greatly more refined parallel exists in the best of sublime landscape painting. What are we to make of a famous picture like Friedrich's *The Sea of Ice* (also known as *The Wreck of the Hope*) painted in 1823–24 in response to the disaster of an actual arctic exploration? Friedrich's art tends to be overly symbolic and is usually interpreted in religious terms. But at the same time, no one doubts that much of it is sublime, since religion and the sublime are, of course, not mutually exclusive. But the inveterate need of critics to heap positive interpretations upon a species of religious art which employs a most desolate mode of the sublime except in glorious terms. In *The Sea of Ice* we view an arctic wasteland of uncompromising inhumanity. In the background endless ice merges with an equally endless, frozen sky. In the foreground an enormous pile-up of jagged ice denies any possibility of life or organic form. Each slab is immense, razor-sharp, and brutal as stone. Beneath this monument of terror we catch the barest glimpse of an overturned ship with, here and there, bits of broken spars, like toothpicks. Nothing else. Certainly nothing human. And that this ship, crushed and buried in ice, should be named the *Hope* is perhaps too patent, but not without point even so. What really terrifies, in a sublime landscape of this kind, is its compelling attraction. The pleasure of Friedrich's art, even the surpassing calm of his dead Christs atop silent peaks at sunset, goes beyond either religious response or mere aesthetic satisfaction. What, then, provokes our attention? Perhaps, among other things, the opportunity to behold in manageable compass the inadmissible encounter within ourselves between terror and our need to assume its power.

Of all the Romantic landscape painters, Turner seems best to catch the spirit, at once calming and disquieting, of the mature, serious sublime. In Andrew Wilton's recent *Turner and the Sublime* (1980) the author observes that "there is a tendency for Turner deliberately to suppress the human element, for, as we know, he was pursuing the ideal of the landscape sublime, in which the brooding hostility of nature to man is a dominant note." But having gone so far, Professor Wilton draws back from going all the way, and will not openly admit Turner's affinity with terror. Instead he sides with Ruskin and suggests that the aim of Turner's art is "to impress us first with the grandeur of nature, and second with the reality of that grandeur as experienced by human beings like ourselves, who live out their lives in the conditions he presents." But at Turner's most intense, there is in fact little or no life at all at a recognizable human level. Professor Wilton's remarks might pertain to a poet such as Wordsworth, but even Wordsworth identified himself with the "power," as he calls it, that rolls through all things.

With Turner the case is otherwise. His early, historical landscapes focus on mass catastrophes such as the plagues of Egypt, the fall of great cities, or wrecks at sea. In his rendering of Hannibal crossing the Alps, even the mountains are dwarfed by the onslaught of the storm. In Turner's more quiet mountain scenes, furthermore, the human image is either absent or minuscule to the point of insignificance. And as Turner's career advanced, all signs of the human figure fade or are absorbed into the swirling energies of nature. The *Deluge* paintings of 1843 are clear examples. And as for identification with terror, what else, even at the level of iconography, can we make of paintings like *Snowstorm—Steamboat Off a Harbour's Mouth* (1842) or *Rain, Steam and*

Speed (1844), in which gigantic human machines blend perfectly into the mass of larger inhuman forces, but where no human *person* is in sight?

I think that in the serious sublime, as contrasted with the naïve sublime, terror is the key element in two ways. First, it provokes the dissolution or disappearance of the human image. Then it transforms the beholder into a participant through a psychic process of identification that, in turn, allows the beholder-participant to transcend terror by partaking of its power. Such, in my view, is the "mental movement," as Kant called it, informing the experience of sublime moments. Longinus summed it up a long time ago when he said: "As if instinctively, our soul is uplifted by the true sublime; it takes proud flight, and is filled with joy and vaunting, *as though it had itself produced what it has heard.*" If we modify that last phrase, which refers only to literary experience, and generalize it to include all modes of sublime experience, it would read: "as if we ourselves were the source of the power we behold."

As I think upon the power of power to attract and calm us even as it threatens, or of terror's capacity to captivate our deepest attention, I am reminded of Turner's great painting in which he fills a significant portion of his canvas with large numbers of people, all of them standing stockstill in excited astonishment. I am referring to his *The Burning of the Houses of Lords and Commons, October 6, 1834.* In this example of the sublime, conflagration is total and encompasses everything else. Flames dominate the sky, but also the river in which they are reflected. Flames likewise dominate the illuminated faces of the silent beholders who are also (at least in Turner's rendering) participants *inside* the scene or event. They must surely feel terror, but also—I cannot doubt it—they must have been struck by strange exultation. And if we ourselves should doubt or not quite fathom the particular depth of emotion among the crowd along the Thames that night, perhaps we can manage a sharper sense of it by comparison with our own response upon beholding the central image of the sublime in our time. I refer, of course, to the atomic bomb as we have seen it, in countless pictures and films, exploding slowly upward into that majestic fire cloud that—with awesome beauty "brighter than a thousand suns"—spreads its mantle of terror everywhere.

Self/Landscape/Grid

Miller owns this field, Locke that, and Manning the
woodland beyond. But none of them owns the landscape. There is a property in the horizon which no
man has but he whose eye can integrate all the parts,
that is, the poet.

—Emerson

Every appearance in nature corresponds to some
state of mind. . . .

—Emerson

I live in upstate New York, rural countryside and lovely hills, a place
my neighbors like to call "the village." It's small, quiet, great for
raising kids. Forty miles to the north, however, lies Griffiss Airforce
Base, known locally as Rome, because Rome is the town the base uses.
Out of there fly the B-52s that control our part of the sky. There too
the Pentagon keeps its brood of cruise missiles. So nobody doubts, in
this part of the country, that Rome (when it happens) will be the spot
where the warheads hit. At one time we thought that the Russians had
size but no technical finesse. That gave us a stupid sort of hope. An
overshot might land on our heads, but if incoming missiles fell short,
they would come down way north, maybe on Edmund Wilson's old
stone house in Talcottville, and we, at least, would be well out of range.
Now we are told that the Soviets have refined their delivery. Their
guidance systems are on target, not least because the Russians have used
American technology, computers, microchips, ball bearings, made and
sold by American firms. That, no matter how we look at it, is ugly news.
And with Rome at the nub of a nuclear arc, we are resigned in our

knowledge that things will start exactly forty miles away. How far the firestorm will reach is what we mainly wonder. We don't know, but we are counting on these upstate hills to block the worst of the blast. If the horizon works in our favor, we shall then have time to consider the wind. In the meantime, B-52s cross and recross above us. They gleam with their nuclear payload. Two or three are up there always, and once I counted thirteen. The air is creased with vapor trails, and in the afternoons, when the sun starts down, the sky looks welted with scars.

That, anyway, is the prospect I share with my neighbors, our part of the nuclear grid. Not a landscape of the mind, no inner weather sort of scene, it's just life's natural place for those who live here. Even so, the bombers overhead keep me reminded that this landscape possesses, or is possessed by, some other will, some demonic grand design or purpose not at all my own. Nor would that kind of death be mine. An all-at-once affair for almost everyone is how that death would come, impersonal but still no accident. That way of dying would be the ultimate instance of political intrusion, for that is what has brought us to this pass, politics, and by political intrusion I mean the increasing unsettlement and rending of our private lives by public force. We do what we can as citizens, but when it comes to nuclear war we can't do much. The hazard is before us and won't budge. How to live with it is our problem, and some of us, at least, resort to magic. We turn to words which give the spirit breathing space and strength to endure. As in any time of ultimate concern, we call on poetry.

I can read *Eccelesiastes* or *King Lear* for a language equal to extremity, but such language isn't of my time, not of my landscape perhaps I should say. I find a little of what I need in poets like Akhmatova or Mandelstam or Milosz, but American poetry? and among poets of the present generation? Not much, in fact hardly anything. I'm writing in early February (1983) and I've just gone through the recent issue of *American Poetry Review*, which offers forty-eight poems by twenty-one poets. Some few good poems, but only two touch upon our nuclear fate, which leaves forty-six in worlds elsewhere. In "Against Stuff" Marvin Bell follows the possibility—this is a night-thoughts poem—that all our forms and habits, including those of poetry itself, may have been wrong, wrong enough to bring us to "the coming instantaneous flaming" of all creatures and things "which could not suffer / that much light at one time." The poem spreads disquiet and resists reply, and in the following lines the pun on "not right" keeps the poet honestly uncertain:

and, if we are shortly to find ourselves
without beast, field or flower,
is it not right that we now prepare
by removing them from our poetry?

Under nuclear pressure, should poetry contract its domain? The other
poem in *APR,* Maxine Kumin's "You Are in Bear Country," moves with
wit and nice inevitability to the imagined moment when the grizzly
attacks—and then jumps to this question in italics:

> *Is death*
> *by bear to be preferred*
> *to death by bomb?*

The question seems to intrude out of nowhere, and the poet closes by
answering yes. The point, I presume, is that any thought of death, even
one so unlikely, recalls the nuclear alternative. And grotesque though it
would be, death "by bear" does seem preferable, one's own at least, and
natural, part of the order of things and an order, too, as timeless as the
wilderness. Bizarre consolations, but once the nuclear element intrudes,
these are the sorts of ludicrous lengths to which we feel pushed. And
the either/or is not even a choice, but only a preference. The absence of
a and *the* before *bear* and *bomb* suggests two categories of death, only
one of which is humanly acceptable.

After *APR* I went on to *Poetry,* where there was nothing relevant,
and after that I rummaged randomly through the library's stock of recent
journals and magazines, all I could manage in two afternoons. I am sure
I read more than two hundred poems, most of them quite short, some
very good, but none informed by nuclear awareness. I realize, of course,
that any successful poem must authorize itself, must utter its world with
self-certainty, but even so, reading so many poems one after the other
left me rather shocked by the completeness, the sealed-up way these
poems deny the knowledge or nearness of nuclear threat. The other
striking thing about most of these poems was their sameness, and especially the meagerness. These observations are not original, of course.
Lots of poetry gets written and published in America just now, and if
one reads even a small but steady portion of it, one starts to see that
the current talk about a "crisis" in our poetry is not unfounded. The

trivialization, the huddled stance, the seemingly deliberate littleness of so much poetry in the last few years—how shall we account for it?

Perhaps the rise of the "workshop" poem has had something to do with it. Maybe also the new careerism among younger poets bent on bureaucratic power in the universities; those who, as Marx would say, have gone over to the management. And surely the kind of literary criticism now in vogue, hostile to the integrity of language, doesn't help. But these are as much symptoms as causes, and the larger situation comes down to this: In a time of nuclear threat, with absolutely everything at stake, our poetry grows increasingly claustrophilic and small-themed, it contracts its domain, it retires still further into the narrow chamber of the self; and we see in this not only the exhaustion of a mode and a tradition, but also the spectacle of spirit cowed and retreating.

The retreat has been swift because American practice invites it. Founded on Emersonian principles, our poetry has drawn much of its strength from an almost exclusive attention to self and nature. Typically we have conceived of the self *as* a world rather than of the self *in* the world. Things beyond the self either yield to imagination or else they don't matter, and the world becomes a store of metaphor to be raided as one can. The "strong" poet turns any landscape to private use, and solipsism wins praise as the sign of success. Emerson didn't invent these attitudes, but he was good at summing them up. "Every natural fact is a symbol of some spiritual fact," he wrote, and "the Universe is the externization [*sic*] of the soul." Thus the road was open for Whitman and poets to come, and thus Emerson delivered his mandate: "Know then that the world exists for you," and "Build therefore your own world." Partly, this is the mythology of our national experience, with its determination to deny social-political limits and focus instead on individual destiny. Partly, too, this is the American brand of Romanticism, part of a larger movement that on the continent peaked in its influential French example. Baudelaire called the world a "forest of symbols," and Mallarmé thought that everything external, *la cité, ses gouvernements, le code,* could be dismissed as *le mirage brutal.*

Stated thus, the whole business seems outlandish—but not really. The Emersonian mandate supports maximum belief in the poet's potency, not in itself a bad thing. Then, too, poets in our century have held some very odd convictions. Yeats for example, or for that matter, Merrill. But in one respect there is no doubting: American poetry has rejected history and politics on principle. Despite Lowell's example and more recent exceptions like Rich and Forché, our poets in the main have been satisfied to stick with Emerson, and few would find anything to take exception with in the following lines from Emerson's *Ode:*

> I cannot leave
> My honeyed thought
> For the priest's cant,
> Or statesman's rant.
>
> If I refuse
> My study for their politique,
> Which at the best is trick,
> The angry Muse
> Puts confusion in my brain.

American contempt for politicians runs deep. As a sort of common-sense cynicism it allows us to go untroubled by crime in high places and, more to the point, it bolsters our belief that personal life exists apart from, and is superior to, political force and its agencies. But also, as Gunnar Myrdal demonstrated in *An American Dilemma,* our sort of political cynicism goes hand in hand with a remarkably durable idealism. We take for granted that governments are corrupt, then feel that some other power, providential and beyond the meddling of men, governs our destiny finally. Where there's a will there's a way, and everything comes right in the end. But does it? Even without the Bomb to put such faith into question, Emerson's example—Poland, for God's sake!— invites skepticism:

> The Cossack eats Poland,
> Like stolen fruit;
> Her last noble is ruined,
> Her last poet mute:
> Straight, into double band
> The victors divide;
> Half for freedom strike and stand:—
> The astonished Muse finds thousands at her side.

The Muse might well be befuddled, given the logic of Emerson's syntax. But of course, Emerson's faith in the future—disaster compensated by renewal—can't mean much to us. With the advent of the nuclear age there is no assurance that anything will remain for the phoenix to rise from.

We have fallen from the Garden, and the Garden itself—nature conceived as an inviolate wilderness—is pocked with nuclear waste and toxic dumps, at the mercy of industry and Watt, all of it open to nuclear defilement. Generations come and go, but that *the earth abideth forever* is something we need to feel, one of the foundations of poetry and humanness, and now we are not sure. That is the problem with nuclear threat, simply as threat; it undermines all certainty, and things once absolute are now contingent. To feel that one's private life was in the hands of God, or Fate, or even History, allowed the self a margin of transcendence; the dignity of personal life was part of a great if mysterious Order. But now our lives are in the hands of a few men in the Pentagon and the Kremlin, men who, having affirmed that they would destroy us to save us, have certified their madness—and yet their will determines our lives and our deaths. We are, then, quite literally enslaved, and assuming that this bothers poets no less than the rest of us, why do they so seldom speak of it? It is not too much to say that most poetry in America is written against experience, against first feelings and needs. Whether the Emersonian tradition is a trap or a last-ditch defense is perhaps a moot point. But the poetry of self still predominates, with nature as its cornerstone, despite Los Alamos, a lovely spot in the mountains.

Nuclear wipeout is possible, perhaps probable, and every day I talk with people who are convinced it will happen. No soul is free of that terror, nor of that knowledge; and simply as a state of mind or way of knowing, it drastically alters how we receive and value our experience. Birth, for example, or one's own death; surely having children troubles us in ways not known before, and we need to feel that each of us shall have a death of his or her own, simply in order to feel fully possessed of our lives. These are common feelings, and it's clearer than it used to be that no man (no, nor woman neither) is an island. Our surface lives are individual and unique, but human existence itself—the being that all of us share and feel threatened—gives us our most important sense of ourselves and, I should also think, gives poetry its most significant themes. Can it be, then, that the shallowness of recent poetry reveals a desperate clinging to the surface?

I do *not* ask for poems directly about the Bomb or the end of the world, although with the Bell poem in *APR* as evidence, a theme of this kind can be as legitimate as any other. I don't expect poems of protest or outrage or horror either, although again, I can't see that they would hurt. I do, however, try to keep in mind that some subjects are more human, and more humanly exigent than others—Forché on Salvador compared to Leithauser on dandelions—and also that poets are often scared off by subjects which, precisely because of the fear, signal a challenge worth the risk. But what I'd mainly hope to see, in this case, is poetry that probes the impact of nuclear threat, poetry informed by nuclear knowing, poems that issue from the vantage of a self that accepts its larger landscape, a poetic diction testing itself against the magnitude of our present plight, or finally just poems which survive their own awareness of the ways nuclear holocaust threatens not only humankind but the life of poetry itself.

Nature, for example, remains the mainstay of our poetry. Natural imagery makes us trust the poem, suggests a permanence at the root of things, and every poem about nature bears somewhere within it the myth of renewal and rebirth. But from the nuclear perspective, these ministrations falter. Permanence? Rebirth? Emerson's response to nature was genuinely poetic, and the measure of our present loss may be judged by the degree of nostalgia rather than assent we feel when he says: "In the woods, we return to reason and faith. There I feel that nothing can befall me in life—no disgrace, no calamity (leaving me my eyes), which nature cannot repair." Well, his notion of calamity isn't ours. And nature, for all its proven renovative power, could never repair the worst that might befall us. Nature suffers the same division we observe in ourselves and in the landscape generally. We are what we are, yet some deep part of selfhood has been invaded by forces wholly alien to personal being, political forces of which the worst is nuclear threat. In the same way, the landscape belongs to us and yet it does not. This concrete place we share is also a site on the nuclear grid. And when, therefore, Emerson tells us that "Every appearance in nature corresponds to some state of mind," we must inquire not only What state of mind? but also Whose mind?

No doubt the crews in the bombers are bored. And no doubt bureaucratic haggling keeps the commander of the base in Rome bogged down in mindless detail. The chiefs in the Pentagon, on the other hand, definitely share a state of mind which must, now and then, get rather dizzy with the glamour of their global strategy. What the Russians have in mind we don't know. But for all of them, we and the landscape are expendable; to think that way, after all, is their job. We cannot say, then, that the landscape corresponds to their minds and to ours in the same way. Rather, what expresses their state of mind, provokes and negates our own. In a traditional landscape, points of correspondence for us would be, among other things, the sky's infinity and the sense of permanence arising from the land itself. But exactly this kind of metaphor-making has been undermined by the transformation of the landscape into a sector on the grid. Or we might look at it this way; the military state of mind becomes an alien element *in* the landscape as we behold it, the B-52s, the proximity of the missile site, the grid and its planners. These forces have broken into our world, they have defiled its integrity, and the new points of correspondence between ourselves and the landscape are the condition of vulnerability and the threat of terminal defacement. Self and world, nature and landscape, everything exists in itself *and* as acceptable loss on the nuclear grid.

I've gone on at length about the landscape in my part of the country to suggest what Emerson's poetic principle—"Every appearance in nature corresponds to some state of mind"—might mean in the nuclear age. Every person has his or her own place, of course, and in a country as vast as ours the variety of landscape must be nearly infinite. The kinds of personal vision to which a landscape corresponds must also, then, be fairly limitless. But all vision converges in the fact that every landscape is part of the nuclear grid. I have the air base in Rome to remind me of this, whereas people living in, say, New York City are reminded by the city itself—its status as a prime target; the difficulty of maintaining life-support systems, water, energy, even in normal times; traffic's five-o'clock entrapment every afternoon, not to mention the way the city is mocked by officials in Washington who suggest that in the event of an alert, nine million people will please evacuate the area. Then too, there are the nuclear power plants nearby; these are also targets, and when hit will spout radiation like the Fourth of July. The citizenry can always avail itself of shovels, as another Washington wit has proposed, but no, there's no real hope. So that landscape too has its message.

Meanwhile, poets write about "marshes, lakes and woods, Sweet Emma of Preservation Hall, a Greek lover, an alchemist, actresses, fairy tales, canning peaches in North Carolina," stuff like that, to quote from the ad for a recent anthology. The apology for poems of this kind (triviality aside) is that by celebrating modest moments of the human spectacle—little snaps of wonder, bliss, or pain—poetry implicitly takes its stand against nuclear negation. To say yes to life, this argument goes, automatically says no to the Bomb. And yes, a grain of truth sprouts here. I expect many among us read poetry that way in any case. The upshot, however, is that poets can go on producing their vignettes of self, pleased to be fighting the good fight without undue costs—except *the* cost, which is the enforced superficiality, the required avoidance of our deeper dismay.

Nuclear threat engenders cynicism, despair, allegiance to a mystique of physical force, and to say no to such destructive powers requires an enormously vehement yes to life and human value. What's called for, in fact, is the kind of poetry we once named "great," and my suspicion is that today the will to greatness is absent. Great poems, Wordsworth's or Whitman's for example, confront their times; they face and contain their own negation. The human spirit draws its strength from adversity, and so do poems. Examples like *The Prelude* and *Song of Myself* incorporate and thereby transcend that which, if they ignored it, would surely cancel their capacity for final affirmation. And having mentioned poems of this caliber, I might also add that the "American sublime," as critics call it, has been missing in our poetry at least since late Stevens. The sublime, as observers like Burke and Kant and Schopenhauer insist, arises from terror, terror beheld and resisted, the terror of revolution for Wordsworth, of the abyss for Whitman, of nuclear annihilation for any poet today who would make a language to match our extremity.

I can see, though, why we try to avoid what we know. Terror will flare up suddenly, a burst of flame in the chest, and then there is simply no strength. Other times the mind goes blank in disbelief. The temptation to retreat is always with us, but where can we go, where finally? Sometimes I let it all recede, let silence be enough, and go for a walk through the fields and apple hedge above my house. The horizon then is remarkably clear, the sky is still its oldest blue. Overhead, the planes are half a hemisphere ahead of their thunder. It's hard not to think of them as beautiful, sometimes; humankind took so long to get up there. I wind my way through milkweed in the meadow and remember how Emerson, crossing an empty field, felt glad to the brink of fear. We know what he means, the elation that sweeps through us at such moments. And then I think of Osip Mandelstam and an old Russian proverb; life, he wrote, is not a walk across a field. We know what he means too, the inhuman hardship of centuries, the modern horror of being stalked to death. But it's all of this, isn't it? the grimness and the glory. Why should we think to keep them apart? We fear, maybe, that dread will undermine our joy, and often it does. To keep them wed is poetry's job. And now that the big salvations have failed us, the one clear thing is that we live by words.

Accident and Its Scene

Reflections on the
Death of John Gardner

> I look down past stars to a terrifying darkness. I seem to recognize the place, but it's impossible. "Accident," I whisper.
>
> —John Gardner, *Grendel*

Around two in the afternoon, one of those extra-clear September days, John Gardner died in a single-vehicle accident on a highway curve just north of Susquehanna, Pennsylvania. It was the fourteenth of the month, 1982. Gardner was riding his '79 Harley-Davidson, the big one called the *hog,* and when the accident happened, something— police speculate it was the stub of the bike's handlebar—hit him very hard in the gut. Death resulted from internal bleeding, or so the coroner determined, but in any case Gardner never made it to the hospital. He was dead on arrival, age forty-nine, the author of twenty-eight books. Next day, Binghamton's *Sun-Bulletin* reported that "the motorcycle, headed north, went off the right-hand dirt shoulder, hit a guardrail and skidded up the road into a grassy area about 20 yards past where Gardner was found." Writing later for *Boston,* a magazine for young professionals, novelist Anne Bernays saw it another way: "John Gardner, an experienced rider of motorcycles, drove his bike into the gravel and onto the shoulder of Route 92 . . . , overturning it and dying." We might almost suppose, from these different descriptions, different accidents. And if something seems odd, some *indécidabilité radicale* as Saussure might have said, the trouble isn't only words. Both descriptions are inaccurate, each depends on myth, but they both say exactly what they aim to. Divergence of views isn't the problem, but rather how the accident's inherent uncertainty, which is indeed radical, can be used to take a manner of dying and make it stamp a life.

The police accident report says that at an approximate speed of fifty miles per hour, bike and rider came out of the curve and then ran off the road, then traveled along the shoulder for eighty-seven feet, at which point, somehow back on the pavement, the motorcycle turned over on its left side. But then, rider and bike "apparently" traveled forward another thirty feet or so, and this does not seem to have been in a skid. Then the rider was off. Then the machine went on on its own, up the roadway and through a guardrail already down, falling finally on its right side, about nine feet off the asphalt. Gardner lay in the road, the Harley far away in the grass, at the edge of a wooded slope inclining downward to the Susquehanna River. So that was the accident. The description sounds clear but it isn't. If you try to imagine it you can't. In other words, nobody knows what happened. Damage to the motorcycle was moderate and the rider, of course, died. But how all this took place, on a clear dry day, at no great rate of speed, on a straight flat stretch of highway past the curve itself, is hard to see.

The motorcycle did not, as the *Sun-Bulletin* said, hit a guardrail, although it makes sense to think so; something must have caused the fatal impact. The police report suggests a slightly different, but no less incomplete, sequence of events. But no law was broken, no one else was hurt or involved; therefore the decent thing, as both police and newspaper know, is to let the dead man rest in peace. They cast no blame nor do they judge. If some definite agent caused the wreck—here is where the myth starts—let it be the bike itself. The *motorcycle* headed north. The *motorcycle* skidded, dumped its rider, and went on up the road. And that is how most people, reading about it in a newspaper, would expect to see an accident like this one described. Myths arise where knowing crosses into the unknown, and so too in this case. How the bike could have crashed, then continued, then thrown its rider, then gone on by itself—it's as if the machine were its own driver. And this is also part of the myth. People who know motorcycles know that the big ones behave with a power never wholly contained. In the range of 1,000 ccs, bikes begin to possess life and will of their own, or so it seems to wise riders. Men and women who ride seriously take this into account; they make a truce with the machine, and if this sounds strange to some, it would not have to Gardner. He agreed (we spoke of it more than once) that what motorcycles are about has very little to do with crazy carelessness, or with loud folly, or with the jumble of sex, speed, and heavy metal that genteel folk sometimes suppose. Respect, as if the machine had a mind of its own, is safety's first rule.

The *Sun-Bulletin* provides the best story it can, respectful, accurate in the main, then moves on to the next day's news. The police also close the case; they write it up, give it an incident number, and file it away. Accidents happen and life goes on. But more recently Anne Bernays has decided, so to speak, to dig things up. She is a writer and that is any writer's job or can be. The problem is that she doesn't know much about the accident itself (there wasn't, for example, any "gravel" to drive into), and I would guess that about motorcycles and the people who ride them she knows little beyond ordinary bias, which has it that anyone on a bike must be stupid or self-destructive. Bernays nevertheless makes harsh charges against Gardner, defining his death in a way that judges his life most unkindly. And she needs the motorcycle to help her. She has, she says, "natural skepticism about anyone who tempts fate by tooling around on a motorcycle." We know what she means, the way seventy percent of bike accidents are caused by people in cars who don't see what they hit. But there is also a touch of put-down here, and it doesn't work. Gardner was not tooling around. He was on his way to SUNY Binghamton to meet his students. He was going about a business he loved in a way he loved, and when he crashed his letters lay around him on the road. For Bernays, apparently, a man on a motorcycle is by definition a fool seeking ruin. If Gardner had been hit by lightning or a bad heart, there would have been shock and lament in response, but no raised eyebrows, no one saying I told you so. He died on a motorcycle, though, and instantly theories zoom out like bees exploding from a thicket.

Because it was an accident, lots of people feel sure that it wasn't. Gardner must have been drunk, which he was not, or racing like a bat out of hell, which he was not, but stuff like that keeps circulating nonetheless. The article by Bernays is hardly special in this regard. She has, however, put herself forward as a witness to what happened, and endorsed what she says with myths both high (art) and low (motorcycles). She says in *Boston,* the December '82 issue, that when she heard of Gardner's death she knew right away it might not be an accident, but more probably a case of "subintentional" suicide. She gives reasons for this conclusion, the Harley first of all, but also a glimpse of Gardner she got some weeks earlier at Bread Loaf Writers' Conference, an impression which convinced her that this man had lost his talent and his grip and was heading for disaster. Thus: "Gardner acted as if something awful were happening to him and he knew it and couldn't do anything to stop it." That is pretty grim. On the other hand, there's no doubt that behavior at Bread Loaf, almost everyone's, tends to be peculiar, though not necessarily in a negative way, and I'll remark more on that later. The point now is this: if Bernays starts with the mad biker myth and connects it with the myth of the mad artist—she calls Gardner "the writer as tamed wild man"—room for kindness and doubt isn't going to exist. As she says, Gardner *drove* his Harley off the road. *He* overturned *it,* a prodigious feat for seven hundred pounds of machine. But that, as some people think, is what bikers do.

Like his father before him, who drove Harleys until he was seventy, Gardner traveled by motorcycle much of the time for more than thirty years. His accident, then, can't be kept apart from personal history and preference. I must also say that Gardner's behavior could be hectic and tormented on occasion, at least at Bread Loaf, which is the only place I knew him. Then too, anyone reading his fiction will see, in addition to fascination with monsters and grotesques, a darker strain in which, at the level of symbolic action and sometimes in theme, the desire for redemption and forgiveness seems caught up by some doom-laden spectral presence hard to define but definitely a part of Gardner's imagined world. None of this, however, yields specific conclusions. Half the important fiction of our time fits that description. Plenty of writers appear more than a little hectic and tormented, at least now and then. And Gardner, I must add immediately, was often tender, sanely as opposed to demonically brilliant, sometimes positively buddha-like. I saw him that way at Bread Loaf last summer.

If a pattern exists it isn't ironclad or even complete. And accidents happen—unexpected, unforeseeable, not at all a matter of intention or will. Unless we abandon practical sense for some cheap or grand determinism, we must allow chance its terrifying role in our lives. I liked Gardner, I was shocked by his death, and gradually the question of specific circumstances (which I've looked into) has led me to consider what an accident is in itself, how it relates to the rest of a life, and how, when things like this happen, we rush faster than usual to judgment.

Unlike ordinary events, which we assess by their causes *and* their consequences, accidents are one-sided; we see them only from the back, blocked by an unaccountable gap keeping past and future discontinuous, the difference, perhaps, between normal evolution and sudden mutation. Between events in the usual sense and accidents there may be more similarity than we typically allow; but in the case of accidents we are more than normally alert to something in the occasion which is indeterminate, uncanny, undecidable, and for this reason accidents invite interpretation more readily than ordinary events. Because we don't know, we cover surprise by talking as if we did. There is, in an accident like Gardner's, an emptiness potent with meaning, or so we feel, and then to read it symbolically becomes a real temptation. Here in particular, anyone writing a life of Gardner will have to be on guard, and it occurs to me that professional biographers must have an infernal job, damned if they make sense of a life (fiction) and damned if they don't (mere massing of fact). In the construction of a biographical design, in search of a life's deeper logic, what will an accident look like? Not, perhaps, accidental.

The mistake would be to think of interpretation as something apart from the accident itself, as if one or another theory might win out as the event's true meaning, when at every moment the enormous element of undecidability leads us to see that any interpretation is part of something larger, a process of understanding that stays anchored in the odd obscurity of the accident itself. The FACTS are always there to start with, but these are at once too many and too few, contrary and incomplete, leading to imponderables enforced by the facts themselves. At this point MYTHS take over, cultural archetypes as well as local stories, all of them rooted in some actual detail or circumstance, but none able to dispose of the others or to cap the increasing flow of uncertainty. The feeling of the inadequacy of knowledge becomes more insistent and first appears as BLANKNESS, a senseless glare without depth or substance. This is part of the accident also, the mindlessness of it, as if facts, myths, the event itself were draining away. But then it doesn't drain away; the accident emerges from its preceding clutter, more real than before, something concrete and undeniable, partly open and partly withheld; and everything we know about it emphasizes what we don't know. At this stage, we are forced to admit that in the accident there is a genuine element of MYSTERY, not mere muddle or temporary lack of information, but something intrinsic to what an accident is. That, at least, has been the order of my own attempt to understand Gardner's wreck. First facts, then myths, then blankness, and finally mystery encompassing the lot.

The curve itself, for example. It's not what my son, who knows motorcycles, would call wicked bad, not anywhere near a right-angle turn, although it does swing to the left, which is to say it's not an inside curve and in the event of trouble a bike could be on the outside edge very fast. It's also blind for about twenty yards, it's not banked, it dips gently downward, and these are conditions less favorable to control than their opposite. Even so, coming into the turn at fifty or fifty-five, braking lightly as a rider might decide, there simply should be no difficulty. And immediately, the curve opens into flat, straight highway ahead. Leaning into it, accelerating out, this curve should not have been trouble. Nor is there any gravel to cause a slide; the shoulder here is gritty dirt, level with the pavement, four to six feet of space between guardrail and road. Nothing, absolutely nothing at sane speeds to signal danger. This, in fact, is what perplexes me: there's nothing there. The strangeness of the accident is partly in the scene itself; no passerby would guess that this is where Gardner died. And he, of course, knew this road like the back of his hand; he'd biked to work this way many times. The other strange thing is that, from the diagram attached to the police report, it's clear that whatever occurred in the curve, the desperate part of the accident unfolded well past the pitch of the turn. What happened happened on the straightaway.

Perhaps defenders of the suicide theory will take comfort from my view of the accident's scene. But *look* at it. This just is not the place to kill yourself. The chances are fine for mutilation, which can happen as well in a supermarket parking lot, but to count on a fatal crash on this particular length of roadway would be very stupid indeed. Take the curve at ninety, shoot off the highway and through the guardrail—even then you'd never make it down to the river. A tree, of course, anything solid would be enough to be lethal, and that, really, is the only clear option—some high-speed plunge off the road, not, as seems to have happened, some sort of drift onto the shoulder. Even at the subintentional level, as Bernays calls it, picking a place to die would seem to rule out this one. I regret talking like this, but failure to imagine the situation allows irresponsible theories their appeal. I guess I should also add that the countryside around Susquehanna offers all sorts of sharp turns and sheer drops, miles of tree-lined pavement and roadway-edging streams. No doubt someone desperate to die will grab any chance that offers itself, but anyone on a motorcycle will see excellent chances mile after mile. This place, by comparison, seems almost benign.

Unless, of course, something was in the road. Truckers usually know what they are doing, but any motorcyclist will tell you that people in cars are a hazard. They are talking, daydreaming, gawking at some signboard or oddity off to the side; they don't watch the road, they don't see motorcycles, and when they do they are often hostile. Coming up from the rear or approaching ahead, cars are always dangerous. But so far as we know (a woman living nearby was fairly sure), Gardner went into the curve alone. Another vehicle in the turn might well push a bike toward the shoulder; but that wasn't it. What about an animal? Small ones don't matter, a woodchuck or rabbit, but deer surely do. If one or more were in the road, or if one leapt from the bush into the path of the bike, disaster could indeed occur. My only objection is that the countryside along this stretch of road doesn't look like the kind of place deer generally use for a crossing; too much human habitation, no fields, the drop to the river too steep for easy access. But a deer there could have been. The nature of an accident is that something not normal, not expected, intervenes. And if it was a deer, or, say, a stray dog, we would never know. The other possibility is the kind of dog that attacks and gives chase, and here the local stories start. Twenty yards or so beyond the curve sits a trailer to the left of the highway. Four people I talked with told me that a big dog lives there, that the dog likes to chase motorcycles, that probably it was the dog that caused the accident. But no one had actually seen the dog. I looked for it, but couldn't find it either.

The accident, therefore, might have a very simple explanation, some small freak danger that, coming around the curve, Gardner would have been upon almost instantly. The point is that we don't know and can't find out. So in addition to the bizarre behavior of the motorcycle after it came out of the curve, there is also the possibility that something was in the road and then gone. This is what I mean by undecidability. Although we must admit that absolutely anything might have happened, our ignorance of what did happen is almost equally absolute. The facts as we know them are just sufficient to spark speculation, and when an accident is fatal, like this one, speculation—by which I mean myth-making—can be wild and even sinister.

Much of the information we have about the accident comes from a woman (housewife, age thirty-nine, the police report says) who was at home that afternoon, her house just above (i.e., going into) the curve, and the windows were open. She knew Gardner and, as often before, she heard him go by. From the sound of the bike, she thinks he wasn't going especially fast. She also thinks no other vehicle passed either way just before or after the accident. What got her attention, first of all, was the sound of a crash in the distance. According to the police report, what happened next was this:

> I ran outside, down my driveway and down the road to where I could see an object lying on the roadway. I thought that a truck which was coming towards me had dropped something on the road. I first seen the truck down by the object on the road. The older model green flatbed truck pulling a small trailer, stopped where I was standing and the driver asked if I had called an ambulance because there was a man lying on the road.

She called an ambulance and when she returned to the road the truck was gone. As the woman says, "I couldn't understand why the driver of the truck didn't stay by the injured man." Nor can we. I can imagine real brutality on the part of the driver, but I cannot see that he had any part in the accident. The police don't think so either. We will never know, but most likely the truck had been traveling south, as it was when the woman first saw it, which means that its driver either saw the accident or came upon it directly afterward, then came on to the woman and asked her if she'd called an ambulance (didn't say she ought to), then left, reasons unknown. Although it must have been a farm truck, and could not have come from too far away, nobody in the area recognized it by its description. And needless to say, it hasn't been seen since.

Those are the facts, such as they are. Now the myth. The flatbed truck almost immediately became, in everyone's reference to it, "the pickup truck" or simply "the pickup." And speculation has been endless. What was it doing out there? Why did it flee the scene of the accident? We see where this is going, yet it might not have assumed the authority it did had the woman not inadvertently contributed the key element: she said, or people say she said, that her first impression was that the truck turned around. If that were so, then we have the *"Easy Rider"* myth full-fledged. The bike and its rider were run off the road by the pickup, which then turned back to vanish as it came, out of nowhere. We remember the pickup truck at the end of the film *Easy Rider,* which after shotgunning one bike off the road, turns around to come back and blow away the second bike. That was, and I guess still is, a powerful image of American paranoia; it's also art waiting for life to follow suit. And it dovetails neatly with the myth of the mad biker and the "wild man" image of Gardner.

The fact that the truck disappeared, that we know *nothing* about it, will never cease to be a sticking point. But of course, the truck did not turn around. The woman's impression, while the situation was at a distance and unclear, was that *if* the object in the road had been dropped by the truck, *then* the truck must have come back for it. This initial impression was corrected immediately, but the woman mentioned that for a moment that's what she'd thought. From that simple slip the rumor spread, never mind that an old truck pulling a trailer could never take any curve fast enough to cause trouble. The truck played no part in the accident, but it did play a role in the way the accident came to be perceived. The driver of the truck was the first person on the scene; his behavior was sinister, and his disappearance leaves a real gap in our sense of what happened. In her article Anne Bernays does not mention the truck, and perhaps she never heard about it. Yet to call the article "Uneasy Writer" seems an unnecessary slam, and whether Bernays or an editor selected the title, it judges Gardner and hurts his loved ones.

Myths like the one about the pickup take their rise in circumstance; their seed is actual, but then they go on to account for everything and in the process fall apart. Their truth value ends up zero. The problem is that the hard facts, as we know them, also end up zero. I try to imagine what happened on that reach of roadway and I cannot. I especially cannot see how the machine could have hit its rider with such concentrated force if both rider and bike were still moving together. The sheer mechanics of it, they don't add up.

I remember talking with one of Gardner's Susquehanna friends, a young man about thirty who knows motorcycles, has a Harley of his own, and more than once had accompanied Gardner on trips. After the accident he'd gone out to the place and looked for tire markings. There were *some,* and from their confused pattern they seemed to reveal an intelligent struggle to get the motorcycle back on course safely. You could see, he told me, that Gardner had been fighting it. We were quiet for a few minutes, and then the young man, who clearly cares about Gardner, sighed and said, but you know, the marks were very faint, they could have been from something else, some other time or vehicle, and it's all, you see, not really readable.

Last summer Anne Bernays spent a few days at Bread Loaf and saw enough of Gardner to convince her that his soul was in terminal pain. The evening she found him "almost alone" and looking "very sad" she did not, evidently, go up to him; but there would have been much else happening, and lots of writers to meet, and it's easy to be swept along by the pleasures of the place. The conference can be like a three-ring circus, several main attractions at once. At least that's how it has seemed to me the four summers I was there when Gardner was. The great enjoyment of it, in addition to the readings and the workshops and the nonstop excitement of so much excellent talk, is the communal atmosphere and the devotion with which men and women of proven talent pass on their craft and spirit to talented beginners. I have seen Gardner work very hard at this. Afternoons, when staff people take a hike up the mountain, or run a Middlebury errand, or just sit somewhere in the shade with friends, Gardner would station himself in the big barn, the central meeting place, and be available to anyone who wanted his help. This was, I think, a point of honor with him, and Bernays concedes that as a teacher—an almost natural force moving young writers to realize their gifts—Gardner was extremely good.

I've seen Gardner steady as noon sun, giving himself with tribal care to any person with the guts or smarts to seek him out, and many did; sometimes it would look like a raid. I have also seen him join the rest of us at 5:30 for cocktails on the lawn or, if it rained, in the barn. And then go on after the evening reading and drink deep into the night. How much alcohol gets consumed at Bread Loaf is an astronomer's guess, and it's not that Gardner drank more than most, but that with him it was an anabasis, a march into the next day's dawn, and mainly for this reason: he loved, sought out, maybe really needed, community of talk. Not every night, but enough, he'd engage in discussion, excitement would spread like a message from the capitol, and a small knot of writers, equal in thought, equal in drink, would gather to fathom Gardner and themselves. Literature, politics, God, no subject smaller would do, and off things would go, Gardner as orator, sophist, inquisitor by turns, talking on and on, elated with ideas and the sport of it, playful, earnest, sometimes as if possessed—and all the time he, like the others around him, would be sipping away, in Gardner's case mainly gin, not noticing how much or how fast it went down. This sort of event wasn't unusual among members of the conference, but Gardner was different in that he'd seldom just stop. The lateness of the hour seemed to mean nothing to him, perhaps because in his other life, as a working writer, his habit was to start writing at midnight and keep on until five or six in the morning. As long as there could be talk, those Bread Loaf nights, there would be, and much of it was very fine. It could also lead to drunken nonsense, of course, but at his best Gardner could be a little like Socrates at the Symposium, talking real philosophy, drinking everyone else under the table. And I can see that if, late next morning, Bernays happened to pass Gardner on his way to the barn for some coffee, she might well get the impression that "something awful" was happening to him because it was—a hangover out of this world, the world itself only starting to return.

Making her case for accident-as-suicide, Bernays offers an outright list of things she thinks contributed to Gardner's subintentional death wish. In truly desperate cases I suppose that any additional small burden, or an aggregate assuming a sort of critical mass, might drive a person past saving. But even at that, some of Bernays's observations seem odd. It's true, as she points out, that Gardner got "dumped on" for writing *On Moral Fiction* and that his last novel, *Mickelsson's Ghosts,* was received with mainly negative reviews. But that's the lot of writers, and the real question about Gardner was whether he intended, like any novelist, to push on. Bernays also reminds us that Gardner "had had cancer," but goodness, any person saved from cancer might be extra glad to be alive. Bernays goes on to point out that Gardner had "been married and divorced twice" and was about to be married again; yet what this reveals, beyond remarkable faith in life, is hard to see. Is any of this, or all of it together, reason for suicide? Bernays thinks so. Her deeper logic is that in every way—literary, personal, biological—Gardner was failing.

Bernays mentions two occasions at Bread Loaf when, in her view, Gardner's performance certified his failure as a writer. One was his reading of his story "Caesar and the Werewolf" to an evening audience. The story was fascinating in idea but pedestrian in style, and also a species of medieval fable-making that Gardner, but not many of the rest of us, liked. To Bernays the story seemed disjointed and overlong, and her mind, she says, wandered. And then it came to her: "What is this monster doing in the core of a straight narrative?" That's offered as a criticism of the story, although it *could* be taken as an intelligent insight into the general structure of Gardner's fiction. Everywhere, in Gardner's novels, monsters and monstrous texts preside at the heart of straight narratives. What this tells us of Gardner might be worth pursuing, but Bernays doesn't see it. Nor does she seem to know that at Bread Loaf the audience regularly sat through this kind of reading when Gardner's turn came. Summer before last he read an openly mindless tale about a female detective disguised in a cheap-laughs beard. Before that it was funny-flat stuff from a child's bestiary. Why Gardner insisted on this kind of reading I don't know. Perhaps he refused to be in competition with his peers, Stanley Elkin and John Irving among them. Perhaps, as in *October Light,* he wanted to see if a sophisticated audience, like the old woman trapped with her smugglers' tale, would find "trash" to its liking. Hard to say, but the reading was standard for Gardner; perverse, but not a signal of defeat. And after the reading I very much doubt that, as Bernays thinks, he "must have realized he'd blown it."

One last item, more interesting than Bernays suggests. Staff people at Bread Loaf give a talk or lecture, usually about craft, and when Gardner gave his he provoked, as Bernays reports, bafflement and anger, at least in some quarters. He started ten minutes late and then only talked for about fifteen minutes, although it wasn't at night, nor did he walk off any stage, as Bernays describes the event. But she wasn't there and has had to rely on secondary sources. He did begin by saying that he was "not interested in literature any more," a statement which Bernays takes as a declaration of Gardner's capitulation as a writer. But that's not the end of it, nor did Gardner ramble on about "political injustice" without point or design. His first remark was meant to shock, which it did, and so did the rest of his remarks, mainly about political awareness as a writing tool, a theme indeed disturbing to writers in the current genteel tradition, as afraid of politics in art as the Victorians were of sex. "You are not writing importantly," Gardner went on to say, "if you're not writing politically." He wasn't endorsing propaganda or programmatic writing; he meant, as one might see, that the overwhelming and possibly fatal dimension of modern experience is political, from our terror of nuclear threat to our deeply personal shame for what our government sometimes does in our name, and if literature doesn't touch this part of our lives it will surely lose its claim to importance. Like many of us, Gardner was alarmed by the way politics disrupts the soul; and for a novelist to be concerned with responsibility and consequence isn't so strange. Gardner also said that "to write greatly you must feel greatly," a judgment that must have sunk many a cloistered heart then and there.

If Gardner's lecture caused a feeling of distress to hang over the conference "like a radioactive cloud," as Bernays reconstructs it, her metaphor is especially insensitive, considering Gardner's urgent message. It also hints that Bread Loaf is exactly the place to go to get away from it all, just belles lettres, some cocktail conversation, and more belles lettres. But that's not the case. If talk of politics in relation to literature upset some people, others of us, that particular summer, had been talking of little else since the start of the conference. The Bread Loaf session of 1982 was different from earlier meetings because, for the first time openly and with a good deal of passion, the idea began to circulate that art can no longer be held separate from the kind of political torment maiming our age and spirit. Some confrontation there will have to be, darker energies distilled, a harder vision of being in the world. So Gardner's lecture did not come out of nowhere. It might have signaled a change in his thinking about literature, but it broadcast no admission of defeat.

The portrait of Gardner that Bernays sketches for us doesn't hold up—not the mad biker, not the writer as wild man, not the failed genius. Concerning Gardner's accident, she is innocent of the facts and blind to the mystery, and she makes her case for suicide in terms of an inner logic such as only myths possess. Of the three accounts of the accident— the newspaper report, the police report, the literary report—only Bernays's makes sense all the way. She is that far removed.

The last time I saw Gardner was departure time, Sunday morning, the end of the 1982 session at Bread Loaf. My son and I were loading our bike onto its trailer and Gardner came over to give us a hand. Then we said good-bye and he was gone. Speaking of his work the year before, he'd said: "When you look back there's lots of bales in the field, but ahead it's all still to mow." The rural metaphor was typical of him; so was the ambition, the natural look forward. The day of the accident, Gardner was planning to meet students in Binghamton, and later that afternoon he was coming back to cast the musical—*Marvin's on the Distant Shore*—that he had written for, and with, his friends at the Laurel Street Theatre in Susquehanna. It was a communal affair, and more people wanted to be in it than there were parts, so Gardner intended to spend the evening writing new roles. This was art for everyone, Gardner had done it before, and the town loved it. So, it appears, did Gardner. He was getting married in less than a week, and years of work on a translation of *Gilgamesh* had just been finished. Soon *On Becoming a Novelist* would appear, and his close friends tell me that Gardner was full of plans of *all* sorts, just like the old days.

And yet, all of us lead more than one life, artists especially. The mind moves at different levels, the spirit is always warring with itself, not content with external terrors only. No one of us is privy to the whole soul's show, not our own, not another's, which is what makes art so valuable and easy usage of a word like "subintentional" suspect. We also know, since it's how we live, that ebb and flow is constant, that decline and renewal is life's first pattern. This is true for artists in particular, who more than the rest of us use their work to live by, charting and steering, coming home and setting forth repeatedly. And even when it comes to the worst, as survivors of all kinds remind us, the fact that a man is down is no sign he's out.

That said, I must now say the rest. Two of Gardner's dearest friends told me that within a month of the accident he had said, straight out, that he felt like he was going to die. One friend feels he said it with a touch of fear, the other thinks his mood was brave and accepting. Neither, at the time, got the idea that Gardner meant suicide. What exactly he did mean isn't obvious; he didn't know, and neither do we. A man turning fifty might indeed sense a sea change upon him. To feel in the presence of death is not uncommon when fundamental transformation begins. And there will be an end—some part of the self sloughed off, past solutions to life and art abandoned to open a future. None of this calls for an accident. We have to be careful in such judgments; the blankness of the accident becomes a blindness in the judging mind, stupid for design and retribution.

There is no life without its mystery, and sorting out the mystery, which is what biographers do, will have to accommodate not only facts and myths and regions of blankness, but also, in the case of a writer's life, the mystery of his works. I cannot do that here, of course, but two examples will be enough to suggest how difficult and fearful such a task might be. "Redemption" is one of Gardner's late stories, published in a collection in 1981, and it opens this way:

One day in April—a clear, blue day when there were crocuses in bloom—Jack Hawthorne ran over and killed his brother, David.

The accident is then described, faithful point by point to that other accident in Gardner's life, when as a boy of twelve he was operating the farm machine under which his younger brother fell and died. The next paragraph speaks not of Jack's grief but of the father's, and in the third paragraph, still with the father, we get this:

> he would ride away on his huge, darkly thundering Harley-Davidson 80, trying to forget, morbidly dwelling on what he'd meant to put behind him . . . or . . . for the hundredth time, about suicide, hunting in mixed fear and anger for some reason not to miss the next turn, fly off to the right of the next iron bridge onto the moonlit gray rocks and black water below.

A psychoanalyst would grab at such a passage, pointing to the father's role as superego and enforcer of guilt, suggesting in the dream of suicide the means of redemption. For the young man in Gardner's story, however, the burden of the accident is lifted through music and the daemon-empowered world of art. He takes up study of the French horn and finds, as his mentor, a figure greatly more powerful than the figure of the father, and it is this stronger spirit's blessing the young man receives. Few of us believe any more that through art our sins shall be forgiven us; but perhaps it's not too much to think that through art a state of provisional grace can be gained, a kind of redemption renewed daily in the practice of one's craft. When Gardner was coming into his stride as an artist and a teacher, his favorite remark to his students was that "art saves souls." I guess we know what that means, in a grand vague way, but in retrospect it points to a darker, more personal vision and might be taken as Gardner's comment on his own career. That he was possessed and driven he readily admitted, and in *On Becoming a Novelist* he put it this way:

> Daemonic compulsiveness can kill as easily as it can save. The true novelist must be at once driven and indifferent. . . . Drivenness only helps if it forces the writer not to

suicide but to the making of splendid works of art, allowing him indifference to whether or not the novel sells, whether or not it's appreciated. Drivenness is trouble for both the novelist and his friends; but no novelist, I think, can succeed without it.

Obviously Gardner believed that art should help us live our lives, the better to enjoy, the better to endure; and it seems clear that he also expected writing to help the writer—art, that is, as *good works*. And now, because of the accident, we ask if Gardner's faith had failed him. But because of the accident, we can't know. Like any accident, this one does as much to break the design as to complete it. And because of it, nothing in Gardner's life is decidable finally. People say he was going through hard changes. People say he was on the mend. Rebirth, too, has its harrowing hours. And what if he wasn't healing, or not yet? What, even supposing enormous pain, does it tell us that on a pleasant afternoon he decided to travel by motorcycle? A man can feel utterly awful and then go out into the crystal day, move through realms of changing light across the road, feel the power of the machine bearing him kindly, surely, and be at home in the homeless wind, the burden abruptly lifted. He can have terrible visions and at moments like this feel beyond them and blessed. I describe it that way because that's the way we spoke of it at Bread Loaf. There are times, we agreed, when a motorcycle clears the mind.

Much of what I've said can be turned around and be made to go the other way. I take the risk because Gardner's death can't be used to measure his life, not soundly or in fairness, and where there's doubt there ought to be kindness. The way Gardner died does not clear or confirm, but rather opens and questions any settled version of his life. Having got this far, moreover, I don't see much choice but to open matters further, and perhaps at this point a poetic image will work best. I quote a passage from the last pages of *Grendel*, exactly as Gardner quotes it himself in *On Becoming a Novelist*, for what it says about accidents, and then, in Gardner's own commentary, for what he says about himself. This is Gardner's monster dying after a fatal wound:

No one follows me now. I stumble again and with my one weak arm I cling to the huge twisted roots of an oak. I look down past stars to a terrifying darkness. I seem to recognize

the place, but it's impossible. "Accident," I whisper. I will fall.
I seem to desire the fall, and though I fight it with all my will
I know in advance that I can't win. Standing baffled, quaking
with fear, three feet from the edge of a nightmare cliff, I find
myself, incredibly, moving toward it. I look down, down into
bottomless blackness, feeling the dark power moving in me
like an ocean current, some monster inside me, deep sea wonder, dread night monarch astir in his cave, moving me slowly
to my voluntary tumble into death.

I suppose the allegorical force of this scene, in retrospect, leaps at us
like the findings of a blood test. After the accident all manner of things
take on meaning where none was before, a circumstance that calls for
going slow. But let us see Gardner's commentary, keeping in mind that
if at the moment of death there is a way in which necessity and chance
become one, this is never seen, by Gardner or his monster, as the logic
of suicide. Here is Gardner's reflection:

> "Accident!"—that is, Beowulf's victory has no moral meaning;
> all life is chance. But the fear that it may not all be accident
> strikes back instantly, prodded a little by childhood notions of
> the cross—blood, guilt, one's desperate wish to be a good boy,
> be loved both by one's parents and by that terrifying super-
> father whose otherness cannot be more frighteningly expressed
> than by the fact that he lives beyond the stars. So for all his
> conscious belief that it's all accident, Grendel *chooses* death,
> morally aligning himself with God (hence trying to save him-
> self); that is, against his will he notices he seems to "desire the
> fall."

The world envisioned here, and the imagination at work to see it, are
as far removed from modern psychology as Gardner's novel is from
literary realism. The vision here is religious, very nearly medieval, and
then not full revelation but only a trace, since it's only in the moment
of the monster's choice that the vision exists. That's as much, I think,
as Gardner felt he could hope for. But it's there, and while it lasts chance
plays no part. Events are informed by the mystery of divine intent,
accidents in particular, because they cannot be accounted for or fully
explained. They come out of the blue, summoned by God's will. And

that is how Gardner's monster, appalled by death's nothingness, eager to feel its necessity, comes to see his fall. The scene doesn't represent a suicide; it enacts the agony of the monstrous soul coming to terms with its death, and it ought to go without saying that any soul, to itself, appears monstrous. Grendel's choice isn't to live *or* die, being fatally wounded already. His choice is to accept the death that is upon him and in this moment—which must, after all, feel ultimate—divine a power greater than himself. Dante's comment in the *Paradiso* was In His will is our peace. The street version is that when your number's up it's up.

Gardner's religious view is valid. But no latter-day reader, having looked closely at the death scene in *Grendel* and then at Gardner's commentary, will be satisfied to let things rest in God's hands. This is perhaps our problem, but the Freudian content can't be denied. The idea of accident, we would say, is overdetermined; it includes childhood notions of guilt and the cross, a boy's desperate wish to be good and be loved, choice as part of dying and death itself as redemption. In view of Gardner's accident these nodes of meaning seem to lock into design, perhaps the structure of Grendel's fate most of all—first a wound got by chance, and then the desire for a voluntary fall that feels compelled. How much weight can stuff of this kind bear? We are again in the realm of uncertainty, but to take it all the way is easy, and we shall end up with just the sort of symmetry most pleasing to our taste, exquisite in its precision, terrible in what it presumes to reveal. Between Gardner's first accident and his last, the life and work of an exceedingly gifted man becomes the long dying of a monster fatally wounded, seeking to fall.

So yes, we can go to that length, all the way and perhaps all the more boldly for Gardner's comment that when he wrote the scene of Grendel dying, he was in a "trance-like state." But if we pull back even a little, it's apparent that something trancelike happens to us as well, the compulsion of metaphor collapsing restraint, urging us onward to sum things up. The coherent design, as I've outlined it, rests on two short bits of texts out of thousands of pages in many books; evidence of this kind would never stand except, of course, in an essay with literary leanings or a case history with clinical intent. We see, too, how we must isolate such passages to make them assume the sought-for significance. And then there remains the actual place on the highway; to go there and attempt to feel the authority of the design is to discover that in saying what happened we seem to believe that to think is to be. And there is still the accident itself, the hole in all our thinking, the piece of the puzzle that rolled off the asphalt into the grass.

Set on by darkness, imagination can go any length, even this: the man who rode the monster in himself, allowing its power to infuse and carry his art, was the man who rode the Harley all his life, staying with the risk and keeping it under good enough control, determined that this monster of a machine, like the demon in the soul, would get him wherever he might need or be required to go. But its power wasn't finally his, neither the horror in the heart nor the big bike he trusted enough not to fear. He saw no accident coming, but in actual fact the motorcycle hit him hard enough to kill him. The most shocking thing about the accident, at least as the police wrote it up, is that at no point did bike or rider collide with *anything*. Except, of course, each other. Living some hundred yards around the curve, the woman by her window heard the crash. What crash? The only possible moment of impact was the instant when, after moving along the corridor of the shoulder, the motorcycle hit the pavement midway in its long careen. Maybe it bounced, maybe went end over end, but it didn't just skid and drag, it turned on its rider with vast force, then was up and went on.

That way of seeing it makes sense to me, as I think it might to others who know motorcycles. In the end, though, it's only one more story— another metaphor ordaining design. And taken to its extravagant limit, it shows the craziness that comes from fighting the void. The sober fact is that what happened that September afternoon is never going to be known. Whatever we think, it will be theory washed in myth. We might understand what we can, and then let it be. Gardner has his death, his dignity, his uniqueness as strange and unyielding as the "accident that took his life." That's how the *Sun-Bulletin* put it. And in some way really, that's what it was, a life that an accident took.

Orwell and the O'Brienists

An Aside on Criticism in the Academy

O rwell's example—his sanity and durable poise in matters of literary-political defeat—has always been an inspiration to me; and if I begin with a set of epigraphs I would like to hold them to a modesty of meaning such as Orwell might have approved. Against the natural excess of signifiers (the fragment being especially wild), I purpose the kind of Orwellian care that would keep language fit for the exigencies of clarity and understand that words are called upon, now and again, to support. My immediate concern is with the wreck of humanism and with what a disaster of this kind might mean to us— to people like myself whose job is working with books; whose expertise is the production of critical discourse; and whose authority in literary matters rests on the traditional, but currently challenged, value of professing languages and literatures. I have placed the following epigraphs inside, rather than before or above, the arena of my argument, as befits the present case. Too late to be shored against ruin, these fragments come together like a fate, like inscriptions on a fallen stone. To ask whose stone, whose fate, is perhaps to inquire for whom the bell tolls:

> We did not ask him if he had seen any monsters, for monsters have ceased to be news. There is never any shortage of horrible creatures who prey on human beings, snatch away their food,

or devour whole populations; but examples of wise social planning are not so easy to find.

>   —Thomas More upon meeting
>   the voyager Hythlodaeus, 1515

So, like a sentinel, he could not sleep. The night was full of wrong,
Earthquakes and executions. Soon he would be dead,
And still all over Europe stood the horrible nurses
Itching to boil their children. Only his verses
Perhaps could stop them: He must go on working. Overhead
The uncomplaining stars composed their lucid song.

>   —Auden in 1939, recalling
>   Voltaire at Ferney, circa 1776

"You are the last man," said O'Brien. "You are the guardian
of the human spirit. You shall see yourself as you are. Take off
your clothes."

>   —O'Brien to Winston Smith,
>   in the Ministry of Love, *1984*

That More's utopian gambit should culminate in an era of embattled
enlightenment and from there descend through savagery and cant into
the Orwellian antiworld describes, I cannot but think, the path of the
humanist's defeat. Thereby also is implied a history, a course of events
sufficiently terrible to render "the death of humanism" rather less the
preferred catchphrase of current literary discourse, and more the exacting
name, as in Orwell's case, for a cause decently suffered and lost. The
foregoing fragments thus enact the arc of tragedy, at the close of which
we find the figure of Winston Smith, whom I would point to as the
emblem for all of us, Orwell included, who in any degree have embraced
or profited from the humanist's stance. That *1984* is based on an out-
moded and too exclusively Stalinist model is perhaps apparent. But
Orwell nonetheless managed to give us a potent image of the worst
world possible—barring nuclear catastrophe, of course—if the superpowers carry on as everyone expects and if, as seems likely, the struggle
of memory against power deteriorates further in power's favor. A warning, then, rather than a revelation; but there is something more to be
said of Orwell's book. He gives us, in *1984,* an intimate portrait of the
humanist destroyed. Here is the measurement of a situation in which

many among us might discern ourselves, a parable of the spirit of *humanitas* caught up in the endgame of a fate already bounded by its final moves. Like all compelling prophecy, *1984* derives its force from alarms already sounded in the heart. To look ahead is to look around, and there is no doubting that one of Orwell's cardinal concerns is the predicament in which he found himself, a humanist committed to the humanist's utopian pledge, in a world not going that way.

Orwell's *1984* is an anti-utopian fiction, a dystopia. It proceeds within, and is an irony upon, the utopian tradition that arose together with the humanist movement during the ferocious excitement of the Renaissance. The two—humanism and utopian thinking—cannot be held separate. Having taken his cue from Plato's *Republic,* Thomas More's *Utopia* is less a prophecy than a critique of abuses then current. It is also, in the Platonic way, an expression of the desire to be in the world but not of it. More's concern for "the future" was decidedly less pressing than it would become for the host of utopian visionaries soon to follow him. But the spark of the utopian impulse, if I may call it that, is alive in More's book and we are right to use his title to identify a way of envisioning the world that takes its form from its futuristic thrust. Central to emerging modernity, coeval with the great Renaissance discoveries, was the increasing seriousness with which imagination turned toward the future, near and far, and began to support visions of change and improvement—worlds new, better, and more finely tuned to desire and the sharing of commonweal. This, the "utopian dream," cannot be overrated; neither can its collapse in our century. Never were so many hopes, so many eggs in one basket; and the result, we see, is not an omelet. Hope for the future has withered; trust in historical progress has been undercut by drastic visions of apocalypse. I do not say that some awful end is upon us, but only that the propensity for great expectations has spent itself, and that this curtailment of the capacity for utopian envisionment translates, for people like ourselves, into a wounding, a damming up, of humanistic faith in literature and learning as engines of moral improvement.

By describing the New World he visited, More's utopian spokesman suggests "possible methods of reforming European society." No one speaks that way now, demagogues excepted; war and the bomb are too much with us. Thomas More wrote his *Utopia* in 1515–16, in the middle of a violent and hyperpolitical age, but also an age of manic energy and opening horizons. By way of fixing a reference point I want to recall two other writers and their books from that time, Machiavelli's *The Prince,* composed in exile in 1513, and *The Praise of Folly,* which Erasmus completed in 1511 while in England visiting More. These are very different works, by very different sorts of Renaissance scholars. But these three men, with their strategic sense of books, were among the front runners in the movement we know as humanism. They were alert to politics and statescraft, keen on the uses to which a library could be put, and each in his way maintained the belief that the human world could be got hold of and changed for the better through secular, rather than divine, inspiration. If I speak of humanism (as I find I must in order to speak of Orwell and ourselves), I have in mind principally the notion that reason and enlightenment are real forces in the world, endorsed by technical advancement; and that with instruction and goodwill, we may trust that human means are sufficient to human ends. Man, said Vico, creates himself. "Dare to think" was Kant's directive. Milton thundered that books are "that seasoned life of man preserved and stored," and that the suppression of books is "the stop of truth." These are articles of humanistic faith. They take for granted that mind and learning count, that the pedagogic power of books is something to be reckoned with. And at the heart of such ideas, directing their energies, is—or was— the hunger for utopia.

Books and the work of enlightenment; truth and the assumptions of moral and material progress—for nearly five centuries these categories informed each other and, not least, underwrote the privileged position of all things literary, on which our present system of benefits, as critics and teachers, continues to depend. When we proclaim "the death of humanism," therefore, we might also keep in mind our debt to that which, while we still expect it to provide dividends, many among us scorn to credit. The first humanists were a band of scholars who fostered freedom of thought and the hope of human betterment through love of literature and devotion to study. To celebrate the Greek and Roman classics was to break the hold of Christendom. To make available the commentaries of the Church fathers was to put choice and judgment into the individual's studious keeping. With remarkable speed, the new sense of human capability took root and spread. By the time of the *philosophes,* in figures like Voltaire and Jefferson, it would stir the beginnings of praxis. Humanism was exactly that: an exalted sense of utopian promise, based in literary vocation both scholarly and critical, aiming to implement its faith that through care for books the truth would prevail and tyranny collapse. That this allegiance would eventually split into two antagonistic brotherhoods, the one radical and bent on revolution, the other ameliorative and given to sweetness and light, no one could foresee. All hoped for a world greatly changed. None saw the catastrophe coming. The innocence of the utopian dream—its abysmal misjudgment of power—was the humanist's own courageous innocence. The cause was noble, and hindsight may lament but cannot condemn the fact that utopian foresight would become the dead-end stare of Big Brother, or that we, guardians of the human spirit that once we were, would end up as bereft of purpose and resource as, in Orwell's view, poor Winston Smith.

We do not, of course, care to see ourselves thus. Yet we in the departments of English and comparative literature are first among the heirs of humanism's destiny, and its contradictions are very much with us. Humanistic values are eclipsed and often reviled, but care for things human must surely still exist. Utopia has given way to dystopia, yet among our larger needs a hopeful vision of the future is not least. In the classroom and in our professional journals, in our monographs, in our books about books, we impute elite command, sometimes rarest truth, to poems and novels merely by taking them as our discourse-occasion. At the same time, much of critical discourse would seem to produce nothing more than more discourse—although again, we proceed as if some other, further gain were forthcoming besides the comfort of jobs surprisingly well paid and, in a world so unstable, secure. Very much we owe our luck to the humanists with their utopian notion of literary potency. Yet here we stand or wobble, stuck in the bell jar of practical criticism, or lost in space with the new breed of high-tech theoreticians, ignoring or flaunting the ruin of our calling. The great Orwellian question, it seems to me, is how humanism might survive its manifest defeat. By writing *1984* Orwell put the question in terms so grim as to rule out any answer less than tragic. We share, that is, the shabby fate of Winston Smith and more than a little his image is ours.

What kind of book is *1984*? In the broad loose sense we call it a novel, and by way of a subgenre, one of the classics of anti-utopian fiction. But when we look to its design and to its author's intention (yes, the author and his intention), we see at once that *1984* is satire, blunt, savage, Swiftian; and that is what Orwell himself called it. All literary modes hide undeclared stratagems and goals, but about satire there is no secret: sometimes open, sometimes oblique, its aim is attack. Satire proceeds by way of mockery and ridicule, by using exaggeration and distortion and hostile irony, its end being to diminish, deflate, or utterly lay flat the power and supposed authority of its object. But if we grant that *1984* is cast in the satirical mode, a curious question arises. What, or whom, is Orwell's central target? If we were dealing with *Animal Farm* the answer would be simple. There Orwell attacks the whole of that gross stupid world. But in *1984* the case is less clear. Is the world of Oceania in all ways silly? Is the average episode more properly risible or disturbing? Given what we know of politics in this century, are Oceania's grotesque exaggerations *only* exaggerations, and if they are deadly do they still provoke disdain? Consider O'Brien; as the story progresses, does his power diminish or increase in our eyes? Does Orwell manage, does he attempt, to deflate O'Brien's emblematic stature? In a word, is the world of *1984* discounted, "put in its place," through satirical means?

I cannot see that it is. That we might like to think so is understandable, but no, the peculiarity of this book is that it does not possess or transcend the darkness it envisions. We might see it as prophecy, as warning, as the dismal vision of a dying man; but what counts is that by the end of the book the Orwellian antiworld is more dreadful than it was when first we entered it. Knowing, as we do, that the book's happiest moments are on film in O'Brien's file, not even the secret delight of Winston and Julia's pastoral lovemaking offers relief. I have never read a book more thoroughly joyless. But by writing *1984,* Orwell gives us a book that surpasses the fate of its protagonist, Winston Smith, and that stands against the world of O'Brien, present or to come. Orwell surpasses victimhood and announces against tyranny. That much we *can* say—no more, perhaps, but also no less. And to view *1984* this way is to glimpse Orwell's answer to the dilemma of the humanist in our time.

I want to suggest, for purposes of judgment, that if we divide *1984* into the realm of O'Brien (who represents the state) and the sphere of Winston Smith (who represents Orwell and ourselves), then it becomes apparent that whereas Smith's world shatters altogether, the realm of O'Brien remains brazenly intact. It thrives on its extremities and is the more terrible for its capacity to withstand satiric attack and to maintain its hegemony not only over the citizens of Oceania but also over the reader. O'Brien survives; the joke is not on him. Winston Smith, on the other hand, becomes more the fool as he plays deeper into the hands of his destroyer. We take him in earnest, of course. We feel that there but for the grace of God goes any one of us. But by the end of the book, having lost his mind and thus his dignity, Smith also loses our respect. The situation is tragic, but not, strictly speaking, a tragedy. The last page of *1984* is not even pathos. Smith's slobbering end is shameful, indecent, and we must concede, I think, at least two points: the main target of Orwell's attack is in fact Winston Smith; and the function of the satirical mode, in *1984,* is to keep us sufficiently detached, and in this way critical, toward the fate of Smith and what he represents. A book without hope is one thing; a book which promotes despair is something else, something from which we are spared by the sort of moral intelligence—tough-minded and ready for hard judgments—that informs the satirical mode in Orwell's usage.

To suggest that Orwell is out to "get" Winston Smith is not the view of most readers, and matters will not be mollified if I insist further that what Orwell is "getting at" through his merciless treatment of Smith is the traditional humanist—the man or woman of reason and goodwill, morally upright, intellectual (for a time), self-possessed, committed to truth, individual liberty and progress through learning, reverent toward books and in love with old things. But also, as in Smith's case, someone unprepared for extremity and, more than a little, an accomplice in one's own destruction. O'Brien calls Winston Smith "the last man." That, in Orwell's notes, was what he originally intended to call the book, *The Last Man in Europe,* a title implicitly tragic but also ironic. My claim is that through his attack on Winston Smith, Orwell meant his book to be a radical critique of humanism in its pre-Orwellian innocence. Orwell also meant to show us the way humanism looks to O'Brien and to those among us who, having gone over to the management, might be called "the O'Brienists." We can even suppose that the antihuman world in which Smith finds himself is, historically, as much the outcome as the cause of the humanist's undoing.

At every point in *1984* the grotesqueries and exaggerations of Orwell's antiworld rub off on Winston Smith and seep into his soul. Two plus two must always be four, and he who would insist upon five must surely be a lunatic. Yet there comes a moment of "luminous certainty," as Winston calls it, when two added to two comes up five. When O'Brien holds up "the fingers of his left hand, with the thumb concealed," he lets us know that *for him* four is not five, but his is the power and Winston finally breaks. On another occasion O'Brien says: "The earth is the center of the universe. The sun and the stars go round it." That is outrageous, but instantly we are reminded of Brecht's *Galileo,* one of *1984*'s great parallel texts (written at the same time), and we see that O'Brien is no fool. He goes on to say: "For certain purposes, of course, that is not true." The issue is power and not truth, or rather, it is *power over truth,* discourse subsumed by its governing institution. And by way of asserting this power, which we can fear but hardly doubt, O'Brien concludes by saying: "But what of it? Do you suppose it is beyond us to produce a dual system of astronomy?" We might, at this point, be reminded of some of our own dual systems, in the academy, in Washington. O'Brien speaks the truth and when he lies he knows what he is doing and corrects himself as he pleases. He never loses his grip on himself, or on Smith, or on us.

Among the most bizarre of Orwell's satiric devices is the daily ritual known as "the Two Minutes Hate." Onto the screen comes the face of Goldstein, archenemy of the state, and almost instantly "the Hate rose to a frenzy. People were leaping up and down in their places and shouting at the tops of their voices." The spectacle is ludicrous and any reasonable man or woman ought to be immune. But as it goes on "Winston found that he was shouting with the others and kicking his heel violently against the rung of his chair. The horrible thing about the Two Minutes Hate was not that one was obliged to act a part, but that it was impossible to avoid joining in." And in the end it is the horrible part—the way dignity dissolves into hysteria—that sticks with us. We have, here, a little parable of the humanist's fall, not to mention the shocking speed with which, in America, the New Jingoism becomes the common cry.

Other aspects of Orwell's antiworld are openly perverse but not, on that count, open to ridicule. To call the headquarters of the Gestapo-like Thought Police the Ministry of Love reveals the same insidious logic as ARBEIT MACHT FREI on the gates of Auschwitz or, for that matter, calling the most deadly weapon on earth the "Peacekeeper." At the root of this kind of naming is "doublethink," the profundity of which goes a good deal deeper than any satirical task to which it might be put. When Orwell describes doublethink as the mind's capacity "to use conscious deception while retaining the firmness of purpose that goes with complete honesty," we think immediately of political leaders the world over, our own Great Communicator among them. And when Orwell goes on to describe doublethink as the ability "to tell deliberate lies while genuinely believing in them, to forget any fact that has become inconvenient," we recognize a universal manner of deception, available to anyone, and not only in matters of politics. Orwell's genius was to reveal the centrality of such thinking to any exercise of power, any extended management of the status quo. Here again discourse bends to power, and while doublethink keeps Winston Smith unnerved and off balance, O'Brien rises above it, untroubled, steady on his course.

Between the realms of O'Brien and Smith there is one crucial point of intersection, such that Orwell's satirical thrust cuts both ways at once. I have in mind Orwell's invention of "newspeak," which allows him to attack the state in terms of censorship and propaganda, while at the same time it permits him to mock Winston Smith in terms of his profession. Orwell's newspeak is not, of course, compounded of airy nothing. Especially in the era of mass media, all governments manipulate language and spread lies; the practice of disinformation is one of power's standard procedures. At home, for example, our State Department has recently removed the word *killing* from its human-rights reports, having substituted the phrase *unlawful or arbitrary deprivation of life*. *Genocide* has been replaced by *consistent pattern of gross violation;* and we are all familiar, from Vietnam and Orwell's famous essay, with the meaning of *pacification*. This democratic version of newspeak aims to blur, confuse, and disperse, whereas newspeak in the Orwellian antiworld reduces and shuts down. In either case, however, it is the intention to which Orwell objects: power's debasement of mind and spirit through maiming of language.

Sometimes this can be almost funny. When Winston's colleague Syme begins to glow with admiration for so singular a language, we are moved—almost—to mirth. "It's a beautiful thing," says Syme, "the destruction of words." And he concludes: "In the end the whole notion of goodness and badness will be covered by only six words—in reality, only one word. Don't you see the beauty of that, Winston?" Winston sees the horror of it, sees that Syme will soon be vaporized, sees also the damage so sinister a fixing of discourse works upon the soul. We might consider newspeak a comic play upon words, except that when the fun becomes lethal—the danger implicit in "ownlife," for instance— the levity stops.

Newspeak is one of Orwell's sharpest satirical creations, one he took quite seriously, and if he used it to take potshots at the state he also uses it to ridicule Winston Smith's status as humanist-defunct. Winston Smith, we are told, is one of the few proficient writers of newspeak and his expertise is sometimes called upon for special Party declarations. He shows us, as the late Foucault would say, that power and discourse easily join in common cause. But Winston's profession goes further than that. He works for the Ministry of Truth, and what he works with are documents and books. Like scholars from the Renaissance onward, Winston's professional commitment is to textual emendation. His job is to produce the "definitive" text, no matter that what counts as definitive changes from time to time. Smith guards, as we do, literature from unauthorized readings; he is a keeper of the canon, whatever it might happen to be at the time, a dealer in a usable past.

Not, of course, that Smith believes in what he does. He is the perfect parody of the humanist scholar, his position is predicated on humanistic principles, but he has not forgotten that the name of this game is betrayal. Like the rest of us, however, he carries on. When by accident he comes across a genuine historical document he is ecstatic—but also terrified, and resorts to the "memory hole" to get himself off the hook. Even so, Winston Smith remains *at heart* a scholar and a humanist, and nothing excites him more than the prospect of getting "the book," as it is called, into his own two hands. About "the book" I shall have more to say presently, but already we see how fixed in mockery Winston Smith becomes by virtue of the profession Orwell assigns him.

We can call Smith the post-humanist, one of Oceania's deconstructionists, busy vaporizing authors and reducing honored texts to writing's perpetual flood. Each day Winston goes into the Ministry of Truth and produces a whole new batch of differences in a world where, as he repeatedly says, nothing makes any difference. What counts is not truth or the referent, but the endless play of signifiers. Words achieve the insubstantial status of momentary images on the ubiquitous television screens, flashing, fading, crowding in and out upon each other, impossible to remember. Winston Smith embodies the spirit of an era that Derrida has named "The End of the Book and the Beginning of Writing." Writing is perpetual, no book can ever be considered closed, and no text has priority over another. With old books constantly rewritten and new books composed by committee, there can be no author and any given text gets lost in the sea of intertext—voice, tone, point of view, and the moral focus of style all alike erased, submerged in the oceanic surge of *écriture*.

Thus are O'Brien and the state served by the likes of Winston Smith. O'Brien knows that without books to anchor point of view, without the voice of the author to bear witness, the self shall never get its bearings nor find ground on which to stand. O'Brien and the O'Brienists take the fundamental character of culture, its status as artifice, and turn it against the human needs it was created to sustain. The only advantage, in this kind of vacuum, accrues to the state. If everything is fabrication, then nothing is true except the fact of power itself. Orwell would counter that some fictions are better than others, inventions like selfhood, dignity, moral choice, fictions necessary to humanness, nurtured and preserved through the culture of the book, on which the human spirit depends for certainty of its own being. When Eric Blair created the style and point of view that became George Orwell, he knew exactly what he was about. And so do we.

Having argued that the humanist and the utopian visionary are of one breed, I have perhaps given the impression that utopian envisionment, in its exuberant innocence, must always be benign. But when we consider that O'Brien is himself a humanist ("Outside man there is nothing") and a true believer in the perfectly ordered society, we must consider also that utopian schemes can work as well to enslave as to liberate. Utopian images point up and challenge the ills of the age, they energize desire for social transformation, but for all these good intentions it must still be said that imagination is not wholly free in its construction of superior worlds. Something will persist and go unchallenged, most especially power in the guise of political necessity. Utopian thinkers either confront or evade the realities they presume to transform, and in every case the outcome depends on how the disposition of power is handled. Plato's ideal state, be it ever so high-minded in its governance and noble in its lies, will still govern and still lie and will end up prescribing classes, regimentation, and the indispensable cement of coercion. There will be police but no poets, and everyone will stay put in his or her place. More's utopian world is far more generous than Plato's, but More does not exclude slavery or penal servitude or, in extreme cases, the death penalty, and his system of surveillance amounts to everyone informing on everyone. How the utopian dream turned to nightmare will not be understood until we grant, if ever we do, that Machiavelli was on the right track. Power, which cannot *not* lie and must rely finally on force, answers its own needs first. Internal order and external threat are constant problems, also constant excuses. And whether we address the body politic or the ship of state, kings and colonels have still to be reckoned with. Power is everybody's problem, and humanism has never been its equal. Marx in his wildest utopian moment could only imagine that the state would, well, pack up and go. Lenin knew better. So did Orwell and so, of course, does O'Brien.

The realm of O'Brien is represented by the myth of Big Brother, the infallible leader who never dies. No doubt Big Brother is being used, by Orwell, to satirize the cult of personality; but within the antiworld of *1984*, Big Brother is one more lie the Inner Party propagates to coerce the populace and mask the truth of power. But the realm of Winston Smith is also served by a myth, in this case the rumor of a revolutionary counterforce known as "the Brotherhood." The symmetry here is a bit much, but we see Orwell's point: against the State a small band of courageous souls will work in secret, will spread the truth that resides in "the book," and as enlightenment takes hold and the ranks of the Brotherhood increase, the grip of the state will wither. We see, in Smith's myth, an image of the eighteenth-century *philosophes,* doing the job of enlightenment, using books as their tool, carried onward by their utopian faith in the revolution to come. And behind them we glimpse the brave band of Renaissance humanists, taking veiled stands against the superstitions of the Church and the tyranny of the Court, passing on to their heirs the utopian hope.

For the age of Erasmus as for the age of Voltaire, the myth of brotherhood was a vital part of the humanist movement. That in our time this Brotherhood would become the Inner Party, the early humanists could not, of course, predict. Winston Smith, on the other hand, might know better; and yet, good humanist that he is, he too dreams of joining just such a brotherhood of conspirators against the state, and his downfall begins the day of the Two Minutes Hate when he first makes eye contact with O'Brien: "there was a fraction of a second when their eyes met, and for as long as it took to happen Winston knew—yes, he knew!—that O'Brien was thinking the same thing as himself." And O'Brien *is* thinking what Winston is thinking, only with a different end in view. From that moment on, Winston is convinced that O'Brien is a member of the Brotherhood, which in fact, as a member of the Inner Party, he is. To join the Brotherhood is Winston's fondest dream, and for this special reason he and Julia go in secret to meet with O'Brien.

Orwell presents the episode in O'Brien's apartment with an irony so brutal as to shock even those among Orwell's critics who would speak of his "sadism." He gives O'Brien full license to string Winston along, to mock him at every turn, and Orwell misses no chance to satirize Winston's romantic yearning to find in O'Brien a brother. O'Brien says:

"Shall I say it, or will you?" Winston answers promptly, "I will say it," and goes on to confess himself an enemy of the Party and profess his desire to join the "secret organization" to which he thinks (rightly, wrongly) that O'Brien belongs. When the butler passes through, O'Brien calms Winston's fear by saying that "he is one of us." Which "us"? And then O'Brien openly tells Winston what the Brotherhood has come to mean. But Winston hasn't the ears to hear. Led on by O'Brien, Winston swears that for the good of the cause he is ready to die, kill, throw acid in a child's face. This moment of folly will be held against him later, as O'Brien knows, and to twist the knife deeper O'Brien turns to Julia and says: "Do you understand that even if he survives, it may be as a different person? We may be obliged to give him a new identity. . . . Our surgeons can alter people beyond recognition." Certainly they can, and as O'Brien knows, certainly they will. Winston, however, cannot at this point know what O'Brien knows. Winston sees what he hopes to see. He looks at O'Brien and beholds in this member of the Brotherhood "an impression of confidence and of understanding tinged by irony." Winston's observation is accurate; what he makes of it is not. Awash in brotherly love, Winston thinks: "When you looked at O'Brien's powerful shoulders and his blunt-featured face, so ugly yet so civilized, it was impossible to believe that he could be defeated." The irony is terrible, and perhaps I should add that whenever Orwell is being particularly hard he shifts to the word "you." It is possible that "you"—meaning Orwell and the reader—sees something, is meant to see something, that is not, or not yet, within the purview of Winston Smith.

What goes on in O'Brien's apartment is something rather worse than cat-and-mouse, and I have belabored the point to stress the extreme degree to which here, but not only here, Orwell ridicules Winston Smith and hits him in ways that only we, and not Winston, can fully register. I mean to say that this relentless undermining irony is not reserved for special moments but operates throughout the whole of the book. For example, Winston feels sure that whatever else happens, he will never betray Julia because, as he says to himself, his love for her is "a fact, known as he knew the rules of arithmetic." That, of course, is before two plus two equals five. And when he anticipates the worst that might become of him in the Ministry of Love, Winston thinks: "They could lay bare in the utmost detail everything that you had done or said or thought: but the inner heart, whose workings were mysterious even to yourself, remained impregnable." This is the humanist's bedrock conviction—that the innermost self is a mystery and inviolate. But as things turn out, no part of Winston Smith remains impregnable, and if he is a mystery to himself, he is an open book to O'Brien, who repeatedly reads Winston's mind and anticipates his reactions.

The point is this: throughout the whole of *1984,* from the moment Winston begins his secret diary (and perhaps long before), he is inside the trap; his file is being built against him, and Big Brother, in the person of O'Brien, is watching. What this means is that everything that Winston Smith thinks and does is undercut, at every point exposed to a view not his own. He is never on his own ground. His existence is entirely ironic, the first or foreground meaning continually subverted or negated by a second or background meaning. In *1984,* the consciousness of the protagonist is undone by another, superior consciousness, and there is no doubting to whom this encompassing awareness belongs. Within the world of the story it belongs to O'Brien, and within the telling of the story it belongs to Orwell. In this deep sense Orwell and O'Brien are in league, and we with them. For what O'Brien knows, Orwell knows, and so do we. Only Winston Smith is left in the dark, yearning to meet someone (he thinks it will be O'Brien) "in the place where there is no darkness." The place where there is no darkness turns out to be the torture chamber, and O'Brien will be there to greet him.

To detect an irony so inclusive and suffocating, we need to read *1984* at least twice—like any other work of complex structure and meaning. A good deal of literary judgment depends on hindsight of this kind, the assessment of modernist texts in particular, and the effect of this doubled point of view in *1984* is shattering. To look back on Winston Smith through O'Brien's eyes is to see the humanist stripped bare, in an arena of irony that, like the torture chamber, brings everything to light. This manipulation of points of view is also a manipulation of the reader, and I consider this Orwell's most profound invention in *1984.* Like a terminal illness, its symptoms are first insidious, then acute, then chronic and beyond salvation. Is this not exquisite and hideous together?

The first time we read *1984* we are quite naturally *with* Winston Smith, who is, after all, the closet humanist in all of us. The second time around, however, we are forced to *go* with O'Brien. We are not on O'Brien's side, but neither can we escape him or shake off his power. There is a certain authentic horror in this predicament, since what first appears as a satiric touch, a harsh joke, now hits us like the gates of hell slammed shut: BIG BROTHER IS WATCHING.

Orwell's satiric tactics operate within an ironic strategy as total as the totalitarian experience he aims to portray. To pursue this much further would be to beat a dead horse, but one last episode needs accounting for, if only because the point at issue—the role of the proles as a possible counterforce in Orwell's antiworld—has been so much disputed in discussions of *1984*. Winston, we know, is attracted to the proles much as Orwell himself was drawn to the denizens of London's East End. And like Orwell, Winston is of two minds. In his diary he writes: "Until they become conscious they will never rebel, and until after they have rebelled they cannot become conscious." But Winston also writes, and repeats more than once, that "if there is hope it lies with the proles." Are we to take these conflicting views as an exercise in doublethink or, more innocently, as the humanist's utopian notion of the noble savage? Either way, Winston Smith's celebration of the proles is as doomed as he is, and in fact they go down together.

Within the structure of Orwell's book, Winston's hope for the proles reaches its peak precisely at the turning point—the moment of reversal— in Winston's own destiny. Winston and Julia, we recall, are in the little old-fashioned room that Mr. Charrington had so kindly (and cunningly) offered Winston as a haven above the junk shop. Minutes before the Thought Police break in upon the solitude that Winston and Julia thought they shared, Winston has his one genuine moment of transcendence, his one clear heartfelt endorsement of the modern humanist's utopian program. In the backyard beneath the window, Winston hears a woman singing a sentimental song while going about the grubby job of doing her wash. This episode, as Orwell renders it, is the most lyrical passage in the book, more so than the first meeting between Winston and Julia in their countryside bower. Here and only here, the grim world of *1984* rises above itself, in an instant of exalted vision that will be immediately crushed. I cannot quote these several pages entire, but let me set down, as in a list, the stages of Winston's mystical rapport with the proles. And let me say beforehand that this vision of the proles victorious, for which the washerwoman is both emblem and substance, fuses in poetic exaltation the central components of humanism—its utopian impulse, its democratic logic, above all its faith in a universal, indestructible spirit of *humanitas*:

> The flagstones were wet as though they had just been washed, and he had the feeling that the sky had been washed too, so

fresh and pale was the blue between the chimney pots. Tirelessly the woman marched to and fro, corking and uncorking herself, singing and fallen silent, and pegging out more diapers, and more and yet more.

It had never before occurred to him that the body of a woman at fifty, blown up to monstrous dimensions by childbearing, then hardened, roughened by work till it was coarse in the grain like an overripe turnip, could be beautiful.

She had had her momentary flowering, a year, perhaps, of wildrose beauty, and then she had suddenly swollen like a fertilized fruit and grown hard and red and coarse, and then her life had been laundering, scrubbing, laundering, first for children, then for grand-children, over thirty unbroken years. At the end of it she was still singing. The mystical reverence that he felt for her was somehow mixed up with the aspect of the pale, cloudless sky, stretching away behind the chimney pots into interminable distances.

Once he has given himself to the figure of the washerwoman, Winston's utopian impulse breaks forth in full splendor, or rather full sentimentality, and in his last minute of freedom Winston Smith indulges himself to the brim:

It was curious to think that the sky was the same for everybody, in Eurasia or Eastasia as well as here. And the people under the sky were also very much the same—everywhere, all over the world, hundreds or thousands of millions of people just like this, people ignorant of one another's existence, held apart by walls of hatred and lies, and yet almost exactly the same— people who had never learned to think but were storing up in their hearts and bellies and muscles the power that would one day overturn the world. If there was hope, it lay with the proles! . . . Sooner or later it would happen: strength would change into consciousness. The proles were immortal; you could not doubt it when you looked at that valiant figure in the yard.

How often have we heard *that*? And out of context, which is to say, out of history and out of Orwell's book, how very fine, how inspired and triumphant it still sounds. In the glare of its glory, reservations fade and once again we feel the excitement of the dream. For what Orwell gives us, in Winston's penultimate moment, is the heart of the humanist's hope for a better world, a resurrection rooted in the coarse but irrepressible potential of humanity at large, life going on and onward, the power of truth unbinding humankind's promethean strength, a vision altogether irresistible *because*—because "you could not doubt it when you looked at that valiant figure in the yard." Seconds later, however, Charrington's "iron voice" breaks in and Winston Smith's demise begins.

To see what Orwell is making of all this, we need only turn six pages forward to the scene in the cell of the prison where Winston is first interned. It is a common jail, not yet the Ministry of Love, and no sooner has Winston settled himself than in comes a prole picked up for drunken disorder. And this, we see with shock, is what the "valiant figure in the yard" looks like close up:

> An enormous wreck of a woman, aged about sixty, with great tumbling breasts and thick coils of white hair which had come down in her struggles, was carried in, kicking and shouting, by four guards who had hold of her one at each corner. They wrenched off the boots with which she had been trying to kick them, and dumped her down across Winston's lap. . . .

The woman curses her jailors, begs Winston's forgiveness, says they "dono 'ow to treat a lady," confides to Winston that she ain't herself, quite—and vomits "copiously." After reviving she puts her "vast arm" around Winston and draws him toward her. Breathing beer and vomit into his face she starts the following exchange:

> "Wass your name, dearie?" she said.
> "Smith," said Winston.
> "Smith?" said the woman. "Thass funny. My name's Smith too. . . ."

So much for the "valiant figure in the yard," for the proles in Orwell's antiworld, and so much, too, for Winston Smith's fantasy of universal

brotherhood. As for the name *Smith,* here is the last stanza of one of
Orwell's poems that he inserted in his famous late essay, "Why I Write":

> I dreamed I dwelt in marble halls,
> And woke to find it true;
> I wasn't born for an age like this;
> Was Smith? Was Jones? Were you?

That the traditional humanist is not up to the world we inhabit is the
deep theme of *1984*: not, that is, the great defeat to come, but the defeat
already with us. We can see, from the long lyrical passage about the
woman singing in the yard, that Orwell genuinely admired the hardy
composure of life in its coarse but stubborn persistence. That *life goes
on no matter what* is a cardinal truth and a real cause for wonder; and
it accounts, I think, for much of Orwell's dedication as a writer, his
peculiar willingness to carry on despite dark times. But at the same time,
Orwell was nobody's fool. At a distance the masses might appear "a
valiant figure." Up close, however, admiration is balanced by an equal
measure of disgust and Orwell is honest enough to say so, as he did
over and over again, in *Down and Out,* in *Wigan Pier.*

The humanist's modern love affair with the people, the proles, has
been central to the utopian adventure, at least since the nineteenth-
century rise of the democratic tide, with its visionary faith that in the
world to come the last shall be first. Rarely, however, have the lovers
of humanity descended to the lower depths, and in this Orwell was an
exception. That he liked and perhaps needed to be down and out, and
wished to see for himself England's "other nation," suggests his closeness
to Winston Smith, who is also a person who likes and needs to move
in the world below the world. But the exceptional hardness with which
Orwell demolishes Winston's mystical rapport with the proles signals
the speciousness of Winston's vision; and in this we behold Orwell's
own determination to face the discouragements of his own utopian
leaning, face the end of easy expectation and yet not be broken in spirit
or give up altogether on the future. Having had his own ideals
stomped—Spain stopped many a lesser commitment—Orwell would
still write, he would still support the English Labour movement, he
would still speak for a possible socialism. He would persist in these
ways, but without the doubtful baggage of traditional myths—without,
that is to say, the usual humanistic consolations. That nothing might

come of such efforts was no excuse not to try. At the same time, however, there can be no illusions about utopian hope, past or future; the defeats and abridgments are real and indicative. But we would be entirely off track to suppose that by his savaging of Winston Smith's pretensions Orwell denies his or our humanity. He lets us know, rather, that we cannot count on much we thought we could; that much we feel to be inviolate about ourselves is vulnerable and can be—to borrow some newspeak from the CIA—"terminated with extreme prejudice."

In "Politics and the English Language," Orwell made his famous plea for defense against political lying. He goes so far as to say that "All issues are political issues, and politics itself is a mass of lies, evasions, folly, hatred and schizophrenia." And in "In Front of Your Nose," another essay from the same period (1946), Orwell spells out what "schizophrenia" means in his observation: "It is the power of holding simultaneously two beliefs which cancel out. Closely allied to it is the power of ignoring facts which are obvious and unalterable, and which will have to be faced sooner or later." *All* issues involve politics? Doublethink is everywhere at work? That is what Orwell says, and he concludes that "To see what is in front of one's nose needs a constant struggle." Surely it does; and if we honor Orwell, if we admire his honesty and moral acuity, we must then go on to wonder why we do not exactly take him at his word. Or, in terms of *1984*, we must wonder why a man as intelligent as Winston Smith, a man who sees things as they are, cannot go further and see through them to the thing itself. Surrounded by lies he knows to be lies, Winston nevertheless persists in misjudgment. He misjudges O'Brien (radically and to the end), Julia (at first), Mr. Charrington (completely), the proles ("the valiant figure"), the Brotherhood (now the Inner Party), and finally himself ("he had hoped to keep the inner heart inviolate"). When at last O'Brien asks him what the truth of power *is*, Winston is as innocent as most of us profess to be. He falls back on utopian logic and prompts himself to believe that for all its lies, power has a human face:

> He knew in advance what O'Brien would say: that the Party did not seek power for its own ends, but only for the good of the majority. That it sought power because men in the mass were frail, cowardly creatures who could not endure liberty or face the truth, and must be ruled over and systematically de-

ceived by others who were stronger than themselves. That the
choice for mankind lay between freedom and happiness [etc.,
etc.]. The terrible thing, thought Winston, the terrible thing
was that when O'Brien said this he would believe it. You could
see it in his face.

That is the Grand Inquisitor's rationale, and from Orwell's point of
view it is the shrewdest of power's deceptions, for it makes the misuse
of power seem but a miscarriage of the utopian pledge, a sort of radical
humanism intent upon the greatest good for the human pool. It is a
rationale not unlike our own, which allows us to believe that while the
power people along the Potomac keep the cold war heated, and transfer
our national wealth from the social to the military sector, and openly
plan for a protracted nuclear war, they do this because in their heart of
hearts they pine solely for peace and national well-being and, if asked,
will say so. The last repression isn't sex or death but the unbearable face
of power, and the most striking thing about Winston Smith's interpretation is that he cannot bring himself *to know what he knows*. He credits
O'Brien with an exercise in doublethink that is in fact his own, Winston's,
which provokes O'Brien to reply: "That was stupid, Winston, stupid!"
And then comes O'Brien's little fire sermon, in which the truth of power
is laid bare:

1. "The Party seeks power entirely for its own sake."
2. "The object of power is power."
3. ". . . power is collective. The individual only has power in so far
   as he ceases to be an individual."
4. ". . . power is power over human beings."

Summed up in the O'Brienist manner, these four points add up to a
fifth: "Imagine," says O'Brien, "a boot stamping on a human face—
forever." And thus, in Room 101, with O'Brien professing Inner Party
truth, Winston Smith completes his education.

Orwell gives us, in *1984,* an old story. And by putting his book in
our keeping, he also pushes us to a choice. Lip service aside, in which
much is said and little meant, what are we to *make* of Orwell's book?
By making it the occasion for still more lectures and symposia, confer-
ences and papers duly collected, we contribute—perhaps unwittingly,
often against our own best intentions—to enhancing its status as a

"ritualized text," the sort of book that is used to certify the rites and rules, the permissions and taboos, of a professionalized discourse whose first function is to certify the books and authors on which it, critical discourse, depends. The process is selective, circular, and thereby many livings are got. Thereby also, as Orwell foresaw, books are dissolved into writing, their power transformed to the army of critics who would speak in their stead. The transfer is effected by filtering the language of the text through the metalanguage of critical vocabulary; and this way of processing literature is at its worst in the academy because within the matrix of institutional power struggles the study of literature justifies itself (pretends to science) by calling itself a discipline. It must therefore comport itself professionally. The *discipline* decides which books count and how much. *Discourse* determines their "truth," what they mean.

Probably, as times worsen and the humanities are harder pressed, the antihumanist proclivities of professionalization will increase. We can expect critical discourse in the academy to join forces with the larger institutional demands of the besieged academy in a world increasingly governed by the mystique of power. But if, as Wittgenstein suggested, forms of life and language games are interdependent, a given form of life does not depend on one game only. Knowing this, some of us might wish to depart in ways more respectful of the integrity and special power that literary artifacts possess. This will be called, is already called, a species of fetishism, but no matter. We can make an effort to recover the humanist's *strategic* sense of books, of their potency as vehicles of conscience and of liberating wonder. We can, in the present case, make a point of honoring Orwell's book over the discourse that would engulf it. And since this particular book is "about" the relation of discourse to power, we can allow its "truth" to penetrate and explode the usual claims of discourse at exactly those points—professional, institutional, political— where critical writing reveals its service not to literature but to its own material base. Meanwhile, too, we can look to the example of outsiders, Orwell certainly, but also Americans like Edmund Wilson and Kenneth Burke or, at this point in time, to the new movement in women's studies.

What needs addressing is our problematic role as carriers of the culture of the book now that the traditional humanist's utopian mission has failed. Do we believe, or do we not believe, that books can awaken, stabilize, and empower moral vision? Can we digest the undeniable observations of deconstruction and go on to affirm that although a book like *1984* is *merely* a fictive concoction of words it can still, nevertheless, help us live our lives and ward off despair? Is literature, as Kenneth Burke once put it, "equipment for living," and do we, or do we not, stand up for the pedagogic power of truth? I realize, of course, that for many among us *truth* has become an unword, a term seldom seen in our professionally authorized publications; but a word nonetheless that in the world of doublethink and the memory hole still retains its archaic authority. We see the pass to which we have come when we see that words like *truth* and *self* only seem certain and beyond meditation in dystopias like *1984*—or, in Zamyatin's *We*, the word *soul*. Like all things human, these words resound against the darkness of their negation. And like all things human, that words like these will prevail is not guaranteed.

That Orwell had no illusions, no object of hope near at hand, can be gathered from the way *1984* is itself left open to satiric assault. The key to Orwell's critique of humanists and their faith in books is "the book," the text within Orwell's text supposedly written by Emmanuel Goldstein, enemy of the state. Winston Smith's reading of "the book" gives Orwell an opportunity for direct political analysis; but "the book" is also the emblem of itself or any important book, *1984* included, and its fate is central to Orwell's message. Whatever might have once been the case, "the book" is now controlled by the Inner Party. Discourse has been suborned by power, and O'Brien confesses to having written some of it (before, or after, he went over to the management?). When Winston asks if what is written in "the book" is true, O'Brien answers yes, that "as description" it is true, but then he goes on to say: "The program it sets forth is nonsense. The secret accumulation of knowledge—a gradual spread of enlightenment—ultimately a proletarian rebellion—the over-throw of the Party. You foresaw that that was what it would say. It is all nonsense."

You foresaw what it would say. At the heart of Orwell's book is "the book," which accurately represents power's antiworld and puts forth, once again, the humanist's utopian program as counterforce. The program depends, for its validity, on faith in the power of truth. But if the humanistic pledge is nonsense, having been smashed by the brotherhood of O'Brienists, then from both the utopian and the O'Brienist points of view the truth shares the fate of the program—it too becomes senseless. As long as "the book" stays in the hands of the O'Brienists, it is powerless and *therefore* void of sense, its call and calling defunct, its appeal reduced to a case of the terminal jitters.

We see, then, how and perhaps also why a humanist like Winston

Smith ends up, in his professional work, a deconstructor of texts. In the grip of power, all hope gone, the utopian becomes a realist. Truth loses its authority and comes to seem nonsensical, at best a bad joke. That is one outcome of the humanist's tragedy in Orwell's estimate. Men and women once dedicated to the potency of the book turn around and willingly deface the book in doubtful hope of securing their own measly power. Better, as Nietzsche put it, to will nothingness than to have nothing to will. At which point the pen and the sword become one, equal in blood.

Channel Fire*

Hardy and the Limits of Poetry

What happens to poetry, and to the poetic regions of self-hood, when the pressure of politics begins to be too much for innocence to excuse? How does awareness of politics, and the peculiar horror of life entrapped and maimed by man-created forces, feel? And how do feelings of this kind "take place" in personal being? Questions like these suppose a vocabulary anchored in words like *self, spirit, soul*— precisely the kind of language that recent academic criticism has ruled out, but which, nevertheless, remains necessary if I continue to believe, as I do, that I exist. I can, furthermore, approach such questions in the abstract or I can turn to the concrete record of interior experience, by which of course I mean poetry. Were I to take the larger historical view, I would necessarily go back to the poetry written in the wake of the French Revolution, which is to say Romantic poetry, poems like Shelley's *Prometheus Unbound*, Wordsworth's *The Prelude*, and Blake's *Jerusalem*. But if I confine myself to the century that is my own, 1914 seems the readier starting point. With World War I, as the name itself suggests, the century entered upon an era of global violence that goes on and on, atrocity compounded exponentially, and almost *all* of it the consequence of human will and conscious effort. Since 1914 the press of politics has borne upon us like a weight of oceans. Under these

---

*"Channel Fire" was still in the process of revision at the time of the author's death. It is reprinted here, in a slightly edited form, as it appeared in *The Yale Review*, vol. 78, no. 4 (summer 1989).

circumstances we can appreciate Thomas Hardy's summary stanza in a poem commemorating the armistice of 11 November 1918:

Calm fell. From Heaven distilled a clemency;
There was peace on earth, and silence in the sky;
Some could, some could not, shake off misery;
The Sinister Spirit sneered: "It had to be!"
And again the Spirit of Pity whispered, "Why?"

The peace did not last long, nor would the sky remain silent ("A screaming comes across the sky," begins *Gravity's Rainbow*). While some among us resort to cynicism, fatalism, the doubtful benefits of immersing in the destructive element, others of us continue to ask why, as if still we could be shocked, unnerved anew by each day's ugly news, surprised, maybe, by a compassion we had thought to be, along with empathetic imagination, in very short supply. What isn't in doubt, though, is Hardy's middle line. Terrible things happen, events too foul to think upon take place, and in their wake we find ourselves divided between those who can and those who cannot shake off misery.

There is, in the general view of twentieth-century poetry, a sort of tacit agreement that Thomas Hardy stands first among our great precursors. He was not "modern" in the Modernist way; his charitable but grim sense of the world, however, and his courage facing dark forebodings make us value him the more as we review our recent past on the lookout for worthy examples of lyrical will. Hardy's characteristic mode is close to ballad and therefore proximate to song where song, given the bleakness of his vision, might least be expected—like the darkling thrush, "frail, gaunt and small," whose "evensong" seems out of place amid "so little cause for carolings." Of Hardy I would also like to say—against the belittlement of nearly all his critics—that Hardy's verse epic *The Dynasts* is one of the few long poems in English that affords me genuine poise in the reading, the kind of poem that not only survives, but bears up and bears me up with it, after the daily rundown of disasters on the news. How to face history unabashed is Hardy's constant challenge. The loss of consoling illusions urges him on. The courage of disenchanted consciousness is his deepest theme.

Alert to the signs of his time, Hardy wrote "Channel Firing," a small poem dated April 1914, first published by the *Fortnightly Review* in May of that year. War broke out barely two months later, and the poem is justly famous for its prophetic acumen. Hardy's pessimism had its reasons, one of which was politics. His poetry is tuned to the larger forces making for human misery, and in "Channel Firing" Hardy dramatizes the sudden brunt of these forces upon a community of sleepers jarred back to life by history's roar. The poem is a parable of political intrusion, worth citing entire:

> That night your great guns, unawares,
> Shook all our coffins as we lay,
> And broke the chancel window-squares,
> We thought it was the Judgment-day
>
> And sat upright. While drearisome
> Arose the howl of wakened hounds:
> The mouse let fall the altar-crumb,
> The worms drew back into the mounds,
>
> The glebe cow drooled. Till God called, "No;
> It's gunnery practice out at sea
> Just as before you went below;
> The world is as it used to be:
>
> "All nations striving strong to make
> Red war yet redder. Mad as hatters
> They do no more for Christés sake
> Than you who are helpless in such matters.
>
> "That this is not the judgment-hour
> For some of them's a blessed thing,
> For if it were they'd have to scour
> Hell's floor for so much threatening. . . .
>
> "Ha, ha. It will be warmer when
> I blow the trumpet (if indeed
> I ever do; for you are men,
> And rest eternal sorely need)."
>
> So down we lay again. "I wonder,
> Will the world ever saner be,"

Said one, "than when He sent us under
In our indifferent century!"

And many a skeleton shook his head.
"Intead of preaching forty year,"
My neighbour Parson Thirdly said,
"I wish I had stuck to pipes and beer."

Again the guns disturbed the hour,
Roaring their readiness to avenge,
As far inland as Stourton Tower,
And Camelot, and starlit Stonehenge.

The community of the dead (they talk among themselves, the speaker refers to his "neighbour") is awakened by the thunder of "gunnery practice," which, if taking place in the English Channel, could be the British or the French navy, or both, as they prepare to take on Germany. The poem begins, that is to say, with a violence that shakes the abode of the dead, that breaks the hitherto prevailing metaphysic (the chancel windows that had conveyed the light of Christendom's truth), that collapses the pastoral scene (Gray's "country church-yard" and, here, the animal kingdom), and causes a fearsome awakening that spreads through the world of the poem. As a general observation about poetry dealing with political experience, I would suggest that the beginning of any poem reveals and locates (cues or encodes) its occasion. *The Dynasts* begins with England bracing for invasion by Napoleon—again locating the moment of political intrusion in events surrounding the French Revolution. Here the occasion is unexpected violence signaling greater violence to come. The event addressed by the poet is the moment of political intrusion and the change in subsequent awareness. The great guns roar, and we dead awaken from our dream of peace.

With the alarm sounded and all earthly creatures on the alert, the voice of "God" intervenes. Hardy was not a believer but divine agencies often occur in his poetry; so do ghosts and other haunting presences, from which we gather an enormous sense of nostalgia, disciplined by Hardy's craft into the lingering presence of a time forever lost—wholly appropriate, or in fact necessary, to a poetry that situates itself firmly between two worlds, the one dead, the other ferociously birthing. The dead are as in Dante's *Inferno*; they are aware of their own past but have no direct knowledge of current affairs. God therefore brings them up-to-date. The notion of Judgment Day is being replaced by the nemesis of modern war, by nations "mad as hatters" striving each against each "to make / Red war yet redder."

As a description of events today, the lines are more accurate than any I can think of. In the poem, furthermore, the warring nations are Christianity's flower, but involved in a politics that utterly negates Christian values. Against this onslaught the dead are "helpless," and, by implication, so is God. The realms of the dead and of the divine overlap, at least in communications, but tradition and the will of the gods are impotent in the event and cannot alter or forestall tragedy even though foreseen. God will or will not be mocked; but in Hardy's poem the hour of God's judgment is in doubt, even to God ("if indeed / I ever do"). The talk about Judgment seems less a threat than does the immediate spectacle of "so much threatening," which leaves God rather more weary than wrathful. In terms of Hardy's mythological spirits, the "Sinister Spirit," or irony, which would be pleased to hear God's trumpet flatten the roaring of the guns, gives way to the "Spirit of Pity," which considers that men have already suffered enough and "rest eternal sorely need." This note of compassion, introduced midway in the poem, is one of the strategies that Hardy uses to overcome the edgy ugliness of raw political events. He shall also, as the conclusion of the poem makes clear, employ a distancing irony.

The first line of the third-to-last stanza—"So down we lay again"— suggests that things shall go on as before, that there will be no apocalypse but rather a return to "rest eternal." That, as we know, is no longer possible. First, however, two voices intervene. The first is Hardy's own, wondering if the world will someday "saner be" than it had been during his own "indifferent century." The diction here is standard Hardy. His question is ironic and rhetorical, ambivalent as Hardy always is when he contemplates the hope of historical amelioration. His suspicion is that the naïve Age of Progress is gone and that now the madness of nations will, like war, magnify beyond all sane proportion. The other voice, surmising the value of beer over preaching, is the Georgian echo of Housman. The diction of both voices is inadequate to the situation (beer and sanity against the vengeful roar), and the occasion that called forth such remarks (which are moments of epiphany to their speakers) shall also overwhelm them. At some point soon the cozy conversation of the dead will be silenced, and is: "Again the guns disturbed the hour."

If we note that the dead lay down "again," and immediately thereafter the guns "again" disturb, it becomes clear that from now on none of us, neither the living nor the dead (which I read as the communal voice of memory and tradition), will know peace. The old order suffers political intrusion, followed by collapse. A state of sleepless alarm sets in, and the new dispensation is announced by guns "Roaring their readiness to avenge."

The last stanza is central to my reading. We can see, to begin with, that the poem starts and ends with the roaring of the guns. What goes on in between—God's little peroration and the complaints of the dead—amounts to a pair of asides. Speech, language, is blotted out by the expanding (encompassing?) noise of destruction. In the beginning the dead are shaken awake by the concussion of artillery. By the end the whole of the cosmos has been invaded, concussion of a greater sort becoming universal. But it is not as simple as that. The last stanza is a careful deployment of ambiguities, meant to keep unresolved the balance between human agency and some other (but not fully known) transhuman power. Hardy could never decide if men and women are responsible for their actions or are only pawns of some "Imminent Will" that "unawares" directs all things to their ruin. Or is it, as I am inclined to think, especially when I read *The Dynasts,* that Hardy finds freedom unbearable, since freedom allows politics its horrific field day; and therefore that he introduces a high, unspecified Necessity to lift the onus from man. He transfers the cause of political agony to a blind or malignant necessity, thereby allowing the detachment and a certain consoling sense of superiority in seeing what others cannot see, the better to salvage a portion of that "rest eternal" which men, Hardy too, "sorely need." In the poem before us, the guns are first assigned to an agent definitely human ("your great guns" and the "nations striving strong"); but at the close it is solely "the guns" we hear. They have taken over the scene, and we are left to decide for ourselves the degree of human agency in the playing out of history.

But beyond that, what are we to make of the way, in the last stanza, line two is left hanging, or the way it falls with vengeful force upon lines three and four? At what is "their readiness to avenge" aimed? Have the guns usurped the role of God's Judgment? Will power be the new dispenser of justice? Is politics the new God? The poem does, I think, suggest a shift in authority from divine (and merciful) to secular (and militant) authority. The ambiguities of the concluding stanza register the change but also Hardy's uncertainty—or is it rather his hesitation to endorse the new dispensation? Yeats, in "The Second Coming," will be more open-eyed and colder about the victory of power over care. Hardy is at least sure of one thing: the coming strife disturbs the time. It creates feelings of persistent alarm and intrudes, with its intimidating roar, "As far inland" as three of Hardy's mythological centers—three locations inside the imagined world of Wessex. Stourton Tower is one of Hardy's invented place-names, suggesting fortitude and vigilance (perhaps also the prepolitical calm of Constable's Stour Valley). Camelot, which folklore and legend put somewhere between Tintagel and Glastonbury (King Arthur's supposed places of birth and burial), embodies the Victorian aspiration for a political order that would glory in a fastidious monarch and warrior class—the glamour of power, in other words, subordinate to humane, courtly values. Stonehenge, of course, recalls an even older order, emblem of energies at one with the cosmos ("starlit") and also, for Hardy, with poetry's primeval source. Against these defenses the guns direct their roar. (During World War I, people along England's south coast could hear artillery fire during the vast, mindless battles of Flanders.)

In the last stanza, therefore, we come upon an emblem of adversity that dramatizes the moment of political intrusion. Hardy's syntax keeps his meanings in motion, but the larger image of the stanza feels altogether final. The disturbance caused by the roaring of the guns reaches as far into the interior of Hardy's poetic universe as his central symbols, and these, in turn, may be seen either as a last line of defense or as under attack and in danger of imminent ruin. Which is it? Both, of course; but in the end, I think, the latter. The powers inherent in tower, court, and sacred megalith are formidable, and these landmarks of Hardy's imagination are of course the bastions of his art, the precincts of poetic, as opposed to raw political, power. But that they are his *last* defense, and that they will be overwhelmed, we can ascertain by settling issues that surround the poem's voice.

Who, we must ask, is speaking, and to whom? The guns express the destructive will of contending nations. They are also "your" guns, and we must concede that the poem is addressed to us, the living, in whose name politics goes forward and wars are fought. This poem is not addressed simply to any reader but to the specific reader whose identity is tied to "your great guns." The poem's first line therefore names us in a way that evokes our public, political character rather than in our private capacity as readers of poems. But we are also, of course, reading the poem in a private capacity, and thus we must suppose that the readiness of the guns to avenge reaches as far inland as ourselves, readers anywhere in time, whose identity (our fate as readers) is doubled, both private and political, with the political determining the private even though it was the private that got us into a position to be undermined.

As God explained things to those jarred from rest in the churchyard, so now the voice of the dead bears witness to what happened that special night, and we might expect some further night to come. The poem begins:

> That night your great guns, unawares,
> Shook all our coffins as we lay, . . .

Thus the experience of intrusion begins, and by referring to *that* night we see that the speaker is looking back to a specific point in time. The poem's voice has a past which informs its present—a past which *is*, in the manner of spiritual meaning, its present. In this connection to mention Freud's idea of "repetition compulsion," first formulated in *Beyond the Pleasure Principle,* does not seem academic merely, for it was the psychic trauma of World War I that called Freud's attention to something—a drive, an instinct, a negative energy let loose and in need of a name—compelling a pattern of apparent self-victimization. This was, for Freudian theory, a momentous turning point, for now the pleasure principle was not the whole of psychic economy. Against Eros has arisen Thanatos, and the specific data that suggested this revision to Freud were the phenomena of recurrent nightmares in war veterans suffering from "shell-shock." They were, Freud noted, doubly the victims of war, first by sustaining the trauma of the trenches, and then by feeling compelled to relive in imagination what had happened in the world over and over again—hence the concept of repetition compulsion. I would suggest that the speaker in Hardy's poem suffers in a similar way. The event to which the speaker returns is as far in the past as the distance between 1914 and now. Since *that* night the speaker has not slept— perhaps a hyperbolic way of saying that there will be no peace, anywhere, for anyone.

If through the voice of Hardy's speaker we discern Freud's traumatized soldiers, we might also make out, just barely, Coleridge's Ancient Mariner. He too has had an experience and witnessed events that he feels must be told. In the telling he intrudes upon passersby; and life, while the Mariner speaks, does not go on. The Mariner, however, speaks with a sense of urgency not to be found in the stoical voice of Hardy's poem. This is, I think, a distinction worth making, for unlike Coleridge, Hardy presents us with a voice that has no trace of guilt. Hardy's speaker is possessed by a knowing but helpless innocence. Victims of political intrusion—think of the children of Hiroshima in 1945, the children of Africa in the 1980s—are in no way implicated by what happens to them. Impersonal forces compel them to die or linger in their damaged lives, by someone's design perhaps, but not by the choice of those on whom disaster falls.

A final note about the form of "Channel Firing." It is, as we would say, a poem in the lyric mode, a form about which Northrop Frye has recently offered some useful observations in a short essay called "Approaching the Lyric." Unlike the epic, which goes on and on and which, like life, is continuous, the lyric is brief and arises partly from a moment of blockage first encountered in experience and then transcended in the voice the poem develops. And yes, in Hardy's poem the "eternal" expectations of his churchyard community are blocked by a moment of political intrusion that becomes, in turn, the occasion for privileged speech. The voice loses its earlier continuity, is awakened or "displaced," in Frye's term, and what might have been narrative becomes instead an act of concentration in which feeling and event, theme and controlling image, amalgamate with new intensity. The poem might at first appear to be narrative but on closer inspection turns out to be a node of experience encompassed by a voice. What might have been a story becomes, instead, an inscription. Uttered in a churchyard by one among the dead, "Channel Firing" becomes an epitaph.

And here Frye's further observations are especially helpful. Speaking of "the epitaph convention that we have had from Greek times on," Frye suggests a sharing of blockage and displacement which includes the reader as well as the voice of the speaker:

> Here the reader is assumed to be a traveler, pursuing his normal course through time and space, who is suddenly confronted with something he should stop and read. What he reads is the verbal essence of a life which has once had its own context in space and time but is now enclosed in a framework of words. He is often told, at the end, that he has been looking in a

mirror: his own context is still in ordinary space and time, but it will eventually disappear, and the verbal essence of *his* life may make an equally short poem.

If we take Frye's suggestion, "Channel Firing" can be read as a public call to private passersby. Intruding in this formal way, it enacts the experience which is its theme. And it is, likewise, a small case of prophecy proposing—one of the impersonal truths of politics—that all of us, speaker and reader, the living and the dead, are alike vulnerable to the poem's occasion. The specific "magic" of the epitaph, as Frye puts it, is its "power of summoning." We as readers are summoned to attend. And what we attend is the prefiguration of our own fate in a world where nations strive "to make / Red war yet redder." In the nuclear age, it seems to me, Hardy's modest little poem is as fit an epitaph as any we might wish. Except, of course, that our century hasn't been "indifferent," and with our own brand of "gunnery practice" so far advanced, it won't be God who "sent us under."

The speaker in Hardy's poem, being dead, can watch and summon but cannot, of course, partake or actively engage in political action of any sort. He represents a type, one that in our time we call the spectator, the bystander, or the witness—the one who, neither victim nor assailant, neither the agent of power nor its object, nevertheless feels morally involved by virtue of seeing or coming to know that terrible things transpire, that political mutilation goes on, now in one place, now in another, nonstop. We know that in many places today, for example, men and women are being tortured at exactly this moment, as I write, as you read. I live with the awareness, furthermore, that my life is shadowed by such ugly goings-on. This kind of knowledge, oblique and depressing, is part of a general political sense that, like any other cultural atmosphere or climate of opinion, everyone now shares (and to say so ought not to be construed as moralizing or casting blame). Somewhere in the world, as Auden reminds us in "Musée des Beaux Arts," "it takes place" while the rest of us are "eating or opening a window or just walking dully along." The peculiar horror of torture is precisely that it takes place within the human universe along with everything else. We speak almost by rote of man's inhumanity to man, a shorthand formula for political intrusion of the grosser sort; but in rare moments, when the weight of those words becomes real, the evil we intuit is more than mere external spectacle. It reveals itself as "a wound in the order of being." The latter phrase is Martin Buber's, made in reference to the concentration camps but with a relevance that feels almost engulfing, politics now being a general tendency toward ravagement that with the bomb can in an instant "take out" everything.

We know the old lament: After such knowledge, what forgiveness? But then we turn to another old saw that in our time sounds almost inspired: Life must, we say, go on. And therefore we proceed with our business, now and then discomforted by intrusions that catch us unprepared, as when, for example, the evening news flashes from some natural disaster (the province of theology) to the sudden spectacle of mangled bodies in the wake of a terrorist bombing (the province of politics). Television is tricky like that: you tune in for the results of an election or a tournament and before you know it you are smack in the middle of mayhem. In its ability to catch us off guard, the medium is mimetic of terror itself, or even, as critics sometimes suppose, a ringside participant—though not, I would add, by special purpose but rather by the nature of the events being "covered."

Terrorism is, after war, the most dramatic and also the most lucidly enacted example of politics intruding. Power and terror go hand in hand, either the state brand of Stalinism and the current death squad or the antistate kind perpetrated by small groups against power systems that cannot be opposed directly. In its dealings with Latin America, for example, the United States has fostered both; in El Salvador the bulk of the killing goes on with government sanction, while in Nicaragua it is the work of the contras, a band of terrorists created by the CIA. Serious political analysis would require hard distinctions, but in terms of spectators like ourselves what hits us first about terror is violence pure and simple, which is by definition unexpected, highly visible to those for whom its message is intended, a moment of instant destruction upon unsuspecting passersby.

Terrorism is inherently political, and its target is always the personal integrity of impersonal flesh. As a phenomenon occurring everywhere on earth, terrorism is specific to the modern age (national in the nineteenth century, international in the twentieth), and it depends for its full effect upon public recognition. Theoretically, at least, the circumstance that gives terrorism its universal character is that both the assailant and the victim can be—in fact must be—anyone. One of terror's functional goals is to create the impression that "anyone" means "everyone."

Terrorism, that is to say, strikes any place at any time, although for practical purposes some situations—airplanes, for example, or areas where large numbers of people gather randomly—are more vulnerable than others. In all cases, however, the "terror" in terrorism arises from the reduction of essence to deceptive appearance, the draining of reliable meaning from places and from persons, as when, potentially at least, the agent of political violence may be the person sitting next to you. In cases of state terror it will not be the stranger but rather your intimate friend who betrays you; an informer is successful only if trusted, as Osip Mandelstam discovered to his harm. In antistate situations, on the other hand, the agent appears to be "merely" a stranger, and since most of the world consists of strangers, the terrorist is, quite literally, anyone beyond one's private circle. With technical advances in explosives, timing devices, and the like, the agent of terrorist attacks is increasingly invisible, the man or woman who plants the bomb and then disappears, in which case the world itself, or certain parts of it, can no longer be trusted. Terrorism aims to dissolve social bonds, to render all of us suspect to each other, and finally to destroy not merely public trust but also that deeply human "basic trust" on which good being-in-the-world depends. In the specific event, violence is randomly visited upon innocent victims for political reasons. But in its wider consequence it touches everyone, intrudes everywhere, damaging private being as well as public order.

Whereas terrorism assumes that privacy does not exist and attacks its victim as a public entity, torture deliberately invades its victim's privacy with the clear intention of destroying the self's interior world. Moments of overwhelming pain obliterate both the self and its world. In *The Body in Pain,* a remarkable study of "the making and unmaking" of the human world, Elaine Scarry observes that in torture the function of interrogation is not to detect lying or discover information but by asking a sequence of questions to determine at what point the victim can no longer speak. Torture takes away from its victims the capacity for language, increasing pain until words collapse into the prelanguage void of nonsensical cries. At *this* stage political intrusion becomes absolute— rather worse, victims testify, than death.

The thing to hold in mind is that both kinds of intrusion, both torture and terrorism, are representations of power; the violence, in both cases, is compelled politically and is furthermore an act of announcement. Both phenomena are worth careful study, especially for what they reveal about the nature of power in our century. What is new is not terrorism itself but that it has entered the political arena as a permanent part of the world, an immediate part of what *politics* means; and we are less than honest to talk as if "declaring war on terrorism" will stop groups encouraged by the international market in arms and munitions, any more than war in general will stop the kind of terror that is government's left hand. Terrorism is here to stay, the more so as, on the one hand, governments keep order by increasing resort to open force, or, on the other hand, as billion-dollar systems of superweapons eliminate old-style conventions of military engagement between superpowers and small nations. We get an inkling of the madness of our time if we simply stop to consider that terrorism is, among other things, a politics of despair.

Torture may also, in the hands of oppressive regimes, turn out to be politics rooted in despair. In her analysis of its structure, Elaine Scarry shows that torture is the end game of governments aware of their own instability, a ritual meant to create the illusion of absolute power. If Scarry is correct, as the world grows more unstable the list of countries using torture routinely, already shockingly long, will grow longer. To think that before World War I torture had all but disappeared! Now it is epidemic, one of the darkest signs of the times. We still respond to instances of torture as if each were an exception, the practice itself being so exceptionally repugnant—but torture has become commonplace, in the "free world" no less (possibly more, as recent reports suggest) than in the Eastern bloc.

Torture is likewise, in state practice, a means of terror. Citizens of Turkey, for example, or Chile or South Korea (places governed by vicious regimes backed by the United States) know that if they speak out they run the risk, terribly real, of having their capacity to speak violently excised. This was certainly the case in Iran under the shahs and during the time of the juntas in Greece and Argentina—clear examples of power in despair, and, I should add, also regimes strongly supported by our own government. I bring up the American connection to free-world terrorism not to moralize in the usual useless way but only to point out that we, who pride ourselves on our democratic institutions and have a "voice" in governing and in the making of policy abroad as well as at home, we are, all of us, thereby granting approval (and sending military and economic aid) when our nation's leaders make allowance for the politics of terror in cases we consider "friendly." To govern by terror, with the torture chamber holding the center, means to silence by generalized fear and specific physical injury the very process of "voicing" that, in America, we celebrate. How much *actual* connection any of us has to political decision making is doubtful, but from the literary rather than the political point of view, what counts is this: the public fact that our government pledges its support to terrorist regimes in many parts of the "free world" increases, concretely, the pressure upon us to know that awful things take place, somewhat like a sea of silent screaming, around this isle of relative peace and plenty. Naturally we are more alert to events in which, at whatever remove, we can feel involved. The shock comes when, one day, we discover that we *are* involved. Thinking on the nature of political intrusion, it would appear that in our time "the shock of recognition" means waking up to politics.

A case in point is the potent combination of American innocence and client-state terror that, until its collapse, was known as the shah's Iran. Reza Baraheni has written a lucid account of that state's use of torture, having himself enjoyed the benefit of firsthand experience. His book, part history, part personal testimony, is called *The Crowned Cannibals* and was published in America in English translation, with an introduction by E. L. Doctorow, in 1977. I stress the year of publication because the shah fell from power two years later, in 1979; yet anyone reading Baraheni's book would know beyond reasonable doubt that the work of SAVAK, the shah's torture team and death squad (advised by our CIA), was making inevitable, by horrid provocation and the need for self-defense, *some* kind of indigenous revolt. Clearly, though, President Carter and his staff did not read reports of this kind. Nor, I would venture to guess, has Baraheni's book—or the hundreds like it—made its way into the hands of most of our poets. (I often wonder what American poets read, I mean apart from each other.) If literature of this kind were to become a part of our general reading, the whole of Whitman's progeny would have to reassess what it might mean to be, in today's world, a celebrator of American language.

Iran under the shah was an example of American-sponsored government by terror that has done infinite harm, not only to its native citizens under the shah, but to those who later suffered under Khomeini, and also accounts for the decline in American political confidence thanks to the 444-day hostage crisis in Tehran (with all that *that* continues to entail). Iran under the shah was truly terrible, and reading *The Crowned Cannibals* we begin to see that the current Iranian madness didn't come out of nowhere, that what we might like to take as groundless fanatical rage has, in fact, practical causes such as one might sit down and itemize in Baraheni's fashion. He gives us, for example, whole pages listing nothing but the names of poets and scholars murdered by the shah's police. And then, too, there is his own story, which starts this way:

> I am given seventy-five blows on the soles of my feet with a plaited wire whip; one of my fingers is broken; I am threatened with the rape of my wife and daughter; then a pistol is held to my head at the temple by another torturer, Dr. Azudi, and, in fact, I hear it fired. I faint.

At one point the following exchange occurs, instructive for the way the issue of "literature" dissolves into "the language of all men and beasts":

> "What were you doing in the United States?"
> "Teaching."
> "What?"
> "Literature."
> "What kind of literature?"
> "English literature."
> "What! What!" he shouts, almost driven from his senses.
> "English literature." It is my turn now to be cool.
> "You mean you were teaching Americans English literature?"
> "Yes, Professor," I answer, as cool as before.
> "Liar! You are a damn fool liar."
> "I taught English literature, and that is the plain truth."
> He turns to Dr. Hosseini, who sits behind his desk almost as lifeless as a tree trunk in freezing winter weather.
> "Dr. Hosseini, do you want to speak English to him? Do you want me to, so that you can see he doesn't even know English?"
> "I don't know, Professor. I cannot be the judge of that. I don't know the language of *az ma behtaran* [those who are better than we], but"—and here he points to the cable whip hanging from the nail on the wall—"if you want, I can make him sing like a nightingale, crow like a raven, howl like a dog. You tell me, and I'll make him speak the language of all men and beasts."

The scene, as Baraheni unfolds it, is highly rendered, an artful representation of what I take to be an actual incident. I might add that Baraheni, when he refers to himself, isn't always "cool." Here, however, he is speaking of literature and has the dignity of his own art to empower him. The scene described above suggests exactly how, in a political situation at its negative extreme, what begins as literature comes down to howling like a dog. And in fact, this particular encounter between Baraheni and his tormentors continues when, after slapping him in the face for a while, they try the psychological approach: they bring in another man, blindfolded, who is taken to a part of the room concealed by a curtain, and the scene continues:

> Then someone is screaming at the top of his voice and saying words that are utterly inhuman and incomprehensible. I know that in the torture chamber people forget humanity's most precious gift—language—and turn into beasts.

We can see, I trust, that the aim of torture is precisely that—to render words "utterly inhuman," to take from us our capacity to speak and in so doing take from us our capacity to humanly be. To me, at least, torture is therefore a key to the connection between power and the politics of despair, on the one hand, and politics and poetry on the other. When men begin to tear the flesh of other men and of women and also children, power stands at its most naked. And the aim of all this mutilation, this radical irreverence toward the physical human body, isn't merely pain or the exercise of power but the use of pain and power's exercise to demonstrably destroy the "soul," the "spirit,"—that within us from which our deepest selfhood flows. And what we learn, observing this process, is that politics isn't only an intrusive force disrupting private being, but also an active force, whose enemy is language—the ability to speak out, to utter accurate words, to simply say.

I bring up these unpleasant issues because in their extremity they illustrate unmistakably what I mean by the experience of political intrusion. Terrorism ignores, torture attacks the privacy of inward being. The victim's specific humanity is denied or slowly leeched out. In one case we are treated as objects, in the other we are reduced to objects by degree. In both cases the personal integrity of the victims is infringed upon and destroyed. My aim, in any case, has been to draw a distinction between *politics* proper, considered as voluntary involvement in power, as active commitment to or against orders of governing, and *political experience,* which is often wholly passive, which like any other experience creates feelings and emotions specific to its kind of occasion, and which, finally, alters the interior world of personal being by virtue of the need to accommodate forces and conditions not, by choice or personal destiny, a part of one's own unfolding.

To consider situations in which the personal realm is usurped by the political realm is to speak of poetry and politics in collision. And this collision, the violence, horror, and possible splendor of its happening, is my direct concern. What becomes of poetry, how does it help us, in such moments? With the extreme case of torture as evidence, it would seem that the human spirit or, less grandly, the autonomous presence of self depends on language, on being able to speak and thereby represent oneself, one's relation to events, one's presence in the world by virtue of the verbal object one creates. In this respect, poetry can be defined (or simply recognized) as language self-consciously deploying the fullest panoply of its resources (material, symbolic, somatic) for strategic purposes. Or, as Kenneth Burke might say, poetry is "symbolic action," each poem a strategy for encompassing a situation. Like it or not, we find our being *in* the world. The great question, to which poetry offers provisional answers, is *how* to be in the world.

The situation of the beholder or the witness, as I have outlined it, is ludicrous in terms of moral obligation but powerfully felt all the same, which is perhaps why Hardy assigned it to one among the dead who may at least be forgiven his or her failure to take action in the face of imminent threat. When it comes to the coming of war or to something as ugly but remote as the system of apartheid in South Africa, there isn't much in any direct or immediately effective sense that can be done by anyone save those with real positions in a real structure of power. Unfortunately, for those in power it can perhaps be said that more often than not there is in the world one grid of power that contending sides uphold even in war—for example, the Cold War embrace which forces all nations to choose sides even though only two, the United States and the Soviet Union, directly perpetuate the global crisis. Those in power can be counted on to defend, first of all, their own claim to power, which often enough means abetting the enemy rather than giving up the deadly game. Those with no power except words, on the other hand, must seem at best no more than mosquitos nipping at Behemoth. So it goes.

Meanwhile, however, we continue to behold, every morning in the press and, via satellite, every evening on the network news reports, the accumulated evils of the time. Insofar as we know about events around the globe, we receive our information in mediated form, as "news," and the news, as we know, gives most of its coverage to disasters. To the complaint that the news ought to be more upbeat, the answer is what it always was. If bearers of bad news are unwelcome and regularly chastised for their efforts, the case is that we still need to know about events and developments in order to alert ourselves to possible dangers and, given the dangers, possible remedies or means of cutting our losses. The news is to society as the nerves are to the human body: they report all sensations, but only pain registers deeply and provokes us to action. At best and at worst, the media—journalism, television, the arts of information—constitute our early-warning system. In the electronic age we receive great quantities of instant information, and with cameras stationed everywhere on earth we are literally wired into the world— the *whole* world—and gain a kind of consciousness never before experienced by mankind. The disturbing outcome is an overload of terrible stories about which we understand little and can do even less. We are, all of us, more than a little like Hardy's dead. We exist quietly among our own but are perpetually shaken by alarms of every sort, until finally we awaken to a kind of passive moral insomnia that can be assuaged only as the speaker in "Channel Firing" handles his or her distress—by speaking out, disburdening by putting the burden into words.

What needs emphasis, with Hardy's poem in mind, is that while at every moment many men and women and children are the victims of unwise policies and systems based on injustice, many more of us are moved by compassion, by imagination's urge to suffer with, to be troubled, often very deeply troubled, by suffering not actually our own and which we might, but somehow do not, put out of mind. There are, then, two kinds or stages of political intrusion. First comes the event, in which some human beings suffer at the hands of other human beings. Second come the moral repercussions of the event, as we receive it into consciousness and therefore, since it hurts to behold others being hurt, into our selves as well. I am deliberately taking for granted that human beings do care about the fate of others elsewhere, at least to the extent that imagination can be made to come alive and allow the spirit entrance to other people's pain. To respond in this way wouldn't seem to take much courage, yet a great many people shy away from this minimal degree of involvement, perhaps wisely in some cases; feeling impotent in the face of serious suffering is an affront to one's own self-respect. Beyond that, the ability to respond rather rapidly transmutes into response-ability, something felt as weakness by those who do or wish to exercise power. Power of the political kind is always impersonal, always takes other people as tools, functions, discardable objects to use and use up. But insofar as I can imagine my way out of myself and across to another's condition, I follow the logic of poetry rather than the logic of power, and in dreamwork of this kind responsibility begins.

Poets like Hardy, Wilfred Owen, William Carlos Williams were blessed with great funds of empathetic imagination—what Keats called negative capability, the genius for perceiving another creature's being. Other poets—Pound, Eliot, Stevens—possessed imagination of a more insular kind, which suggests that not all poetry arises from the kind of imagining that takes the self out of itself into the world. Imagination can just as well compel the self into a world of its own making. Either kind can be useful to poetry which takes on political experience. One can focus exclusively on one's own encounters with power or on one's own reaction to political intrusion at the level of the spectator and go as far as those who say, with Nietzsche, that the world is bearable only from an aesthetic point of view. This latter strategy has served well enough in the past but may now have reached its limit—for with electronic overload, how much information, how many political events of hateful consequence can even the most solipsistic imagination process aesthetically? The end of pure aestheticism is despair. That imagination is excited by power I take for granted, and the old solution, Shakespeare's for example, was to make the leap from terror to the sublime. But as Edmund Burke reminds us in his treatise on beauty and the sublime, vast and terrible things appear sublime only *at a distance*. Mystification, power's majestic mumbo-jumbo, works its magic from afar. At some miles distant, to judge from film and pictures, the spectacle of a nuclear explosion comes at one with a grandeur that surpasses understanding. I have also, however, seen films and pictures of the victims, and then the terror, which is the secret heart of the sublime, is restored.

On Governing Narratives

The Turkish-Armenian Case

> . . . the struggle of man against power is the strug-
> gle of memory against forgetting.
> —Milan Kundera

It has been suggested—by Umberto Eco, by the loquacious diner in *My Dinner with André*—that a new Middle Ages is coming or perhaps upon us even now. With the superpowers locked into battle formation, the world becomes a global patchwork of enclaves and vassal states, very like a feudal order. Political behavior is determined less by reason than by martial dependencies, and the integrity of knowledge is preserved, if at all, in ways resembling the monastic practices of medieval Europe. The emergence of a new feudalism threatens many older dreams, not least our hope in progress through enlightenment (that the truth shall make us free), now being displaced by a more recent faith in salvation by force (that godlike weapons will prevail). A further consequence is that knowledge is no longer honored for its utopian promise, but valued for the services it furnishes. These developments have already done much to define us. What they signal is a wholesale shift in our story of ourselves, a turn in worldview that can be formulated this way: Our earlier narrative of enlightenment, in which knowledge is the privileged agent of liberty, has been set aside as more and more we take our sense of things from the nuclear narrative of armageddon, a story in which all privilege, including the privilege of truth, depends flat out upon power.

The figures of enlightenment and armageddon are examples, as I would call them, of *governing narratives*. They are presiding fictions that allow us to behold ourselves and make sense of the historical world, and by them the status of knowledge is affected in intimate ways. A striking illustration (I shall use it throughout) comes from the conflict surrounding Turkey's determined effort to deny that the Armenian genocide of 1915 took place. The academic-political quarrel between Turks and Armenians—which has included intimidation on the one hand, terrorist attacks on the other—is not a special case but rather, in its sad remorseless way, a compact sign of the times. Our own government, furthermore, sees fit to be involved; and if we rule out (or at least bracket) villainy pure and simple, we are free to consider the role of governing narratives in a case where the central issue is power versus truth.

Until recently the facts of the Armenian genocide were thought to be certain beyond dispute—more than a million people destroyed in the space of a year, the men cordoned and shot, women and children scourged, ravaged, force-marched across the Anatolian plain and into the deserts of Syria to die of thirst and starvation. Our own official archives are thick with firsthand evidence, and many additional sources exist, including the state papers of several nations, eyewitness documentation, journalistic reports, and testimony by survivors and their children. As much as any historical event can be known, this one is known. What then has happened? How has it come about that increasingly we hear there are "two sides" to every issue, including even this one, and that the time has come to give the other side—the Turkish side—its rightful hearing? Can there be a full alternative? Or has the old and honored method of hearing both sides become a gimmick for turning history on its head and allowing the interests of the Turkish government to occupy center stage? Two sides, the revision begins—and then we are told no genocide took place but only a vague unfortunate mishap determined by imponderables like time and change, the hazards of war, uncertain demographics. There is a commonsense sound to the Turkish proposal, but to simply insist on "equal time" cannot be the whole of it, especially when the Turkish side (as we shall see) bolsters its case by exploiting its position as part of a global power system that reaches from Ankara to Washington, a Western system that stands in a posture of war against a second, Eastern system, with both sides dedicated less to truth than to power. Turkey's denial of the Armenian disaster is backed by something larger than mere doubt, and it's here that the connection between contempt for truth and the requirements of Cold War politics come into view.

Historical revisionism is at present very much in the air. If the Holocaust was a hoax, why not the Armenian catastrophe also? If Anne Frank's diary was faked, who's to say that certain documents signed by Talaat Pasha weren't forged as well? Over particulars there can, of course, be endless quibbling. If one wishes to contest a footnote, or to dispute some fact in isolation, one can bring the process of historical recovery to a halt. But verification of past events does not depend on one kind of information merely. It is precisely the convergence of different orders of evidence (official, private, institutional, material) that gives history its substance, and, in the end, problems specific to historiography will be handled by historians.

There are, however, other issues at stake, in particular these: What has happened to the argument that there are two sides to everything, which once worked to foster truth but now works against it? How does information overload undermine the older, critical role of knowledge in favor of newer practices that are more commodity-oriented? What does it mean when a client state like Turkey can persuade a superpower like the United States to abandon its earlier stance toward the genocide of 1915–16? And finally, what is happening to the university if increasing numbers of scholars occupy positions funded or promoted by governments and have no ethical or professional qualms about work that aims, sometimes less, sometimes more, to shore up the official claims of nation-states? These are among the developments that allow Turkish denial to go forward. In ways like these the pressure of Cold War politics distorts information, demotes the university to a station of service, and redefines "truth" as that which can be made to prevail.

That there are two sides to every issue is not in itself a bad thing. Liberal education and the democratic process both require a critical survey of options before the process of judgment can be counted on to get to the heart of the matter. The two-sides method ensures a margin of fairness, although of course the vantage of detachment is sometimes abused—as when the passions of advocacy are held to be ungainly or naïve. Still, this essentially critical method has had a long history and important applications. Its origins lay in the eighteenth century, where the two-sides argument worked to discount the constrictive authority of Church and monarchy, and thereby encouraged liberties essential to capital in its open-market phase, to liberalism as a political philosophy, and to the new notion of progress through education. Before its wedding with the state, capitalism offered critical habits of mind an important power base, but critical thinking grew quickly to be its own champion. Pluralism was good for business, business was good for pluralism, and both helped liberal ideas—one of which was that official views ought to submit to critical examination.

At the onset of the modern age, therefore, insisting upon the existence of two sides to every issue helped limit established power and allowed for the nurturing of liberties, among them liberty of thought. Thanks also to the new prestige of science, knowledge took on the character of an autonomous enterprise and truth became a power unto itself. Intellectual confidence grew strong enough to contradict the state, and the modern enterprise of critical thinking got off to a goodly start. The further development, however, is that our Enlightenment heritage now finds itself endangered. A new kind of despotism begins to make itself felt, one in which endorsement of the two-sides argument works against the freedoms it was meant to foster. There are still, of course, different sides to the issues we confront, but increasingly the side that counts is the one that speaks with power's voice.

What has happened is that the two-sides argument has degenerated into mere relativism on the one hand, and on the other into the mechanical belief that there must always be "another" point of view. A sort of emptiness has developed at the heart of the critical enterprise, and power has been quick to fill the vacuum. We can say, I think, that the kind of care for truth that insisted on reviewing the evidence has given way to a bewildered skepticism that ends up accepting official positions. Skepticism of this sort is widespread and is part of the revolution in knowledge itself. This is, after all, the age of information, and the program of liberal education, which cultivates the virtues of a definite point of view, has been ambushed by information overload and by the ways flow charts and data systems scatter critical focus. There is no center and nothing holds still. Information becomes fluid and facts dissolve into digital codes. The world comes at us from all sides, and how we handle it depends less on thinking and judging than on the computer programs someone (someone?) writes to do our thinking for us.

None of this defeats historical knowledge, but truth becomes harder to pin down and disinformation easier to spread. One's ability to distinguish fact from propaganda falters amid the nonstop flow of images, printouts, publications, and media events from every corner of the globe. With so many sides to so many issues, we are susceptible to any voice more insistent than our own that tells us which side counts. At this point, unfortunately, we abnegate the rights and duties of critical questioning and turn the making of decisions over to experts and technicians or to officials in high places. Humbled by those who possess "the big picture," we lose our conviction that independent learning leads to truth. Knowledge is no longer the mind's ground of judgment but a commodity for hire. What one knows is neither true nor false, but rather what happens to be worth knowing.

And thus we reach the point of full reversal. The belief that there are two sides to every issue once supported liberty and set earnest minds in contest with the status quo. Now the two-sides method opens up a multitude of perspectives and allows every position its expert opinion. And of expert opinion—backed by talk-show glamour and political clout—there is no end. As John Newhouse put it in *The New Yorker* (July 22, 1985), "Reality in the nuclear age tends to become what people whose voices carry say it is." At worst, the predicament of knowledge comes down to this: When we turn to examine hard questions, we discover that smart people with impeccable credentials can certify any side of any issue.

If, then, we ask how an American client state can contravene historical truth and dissolve knowledge into a productive uncertainty—how the government of Turkey finds the resources to pursue its program of denial—we must start with the fact that deep changes are occurring in our attitudes toward knowledge. And here I come back to the notion of "governing narratives." Those of us in the knowledge industry must now accommodate two unconnected stories of ourselves, two grand designs of worldly destiny in which very different roles are assigned to learning and its uses. To anyone schooled in Enlightenment values, the older narrative is familiar. Its protagonist is *the hero of knowledge,* one whose task is the pursuit of truth in the cause of progress, especially the kind of moral and social advance that increases general liberty. In the new narrative, on the other hand, the central figure is *the hero of power,* one whose professional skill enhances the political charisma and technical capacity of the state to which—East or West—one happens to belong.

These narratives are mythical, of course, but that does not diminish our need to have them inform our thinking and organize our actions.

The real point is the difference between them. The older story depicts history as an upward struggle that one day allows knowledge to overcome ignorance and create a world in which truth and liberty are available to everyone. The hero of knowledge is heroic because his or her learning becomes the means through which the retrograde forces of established systems can be opposed and overcome. In this narrative, therefore, knowledge is not merely a tool but an active agency converting little by little. Leviathan itself—the whole dense mesh of circumstance that stands in truth's way.

The new narrative, on the other hand, is Manichaean and militaristic, and the hero of power is heroic because he or she assists the state in the urgency of its needs, needs called "security" or "national interest" or whatever, but always exaggerated with crisis and magnified still further by the apocalyptic stance of the superpowers in their bid for global supremacy. Within this framework history is static and events are tactical. Nothing substantial changes until, in the moment of armageddon, everything changes. Then the battle will be fought and the other side will fall. Meanwhile the superpowers strain to enforce their spheres of influence, and what we behold are two very similar empires staking out the world between them. They do not attack each other directly, but keep the conflict going symbolically (through spectacle and image) and by proxy (through strife between respective client states). The militarization of the world accounts for the latter. The suborning of knowledge is part of the former.

Our governing narratives oppose each other, but their function is the same in either case. Both assign the flux of human energies an order and a destiny. Both are also utopian, since in both cases a victory is projected that will someday turn the world into a wholly good place. But while the future justifies everything, it accounts for nothing; each narrative therefore must be judged by its present impact. The hero of knowledge, for example, is decidedly more discerning and more wary of force than the hero of power. In the story of enlightenment, furthermore, truth plays a leading role, whereas in the story of empire the truth is at best a reckless element, a sort of wild card in a deck that otherwise is tightly stacked. Power, it goes without saying, is hostile to unindentured knowledge. Both narratives, finally, are vastly abstract, but this does not mean that they lack actuality. Their base, in fact, is history itself.

Looking back, we can see that the narrative of progress was substantiated by an array of positive changes, among them the rapid expansion of capital and the rise of an educated middle class; the general increase in wealth and material well-being; the success of scientific method with its steady advances in technology; and not least, America itself, the New World endless in opportunity. The narrative of confrontation, on the other hand, is founded on conditions almost systematic in their negativity, including the recolonization of the globe by the superpowers; the decay of human rights and increased reliance on force; the end of openness on earth and the consequent move to occupy the sky; and finally, the shutting down of the future that results from nuclear threat. If this sounds overly dramatic, it may be that the narrative of power is inherently hysterical. Its signs point always to crisis and danger.

Narratives that make purposive sense of the world are fictional, but their challenge is real. How, for example, shall the patient narrative of enlightenment survive the more urgent narrative of confrontation? How do we in the academy expect to be heard against the shouting of Cold War alarms? I mean to say that knowledge is in trouble because historical conditions have changed and a situation has arisen that no longer sustains a story of ourselves in which truth is the principal agent determining our destiny. Now it is power that rules, and destiny gives way to fate. We live in the nuclear Cold War world, where knowledge is power's servant and truth is what the state decrees. That, at least, is how things look to those who have moved from the narrative of enlightenment to the narrative of armageddon. With the superpowers ready to annihilate each other, many among us believe that what counts is the battle itself—the earth, after all, is at stake—a struggle to be won by every means that power can summon. And knowledge, of course, is among the means that power summons.

Our universities and research centers are therefore caught between governing narratives and can be useful to either. This means that we have come to a parting of ways. In the nuclear era there isn't room for ivory-tower innocence. As politics invades our lives, our professional lives especially, we cannot escape the necessity of commitment, and our choice will depend on the governing narrative that seems to each of us more real—or more worthy. One solution is to take a position inside the structures of power and speak with the authority that power confers. Those who take that path subscribe to the narrative of empire and may honestly think that the function of knowledge is to support the state in its hour of ultimate need. The other solution—the militant course in a militant time—is to set one's work against any approach to, or from, the agencies of power, eschewing ideologies of every stripe, left, right, or deceptive middle. The unpalatable fact today is that political order requires the subservience of knowledge. For scholars repelled by politics, the best solution may be to revive the adversary stance of eighteenth-century *philosophes* like Voltaire or Diderot and take up an oppositional or antithetical style of inquiry. What this means in practice is to proceed with doubt toward all things official. Suspension of belief has always been our right, but like other rights, this one needs defending.

The political control of truth quite naturally calls up Orwellian impressions, but in fact the manipulation of knowledge goes deeper than censorship and is more subtle than outright propaganda. It can include conditions under which research will be funded and given a forum, and also the designation of legitimacy to be conferred or withheld in specific fields of inquiry. Jobs, tenure, professional advancement, all can come to depend on taking the approved line. Along with these comes the adjacent phenomenon of the "institute" and "think tank," in most cases with official backing of one sort or another. And then too, there is the way universities pressure their faculties to bring in big money by securing government projects. What all this scrambling means is that in the struggle of memory against forgetting we must compete with official versions and special interests, with public and private demands for serviceable knowledge, with the kinds of on-line information geared to short-term needs. Amid this din the scholar's independent voice is hard to hear.

We who pride ourselves on learning must now decide if research is to become the service industry that governments require. We are accustomed to denigrating Marxist distortions, and we point with scorn to situations in which Soviet scholars produce results useful to the state. Such cases are highly visible, and the machinery of coercion, which includes exile and imprisonment, makes the Soviet example impressive. But coercion may take other forms as well. I've mentioned appointments and grants, which reminds us that the economic factor is always active. We might also recall the general bias of professionalism, which opens its best avenues of advancement to those whose methods are duly authorized. And not least, there is always the influence of nationality, by which I mean the need to display in one's work a patriotic spirit, especially in times of political stress. At its worst, pressure of this kind becomes McCarthyist; at its best, the gentle nudge of commonweal. And over everything, the profounder nudge of the governing narrative.

The political manipulation of truth is ruinous to any free society—to the scholarly community especially, for if we cannot trust our standards and each other, our enterprise is groundless. Perhaps, however, my description of this threat is too extreme. Perhaps the clash of governing narratives cannot breach the kind of above-the-fray practice that has always been our pride. We can agree that things go badly behind the Iron Curtain, and the example of Nazi Germany is ever before us. But surely in our academies and among our intellectuals, the life of the mind bends to no one. At least among peoples of the Free World, research and learning go forward without interference or intimidation, or so we presume and often boast. But of course our "academic freedom" is abused, sometimes grievously. When it comes to examples of power ordering knowledge, there is no shortage East or West; and in fact, as Edward Said suggests in *Covering Islam,* these coercive namings of empire—"the West" in contest with "the East"—underlie our failing capacity to make sense of current events. Even so, the Turkish example seems worth remarking, not only because Turkey is high on the list of Free World defenders (second only to Israel and Egypt in American military aid), but because the Turkish attack on truth exemplifies the triumph of the new governing narrative, the one in which truth is fugitive and knowledge consorts with power.

It was once fashionable to expend one's pity upon the "starving Armenians," a sort of teatime sympathy requiring no action but at least recognizing Turkey's attempt, during the war, to exterminate its Armenian population. It is now fashionable to be shocked at Armenian terrorists and to sympathize with "the Turkish side of the story." This sort of windblown compassion, as I have suggested, is not autonomous; it is, rather, an expression of changes in political climate. During World War I, when Turkey was allied with Germany, the governments of Great Britain and the United States vigorously condemned the genocide then in progress. By 1923, however, when Turkey achieved its status as a modern nation-state, political allegiance began to shift to accommodate the Cold War alignment. As a traditional enemy of Russia, Turkey was worth wooing; and as the Cold War warmed up, the geopolitical importance of Turkey—its strategic position on the border of the Soviet Union, its willingness to transform Mount Ararat into an outpost for Western surveillance—worked to inhibit criticisms of official Turkish policy then and now. As Jeane Kirkpatrick made clear in her defense of American client states, political regimes "friendly" to the United States are generally acceptable, no matter what military abuse or contempt for human rights might then require coverup. Kirkpatrick's distinction between "authoritarian" and "totalitarian" governments is a prime example of how the narrative of empire works to sort out the world. And so it comes about that, at a time when Turkey refuses to admit a genocide occurred, our State Department backs off from its own extensive records and designates the Armenian affair as "alleged"—something in the manner of a back-country rumor.

Officially, that is what the Armenian genocide has become—a sort of distant rumor. Nothing that happened in the hinterlands of Anatolia so long ago can matter to the balance of power in the nuclear age. Governments have always required short-term memory, but never more than now. The historical record either enhances or it hinders the ongoing process of propaganda, and the Free World doesn't need ugly events to question its virtue. At a time when the charisma of national images plays a key role in the symbolic conduct of Cold War encounters, events that contradict the image are officially *not true*. This, in fact, is the definition of *truth* for those who subscribe to the narrative of power, and the new criterion is this: *consistency with system*. Truth bends to that which is consistent with the program of empire, and what we see, when we observe the Turkish denial of the Armenian tragedy, is a small but vigorous example of the program in action. We see an American client state trading its loyalty for American endorsement of an image that it, the client state, thinks it has a right to. This image then becomes integral to the world order it helps to uphold. And it is, finally, consistent with the general pattern of righteousness that Western power uses to promote itself. We begin to understand, therefore, why the Turkish denial of the Armenian catastrophe involves more than Levantine intrigue or the usual deceit among nations. We are confronting a coherent way of representing the world, not specific to Turkey, but in the Turkish case too visible to overlook.

When it comes to power ordering knowledge, there could hardly be a more open example than the circumstances surrounding the International Conference on the Holocaust and Genocide that took place in Tel Aviv in the summer of 1982. As Israel Charny and others have documented (in a commentary on the proceedings entitled *The Conference Program and Crisis*), when the conference was being planned, officials of the Israeli government importuned certain scholars to stay away. This extraordinary action was in response to messages from representatives of Turkey who had approached the Israeli foreign ministry with remarks about the well-being of Turkish Jews, remarks that might have been vague and indirect but that caused officials in Israel to attempt to abort the conference. "There was a sense," says Charny, "that actual Jewish lives were at stake." Suddenly, leaders of Jewish communities in the United States and elsewhere were advising that the conference might better be canceled. The spiritual head of the conference, Elie Wiesel, decided (after a visit from Turkish representatives and messages from the Israeli government) that he could not attend, citing danger to the lives of Jews in the Middle East. According to *The New York Times* (June 3, 1982), which interviewed Wiesel in Paris, "the Turks let it be known there would be serious difficulties if Armenians took part in the conference."

The conference took place as planned, which speaks well for intellectual courage, but the point to keep in mind is that *political* interests were mobilized against an *academic* meeting. It was a gathering of scholars, nothing less and nothing more, learned men and women convening to pursue understanding. The larger import of events in Tel Aviv is that they reveal the conflict now in progress between the governing narratives that plague us generally. We can feel grateful that in this case the heroes of knowledge withstood the minions of power. But we cannot, I think, afford to call it victory.

The point is that as politics goes, so goes a goodly part of what passes for knowledge. And far from being something as simple as hypocrisy, the current predicament of scholarship reveals a terribly complicated modus operandi. One of the best commentators on the relation of knowledge to power has been Michel Foucault. The bearing of politics upon learning becomes, in his later work, a function of the services knowledge and power perform for each other. Some reciprocal trade-off, in Foucault's view, is always in the works. He argues that more than we have cared to admit, scholarly discourse depends upon institutions that are locked into the larger grid of power relations on a spectrum running from the lowliest academic squabble to the nuclear terrorism of the superpowers.

The myth of detachment is dead, and it seems unlikely that we can go on ignoring problems that arise from the deep entanglement of knowledge in the agendas of power. At the same time, we need to keep in mind that truth is now defined in two ways, in accord with the governing narrative to which one subscribes. Truth can be, in the old high sense, the goal of a critical striving to cut through the realm of appearance. Or truth can be the goal of procedures that aim to organize appearance in ways consistent with system. There is a beauty, an aesthetic, to both. But between them an endless irony obtains, an irony to which Foucault is fully alert when he reminds us that "truth is a thing of this world," not a Platonic entity above and beyond history but very much a bargaining chip in humankind's struggle with power. That might be truth of either kind, but finally Foucault opts for the historicized version, the kind that arises from "a system of ordered procedures," as when he says that "each society has its regime of truth," to be understood this way:

> that is, the types of discourse which it accepts and makes function as true; the mechanisms and instances which enable one to distinguish true and false statements, the means by which each is sanctioned; the techniques and procedures accorded value in the acquisition of truth; the status of those who are charged with saying what counts as truth.

These "regimes of truth," as Foucault calls them, are intrinsic to the governing narratives of one's historical period. Until some fairly recent date (perhaps midway through the eighteenth century) educated elites openly served their political masters. Then the Age of Enlightenment, announced by Kant's courageous "Dare to know," launched the era of independent knowledge. But after only two centuries of intellectual liberty, of critical thinking vis-à-vis the ruling powers, the politicization of knowledge is again gaining ground. We cannot escape this predicament, but neither are we necessarily its absolute victims. If knowledge caters to power, the case is also, as Foucault makes clear, that power depends on knowledge—a small wedge of hope, but one we cannot surrender. At stake is whether or not we wish to be menials, for at the very least, scholars who spend their resources defending the honor of nation-states serve something other than truth.

With what general courage we comport ourselves remains to be seen. In an immediate way, however, our conduct is put to the test by this question: Will the Armenian genocide in Turkey be recognized, or will it go down, with much else, into Orwell's memory hole? Or again, at Bitburg in the spring of 1985 President Reagan called upon the world to forgive and forget, to conflate a killer elite with its victims and let the memory of past events fade. Neither history nor conscience was as important to the leader of Western power as a quick fix of relations with German leaders, West Germany being a vassal state to be kept at almost any price. Reagan's symbolic gesture is of course less acute than attempts to cancel the Armenian agony. What needs emphasis is that these separate cases—Turkey's denial and Reagan's dismissal, of two of the century's worst crimes—are not only related, not only connected intimately, but are identical *as signs* of the narrative of power, in which knowledge serves the state and truth is what world leaders say it is.

Sisters to Antigone

A Review of Wendy Wilder Larsen and Tran Thi Nga's Shallow Graves: Two Women and Vietnam

About the Vietnam War, its politics and battles, we know a great deal. Civilian life inside the war is less certain. The noncombatants, those whose land we laid waste—who were they? Who are they now and how does their fate dispute ours? Vietnam was an enclave of Western empire for many years, under the French and then under us. We fought hard and caused irreversible ruin to keep Saigon, the pearl of the Orient, a Western outpost. The grave misfortunes of that time and place are still unsettled. Its memories are still to be acknowledged. With its miraculous memory hole, the Reagan era leaves remembrance to the more recalcitrant among us, to poets, artists, here and there a scholar. But like all things human, recovery takes time.

In the case of *Shallow Graves,* a verse narrative by Wendy Wilder Larsen and Tran Thi Nga, it took a full decade. That was, however, ten years well spent; and I can imagine the flack and dissuasions that had to be faced before poetry of this kind made its way into print. The civilian experience in Vietnam is directly the heart of it, told by two women who were there, one American, the other Vietnamese. Their stories are separate, each unfolding in anecdotal increments, through a sequence of short poems. But then paths start to cross and connections emerge until the different sets of circumstances compose one story, one world behind, underneath, or siding up against the more newsy and prestigious military drama. Larsen simply tells what happened to her and then what happened to Tran Nga. She bears witness in the plainest of plain styles. This unadorned stance permits modest victories along the way and gives the whole a steadfast candor.

In the way it came to be written, as a collaboration from different sides of the war, *Shallow Graves* seems one of a kind. But it is also one of several books of poems in recent years to inquire, in the wake of American policy abroad, about the cost to ordinary people. The Salvador poems, a sequence in Carolyn Forché's *The Country Between Us,* open a window on El Salvador's horror show in progress, the death-squad governance that has for years enjoyed our government's support and instruction. Another sequence of this kind, Marc Kaminsky's *The Road from Hiroshima,* revives the testimony of survivors of the Bomb. Out of the whirlwind come voices like Eumenides, strong in expiation for the evil upon them. Both Forché and Kaminsky use language that allows the mutilated soul a dignity that otherwise, with newsreels and glossy photos revolting the mind, is hard to perceive.

The right to witness such "foreign" experience is one of the darker blessings of the American Connection, by which I mean our government's perpetual business of intervening violently in other nations' affairs. The idea of U.S. poets tracking U.S. transgressions will bother those for whom the nuclear standoff of the superpowers looks like Armageddon; they will remind us that we crush whom we must to get on with our mission. There is something to be said for that, although not much that's decently human, and not in the rabid way it usually gets said. Those of us who take a less jingoistic, or less grandly cynical, view will insist on accounting for the damage done. This, in turn, becomes a mode of contact with events in places like El Salvador, Hiroshima, and Vietnam, a connection based on the claims of solidarity and on the fact that small people being smashed by large powers is foremost among the signs of the time.

Something of both these conditions (the American Connection, the representative aspect of political torment) impelled Larsen and Tran Nga to write *Shallow Graves*. People go about their lives, they carry on as best they can, then one day find themselves caught up in events not of their making nor even of their understanding. This was true for Tran Nga, true overwhelmingly. In its lesser way it touched Larsen as well. She goes where her husband's job takes her and it takes her to Saigon. Her larger situation is like the incident recorded in "Letter to My Sister":

Yesterday on my way to the market, I was walking along like a true colonialist in my straw hat, when a cyclo man jumped on my back. I don't know why I didn't buckle to the pavement—but those cyclo men smoke so much opium they weigh nothing. His egret legs wrapped around my waist as he pounded on me yelling, "Get out. Get out. Get out of my country."

Any American in Vietnam, even those living at ease in Saigon's cozy compounds, might now and then feel the burden created by the war. But for someone like the "cyclo man," one of those who pedaled the rickshas, the pressure of the war would be relentless. Political intrusion, for Vietnamese civilians, was a steady stream of assault. The Vietminh order Tran Nga's brother to burn down the family house near Hanoi—"When he realized he could not save the piano, / he began beating it with a hammer." Her family is forced to run "from the bombing, from the French, from the Viet Minh, / it did not matter." They are "caught in the middle" in the North, and after immigrating South they are still caught:

> The family hiding together in our house in Cholon
> sunlight coming through the bullet holes.

Events in Vietnam were no longer growing naturally from the past, but arriving suddenly, by fiat. This is an old story, the great emblem of which is *Antigone*. When she goes out to bury her brother, Antigone acts for reasons that are private, at most a family matter. She is stopped by Creon's decree—a decision made for reasons of state, a law imposed for political purposes having nothing to do with Antigone but which, as law backed up by force, is now the potent reality that determines her story. She never gives in to Creon's authority. She is never "political." But she is trapped by a political imposition that robs her of her private fate and sends her to her tomb alive.

We've got beyond the Age of Oedipus, when sons fought fathers for social control, and are now far along in the Age of Antigone, where individuals find themselves set upon by the state. It seems fitting, moreover, that the central figure in this story is a woman, one whose traditional role has so often been assumed in terms of privacy, and one whose strength in the political arena stays rooted in personal needs. In

Vietnam, families like Tran Nga's strained to keep themselves together by holding to the old ways even as troops from the North and B-52s from the South pounded temples, homes, the familiar streets to ash. All this ought to seem remote. That it isn't is the problem. As Tran Nga's husband says when things look bad, America is

> Number one in the world. She will never desert us.
> She cannot. She is in too deep.
> She will send more ammunition.
> NBC and CBS say so.

In 1970–71, Wendy Larsen spent a year in Vietnam while her husband ran the Saigon bureau for *Time* magazine. A job teaching English to Vietnamese exposed her to a sensibility different from her own. And with the resources of *Time* at her disposal, she was able to move around, to meet a variety of people both civilian and military. One whom she met was "Mrs. Nga," the magazine's bookkeeper. In Saigon they never managed to communicate. After Tran Nga and her children got out on one of the last-minute flights, and after a chance meeting on the streets of New York in 1975, the two women became friends, able at last to share stories.

Larsen could not have written about Vietnam in the way she has if Tran Nga hadn't provided authority and blessing. Nga's story enables Larsen to judge American involvement not as foiled policy only, but also in terms of foiled lives. With Nga's life to question her own, Larsen's narrative gains a necessary irony, some of it available on first reading (or first encounter, in terms of Larsen's experience in Saigon), some of it revealed only after Nga's account adds perspective. In "Advice," the irony is pat:

> "You'll like it there.
> Saigon's not scary at all.
> All that humidity's marvelous for the skin
> and those wonderful little seamstresses
> come to your house, work all day
> and eat like gerbils."

What Scott Fitzgerald called "the vast indifference of the rich" became, in Vietnam, the vaster indifference of power for anyone who shared the pleasures of the ruling elite. That's clear enough, but after Tran Nga reminds us of the hunger and hard choices—in this case sewing or prostitution—the poem's small barbs pick deeper. The Vietnamese side of the story extends the American view. In Saigon, Larsen was quick to catch the small slips revealing deep disjunctions, and could guess what these tremors of dissonance might mean. In "Consciousness Raising," for example, the "wives of journalists" gather thus:

> I remember sitting in a hot small room
> a punkah fan creaking overhead,
> our knees forming a circle
> as we discussed why baby girls
> are dressed in pink,
> boys in blue.
>
> Outside, a peasant woman
> driven into the city by the bombing
> slept in the street
> on a newspaper
> a child pulling at her breast.

The visitors indulge in aesthetics, but in the streets the ugliness goes on. These "wives of journalists," like their men who groom the news, see what internal censorship permits them to see. Those on top exercise status by not looking down, a posture often expressed—mainly by women with no purpose—through boredom and trifling with art. This is one of the signs of empire; it shows up in a number of Larsen's poems. Here is "Recalled":

> Sitting in a lounge chair by the pool,
> the wife of a TV correspondent said,
> "We've just been recalled.
> I've got to beat it down
> and pick up some of those silver animals,
> those gorgeous little elephants,
> before the plane takes off."

This sounds like a scene from a travel brochure, an aesthetic imperative blocking out the world. The last line, moreover, cannot be fathomed until we have Tran Nga's nightmare account—what she has to do "before the plane takes off"—of her rescue. *Shallow Graves* owes much of its frankness to the fact that its authors are women. Their perspective is dependent on their gender and vulnerable in revealing ways, ways not usually recorded in reports of the war. We see, for example, American wives constrained to speak as their husbands do, but in a language more guarded. They affect "feminine" innocence while privy to men's excitements, for example this morsel of masculine wit in the war zone:

> Downstairs, at the embassy party,
> there were place cards with embossed gold crests
> antimacassars on the backs of stuffed chairs
> talk of commitment.

> Upstairs, in the bedroom after dinner,
> there was a refrigerator filled with champagne
> and bar-girls dancing
> to Mick Jagger's rock 'n' roll.

> "Welcome to the turd world,"
> the diplomat winked.

Despite the last line's stumble, a situation is suggested in which members of the ruling clique can mock official images. At the same time, they discount the reality of two worlds in one as much as they can. In *Dispatches,* Michael Herr suggests that American occupation of Vietnam created a schizophrenic arena in which the distance between decadence and terror, or between aesthetic and political kinds of awareness, was never very great. You could move from one to the other as easily as passing from one room to the next. It's exactly this false partitioning, and the notion that one can pass in and out with immunity, that Larsen and Tran Nga challenge. They work to put the two worlds back in touch, each as it impinged upon the other, back to the one world all sides shared. This happens as the book progresses, as the two stories discover each other. Not least among its virtues, *Shallow Graves* illustrates the way aesthetic resolution (rather than aesthetic indulgence) depends on political consciousness (as opposed to partisan bias and diplomatic bad faith).

While Larsen must wait on Tran Nga to understand fully, she had opportunity for insight through contact with Vietnamese and their culture in the classroom. She teaches English literature by the old thematic of "appearance and reality," but when the class looks at a Vietnamese poem, Larsen's innocence is countered by a young man who tells her that "appearance" is for those "who do not know our land." For example, in the following Vietnamese *ca dao,* what's to be made of these lines?

> "Oh, my darling, over there by the side of the path, why do you scoop up and throw away yellow moonlight shining on the water's surface?"

It might be that the speaker praises beauty's fleeting moment or envies the chance to dally in its rapture. It might be so. But here is Larsen's comment: "This is a question on a summer moonlit night asked by a passer-by to a hard-working young girl using her draining can to take water from a flooded field to a dry field." If Larsen were the one on the path, the hard-pressed girl might be Tran Nga. If the girl is a figure for the nation, the passerby is any American in Vietnam—perhaps Larsen's friend Jeannette, who "stopped by 'the Nam' / on her way home / from temples in Burma" to say:

> "Darling, why bother teaching them English?
> We taught them French.
> Next they will have to learn Russian."
> She knew her antiques.
> "Not that one," she'd roar,
> pointing to a blue-and-white teapot,
> "that's early Chiang Kai-shek."

That is, I suppose, a kind of political chic, a language grounded in geopolitics but devoid of political sense. For this woman, who "wore a Nikkormat / around her neck / like an ornament," political suffering is an excuse for tough detachment. To bolster contempt she professes a brittle aestheticism that takes the world in silhouette. Again, in Larsen's view, the moral drama resides in the division between an aesthetic adjustment to surfaces, and political response to deeper connections. More generally, this division separates poetry of the sort that evades politics from poetry that rises to real-world impingements. These are two ways of seeing, but only one can claim to be complete.

At one point Larsen asked her students to compare William Blake's "London" to Saigon in 1970. She then sets Blake's poem among her own. In this context the poem's impact is tremendous, like shock waves absorbed and sent forth anew. Larsen, unlike others of her American circle, had an extra resource—the poetry she was teaching—to count on for clearing her head. It's true, of course, that poems don't always work this way. Here at home Blake's alarm may still seem excessive, his voice unduly raised. But in Saigon, where harlots cursed the midnight streets and woe really did thrive, the poem recovers its prophetic force. Like the Vietnamese poems Larsen quotes, Blake is one of her touchstones.

Even so, she could sometimes be as blind as the rest of us. A poem near the end of her story records an incident that cannot be understood until, 125 pages later, Nga tells her version of the same event. Entitled "The Noodle Cart," the poem is about the American urge to collect the world and ship it home, about seeing only the aesthetic side of a political situation. Thus in stanza one:

> My friends sent back drums from Laos,
> lacquered trays with goldfish, ceramic elephants.
> Once I knew we were leaving
> I wanted a noodle cart,
>
> the old kind . . .

The "old kind" is more exotic, of course. It is street-worn and decked with the emblems of a culture—"stained-glass panels / of dragons and oceans and mythic sword fights"—that another culture is destroying. Telling us why she wants one, Larsen sounds like any other tourist: "I loved the giant ladles / the blue-and-white bowls in racks." But to go about actually getting one, she must rely on someone who knows more than she knows:

> I asked Mrs. Nga to help me find a noodle cart.
> After a month she said she had.
> To buy one, she had to talk a family out of theirs.
> The son was all in favor, but not the father
> who was dead against selling the family business.

Now the noodle cart stands
on my brother's porch in California
stocked with little green bottles of Perrier water
Mr. and Mrs. T's Bloody Mary Mix.

On first reading we might be satisfied with the clash between Saigon and California, or the ironic fate of another objet d'art. But then we might also wonder what's meant by "After a month," or what the cart was worth if the owner was "dead against selling." Only when we get to a poem from Nga's story, also called "Noodle Cart," does the scene deepen and take on tragic dimensions that cancel the earlier poem's delight in acquisition. When Larsen asked Tran Nga for help, Nga says, "She was my boss's wife. Of course I would do it." Thus begins "three weeks of searching" through the city and into the dangerous countryside "where I had never been." Much time is spent with "the same noodle man / pretending I went for noodles," until one day, "after 14 bowls, he told me where to go look." He did not tell her right, but at last a cart of "the old kind" turns up:

The father and son fought.
The father refused to sell.
The son said he had to. The father cried.
The son told me to sneak back in the evening
and take the cart.
I had to find people to push it to the warehouse.

"It's perfect," says Larsen to Tran Nga. She means the cart. This is not irony for its own sake, or art's sake, or to allow the poet a margin of detachment. Discontinuity points up the conflict between aesthetic and political viewpoints, and settles, at Larsen's expense, her major theme. Politics breaks the world into Us and Them, the few whom power serves, the many whom it hurts. The predicament is so constant and inescapable that it moves some of us, the lucky ones, to "transcend" injustice by viewing the world "poetically." As Nietzsche put it, history is only bearable from an aesthetic point of view. That's true enough, once religious solutions are lost. But is the poetic solution really that— a solution? Those on the bottom don't think so. Even for those on top there is a cost. Larsen's wives and world travelers detach themselves, develop a cynical style, give up on care.

The labor of *Shallow Graves,* as I've suggested, is to summon the one world from its disparate parts. It is a task at which Larsen and Tran Nga succeed, thanks partly to Larsen's courage. She puts herself among the "wives of journalists" she faults. Against the cant of the Reagan era her own push is constant and brave. In one particular, however, she falters. Larsen does not manage the poetic confidence to possess another's story, with the result that Tran Nga's voice is often as colorless as Larsen's voice is not. But then the usual response to survivor testimony— and Tran Nga is certainly a survivor—is to keep mediation at a minimum, downplaying art and authorial choice. One wants the very voice one hears.

I am guessing, in Nga's case, that Larsen prized fidelity more than enhancement. Anyone who has listened to stories burdened by political torment will know this voice. From Tran Nga's girlhood, here is a stanza from a poem called "Politics":

> I never understood politics.
> In the highlands Father warned us
> not to take any leaflets.
> They were guerrilla propaganda
> would ruin our family's name.
> His look scared us into silence.

As a provincial administrator in the time of the French, Nga's father had to appear accommodating, even though, like most of his neighbors, he despised Western power. But what worked with the French was worse than useless when the colonial order collapsed:

> We heard the Viet Minh buried the French alive.
> We were nothing now.
> My mother read her Buddhist prayers
> over and over.
> She would not go to the door.

Later, after the politicians in Geneva split Vietnam in two and Tran Nga's family moved South, she discovered that immigrants from the North were seen as opportunists and reviled. In the Saigon market— the same place Larsen strolled to enjoy the smells and colors—a small mishap involving an upset basket becomes the end result of global politics:

> She scolded me until a mob came
> and started ripping my dress
> calling out: "Hurt that Northerner.
> They have come to make us suffer."
> A policeman came.
> When they saw he too was from the North,
> they yelled, "Kill him. Kill them both."
> Finally a third came, from the South.
> He tried to calm the mob, saying,
> "This lady is your countrywoman.
> She has left everything behind.
> She suffers too. Please."

Whereas Larsen's narrative derives its political subtext from its irony, segments of Tran Nga's story reflect on themselves in the manner of a parable—as episodes to be looked into. But what, one wonders, would a Westerner, a tourist without the language, make of the scene in the market? There would be no distinction between North and South but only unladylike women in a shouting match as proof, maybe, of formless Asian ways. Some less civilized nation's primitive conduct, perhaps. Without its political context the scene is not what it is. In general, Larsen does the "looking into" herself. Through Western eyes is not the way she wants Tran Nga to be seen. Dignity is at stake, and Larsen is good at revealing the politics implicit in dramatic situations.

Larsen succeeds at this part of her task; Tran Nga's testimony is secured and passed on. At this level, however, a prose narrative might have served the same purpose. What is gained by verse? Perhaps the immediate leap to large issues, and then the freedoms of speed and precision. Larsen's poetic strategy allows her to jump to turning points and epiphanies, to build detail into design, to braid a life's travail into essential strands. She is able to weave the two stories in and around each other without the explanatory baggage that prose would require. Poetry, that is to say, allows both economy and homage. These are humble virtues, but Larsen makes the most of them and Tran Nga's story is never less than compelling.

She was born in 1927, twice married (her first husband died fighting

Mao), and her life included, or rather was included in, the war between
the Chinese and the Japanese, partly fought in Vietnam; the colonial
struggle between the French and the North Vietnamese; the conflict in
South Vietnam while the Americans ran the war; then the debacle of
withdrawal, the randomness of evacuation, and finally relocation in the
States through church sponsorship. Apart from the period of her first
marriage, Tran Nga's family was always the center of her life in Vietnam.
At every point events surrounding her were vast, but in the telling their
imprint is personal. On the night of April 30, 1975, here is Nga alone
with her children in a refugee camp, listening to news of the fall of
Saigon:

> Sitting on the floor of the blue tent in Guam,
> all of us cried, even the boys.
> We had thought we would be gone only a short time.
> Now we knew we would never return,
> never see our friends and family.
> Our country was lost.

Like Antigone, she is simply cut off. Her mother remains in Saigon
and dies there unattended. Is it coincidence that Antigone is ruined by
a political decree against last rites? Tran Nga thinks not. *Birds have nests,*
she says, *and people have ancestors*. When her father died, his death was
sanctified by traditional ceremonies lasting one hundred days: "We believe the dead must be buried deep and tight / so the soul will be secure."
People are not birds. That she cannot visit the graves of her parents
becomes Tran Nga's deepest grief. The following lines are artless and
can be faulted to that extent, but not for their plight beyond closure or
their knitting of politics and private sorrow:

> O my country!

> O my countrymen
> so many of you left in shallow graves
> in time of war
> your souls wandering ceaselessly.

The final entry in *Shallow Graves,* a sort of coda entitled "In the
American Museum of Natural History," is the only poem about both

women together. A spirit of anger and pathos—mindful of decorum but still unsatisfied—has all along haunted the book, and now it comes to the fore. The poem remembers a day in New York when "Ba Larsen and Madame Nga" went to the Museum of Natural History for an exhibit of Eastern cultures. The women go toward the Hall of Asian Peoples, passing first through the Hall of Asiatic Mammals:

> We stop before a leopard killing a peacock.
> The bird's neck is broken
> snapped against a rock.
> The leopard stares straight ahead.

The irony has become symbolic, suggesting that images of power taken allegorically—for their "natural history," so to say—tell us why, as Tran Nga puts it, "your country wants to forget about mine." Thus they come to the Vietnam display:

> one small window
> buried between India and China.
> Black-and-white drawings show
> a traditional wedding procession,
> a typical farmer plowing with a water buffalo,
> rice growing in a Vietnamese landscape,
> four Vietnamese faces.
> The only statue is a grinning Money God.
> Its caption says
> small change is dropped in his back for good luck.

Birds have nests and peoples have histories. Or maybe all of that's behind us now. Reading through *Shallow Graves,* I thought at first that Larsen's simple verse would be too meager, too empty of metaphor, for something as large as the war in Vietnam. I was mistaken, mainly because I didn't see the web of ironies, because I was not expecting the difference that gender makes, nor, before careful reading, could I value the integrity of Larsen's and Tran Nga's narratives working together. The language of witness, with its will to get the record straight, tends to avoid expansive options. Figuration would damage a diction as sternly mimetic as Larsen's. As it is, you read this poem and come away enlightened, strangely pleased that truth survives a time as lied-to as this one.

Holocaust Laughter

Dduring recent years we have become increasingly alert to the fact that academic disciplines constitute their respective "fields" by resorting to "fictions"—myths or principles accepted without question and endorsed by the community, but not susceptible to proof. To ask if the field of Holocaust studies is, like other fields, founded on fictions, is to conclude that it is. Now, survivors and their testimony have no care to organize a "field," and are exempt from arbitrary rulings of this sort. So are the poets and novelists among us who, I presume, proceed in any way obsession compels or invention points. But those of us who "interpret" these things, if we want our ideas certified by a community of academic peers, conform to the fictions that underwrite our enterprise. It's true, of course, that fields reconstitute themselves. New fictions supplant others no longer helpful or exciting. It seems possible that the field of Holocaust studies will modify itself in this way—or even, forty years after the event, that a transformation is in progress. My concern, however, is not to chart new directions but to establish the class of fictions that plays a cardinal role in critical writing about the Holocaust. Here are three—three inclusive rulings—that at present set limits to respectable study:

1. The Holocaust shall be represented, in its totality, as a unique event or special case or kingdom of its own, above or below or apart from history.
2. Representations of the Holocaust shall be as accurate, as exacting, as unfailingly faithful as possible to the facts and circumstances of

the event itself, without change or manipulation for any reason—
artistic or literary reasons included.

3. The Holocaust shall be approached as a solemn, or even a sacred
event, admitting of no response that obscures its enormity or dis-
honors its dead.

These fictions aren't perfect or perfectly tyrannical. Even so, they foster
strong restrictions. They become regulatory agencies that have influ-
enced how we conceive of, and write about, matters of the Holocaust.

Because these informing fictions are so fundamental and widely
shared, we tend to accept them silently, without question, in full belief.
We might also see them, therefore, simply as "the truth." Here I would
like to enlist the help of Michel Foucault, one of our more incisive
commentators on the ways in which fields of discourse unify themselves.
Foucault reminds us that "truth is a thing of this world," not a Platonic
entity beyond the reach of history and struggle. The "truths" of knowledge, moreover, depend on "a system of ordered procedures," for how
else shall a field of discourse know itself to be a field, with its own rites
and validating processes? Knowledge cannot exist without order, and
order depends upon informing fictions accepted as true. Every field of
knowledge therefore has its "regime of truth," as Foucault calls the rules
of discourse, including "the techniques and procedures accorded value
in the acquisition of truth [and] the status of those who are charged
with saying what counts as truth." The "regime of truth" that controls
knowledge in the field of Holocaust studies includes the rulings I cited
earlier.

It seems clear that fictions informing the field of Holocaust studies
force upon us a set of rules, a decorum, a sort of Holocaust etiquette
that encourages some, rather than other, kinds of response. One of these
fictions dictates that anything pertaining to the Holocaust must be serious, must be reverential in a manner that acknowledges (and supports)
the sacredness of its occasion. This imperative appears natural, and at
first may not seem limiting. Only when one comes to questions of artistic
treatment, especially to the propriety of literary modes, do problems of
response come into view. In literary treatment of the Holocaust, is
laughter possible? Is the comic mode ruled out by the nature of the
subject matter? Or is the general absence of humor the result of Holocaust etiquette? To ask this set of questions is immediately to recognize

the problem and also, perhaps, to foresee a part of the answer. For without doubt, most of us in the field of Holocaust studies take a dim view of jokes or comic indulgence of any sort in matters so laden with pain.

On the other hand, one of the first treatises on laughter, written by Hippocrates, the father of medicine, tells us that laughter is medicinal, a healing agency. But can laughter be restorative in the case of the Holocaust? To this question we know what will be said because we know what has been said, namely, that toward matters of the Holocaust the comic attitude is irreverent, a mode that belittles or cheapens or denies the moral severity of the subject itself. In the presence of evil so vast and suffering so endless, laughter is simply taboo. At the same time, of course, we know that one of laughter's virtues is its survival value. In difficult times, laughter lightens the burden. The importance of a comic response to disaster is verified by Emmanuel Ringelblum in his *Notes from the Warsaw Ghetto,* where he records the jokes that kept people going in the ghetto. And most of Ringelblum's jokes, as we shall see, reappear in Leslie Epstein's *King of the Jews,* a comic novel about the Holocaust.

Whereas tragedy and lamentation affirm *what is* and proceed largely in a mimetic mode that elevates, the comic spirit proceeds in an anti-mimetic mode that often mocks *what is,* that patiently deflates, demotes or even denies the authority of its subject matter. Tragic seriousness, with its endorsement of pity and terror, affirms the hegemony of historical fact. And it seems to me that of all the imperatives informing Holocaust studies, none is so absolute as the need to affirm historical authority—by which I mean, in the case of the Holocaust, fidelity to the memory of the death camps. We say "Never again" by insisting not only that the Holocaust happened, but also that its unique evil and suffering are very much with us even now. It would seem, then, that we presume to guard the historical truth by saying yes to the authority of the Holocaust over our spiritual lives. Anything that detracts from this authority we rule out on principle. We presume to liberate the future by placing ourselves in bondage to the past.

One of the surprising characteristics of the film *Shoah* is how often Claude Lanzmann, and some of his witnesses, take up a sardonic tone, a kind of mocking irony that on occasion comes close to laughter: his satiric handling of the retired SS men; Rudy Vrba's breezy style of bitterness; the Polish survivor of Chelmno, silent and faintly smiling, who stands in front of a church while surrounded on all sides by townspeople whose babbling is informed by various degrees of anti-Semitism, most of it comically naïve. This is, of course, dark laughter, but it is comic all the same and Lanzmann, moreover, seems deliberate about it. If *Shoah* is a sign of the times, we may suppose that artistic representation of the Holocaust is changing—that it is trying more flexible modes of response.

I would like, at this point, to cite three works of fiction that span the duration of literary reaction to the Holocaust, all three of which are comic in degree, although by no means alike or even similar. The books I have in mind are Tadeusz Borowski's *This Way for the Gas, Ladies and Gentlemen,* first published in story format in 1948; then Leslie Epstein's *King of the Jews,* published in 1979; and most recently, published in book form in 1986, Art Spiegelman's *Maus.*

Whereas *King of the Jews* is comic in a multitude of ways including tone and management of character and scene as well as play of language, the other two books are comic mainly in conception. The literary conceit at the heart of *This Way for the Gas* is the narrator's pretense of normality. In *Maus* the governing conceit is the cartoon itself, the comic-book pretense that Jews are mice and Nazis cats. In all three cases, however, the world depicted is grotesque and exaggerated by virtue of its comic perspective. Of course, the actuality of the Holocaust is already exaggerated and grotesque. Here, however, actuality is displaced by a fiction that in its conception is durable enough, and skillfully enough imposed, to inform the narrative with its own invented principle. This might be said of any story, in degree; all fiction aims to usurp the real world with a world that is imagined. In comedy, however, the revolt is more pronounced. Without Borowski's pretense of normality, without Epstein's larger-than-life figure of the trickster, without Spiegelman's game of cat-and-mouse, these books would be as grim and horrid as the world they refer to. It's just for this reason, by the way, that mimetic fiction so often fails when its subject is the Holocaust. In its homage to fact, the mode of high seriousness has no option but to attempt convincing likeness. It's this "realism," this compulsion to reproduce exactly, that almost necessarily ensures defeat. Comic works, on the contrary, make no attempt at actual representation. Laughter, in this case, is hostile to the world it depicts. It is free as tragedy and lamentation are not.

In the realm of art, a comic response is more resilient, more effectively in revolt against terror and the sources of terror than a response that is solemn or tragic. The mimetic mode is proper to high seriousness because tragic art accepts that which has come to pass. The antimimetic mode is proper to comedy because comic art resists that which has come to pass. The point, here, is that the three books I've cited refuse to take the Holocaust on its own crushing terms. They insist on their own imaginative integrity. And it's these powers of self-possession that grant us, finally, the liberty to take heart.

Of the three works, *This Way for the Gas* affords the least amount of breathing space, the least distance between actuality and comic displacement. Tadek, the principal character, tells us that "having, so to say, broken bread with the beast," he has become one with the world of Auschwitz. The horror of the camp, for such as himself, has become normal. He and his fellows speak with easy familiarity of "the ramp," "the Cremo" and "the puff." When things are going well they say, "*Keine Angst*"—"No problem." The German phrase is perversely funny. Its humor resides in the incongruity of superficial meaning (as in "No problem") and meaning profoundly horrible (as in *Totesangst,* a term for extreme fear). In *This Way for the Gas,* behavior of the most ordinary sort mocks and is mocked by simultaneous behavior entirely inhuman, as when, on the ramp, Tadek and his comrades take pleasure in eating even as they brutalize children.

Horror and banality combine, in Borowski's narrative, to produce a central ludicrous moment that repeats itself each time the main character slips, each time Tadek loses his ironic grip and falls back into his humanity. In one instance a woman, Mirka, has hidden a child she is trying to save. Of course the child will not be saved, and seeing the stupidity of the attempt Tadek is suddenly possessed by "a wild thought" and says to himself: "I too would like to have a child with rose-coloured cheeks and light blond hair. I laugh aloud at such a ridiculous notion. . . ."

This Way for the Gas is a ferociously ironic book. Nothing so genteel as humor can be said to exist within its pages. The kind of laughter that confers charity and saving grace is altogether absent. Borowski sets his comic energies against the world of Auschwitz but also against the world that allowed Auschwitz to happen, and then against the self's impotent decency as well, and thus, in the end, his laughter is set against life altogether. Back home, having survived the camp and the war, Tadek feels "full of irreverence, bordering almost on contempt." That is *one* kind of Holocaust laughter. Almost wholly negative, it can be called demonic, a kind of ridicule without redemptive power except for the vigor of mockery itself. The comic spirit is always ambivalent, cursing and blessing at once. In *This Way for the Gas,* however, the curse is more or less total. Reviling that which overwhelms him, Borowski is in hopeless revolt, hence his inflexible stance and grim disregard for the reader.

By contrast, in Epstein's *King of the Jews* the narrator's voice promotes a wonderful civility, a sweet insistence on decorum in a world where decorum sounds out of place and funny. The narrator addresses the reader as "ladies and gentlemen," and assumes that those to whom he speaks are an extended part of the community. This emphasis on community is part of the fiction and a cardinal point to keep in mind. Epstein's novel is comic for its crazy naming—for Phelia Lubliver, the Ghetto Queen, or Urinstein, Minister of Vital Statistics; for the abstract Totenkopfers and the Big Man in Berlin. And it is hilarious for the bizarre and often frenetic behavior among the ghettoites of Suburb Balut. But Epstein's novel is comic in a more comprehensive way as well, touching on a kind of folk or communal laughter that Mikhail Bakhtin, in his book on Rabelais, calls "carnivalesque."

I do *not* mean to say that the Holocaust becomes a carnival, but rather that in a world of death the spectacle of life defending itself is open to unusual perspectives. In Bakhtin's view, carnival laughter draws its authority from the utopian hunger of humankind in general. Such laughter is in revolt against everything fixed; it is hostile to rules, regulations, hierarchies, anything closing down life. It celebrates the regenerative powers of human community as such, life and the plenitude of life, at the expense of particular forms. Against internal as well as external threats to communal well-being, this kind of laughter is ruthless. It pulls everything down to earth, officialdom and worldly power especially.

Nothing that sets itself above the community escapes ridicule. Enactment of the comic spirit, in this case, proceeds through vulgarity and exaggeration, through grotesque and monstrous forms. Food and sex take on exaggerated significance as the functions of the belly and genitals are magnified. The lower forms of humor prevail—jokes, puns, slapstick, and clowning. The official world is empty, power is stupid, selfimportance of any sort is the bedrock of folly. Here, in short, is a great feast of fools. Here is neither terror nor pity but only fearless affirmation of life against death.

By way of connecting this notion of laughter to representations of the Holocaust, let us go back for a moment to Ringelblum's *Notes,* in particular to jokes circulating in the ghetto. Here are three:

A Jew alternately laughs and yells in his sleep. His wife wakes him up. He is mad at her. "I was dreaming someone had scribbled on a wall: 'Beat the Jews! Down with ritual slaughter!'" "So what were you so happy about?" "Don't you understand? That means the good old days have come back! The Poles are running things again!"

Horowitz [Hitler] asked the local Governor General [Hans Frank] what he has been doing to the Jews. The Governor mentioned a number of calamities, but none of them sufficed for Horowitz. Finally, the Governor mentioned ten points. He began: "I have set up a Jewish Self-Aid Organization." "That's enough; you need go no further!"

H[itler] is trying to imitate Napoleon. He began the war with Russia on the 22nd day of July [*sic*], the same day Napoleon invaded Russia. But H. is already late. . . . They say that at the beginning of his Russian campaign Napoleon put on a red shirt, to hide the blood if he should be wounded. H. put on a pair of brown drawers.

In the first two examples, the community laughs at itself. In the third example, the community laughs at its enemy, exploding its fear with an off-color punch line. Three points about these jokes: they were the communal property of ghetto Jews at the time of the Holocaust; they are examples of carnival humor, in which bodily existence is emphasized and disaster is absorbed by the community at large; these jokes reappear, along with others from Ringelblum, in *King of the Jews,* a novel in which Hitler is referred to as "Horowitz." In this novel, too, the one time the ghetto population asserts itself as a community, with an energetic if short-lived surge of solidarity, is during the period of the General Strike, led by the "fecalists." The artist Klapholtz has just been shot for painting the French tricolor on the ceiling of the Church of the Virgin Mary for the Jewish wedding of the ghetto elder. The execution of Klapholtz provokes an uprising among the citizens of the Balut, and thus they proceed:

Hundreds of workers broke ranks and raced across the street. Even the shirtwaist girls were coming. They surrounded the excrement wagons and turned them around. Then they began to march behind them out of Jakuba Street. Their voices rang out: "Food! Fuel! A better life!" Their fists were in the air. . . .

What a spectacle it was. A procession of resolute Jews! They seemed to themselves to consist of an irresistible force. The world, which had been snatched from them, would be seized once again. . . .

The broken body of Klapholtz draped over the wooden staves of the leading wagon, rocked back and forth. His arms and legs and the head on his neck seemed full of energy. Someone ran up and attached a flower to his trousers. He was their martyr, their hero. Ladies and gentlemen, what other artist— not even Victor Hugo, not Michelangelo—has moved men so greatly, or filled them with the conviction that they could change the course of their lives?

So began the first day of the Five Day General Strike.

I have selected the foregoing passage because it stands as a comic image for the novel overall. The great scenes in *King of the Jews* are all communal, from the early demise of the first *Judenrat* in a lethal game of leapfrog, to the death and resurrection of the later *Judenrat,* splitting hairs over how to make up "the list." In the scene above, which extends over many pages, the ghettoites join forces behind the "excrement wagon" on which their dead hero flops along "full of energy." In these lowly circumstances they feel possessed by "an irresistible force," which is the power of life itself and thus of imagination when concentrated and magnified by an action of the community as a whole—the same power that they, the citizens of the Balut, invest in I. C. Trumpelman, a heroic figure who in the eyes of the ghetto is messianic and immortal. Trumpelman is in fact a monstrous benefactor, a medicine man and a quack, a savior and a betrayer who ends up destroying the ghetto in order to save it. His behavior, like the predicament of the *Judenrat,* is radically ambivalent, a blessing and a curse together. It is, however, precisely this ambivalence, pointing to life and death at once, that is the carnivalesque element and the sign of Holocaust laughter in *King of the Jews.*

Ringed round by its destroyers, caught up in a perfect net of death, the community of Epstein's novel nevertheless conducts itself in such a way—with a carnival freakishness and frenzy—so as to revolt against the darkness closing in. They know what is in store for them, and so do we. Against their fate the ghettoites embrace an antimimetic counterworld that shuts out terror and pity together. During the European Middle Ages this kind of behavior was allowed in ritualized form on certain feast days or days marking the change of seasons. During the Holocaust it could only occur in places where the community still felt itself to be intact, which is to say in the besieged ghettos. Even then, as Ringelblum's collection of jokes suggests, the spirit of carnival laughter was fitful and appeared in small ways only.

The proper place for comic enactment of this encompassing category is not of course life, but life reenvisioned through art. In *King of the Jews,* the actual world of the Holocaust is evoked by a multitude of allusions to the historical record, including not only Ringelblum's *Notes,* but the rickshas of the ghettos and even, on one occasion, Czerniakow, the leader of the Warsaw ghetto—not to mention Trumpelman's historical double, M. C. Rumkowski, head of the *Judenrat* at Lodz. But Epstein does not stop there; he goes on to create, *inside* the historical world alluded to, an antiworld, the communal world of Baluty Suburb, informed by the antimimetic humor of the carnival style. This secondary world is in full revolt against the world that encircles it. The actual world is recognized but not accepted as final, even though, of course, it is final. But human beings do not live by actuality only. And it is this kind of comic enactment, in this kind of double-world art, that we can justly call "Holocaust laughter."

By way of conclusion, a few words about *Maus.* The idea of a cartoon about the Holocaust is rather shocking. At least I thought so when I first encountered it. But in fact the cat-and-mouse notion is daring and sad at once, and therefore funny in a wry sort of way. This has everything to do with the book's artistic reliance on distorted visual representation, which provokes a remarkable kind of melancholy, and then a pathos that is humorous. By portraying the victims in this way, we see them at a distance, and they, in turn, are able to say things that long ago were clichés in Holocaust fiction of the standard sort—for example, "synagogues burned, Jews beaten with no reason, whole towns pushing out all Jews." There is, moreover, the way *Maus* makes light of itself by incorporating the actual circumstances of its origin. On one level, the artist-son engages his father-survivor at home in Queens. On another level, the father's story unfolds with grim finality during the years of the Holocaust. Both stories are autobiographical, and again there is a two-world situation, one part funny and one part terrible, with each afflicting the other. The cat-and-mouse idea, finally, together with its comic-book format, is a Brechtian device that alienates while provoking a discerning look.

In *Maus,* as in the other books I've cited, pity and terror are held at a distance. This is not, in my view, altogether a bad thing. It's not fear and sorrow we need more of, but undaunted vision. The paradox of the comic approach is that by setting things at a distance it permits us a tougher, more *active* response. We are not wholly, as in the high seriousness of tragedy, forced to a standstill by the matter we behold. At the same time, however, the books I've cited manage to respect the three "fictions" with which I began. They take the Holocaust seriously, they allow for its specialness and even for its factual particularity. All this they assume and point to. But they do not, on the other hand, capitulate to terror. As comic works of art, or works of art that include a comic element, they give us laughter's benefit without betraying our deeper convictions. They foster resilience and are life-reclaiming. For these reasons, comic treatment of the Holocaust seems valuable. To say "Never again" is to ask for all the help we can get. That laughter can be helpful is the point I've tried to make.

Memory of Boyhood

In the Missouri I knew as a boy, nobody called fishing a sport. Life was rooted in the land and fishing was mainly for food. To me, anyway, it was as natural as cutting wood, as sacking nuts or watching the men make whiskey. It was exciting, too, with strong pleasure and sometimes the splendor of magical events, like the Sunday afternoon we seined deep holes and took more fish than sacks to hold them, carp and catfish sliding from the truck bed as we bounced up the rut-torn hill. Or those November nights on the river with boats and lanterns and gigs pronged wide as pitchforks. I no longer fish, and the boy who did is twenty years into the past. Yet memories of that time come constantly to mind. They return to me, or I to them, as if they were my source, a keel of sanity in a world more gnarled and rotted than—at a right-angle bend in the river—the gigantic pile of driftwood and tree trunks we used to call Snake City.

Remembering begins with noon and the sun's raw glare. With hot fields and ridges adrift in the haze. Trees, bluffs, the land transfixed in windless air. And through the rinsing heat, a boy heading down to the river, down the dust-still road toward spots where rocks jutted into the stream or where a tree had fallen and jammed near the bank. He would know beforehand that big fish—bass and buffalo, carp and catfish and drum—were never caught that time of day. But there against stone or bunched roots the water rushed and swirled and dug out a hole. And there with cane pole and worms he would catch thirty, sometimes forty, fish.

Perch, bluegill, pumpkinseed, the spread and thickness of a man's full hand. Sunfish with colors so finely gray-orange and green that holding one for a moment in his hands, careful of its spiny erections, he could not but wonder at the beauty of these small dumb creatures, so swift to strike, to jerk down the cork and be caught. They rose into sight and hit in a mass. They flashed fins and bright bellies against the hook's hold, fish after fish all afternoon. It became a small rite of plenty, of rapport with life at its ravenous source. The fished-out hole stayed empty but there were always others, always a piece of river secret and untouched. And now, going home, his worth was plain in the fat full stringer. The weight of his catch was proof of luck, of that primeval blessing which fishermen seek.

Almost all his free time he spent on the river. He came to know every hole, slough, creek mouth, and gravel bar, every bridge and crossing down or upstream for miles. Where he went on any given day depended on the fishing he wanted to do. He loved best to take his fly rod—a ferruled cane pole to which he'd wired eyes and a reel—and start for the river at dawn. To enter the wet gray stillness of day before sunrise. To turn downhill from the sleeping town, with no sound but footfall and the waking cry of birds. Across pastures, thickets, fencerows, to come out finally on a mud road winding through dark trunks of timber in the bottoms. The world then was suspended in shadow and half-light, dense with the being of earth before man: unmoving quiet shapes and smells—of cattle and cut hay, of wet stones and dew—that in the keen air were like another language, older and more true. At moments like this he felt that nothing in the world was not essential. And when at last he came up on the bridge—a single span of iron rail and loud loose planks—he stopped to watch mist rise and drift above the silk black surface. He stood stock-still and let the purl of water come into his heart, until all the river, its force and grave repose, its life apart from human life, was in him, too.

Upstream the river narrowed with many rapids spilling into depth. Water sprawled spuming through willow and beds of blunt rock to deepen abruptly, six feet, ten feet, and then go shallow again. It shot in chutes past sandbars and mudbanks to gradually grow broad and still in deep pools. To places like these he made his way, beneath trees arched like a vault, wading sometimes waist-deep to get around brush and the wreckage of trees. He worked then to set his fly down perfectly. It would drop and settle slowly, its small spinner flickering, and instantly his body was alert with waiting for the sudden pull. It came soon or not at all. When it did, up through the tremor of the bending rod sprang shocks of primal life. He could feel the fish as it fought, feel its veering thrust and surge. Each strike felt firm, deliberate, as if each time a bond were being joined. While the outcome was in doubt he wooed with magic and prayer the fish he could not see. Then it became visible, its dark shape forking toward him. He caught rock perch, crappie, and bass, none of them so very big. And yet, through the mystery of that first contact, they seemed somehow huge.

He worked each place patiently, and as he fished the sun spread golden through the mist. It climbed, and light cut in shafts through the trees. The water turned from black to gold to transparent green, and then a different kind of fishing began. He replaced the fly with a hook and no longer stopped to try each tempting spot. He moved upstream, on the lookout for holes in which there would be a single big fish—a small-mouth bass charging back and forth in a rage. For some reason these warlike fish took over smaller pools. They did not defend a nest, so far as he could tell, but only the hole itself. They attacked intruders, they stayed in plain sight, and for a long time they were impossible to catch. Minnows, poppers, crawdads, too, he tried without luck. What worked he found by chance. He was watching one of these fish when a frog about three inches long jumped away from him into the water. It started kicking across the surface, and in a flash the bass was under it, churning in tight circles. The longer the frog swam the more enraged the fish became. It rushed to the end of the pool and shot back. It rammed into the frog with a vicious shake of its head, gulped, and went back to its irate patrol. That was how to do it. He would catch a frog and jab the hook through its belly. A minute later he had the bass on his line. These were big fish, five and six pounds, and more than once he splintered the bamboo rod.

He would take three or four bass like that and start home with tails dragging the dust. He stopped again on the bridge, this time to stare down through his own image and gradually make out, in the dark hole under the bridge, the most enormous bass he'd ever seen. It weighed ten or more pounds, or so he guessed. It was there each time he passed, hovering mid-depth on the upstream side. And nothing, not lures, not live bait, not the many movements of men, disturbed its perfect calm. It seemed never to move, merely to appear and vanish, as if part of the river itself. He had seen men shoot fish from bridges (though not this bridge), especially the slow-moving carp that nosed along the bottom in bunches of five or ten. When one was hit, it zigzagged madly, its thick back cutting the surface, its wound white and pulpy, like a ripe rose. This fish, though, seemed apart from harm, beyond guns, dynamite, the unfair things men used to take fish, electric shock cranked into the water from an old box telephone. Maybe it knew, the same way crows or deer know, men armed from men unarmed. It seemed inviolate and wise, not at all like the brazen, nervous bass he caught with frogs. It seemed, in fact, the spirit of this place to which he came at dawn, and every time he saw it he felt deeply at peace.

The boy, of course, is myself, a self more vital, compact, pure, like wood within the inmost ring of a tree whose life has reached to many rings. Once, out for firewood, another boy and I crosscut a trunk of walnut that had lain barkless and rotting for maybe fifty years. When the yard-thick halves rolled clean we found the ooze of sap still live at its heart. Time remakes the meaning of such moments. They grow in memory and come finally to speak for the whole of one's life. I try, anyway, to stay loyal to those times on the river. Amid the damage of living I find purchase in that uncluttered coming to selfhood of a boy whose serious solitude began on clear-water streams, the Maries and Little Maries, the Osage, St. Francis, Castor, Huzzah, Black, Blue Tavern, Jacks Fork. Most of them were small enough to flashflood after a night's downpour. They fell to almost a trickle in late summer, and you could hear a boat coming miles off as it bumped and scraped through the shallows.

I fished alone often, but not always and not at first. Like any beginner I had to learn from someone: techniques, judgments, places. I had to receive a code of simple conduct, or merely an essential feeling, and this was my father's gift to me. It was a deep, unconscious giving, the only thing, I sometimes think, entirely his to give. He was a carpenter turned schoolteacher, moving from job to job, small town to small town, leaving friends, enemies, a string of half-built houses. Nothing much worked out, which might, perhaps, be said for most men. But my father, at least, knew how to retrieve himself from the debris of his life, and that knowledge became mine through him. From the time I was six we would dig worms and with an armful of poles take off at evening for the river. We would bait up and cast out to the channel, then sit back in the calm and watch the sun slant downward.

Sometimes we got ambitious and drove to special places, most often to one of the big dams—Bagnell, Wappapello, Clearwater—where fish gathered in great bunches along the edges of the spillway. You could see them, dark flashing shapes crowding the bank to escape the pounding of the water where it churned up from the floodgates. To fish close to the dam was forbidden, but with a treble hook—three big hooks welded back to back—we could cast upstream into that swarming mass and snag them with hard jerks on the line. Or else we fished the channel with heavy sinkers that dragged slowly downstream. Along the embankments of towering concrete, six-foot gar floated like logs in the sun, and at Bagnell, on the Osage, catfish large as men were said to lie at the base of the dam. The biggest one I saw was four feet, a blue cat with slit belly and guts cleaned out that pulled loose from the stringer and swam off. There we caught crappie, channel cat, and, sometimes in great batches, the silver-bright humpback drum.

For a time, too, we fished small streams with trotlines, cord strung from log or rock across the river with a dozen hooks baited and left overnight. We took nice catfish that way, and now and then a soft-shell turtle. Better than any catch was the excitement of going to check it in the morning. If a ten-pound flathead was on, the water fairly boiled. Mostly, though, we just put out lines and settled down to wait. I'm amazed now how broadly satisfying that was. Once we fixed the poles, propped them with stones and forked sticks, we felt that simply being there was enough. What we caught or didn't catch was up to luck entirely. Luck meant a mess of fish, of course, but on those soft evenings it meant something more: participation in an order as slow and patient as the earth itself, a harmony whose silent moving depth was like the river. Shadows spread, and across the hills came ringing of far-off church bells. Walls of trees massed darkly from high banks over the water, and upstream pale-limbed sycamores grew ghostly in the twilight. The air cooled and dew damped our clothes. Nothing stirred. First one, then another whippoorwill began to call, and as night rose the peace got so intense that to reel in and leave seemed almost sacrilege.

And then there was grennel fishing. That, anyway, was what we called it. Grennel are also known as grindle or bowfin, and in Mingo Swamp they grow ungodly large. Eight to eighteen pounds, two to three feet long and thickly lean with wicked teeth and a flared fin running the length of the back. They hit best on cut bait—we used chunks of carp— and they fought with brute fury. Mingo lay in one of the old channels of the Mississippi north of the Arkansas line. It was banked for water control, and the only way in was to walk, two, three miles along dikes and levees, cutting through brush with machetes, sidestepping the cottonmouths and rattlers that everywhere thrived in the mud and mud-thick waters. That place was nothing human, and when the reeds ahead began to shiver and slowly part, you stopped and allowed time for what was moving there to make up its mind.

We used cane poles, fifteen-footers cut new each time we went in. Carp swarmed so thick in some of those sloughs that for bait we just clubbed what we needed and sliced them up. Then we waded in waist-deep, huge fish splashing around us, the gumbo sucking at our feet. We set out the poles in a wide circle, rammed them into the bottom so they stuck out of the water at an angle, with the chunks of fish meat on hooks a foot below the surface. We stood then at the center and waited for strikes. We never waited long. Grennel hit like locomotives and moved on without slowing. The pole would heave and begin slapping the water in wild arcs, sometimes two at once, and the only way to take those fish was to scoop them into dip nets as they swept past our legs. There was no end to what we could catch that way. They piled up on the bank, fish after fish, as many as we could carry. Getting back to the car with a hundred pounds of fish was hard going. We decided finally to build a makeshift wheelbarrow, wooden so we could float it. We hauled out our catch in that and left it there for the next time.

That was when we lived in Glennon, in the southeast end of the state. The town had a population of about thirty people. There was a gravel lane flanked by eight or nine houses, some of them empty, and a wooden church that later burned down. We sat steep on a ridge over swampland and canebrake twenty miles from Marble Hill, the county seat, and ten from Leopold, where the school was. Every spring high water half destroyed the roads—dirt, gravel, blacktop torn into potholes—that bound the country together. Farming was all there was, and each farm took its bearing from the closest town. If a man said he was from Zalma or Clubb he most likely meant from a farm nearest the junction with that name. The towns were small indeed, often no more than a church, a couple of houses, and a general store that was also the post office and gas station. I gradually came to know these places, but at first their names alone were real, names like Advance and Arab and Gipsy and Drum, like Loose Creek or Folk or Rich Fountain, from which I got my first notion of the backwoods as a community. I did some of my best fishing while we lived in Westphalia, where in addition to a paved street there was a stone church, a tavern much used, a school, and a mill for grinding feed. The town was strung out on a mile-long bluff above a river that cupped it on three sides. From our house you could look off and see it winding beneath the trees and sky, cutting through hills and valleys as it disappeared and then appeared again to vanish finally in a distant stand of gum and cottonwood.

The life we lived was failing even then—the land wearing out, the young people leaving—but communal customs still survived. People got together to build a corncrib, to work on cars, to meet at sunrise on a neighbor's farm and bring in the whole crop in one day's time. Every gathering had a purpose beyond mere meeting, and so, too, with fishing on Sundays. After church, talk went from farming to the weather, from that to fishing, and in the afternoon maybe thirty people and a dozen dogs would gather on a farm near the river, the women to start the meal, the men to pile everything—nets, sacks, dogs, kids—onto a wagon or into the back of a pickup and take off for stretches of water where the big fish were. We would bump along through the bottoms high in corn and sorghum cane, the air sultry, the sun blazing stubbornly down. Heat lightning flickered faintly without sound, and beyond the rim of hills loomed massive thunderheads. They would stand there for days, miles high and motionless.

Once on the river we planned our strategy, unraveled the nets, and took our positions. Then real fishing began. In overalls and old shoes, hats cocked tight, we waded in with forty feet of spread seine. We dragged the length of channels, we circled snags and deep holes and went in to drive the fish from hiding. We splashed, poked, danced on the limbs of sunk trees. Ten-pound carp shot headlong into the net, bass darted up and down its length, catfish swaggered slowly back as we fought to bring the deep end around and outflank them in the shallows. Then into the mass of seething fish we charged, clubbing, grabbing, digging fingers into torn bloody gills. We hugged heaving fish bodies against our own, scales like silver dollars rubbing off on our skin, clothes, hair. The men were left the catfish, whose teeth did real damage, whose erect side fins stuck out like pointed knives. There was only one way to take a cat bare-handed: ram your fist straight down its throat and grab, fast, before it could bash into you or grind its teeth across your arm.

And afterward, supper. The fish were skinned and filleted, each piece finely cross-sliced so small bones would fry to a crisp. Wood stoves roared with flame in the cook shed, and into kettles of boiling lard were dumped pounds and pounds of fish steaks. They had been rolled in cornmeal, and when they were done the crust was hard and golden around meat white and tender and unbelievably sweet. There was always a fish fry. But when the haul was great each man took home a share as well. When this happened the fish were sorted into a circle of glistening heaps on the grass. Everyone helped except one man, who stood apart with his back turned. His job was to answer with one of our names each time another man pointed to a mound of fish and called out "Whose?" The pointing started at random, but once in motion it went from pile to pile in order. An enormous catfish might by itself be a share, and it went in the order of the circle to the next name called.

There was one other kind of fishing—on winter nights, with twenty-foot gigs, from boats along the deepest stretches of water. It took skill, it took a man's whole strength, and my own first time with the gig—not just being in the boat but actually doing the spearing—was a moment of fear and exulted entry into that much, at least, of manhood's joy. In winter big fish came to settle in the wide, long parts of the river, not in the channel but in sloughs and elbows of backwater, six, eight, ten feet down among logs and pockets of mud. Spots like these were too deep to seine, and to try with hook and line was useless because of the snags. But here the river's biggest fish were found. You could look down from the boat and see them, their bellies pressed to the bottom, their dark shapes still in the shadows. The trick was to jam steel barbs into one of those backs and then get it up through ten feet of water. And you had to do it right, otherwise you lost the gig and maybe swamped the boat. Twenty pounds of fish caused fierce commotion. It appeared to sleep, to be mesmerized by the cold. But the second you touched it, it sprang to violent life.

We used a twenty-foot flat-bottom boat, and once on the water—there were never more than three of us—we poled with the shaft of the gig, its ten-inch teeth upturned and gleaming. We hung out a kerosene lantern and glided in a globe of light, a coppery glow that lit up the bank as we passed. Things came out of the dark and fell back again, tangles of root and stone, fallen trees, the jagged rock face of bluffs rising hundreds of feet from the water. The lantern hissed softly and nobody spoke. We watched the silt-gray circle of light slide over the bottom. It cut into darkness and spread through the river's debris. We examined each clutter of rock and logs until, at first sight just a log, we found the object of our search. In that instant the night became vibrant with life. Far off a dog barked twice, tires spun gravel on the ridge road, and below, in the river's silence, great gills flexed slowly.

You stood then on the seat at the tip of the boat, your mind fixed on the fish, and began to lower the head of the gig. The distance had to be judged with care: too close and your thrust would not gain momentum, not close enough and you would be off-balance when you hit. With about two feet to go, you stopped, gathered your body like a fist, and came down with all your weight on the fish. It was like plugging into a dynamo. A cloud of swirling silt arose, an explosion of hurt heaving life at its center, and everything—the boat, the light, your own flesh—began to tremble against the violent shudder of the gig. At such a moment, ever to get the fish into the boat did not seem possible. If it got off the bottom it would start to swim, and if that happened it would be too strong to hold. You just leaned on the shaft of the gig and bore down, waiting for the fish to spend its strength. Eventually it did; it fell suddenly quiet and then you could lift it to the surface. In the boat you stepped on its head and yanked the barbs free. It lay there, its tail twitching slowly, its torn flesh hanging in tendrils.

Fishing was brutal, savage, cruel, but none of that was the point. Joy was what counted, the rush of deep delight that came, I think, from rites that for a million years kept men living and in touch with awe. On the river I felt untroubled and at home, as if creation were a living whole in which I, too, took part. At such times I *loved* to fish—that is the word. I felt thankful for my luck and in wonder at the mystery I touched upon. That was the blessing of boyhood. It depended on a way of life now largely vanished and to which in any case I cannot return. Perhaps that is why I no longer fish. Except in memory, a grace that is lost stays lost.